The Jackson MacKenzie Chronicles

IN THE EYE OF THE STORM

by
Angel Giacomo

1st Battalion
Publishing

Copyright ©

First publication in 2020 by 1st Battalion Publishing
1stbattalionpublishing@gmail.com

ISBN 978-1-7345674-0-3

Printed in the United States of America.

First Edition: 2020

DISCLAIMER-FICTION

DEDICATION

This book is dedicated to all who have served in every branch of the military. I write it with extreme humility. It is to honor the veterans of the United States who fought in our conflicts, both past, present, and future.

Do you give the horse his might? Do you clothe his neck with a mane? Do you make him leap like the locust? His majestic snorting is terrifying. He paws in the valley and exults in his strength; he goes out to meet the weapons. He laughs at fear and is not dismayed; he does not turn back from the sword. Upon him rattle the quiver, the flashing spear, and the javelin. With fierceness and rage he swallows the ground; he cannot stand still at the sound of the trumpet. When the trumpet sounds, he says 'Aha!' He smells the battle from afar, the thunder of the captains, and the shouting.

JOB 39:19-25

ACKNOWLEDGMENT

Thank you to those who have believed in me. Especially Sally.

CHAPTER 1

January 15, 1972

The late midday sun beating down on him, Jackson MacKenzie walked across the packed earth of the Phước Vĩnh forward base camp. A distinctive growl broke the silence. Close enough to feel the pressure wave, a low flying fully laden F4 Phantom flashed over his head like a lightning bolt. Sunlight glinted off the camo-painted wings as it banked sharply west. The air exploded with the sounds of bombs and machine-gun fire. *Charlie must be close to the perimeter.* He flipped off the safety on his M16 with his finger on the trigger.

Jackson strolled into Colonel Matthew Johnson's outer office, shouldered his M16, removed his Green Beret, and tucked it under his belt. The colonel's aide, Captain Colin "Knuckles" White, ushered him into the inner office. He smiled at the former Golden Gloves boxer as he passed and came to attention in front of his superior officer. "Lieutenant Colonel MacKenzie reporting as ordered, sir."

Colonel Johnson finished his signature before acknowledging him with a nod. "At ease."

Jackson snapped his hands behind his back and waited for further instructions.

"Take a seat, MacKenzie."

"Yes, sir." Jackson sat on the chair in front of the desk and laid his weapon on the floor.

"The Pentagon brass and the CIA have a new mission for you." Colonel Johnson drummed his fingers on the desk.

"What do they want us to do, sir?" Jackson ground his teeth together. "And why is the CIA involved?"

"I know you don't like to work for them. It's a broken record every time it comes up."

"Yeah, too many chances of getting screwed over."

"Well, this operation came directly from the Pentagon. The information on the black market art dealings came from the CIA."

"Well, sir, what's the mission?"

"The North Vietnamese government has been selling their rare artwork on the black market to finance their war efforts and replacing them with fakes. One piece went for over three million dollars in an underground auction last week." Colonel Johnson tapped a light green folder on his desk. "The brass wants your unit to recover four of the most expensive originals and replace them with counterfeits. This would deny them money and their troops needed weapons and ammo. You would save the paintings for the people of Vietnam and the lives of American troops. It could even shorten the war. The art dealers will know the canvases are reproductions, and the North won't get paid."

"They want us to what?" Jackson hit the desktop with a closed fist. "We're supposed to be winning the hearts and minds of these people."

Colonel Johnson's narrowed eyes stared over the top of his reading glasses, his forehead puckered in the center. "From your reaction, MacKenzie, you don't like the idea."

Unwilling to back down, Jackson shook his head. "No, sir, I don't. It smacks of hypocrisy."

"Your dissatisfaction and reservations are duly noted." Colonel Johnson leaned forward in his chair. "I will not tolerate insubordination." His voice became lower and louder. "You have my permission to forward your doubts up the chain of command. You will follow the order as given or be relieved of command."

"I may do that, sir. Will anyone else even take the mission?" He already knew the answer.

"Probably not. You were the only choice given your current track record of pulling off the impossible. You're the best chance of it going off without a hitch as the US Army's absolute expert in small unit tactics."

Jackson resisted the urge to give an eye roll to his superior officer. "Sir, I don't agree with the mission at all. However, I will follow my orders unless my doubts find the right ears in the chain of command."

"Fair enough." Colonel Johnson opened the folder. "Let's go over the plan."

Jackson flipped his chair around and sat straddle-legged across it. For the next three hours the two men went over the operation, line by line. The more they read, the more Jackson hated the plan. *Whoever came up with this needs their screws tightened to stop their marbles from falling out.*

"Any questions, MacKenzie?"

"Not for you, sir."

Johnson closed the folder. "Then you're dismissed."

"Yes, sir." Jackson exited the office and closed the door. In the outer office, he pointed at the typewriter next to Captain White's desk. "Mind if I use this, Colin?"

"Nope. Help yourself."

"Who beat your nose flat?" Jackson rolled a piece of paper onto the roller.

Colin wiggled his nose back and forth with his finger. "That bad, huh? Al 'Tiger Cat' Jones. He won a bronze medal in the '68 Olympics."

"What happened?"

"He knocked my happy ass out in the second round when I fought him in Detroit. I'm headed to the latrine. Be back in ten."

"Don't let the flies carry you away." Jackson went to work on his letter to General Thomas. He bullet-pointed every reason for his misgivings and signed his name.

Duty, Honor, Country – Those words, steeped in lore and tradition were the motto whereby every West Point cadet patterned their lives. That honor code meant everything to Jackson. It was the direction. The North arrow toward which he pointed every day of his life. He knew the meaning behind that call to arms. To fight with courage and die with honor, all for the love of his country.

Jackson placed the letter inside an envelope with a certified copy of the orders.

Since it was time for the mail run, Colonel Johnson forwarded the entire packet via the nightly courier junket to Da Nang.

For his records, Jackson slipped the carbon copy of his letter inside a binder under his arm with the mission plan. He shouldered his M16 and glanced at his watch. The hour hand pointed at eight. *Crap, the mess hall closed thirty minutes ago. Harry will jump my ass again. Not the first time. Won't be the last. It doesn't affect my ability to command. I have a one hundred percent completion rate. Colonel Johnson doesn't care how much I weigh as long as I get the job done.*

As Jackson walked around the edge of the ammo dump into a row of small steel Quonset huts, a beam of light caught his eye. He followed it. Major Harrison Russell, his executive officer, stood in the doorway of their living quarters with a flashlight in his hand.

Jackson chuckled. "You looking for me, Harry? You're such a mother hen." *I appreciate his insistence as my sounding board. Ever since the POW camp, I need someone to double-check my decisions. What did his ex-girlfriend call us? Oh yeah. The yin and yang of each other's existence. We're best friends.*

"Yeah, you missed chow again." Harry pushed two chocolate candy bars into Jackson's hand. "You know what General Thomas said. Do you want to go home on forced retirement? That's going to happen if you don't follow orders."

Jackson gripped the candy bars then looked his friend square in the eyes. They were nearly the same height. "No, I don't, but I can't leave, not yet."

"We escaped that damn camp two years ago. You need to let it go." Harry ran his hands through his short brown hair. "Maybe you should go home, my friend. What Dung did to you is eating you alive. I'm worried about you."

"I'm fine, Harry. Really." Jackson tore the wrapper off the candy bar with his teeth and laid the folder on the table, setting the second chocolate bar on top. Unslinging his M16, he placed it in the rack. "We have a new mission and twelve days to get ready for it. Go tell the others the briefing is at 0800 tomorrow."

"Where are we going?"

Jackson bit off a chunk of the mushy chocolate. He wiped his lips before replying. "Tomorrow. You won't believe this one. The brass has lost their minds."

"And you haven't? I've heard the words coming out of your mouth when you manage to fall asleep. Dr. Nicholson should pull the trigger on his threat to send you home. Then you can get some help and go on tour as a recruiter. General Thomas called you the living image of a Green Beret. That dark blond hair, your tan, those dimpled cheeks, and sapphire blue eyes will make you a hit with the babes in your dress uniform. Especially with that Marine Corps high and tight you're sportin' on your head."

Jackson gave Harry a bemused sneer. "Yeah, right? Like any woman would want me now. I'm okay. Go tell the others about the briefing. Since you're so worried about me, we'll meet in the mess hall for breakfast at 0730. Satisfied?"

Harry nodded in agreement. He took two steps to the door then spun around. "Yep, that way, you'll eat more than a piece of toast and drink a gallon of black coffee. I know you're committed to staying in 'Nam, but I see what it's costing you." With a two-finger salute, he turned on his heel and left the hut.

Jackson looked up from his paperwork when the door shut. *Harry's right. I should stop pulling strings to stay in 'Nam. But I have nothing to go home to except a room at the BOQ. Doesn't matter. I'm headed home after the next weigh-in. I lost a pound this week. That means forced retirement, and there's nothing I can do about it.*

Four hours later, Jackson still stared at the mission plan as he lay in his bunk under his overhead light. A dirty, stinky, wadded up sock landed next to his head.

"Turn out the damn light. It's keeping me awake. If you don't, I'll toss your bloody colonel's ass outside. It's late. If things go according to plan tomorrow, we have a long day ahead of us. Go to bed, you knucklehead!" Harry pulled his blanket over his head.

Unable to find another reason to stay up, Jackson ate the second candy bar then surrendered to his friend's good sense and his own exhaustion. He threw the sock back at its owner and switched off the lamp beside his bunk. In the darkness he mulled over the plan on one side of his mind while a small voice yelled at him from the other. *Don't go. Something's wrong. Tell Colonel Johnson no. I'll put myself on sick call and let Dr. Nicholson send me home.* What was he thinking? That damn POW camp was messing with his mind. His heart's throwing a red flag. *Forget it. Duty requires me to follow all reasonable orders, no matter how much I don't like them. This mission will save lives. That makes it important and why the brass gave it to me—again.*

January 16, 1972 – 0600 hours

Reveille sounded over the base loudspeakers. Jackson rolled out of bed for his workout. A leader by example, he was fanatical about staying in shape, even if it caused most of his weight loss. He jerked the blanket off Harry's body. "Time to get up, sleepyhead."

"Ugh." Harry wiped the drool off his chin as he sat up.

"What did you say?" Jackson bent over to tie his sneakers.

"Never mind." Harry stretched his arms over his head. "You spoiled a wonderful dream. I was in bed with Tina Louise."

"Don't want to hear it. Unless you send her my way."

"Nope, she's mine. Why don't you stay here today?" Harry slipped on the sneakers next to his bunk. "I can run by myself this morning."

"Can't do it, Harry. I need to stretch my legs. You'll just have to put up with my jokes again today." Jackson tucked his dog tags under his t-shirt.

Jackson turned to run backward. "Hurry up. You're lagging behind. We've gone three miles, one to go. I'm not going to be late for a meeting I scheduled."

"Who kept whom up last night?" Harry panted with each step. "It's your fault. Turn around before you trip and break something, you nincompoop."

Jackson fell back to jog with his best friend. Fifty yards from the wooden post designated as the finish line, he sprinted ahead then clapped as Harry passed him. "You haven't changed since selection training. I'm still the champion."

"True." Harry pinched his nose. "A champion at world-class body odor. Pee-yew."

At the showers, all the stalls were full. Jackson stood in line with his towel, uniform, and shaving kit. "What's taking them so long?"

"You know it's the one place where rank doesn't matter. It's all about the hot water." Harry snapped his towel against Jackson's butt. "We get cold showers today."

"Thanks to your slow ass feet, Major Russell. We're going to be late."

"Blame yourself and your light, Colonel."

Still damp a little later, both men grabbed their rifles from their quarters then double-timed to the mess hall. They came to a sliding stop at the doors.

Jackson glanced at his watch. "Five minutes to spare. No thanks to you."

"Whatever." Harry wiped the sweat off his forehead. "Get your ass in the building." He opened the door. "Rank before beauty."

"Hmph!" Jackson slung his rifle and walked into the building. Harry let go of the door, pivoted, and fell in step at Jackson's side. They stood at the back of the line, but the lead mess cook waved them to the front.

Harry shoved his way in front of Jackson and loaded his tray down with pancakes, sausage, and eggs to go with the black coffee.

Jackson rolled his eyes. He couldn't eat that much It would make him sicker than a dog. *I can't spend one day hunched over in the latrine or laid up in the hospital with diarrhea. There's too much to do for the upcoming mission. Dr. Nicholson will send me home.*

Nicknamed "Chief," Sergeant First Class Dakota Blackwater was already there, wolfing down biscuits and sausage gravy from his fully loaded tray. He'd reserved the table for the rest of his unit.

The two officers carried their trays to the table and sat across from him.

Chief acknowledged their presence with a scowl and returned to his meal.

Throat parched from their little jaunt, Jackson guzzled his coffee then gawked at the food on his plate. All mixed together, it looked like a weird colored science experiment from his high school chemistry class.

Harry jabbed at the tray with his fork. "Are you going to eat that, or do I have Chief sit on you, and I feed you like a baby, one spoonful at a time?"

Chief looked up. "Stay on him, Major Russell. The colonel's too skinny for his own good."

"You could sure try. But neither one of you could keep me down, and you know that." Jackson stuck a forkful of eggs into his mouth, frowned at the bitter taste, and spit the half-cooked wad of unsalted yellow goo onto the plate. *Yuck, powdered eggs.* He pushed them aside. The pancakes looked tastier. He took a bite of the syrup-soaked, round, half-burned bread and wanted to throw up. *If I don't try, Harry won't leave me alone.* Instead, he drank coffee and pushed the food around the plate. *Maybe Harry won't notice.*

Harry covered his mouth. "Ahem!"

Jackson paused, eased another bite into his mouth, and shoved the plate away. *If I eat that crap, I'll puke and kill my image in front of all these enlisted men.*

For his next act, Harry replaced Jackson's coffee cup with a bowl of oatmeal. In the middle of the gray goop, a spoon stood straight up.

Shaking his head, Jackson thumped the utensil with his finger. When it didn't move, he glared at Harry, who poured milk into the bowl then added several tablespoons of sugar. Jackson didn't take a breath as he consumed the container of gray porridge, downing it like a thick milkshake.

Once that bowl was empty, Harry shoved another one in front of him, complete with milk and sugar this time.

With his executive officer as pig-headed as him, Jackson chose the route of least resistance. He ate the second bowl without an objection, wiping the sides clean with a piece of toast.

Chief's eyes crinkled at the corners across the table.

Harry set Jackson's full mug on his tray. "Now you can drink your coffee."

Staff Sergeant Michael "Mikey" Roberts sat next to Chief. "Top of the morning to ya."

Jackson glanced at his watch. *0740, they're ten minutes late.*

"Do I smell a Jayhawk somewhere?" Chief grumbled then shoved a gravy-soaked biscuit into his mouth.

7

"Nah, that's pony crap." Mikey stuck out his tongue.

First Lieutenant Taylor "Ty" Carter took a seat next to Major Russell. At the same time, Captain William "Bill" Mason sat on the other side of Lt. Carter.

Jackson gave the men a hard stare. They ate with their heads down, avoiding his eyes. *After mission prep this afternoon another one of my lectures about promptness. And a few hundred pushups. No, a thousand. They know better.*

At 0800 hours, the men adjourned to the unit meeting area—a cleared space in front of Jackson and Harry's quarters. A makeshift table and four chairs constructed out of old wooden transport pallets stood in the center. Jackson grabbed the chair with a piece of foam to protect his butt from splinters. Harry claimed the chair with a canvas bag stuffed with hay as a seat. Bill sat on the one with a toilet seat. Ty pulled a faded out, half-rotted canvas red camp chair from under the table. Chief took off his shirt, folded it, then laid it on the seat of the last chair to cover the knots and broken staples before easing his big frame into it. Mikey used the only thing left— a wooden milk crate.

"Where are they sending us, JJ?" Harry tipped his chair back on two legs.

Jackson tried to remain expressionless. The mission was that ludicrous. Unable to maintain it, he rolled his eyes. "Believe it or not, Hanoi."

Harry's front chair legs came down with a bang. "What?"

"Why would they send us there?" Chief asked with disbelief.

Jackson held up his hand to stop all conversation. "I didn't like it either. Let me explain the mission. According to our intelligence—" He stopped as groans came from his men. "I know, I know, it's counterintuitive. What intelligence? These are generals we are talking about here. Let me finish, then you can chime in. The North has been selling its rare artwork on the black market to finance its combat and guerrilla operations. We are to recover four original paintings and replace them with forgeries. We'll be saving them for the Vietnamese people and give the North Vietnamese government the finger in the process. Think of it as taking out an enemy position. That's how Colonel Johnson pitched it to me. Not that I agree with him. But unless we get orders to the contrary, we go."

"Okay. Let's say the mission goes as scheduled." Harry raked his fingers through his hair. "How are we getting into Hanoi?"

"Oh, you're going to love this one." Jackson leaned forward in his chair. "HALO jump at night."

Bill banged the table with his fist. "HALO at night. Why?"

"Because at a normal jump altitude, the plane is too loud." Jackson tapped his right ear. "A HALO gives us a fighting chance once we hit the ground. If the enemy troops hear a low-flying plane near Hanoi, we'll be sitting ducks in our chutes for the guys on the anti-aircraft guns." He drew his thumb slowly across his throat from ear to ear. "And dead before we hit the ground."

Harry crossed his arms. "Okay, that makes sense. Now how do we get out? If an alarm goes off, we'll need a quick getaway, provided the NVA doesn't capture us first."

Jackson snorted, stone-faced. "I'll fly us out in a helicopter hidden by the CIA near the coast." He stopped at the full-blown snickers. "Yeah, I know, it's a load of crap. But, for the sake of argument, say it's there. We should make it out of North Vietnam without any difficulty unless a patrol spots us. If that happens, plan for a fun-filled time haulin' ass back to our lines. Since we agreed to the pact, you know my decision if we're caught I will not go through what I did before. Winding up a POW again is out of the question."

Harry's eyes narrowed. "Does that mean what I think it does, JJ?"

"Major Russell, are you asking if I will put a bullet in my brain rather than let the NVA capture me a second time?" Jackson slammed his hand on the table. "That's exactly what I mean."

Chief placed his Colt M1911A1 .45 caliber service pistol next to Jackson's hand. "Colonel, I'll be there right beside you if it comes to that."

Jackson acknowledged each man with a nod. "Okay guys, now that we've been morbid about what if the worst occurs, let's talk about the best-case scenario. We get in and out, and no one is the wiser. We have to wait for the CIA to deliver the forgeries. I need to arrange the HALO to avoid any snafus. I don't want the paperwork lost and leave us with no ride. It will take at least three days to get into the pipeline. Our backup plan for getting out if the chopper isn't there or poops out on us is to hump out. We need to prepare for both contingencies in regard to ammo, food, and water."

"And medical supplies," Mikey, the unit medic said emphatically, pointing at his CO. "You know how good ol' Murphy likes to jump us and your little quirk of obtaining injuries when we least expect it, sir."

"Of course, medical supplies. I don't intend to need any this time around. If we get in without attracting attention, we should get out the same way. It should be a piece of cake for a suicide mission."

Harry punched Jackson in the shoulder. "Right. When was the last time you had a simple mission in 'Nam? One word, never. You always get the *point-one percent chance of pulling it off* complex operations. The problem is every time you complete one of them, someone gives you a harder one. Mikey's right, you always wind up with pieces of metal embedded in your body."

"Major, stop being a drama queen. I'm not that bad. Okay, guys, we've been together a long time. You know what to do, so let's get it done. Major Russell and I are headed to flight ops to get the HALO in the books. We'll meet same time and place tomorrow morning for our next briefing. If the dumbass who came up with this harebrained plan has anything new, I'll let you know. Or maybe the brass will call it off. I don't give good odds on that happening." Jackson stood, and Harry followed.

The other men came to attention and saluted.

Jackson returned the salute. "At ease. Get to work." He pivoted on his heel, and Harry fell into step beside him.

CHAPTER 2

Colonel Johnson glanced up at the knock on his open office door. "Enter."

Captain White stood in the doorway. "Colonel, there's a special courier in my office. He will only talk to you."

"Tell him to come in." Johnson sat on the edge of his desk as the man walked in with a briefcase handcuffed to his wrist. "Do you have something for me, Lieutenant?"

"Yes, sir. A confidential packet from the Pentagon." The lieutenant handed Johnson a metal clipboard. "Sign here, sir."

After Johnson signed his name, the soldier unlocked the briefcase and handed him a large manila envelope. Johnson checked the intact seal on the flap. "Dismissed." Once the door closed, he broke the seal. "It's about MacKenzie's letter." As he read through the document, he laughed to himself. *They ignored MacKenzie's reservations altogether. Even I know that's not in the army's best interest.* He flipped to the next page. The new promotion list. *MacKenzie's a full Colonel. At thirty-seven? What else?* His fingers wouldn't catch on the slick paper, he licked them and turned the page. Those words meant even more. MacKenzie's immediate transfer orders on the next available transport. And his new command, the 5th Special Forces Group. *Why did they send this to me, not him?*

The header on the last page stood out. Army Chief of Staff. The Pentagon wanted MacKenzie to go to Hanoi. The promotion was to remain hidden until he returned with the paintings. Then he can get his command. What a lucky break. MacKenzie's a pain in his ass. His small and experienced unit pulled off every mission instead of getting captured or killed. *I want them gone. Now I gain legitimacy with the CIA and North Vietnam. I can sell Army weapons, ammo, and food on the black market, and play them against each other.*

Carefully, Johnson fished a small, black-and-white picture out of his wallet. A tear dribbled down his face as he ran his finger across the worn-out, dog-eared surface. "Hi, Dad. I miss you." He pounded his fist against the wall. *I hate this country! They let stupid people immigrate but not us.* All they wanted was to escape Hitler. With a name like Balabnov, that didn't happen. Everything worked against them. The Germans were fighting the Russians. His father gave up his life savings to smuggle him into England. Then the SS took his dad, mom, and sister away. *I was lucky when that American couple walked into that rat-hole of an orphanage. I told them I lost my family during a bombing raid in London. They adopted me on the spot. Not sure why. Perhaps because their son died at Normandy.*

Johnson looked at the picture again. His graduation from Marshall, and later Army OCS would have meant more if his dad had been there to share it with him. He laughed at the irony. On his first assignment as a Second Lieutenant with the 205th Military Intelligence Detachment, he learned his father died in a concentration camp gas chamber. All because of a name.

My revenge. Ten pounds of C-4 and a walk around the camp ought to do it.

A knock at the door broke the silence. Johnson opened the door. "I'm busy, Captain. It can wait." He shut the door, locked it, and called his handler.

Jackson and Harry strolled across the compound past headquarters to a steel Quonset hut next to the airstrip. They watched a C-130 take off then Harry opened the door for Jackson and followed him inside. Both officers stopped in front of the counter.

Jackson handed the airfield commanding officer a letter embossed with the Department of Defense seal. "We need to get a flight on the books."

"Hanoi? Really?" The captain pointed at the city name on the page.

"Yeah, don't ask me why, Captain Stewart. It's classified." Jackson hitched his hip on the counter.

"You know the drill, sir. Fill out the paperwork." Stewart handed Jackson a paper-clipped half-inch thick bundle of papers.

Jackson looked around the room. "Got a pen?"

"Yes, sir." Stewart pulled a pen from his shirt pocket.

Jackson filled everything out and pushed it across the counter. "Make sure the date is correct on the log."

Stewart slammed a stamp on the first page. "January 27th. Yes, sir."

Jackson dusted off his hands. "Okay, now let's go make sure the parachutes and oxygen masks for the HALO are in stock."

Harry adjusted his Green Beret. "Yeah, since the new guy took over, it's been hard getting anything around here."

The two men jogged over to the quartermaster's office. Jackson walked up to the counter. The soldier on the other side came to attention. Harry stood to his right.

"At ease, Lieutenant. I need these items." Jackson slid a piece of paper across the counter.

The young man glanced at the list, then rolled his eyes. "Sorry, sir. Don't have any of it."

"Then get on the phone. That's your job."

"Okay, sir, but I can't guarantee anything." The lieutenant picked up the phone.

Jackson leaned with his back against the counter. "Harry, we may need—"

"The guy in my office is an ass... No. I don't know... He wants parachutes, oxygen masks, ammo, rations, grenades... Who is it? MacKenzie. You know the guy who killed a dozen Cong two weeks ago by slitting their throats. Word has it the POW camp screwed him up. He's glory-seeking asshole and FUBAR broke-dick drunk ass crazy colonel who needs to go home for good."

Jackson flipped around to face the lieutenant. "What did you say, Second Lieutenant Winter?"

"Nothing, sir." The man set the phone receiver in the cradle and took a step back.

Jackson leaned across the counter until he was nose to nose with the young officer. "My hearing is perfect. You sure you want to go there? All I need to do is call JAG and court-martial you for insubordination. Do I need to do that?" His voice could drown out a jet engine at full power.

Harry slapped both hands on his head to protect his eardrums.

Lt. Winter melted back as Jackson's hot breath hit his face. "No, sir." His voice sounded like a tiny mouse squeaking as it ran from a large tomcat.

"Am I going to get my equipment on time, Lieutenant?" Jackson, his tone low and growling, eyes narrowed to crinkled slits, slammed both hands on the desk. In his right one, a large, fixed blade combat knife.

Lt. Winter's eyes widened like saucers. A large spreading wet spot appeared over his groin. "Yes, sir."

"Good! Make sure of it, or I'll take it out of your miserable hide! Good day!" Jackson spun on his heel and stormed through the door, slamming it against the doorframe with a loud bang. For several seconds it swung back and forth on the hinges.

Outside the building, Harry stopped Jackson with a hand on his shoulder. "You okay?"

Jackson drew a deep breath to relax and slid his Marine Corps KA-BAR into the sheath on his belt. A gift from his godfather after his first deployment to Vietnam. "Yeah, I think so. He pissed me off. *A glory-seeking asshole and FUBAR broke-dick drunk ass crazy colonel.* Really? Do people around here actually think of me like that?"

"No, they don't, at least not as far as I know. We sure don't think of you that way. He's probably getting an earful from every combat unit in the area because of the equipment shortage and took his frustrations out on you. Lieutenant Winter should've done as you asked without the comments. I agree he needed a dressing down." Harry chuckled as they looked through the open door. Lt. Winter had a phone receiver in one hand and a towel in the other. "I bet he makes sure we get everything we need for the mission."

"Me too." Jackson grinned as his anger abated. "Let's go check the guys' progress on building the art museum mockup."

Harry pointed in the direction of the kitchen. "No, lunch first, then check on our unit."

"I'm not hungry. I ate two bowls of oatmeal this morning."

"Just eat something for me, anything. Other than drinking coffee, and I'll keep my mouth shut."

"Promise?" *Harry's statement could bite him.*

"Yeah, promise. As long as you eat something."

Jackson nodded as they reversed direction toward the mess hall. Upon seeing a worn-out copy of Stars and Stripes on the table next to the door, he picked it up and went through the line. *I'll get Harry for his big mouth.* He waited until they arrived at the limited fresh fruit section, grabbed an apple, a banana, and a coffee cup.

Harry carried his tray to the same table and sat across from his friend. "Nice little stunt, there, JJ."

Jackson spread out the paper and munched on the apple. "Uh-huh. Remember the promise."

"Okay. Anything interesting in the paper?"

"Well, let's see." Jackson scanned the paper with his right index finger, taking a swig from his coffee mug with his left hand. "Nixon is running for re-election. No surprise there. Oh, wait, here's one that affects us,

Nixon is pulling 70,000 troops out of Vietnam, cutting the force in the country by half. That's just great."

"We knew that was coming. They sent the 5th home last year. The State Department is trying to work out a deal at the peace talks to send us all home for good."

"Yeah, I know. But cutting us in half, that's a bit much."

"I agree, but there's nothing we can do about it except our jobs." Harry shoved his plate away.

"True." Jackson peeled the banana. "Don't you like those potato chips or the ham sandwich?"

"No. It's like eating from a salt lick, and the bread tastes like mold." Harry picked up his coffee mug. "Anything else?"

Jackson flipped through the rest of the pages. "No, that's about it, but the paper is several days old. We don't get the most recent copies out here." He folded the paper, ate the banana, and drank the rest of his coffee.

"True." Harry placed his hand on top of the paper as Jackson chucked the apple core like a basketball into the nearest trash can. "Hey, knucklehead, nice shot, and three points."

"Always." Jackson wiped the sticky juice on his pants.

CHAPTER 3

January 25, 1972

Cutting it close with two days to go, the Vietnam II Corps CIA station chief delivered the counterfeit paintings to Jackson in front of his quarters. He tossed cardboard tubes on his bunk, stepped outside then shut and locked the door.

We don't have a choice now. "What about the sampans? Are they at the drop zone? We need them to get into the city. We aren't going on this mission without them. Sneaking into Hanoi on foot is a suicide mission!" Jackson waved a tattered copy of the mission plan in the man's face.

The agent was dressed like a tourist. His pink-flowered Hawaiian shirt and floppy straw hat were out of place on a forward firebase.

"Yes, Colonel MacKenzie. Our contacts hid them yesterday. Don't worry about it," the agent replied in a tone devoid of emotion.

"It's my prerogative to worry. Our necks are on the line, not yours. What about the helicopter? We need it to get out of North Vietnam." Jackson glared at the shorter man, using his six-foot-one-inch height to his advantage.

The station chief stared off at the horizon instead of answering. He refused to acknowledge Jackson's presence with even a glance in his direction.

"Hey, look at me. I'm not going to talk to your back." When the man turned around, Jackson let his anger drip from his voice like rancid butter. "I said, what about the helicopter? I don't trust the Company. Your lousy intelligence has burned my unit more times than I can count." He took a step toward the man. "It was so screwed up on our last seek-and-destroy mission we were almost captured parachuting into the middle of a bivouacked NVA platoon."

The agent stepped back.

Jackson pressed his dominance and stepped closer with his right hand on his KA-BAR. "Are your analysts so blind they need a seeing-eye dog? How do you miss fifty men camped inside a clearing? We were lucky to get out with our lives."

The agent almost crouched, as if to run. The blood drained from his face leaving it a ghostly-white pallor.

Good, he knows my reputation. "Count this as the last time I work for the CIA. I won't be double-crossed again."

The agent pulled a map out of his back pocket and handed it to Jackson. He stuck his other hand in his front pocket, next to his plainly visible .38 Special revolver. "The helicopter will be delivered tomorrow at the spot marked on the map. Memorize the location and destroy the map. It's for your safety and ours. Trust no one outside your circle of friends. Good day."

Jackson watched him walk toward the airfield, his untucked shirt waving back and forth with each step. His shoulders were hunched over as if protecting his pencil neck. *He's lying to me. There's no helicopter. We're humping our way out of North Vietnam until we find an alternate form of transportation. I hope it's a truck. My feet hurt for a week the last time.*

A soldier ran up to him, came to attention and saluted.

Jackson returned the salute. "What can I do for you, Corporal?"

"Colonel Johnson wants to see you for an update on your progress, sir."

"Thanks. You're dismissed."

Jackson studied the map on his way to headquarters. At the door, he tossed it into the burn barrel and shouldered his M16. Once the map disappeared into flames, he entered the building.

Captain White pointed at Colonel Johnson's open door. "He's waiting for you, sir."

Jackson nodded, marched into the inner office, and came to attention. "Lieutenant Colonel MacKenzie reporting as ordered, sir."

Johnson looked up from the report in his hands. "At ease, MacKenzie."

Jackson snapped his arms behind his back. "Has anyone from HQ replied to my letter, sir?"

"No responses have been forwarded to my office. How's everything going?"

"According to schedule. The chutes and masks arrived yesterday and the paintings today. We spent the morning on the range. This afternoon is our final dry run with weapons. Is the mission still a go?"

"Yes, Captain White confirmed it with General Thomas' aide at brigade headquarters this morning. I want you in my office an hour before your departure for the signing of your final operational orders. You're dismissed until then, Lieutenant Colonel MacKenzie."

17

"Yes, sir." Jackson gave his commanding officer a crisp salute, turned on his heel, and left the building. "They consider me such an expert you'd think they'd acknowledge my reservations. Generals and their holier-than-thou attitudes," he mumbled under his breath on his way to their makeshift training area.

Unit tradition dictated the men meet for their pre-mission bull session. As the sun crossed the horizon to the west, Jackson propped his M16 against the wall with the others and relaxed against the doorjamb of his quarters. He observed the festivities from afar until Harry pulled him into the circle by his shirtsleeve. They sat on two upturned shell boxes.

Bill handed them turkey and cheese sandwiches, potato chips, and chocolate chip cookies.

Jackson sniffed the bread. "Mmm. Where did you get the fresh-baked stuff?"

"Don't tell anyone, sir. I intercepted Colonel Johnson's morning delivery from Da Nang. Maybe he'll eat the slop in the mess hall tonight like everyone else." Bill blew on the fingernails of his right hand then buffed them on his shirt.

Jackson made a zipping motion across his mouth. "My lips are sealed. He always eats better than his men. It'll grow some hair on his flabby chest to eat that crap if he doesn't puke it up first." He crammed bites of the delicious sandwich into his mouth between handfuls of potato chips.

Ty held up a large Styrofoam cup with a lid and straw. "This is for you, Colonel." At his feet, an artillery shell box filled of ice. Next to it, a full case of beer.

"What is it?" Jackson shoved the last bite of cookie into his mouth.

"A surprise."

Jackson stuck the straw into his mouth. "Mmm." *A vanilla milkshake.* He sucked until the straw stuck to the bottom of the cup, then pulled off the lid and wiped the sides clean with his finger.

Harry gave Jackson a small shove. "That's more food than you've eaten in the last five days. Did you figure out you need to build up your strength?"

Jackson stuck the straw between his teeth and chewed on it. "Nah. The cookies tasted so much like Mom's it felt like I was at home. Everything was good for a change. Why not enjoy it? But I have to ask, where'd you get the ice cream, Lieutenant?"

Ty rubbed a hand over his stubbled chin. "It's better you don't know. I don't want you to wind up in the brig with me."

"Kinda like Bill's little raid, huh? The Seabees were in camp yesterday. Did you appropriate it from the Navy along with the beer?"

"Ain't going to say another word, sir."

Jackson looked at Harry. "The Navy," they echoed.

Chief gulped down a beer and grabbed another before the other men could drink one. "Thanks for the good beer, Lieutenant." He let out an extra-long loud belch.

"Tell me again, Chief. Where'd you go to high school?" Mikey did a war dance in front of the table.

"Little River!" The big Osage Indian stood, his six-foot-two-inch, 250-pound frame towering over the five-foot-nine-inch, 150-pound, corn-fed, dark-haired kid from Kansas.

Mikey didn't cower. Instead, he made like he was riding a horse in a circle around Chief. "Do you still ride horses to school?"

"Nah, we drive cars. I had this sweet candy apple red '58 Impala. Boy, it could move. Tricked it out myself. Drove it at Main Street drags every weekend, and beat all comers. Right before I shipped out, Skyline Amusement Park finished a wooden coaster called the Nightmare. I must've ridden it a dozen times that night. There's nothing like the clickety-clack of the rails and the groan of a wooden coaster. They have a ride called the Tornado." Chief made a whirling motion with his finger. "It spins you round and round. I rode it twice before I puked." A boisterous snicker escaped Chief's lips. "I ate Mexican food before I got to the park. After spilling my guts into a trash can, I rode it four more times. It was a fun night. Boarded the plane for 'Nam the next morning. Haven't been back since."

Jackson leaned back until his box almost tipped then caught himself. "Sounds like a nice send-off. Much better than my last night before shipping out for my first tour in 'Nam. I watched television and wrote out my will. I left everything which wasn't army issue to my now ex-wife. Due to my family history of dying in a combat zone, I expected to return inside a body bag." At everyone's sad look, he winked at them. "Not that she would have gotten much. I crammed it all in two standard footlockers."

Mikey, beer in hand, poked Chief in the chest. "How'd that school song go?"

19

Chief's nose whistled as he drew in a big breath. "Strike up the band. Unfurl our banner and raise it high." Every word sung to the melody of *Anchor's Away*. "At Little River, we stand as one, no matter where we may be. Fight! Fight! Our teams never quit. We always take the field. May our courage always triumph. It is our knack. It is our quack to fight for victory!"

Several soldiers en route across the compound looked in the Chief's direction. Jackson tracked them with his eyes as they kept walking. *Good decision. Not in the mood for onlookers. Especially with Chief half-drunk. Don't want him punching someone. Or throwing them across the compound like a child's toy. I'd have to call in favors to secure his release in time for the mission.*

At the end of the song, Chief smiled, his white teeth flashing in the moonlight. "I sound like the lead singer of Three Dog Night, right Mikey?"

"Nope, one of the Andrews sisters." Mikey waggled his eyebrows. "Quack?"

"Yeah. Quack! Little River's the home of the Fightin' Ducks." Chief popped his knuckles. "Got a problem with that, Mikey?"

"No problem at all, Sergeant." Mikey handed Chief another beer and picked one up for himself. "Since we know Chief's proud of his school. Is there anything you're proud to have been a part of, Colonel?"

Jackson paused for a moment. *Why not?* "Making the Olympic team."

All five men said "Huh," almost in unison.

Harry leaned forward on his shell box. "What sport?"

"Equestrian. I made the team in dressage and jumping on my academy horse Firefly. He was a donated former thoroughbred racehorse. Bright red. What we call chestnut with a blaze and four white socks. No one thought Firefly was anything special. As a dressage horse, he wouldn't learn the patterns and as a jumper, refused to jump. Our coach believed all Firefly did was eat and shit. I made the team as a plebe. They assigned him to me because he was the worst horse in the barn." Jackson stopped as his men howled with laughter.

Harry patted Jackson on the shoulder. "Sorry, but you have to admit, it's funny. A jumping horse that refuses to jump."

"Yeah, I get it, Harry. Now can I continue, unless you guys don't want the rest of the story?"

Mikey scooted his chair closer. "No, keep going, sir. I really want to know how you made it to the Olympics."

20

Jackson's grin grew wide. "We won a lot of meets. Even several big ones at the Kentucky Horse Park against Olympic riders from other countries. As a result of Firefly's blue ribbons, the US coach invited us to the Olympic trials. In '56, the Olympics were in Melbourne, but Australia wouldn't change the importation laws. They held the competition for us in Stockholm. As an alternate, I didn't get to compete. I could've won a medal in jumping and dressage. Firefly was better than any of the other horses. We beat most of them earlier in the year. There's a picture of us at the West Point stable taken in front of the Olympic rings."

Surprise lit Ty's face. "Wow. I would've never pictured you on the back of a horse. You don't seem like the cowboy type."

You don't know how wrong you are, Ty. "I started riding when I was seven on a pony. My dad bought me a dark bay quarter horse when I was ten. Since Dad was a Medal of Honor recipient, the Pendleton stable gave me a stall, free of charge. I competed with Taco until he bowed a tendon. Dad wanted to buy me another horse. He didn't have the time when the 1st Marines shipped out for Korea two days later. Mom asked my riding instructor to find me a new horse. He came to me first. I nixed the idea. I was already on schedule to graduate a year early from high school. The day after my seventeenth birthday, I enlisted in the army and deployed to Korea with the 101st a few months later."

Ty quirked an eyebrow. "Your dad has the Medal of Honor like you? Wow. Father and son. Bet that's never happened before."

Jackson let out a huff of barely repressed humor. "Actually, it has. Arthur MacArthur received one during the Civil War and Douglas MacArthur for the defense of the Philippines in World War II. There's controversy over the subject. Long story short, they changed the standard for him. Instead of an incredible act of bravery like everyone else, General MacArthur's nomination stated for conspicuous leadership in preparing the Philippine Islands to resist conquest. His statement said he accepted it in recognition for the indomitable courage of the gallant army he commanded."

Harry pointed at Jackson. "Quite the history lesson there, JJ. That last bit sounds familiar. Doesn't it, guys? I read something like it in your interview with Stars and Stripes."

"Oh hush up, Harry." Jackson winked at Ty. "What about you, Lieutenant? Since I joined the conversation this time, anything to add about your life?"

"Nah, I'd rather stay silent, sir. I'm more mysterious that way." Ty drank a large swig from a half-empty beer can.

Jackson laughed. The sound rolled up from his gut and rocked through his body. He jammed his foot into the ground to keep from falling off his shell box.

Chief doubled over, cackling like a rooster. He held his beer above his head.

Mikey, Harry, and Bill clutched their stomachs.

"Sure, Mr. Base Casanova from Charleston, South Carolina. Where's your date for the evening? You normally have a nurse stuck like honey on each arm. They love your southern drawl, running their hands through your dark, curly hair and kissin' that mouth of perfect white teeth." Harry pursed his lips and made kissing noises.

"Haven't found the perfect woman to take home to Mom yet, Major." Ty tossed his beer can into the trash and grabbed another one.

"Yeah, I bet. Not in the battlefields of 'Nam."

Bill jumped in next. "Did I tell you guys about my last year as a chemistry teacher in Palmyra? I was doing this neat experiment called elephant's toothpaste. You drop hydrogen peroxide into a beaker containing dish soap and iodine. It shoots a volcano of foam into the air. Looks really cool with red food coloring added. Instead of oohs and ahhs by the class, the jocks threw spit wads at me. Kids today don't want to listen. I quit that afternoon and joined the army."

Everyone in the circle groaned low in their throat. They'd heard the same story ad nauseam for two years. Empty beer cans flew in Bill's direction.

The party continued for the next three hours with small talk and rambunctious jokes. Chief wound up with laryngitis after belting out tune after tune at the top of his voice. When the beer ran out, Ty, Bill, Chief, and Mikey stood.

Jackson and Harry watched until the men staggered safely into their little steel huts. They went to bed to get what little sleep they could until reveille.

January 26, 1972

Jackson pointed downrange over the berm of the grenade course one-hundred-yards north of the firebase rifle range. "Sergeant Roberts, throw harder. You missed the target by ten feet."

"Colonel, I'm a medic." Mikey patted the olive green pouch on his hip stamped with a red cross inside a white circle. "Why do I need to do this? Chief's the heavy weapons guy."

"Yeah, I know. That's why he hit every target today and poked large holes in the paper bad guys with the M60 yesterday. But we're all training today. Try again."

Mikey picked up a practice grenade, pulled the pin and lobbed it into the field. It landed five feet away from a large wooden cutout of a Cong soldier with a rifle then popped with a loud bang.

"Better, but throw a little harder." Jackson checked Mikey's pupils. They were slow to constrict in the bright sunlight. "You're hungover, right, Sergeant?"

Mikey rubbed his head. "Yes, sir."

After a long morning in the grenade pit and an impromptu tabletop exercise in front of Jackson's quarters to cover all contingencies in the afternoon, it was time to relax. A poker game broke out during the evening using different colored small rocks as chips.

"Fifty bucks to you, Major." Chief placed his bet in the center of the table.

Harry tossed two green rocks into the pile. "Call. JJ, you've got to eat more than a roll and drink a gallon of black coffee if you want to avoid a forced trip home."

Jackson glanced at his cards. *Nice, two pair, aces over kings.* "Whatever, Harry. The dog crap they served us in the mess hall tonight is the least of my worries. This mission plan is about to give me an ulcer. Unless you wanted me to puke in your lap." He flipped a black rock next to Harry's bet. "Raise you fifty."

The whistle of shells pierced the air overhead. Jackson's heart lurched. Harry's eyes went wide. The men dropped their cards as they scattered for the closest foxhole. Jackson and Harry grabbed their rifles and ran to one twenty yards away. As they dove in, a shell hit nearby, sending shrapnel flying in every direction.

Jackson struggled to sit up. His vision was obscured with stars from hitting the bottom headfirst. He covered his head with his arms.

"Owww…"

"Where's Harry?" Jackson blinked and tried to focus on the direction of the moan. In the smoky darkness a man leaned against the opposite wall. On hands and knees, he scrambled over. "Shit!" He pulled Harry out flat and looked him over. Harry's left foot was turned sideways at an unnatural angle. Bone poked through the deep laceration above his ankle. Blood pooled around his foot.

"How bad is it?" Harry tried to sit up.

Harry was alive. "Stay still. Let me work." Jackson pushed his friend on his back then yanked a tourniquet tight around Harry's thigh to slow the bleeding. He wound a pressure bandage from his belt around Harry's foot to stabilize it for transport.

"JJ…"

"Hang on, Major." Jackson poked his head above the rim of the hole. "Looks like it's stopped." He jumped out, lay on his stomach, and extended his arms. "Give me your hands." Once Harry was lying next to the foxhole, Jackson pulled him over his shoulder in a fireman's carry. He took off toward the hospital.

Two steps later, the bombing started again. Jackson ran across the base as shells rained down like a thunderstorm. Screams filled the air. Fire lit the night sky. Explosions rocked the ground in an unrelenting earthquake. A blast wave knocked one leg out from under him. With his hand on the ground to maintain his balance, he kept running.

In the hastily erected triage area, Jackson dumped Harry on an empty gurney. "Medic!" He pulled out his knife and slit Harry's shirtsleeves to gain access to his arms then grabbed an IV setup from the cart behind him.

Harry lifted his head. "Ouch."

"Hush. Your foot's half-gone and you're complaining about the IV catheter in your forearm." Running footsteps signaled someone's approach. Jackson glanced over his shoulder. "Dr. Nicholson, hurry."

The doctor came to a sliding stop next to the gurney. "What do you have, Colonel?"

"Shrapnel in his left foot." Jackson checked the blood-soaked bandage then pulled the tourniquet tighter. "It may have hit an artery."

"Let's get him inside." Dr. Nicholson pushed the gurney through the hospital doors.

Jackson trotted alongside, holding Harry's hand.

At the treatment room door, Dr. Nicholson shoved his hand flat against Jackson's chest. "Stay out here. You'll get in the way."

Jackson leaned against the wall. After-images of the bombing appeared in front of his eyes. A hand fell on his shoulder. He spun to see who it was. "Huh?"

Dr. Nicholson stood beside him. "Finally, I can see your eyes. Are you okay? I've been shaking you for two minutes trying to get your attention."

"Yeah, I'm fine. How's Major Russell?" Jackson glanced at his watch. *Three hours?*

"If you didn't apply the tourniquet when you did, Major Russell would've bled out in a matter of minutes. The shrapnel sliced through every tendon, muscle, and bone in his ankle. I will do everything I can to save his foot, but I'll be as honest with you as I was with him. I think we'll have to remove it. You can see him for a few minutes. Then I'll give him some additional morphine to manage the pain until we ship him out to the 95th Evac hospital tomorrow. He's going home for good."

"Thank God Harry's still alive to go home." Jackson straightened his shirt. As he took a step toward the room, Dr. Nicholson stopped him with a hand on his arm.

"I should be sending you home with him."

"Yeah, I know. Harry's been on my ass since you warned me last month. Just this last mission, then send me home. I need to gain a bunch of weight, and I'll never do it here. He's my best friend. I can't let him go through this alone."

Dr. Nicholson dropped his hand. "Is the sky falling, sir, because that's a first? But, okay, if that's what you want. I'll cut the orders when you get back."

"Thanks, Doc." Jackson pushed the door open with his dirty hands. *I have Harry's blood all over me.* He stopped, wiped his hands on his pants, walked to the bed, and leaned over the rail. "Hey, Harry."

"Hey, JJ. Guess you heard." A tear rolled down Harry's cheek.

Jackson brushed it away with his thumb. "Yeah, you're going to beat me stateside. I'll be right behind you when we get back. I told the doc to send me home. Expect to see me snapping the whip on you at rehab."

"You did what? Really? For me?"

"Sure did. I'll be there for you in the same way you've been on my ass these last few months keeping me alive and sane."

"Thanks. I couldn't ask for a better friend." Harry held out his right hand, which Jackson clasped in a tight grip.

Dr. Nicholson dug his fingernails into Jackson's forearm. "Colonel, did you hear me?"

"Ouch." Jackson jerked his arm away. "Sorry, Doc. I was thinking about something."

"Yeah, I noticed. You've done that twice. Is something wrong?"

"No. What did you want me to do?"

"Let go of Major Russell's hand so I can check his blood pressure."

25

Jackson complied then backed up. He peeked around the doctor's shoulder. "I'll be back tomorrow before they send you to Da Nang."

Harry craned his head above the bed rail. "I may not be too coherent, considering what they're pumping into me, so I'll say it now. Good luck tomorrow. Keep your head out of the line of fire and get everyone home safe."

"I'll do my best, Harry. Thanks for everything."

"I'll see you stateside in a couple of weeks."

Jackson watched the doctor inject a sedative into Harry's IV line. He waited until Harry's eyes closed then left the hospital. The bomb craters slowed the walk to his quarters. He had to weave his way around them.

At the door to his hut, Ty, Bill, and Chief sat on the ground. They stood at his approach. *Oh no!* Jackson's stomach plummeted. "Where's Mikey?"

"Here, Colonel." Mikey emerged from the darkness. "How's Major Russell? I got stuck in the triage area taking care of wounded so I couldn't check on him."

Relax. Don't let them feel your anxiety. Jackson straightened. "Not too good. Dr. Nicholson's pretty sure they'll have to amputate Harry's foot. They're shipping him to Da Nang tomorrow and sending him home once he's strong enough to travel."

Ty shook his head. "Aww, shit. Poor Harry."

"Lieutenant Carter, you know how I feel about that. The only thing you accomplish by swearing is making people mad at you." Jackson winked at him. "But tonight, I agree with you."

Bill raised an eyebrow. "Aww, come on, Colonel. You cursed like a sailor in the POW camp. Where'd you learn those words?"

"My dad when I was little, but only out of earshot of Mom. She would've washed our mouths out with soap if she heard the things coming out his mouth."

"There goes the unit good luck charm. Major Russell never gets hurt." Chief shifted his M16 to his left hand. "Is the mission still a go, sir?"

Jackson sagged against the door to ease the pressure on his tired legs. "As far as I know, yes. We'll have to cover for Harry's loss. After we get back, I'm going home."

"For real, sir? You agreed with a doctor for a change. That's a new one for you. Don't worry about us." Mikey pointed at Jackson's rank. "I hate losing the best commanding officer in the army."

"Thanks, but I'll worry about all of you. When Dr. Nicholson gives me the official word, I'll take care of your transfer orders. I want you guys stateside, not here."

Ty spoke up. "How about we go see Harry at the hospital together once we get home. Show him we're safe."

"He'd love that." Jackson took the M16 Ty handed him. "Let's make this last mission one for the books."

"What's the plan for tomorrow, boss?" Chief asked.

"We'll meet at the mess hall at noon for lunch, then get our equipment ready. Once that's done, I'll check on Harry and report to Colonel Johnson at 1900 hours. If the mission's still a go, we take off at 2100 hours and jump at 2345." Jackson paused as his gut churned. "Since Charlie mortared the base tonight, we'll hit the museum a day earlier than scheduled. Something doesn't feel right. I don't want us to get caught with our pants down. Plan accordingly. Don't tell anyone. I'm not even going to tell Harry. Got it?"

"Yes, sir," they echoed together.

"Let's get some rack time." As the men walked toward their quarters, Jackson watched a falling star as it streaked across the sky. *Take care of Harry. Bring us all home alive.* He sat on his bunk and stared at the empty one next to him. *I can't sleep. Harry's not sawing logs next to my ears.*

January 27, 1972

A closet insomniac, Jackson climbed out of bed before reveille. He glanced at Harry's unmade bunk, shook his head, and put on his sneakers. For an hour, he jogged the loop around the base. *I miss Harry's constant babble. He's right. I need to go home.*

After showering and changing into a fresh uniform, Jackson headed to the chow hall. His stomach churned as he went through the line. The only thing he could keep down, a piece of toast and coffee. *This mission feels off. Why don't I trust my instincts? I do. But I have to follow orders unless another option falls in my lap.*

Full of nervous energy, Jackson returned to his quarters to prep his gear. Meticulously, he cleaned and oiled his M16 and Colt service pistol, twice. He loaded his magazines and sharpened his combat knife against a whet stone until it would cut flesh at the slightest touch. *Better for my victim to not feel it going through his neck.*

His personal pre-jump checklist came next. One, the inspection of the harness straps, risers, and suspension lines for frays or wear. Two, the ripcord securely attached to the main canopy. Three, the reserve chute and cutaway system properly packed. Four, the facemask and oxygen bottle for any irregularities. *Don't want to pass out at 30,000 feet and hit the ground at terminal velocity. I won't feel the impact, but my body will make a large hole in the process. The guys will be escorting a bucket home.* On edge, he went for another walk to burn off his nerves.

Rifle slung across his back, Jackson entered the mess hall at noon. Chief waved at him from their usual table as Jackson picked up a tray. The selections on the buffet line looked like gray dog food. He chose the safest option, a foot-long turkey sub, chips, and a bowl of red Jello.

Chief gave him the stink eye from across the table.

Jackson picked up the hoagie. As the bread touched his lips, he sniffed. *Yuk. Where did the mess guys find the roadkill? The bread tastes like mayonnaise coated mold, and the meat smells spoiled.* A burning pain erupted high in his chest. He pushed the plate aside and ate the Jello to soothe his throat. His willpower failed as he tossed his dirty utensils in the bucket next to the door. "Oooh…" He slammed his hand over his mouth and ran for the nearest latrine.

A loud knock on the door echoed in the small wooden building. "You okay, boss?"

"Yeah, Chief. Give me a minute." Jackson rinsed out his mouth with water from his canteen. He opened the door, shoved Chief back a step then stepped out onto the muddy ground. "Go get your stuff ready. Mine's packed and laid out on my bunk. I'm going to visit Harry."

"Good." Chief tapped under his eye with his finger. "The doc can take a look at you."

"Not on your life." Jackson wiped his mouth on his sleeve. "Get moving."

"Yes, sir." Chief ran off toward the living quarters.

Jackson went in the opposite direction to the hospital. He stopped at the front desk. "Page Dr. Nicholson to Major Russell's room."

"Yes, sir." The nurse picked up the microphone next to her hand. "Dr. Nicholson to room three. Colonel MacKenzie is waiting."

Jackson leaned on the wall outside Harry's room. He stood up straight as the doctor walked over to him. "How's he doing, Doc?"

Dr. Nicholson flipped to the last page on his clipboard. "As good as can be expected. Major Russell will definitely lose his foot above the ankle. There's no way to save it. The damage is too extensive."

Jackson jutted his chin toward the door. "Does he know that?"

"Yes. He's pretty upbeat, considering. I think it's because you decided to go home. So, I have to ask, were you serious about me cutting the orders?"

"Yes, I was serious. It's time I went home. I've been in this damn country far too long. Four tours is a lot to ask of anyone with one year as a POW on top of it. So yes, once I get back from this mission, send me home. Harry's going to need the help, and I need the break."

Dr. Nicholson pointed at the front of the hospital. "Come by my office when you return, and I'll forward the orders. Don't get yourself killed, please, Colonel MacKenzie."

Jackson grinned. "Won't happen if I have anything to say about it."

"Good, but people who get wounded or killed normally don't. You can stay with Major Russell for a few minutes. He's awake. Be warned he's on heavy pain medication. We're shipping him out by helicopter in thirty minutes."

"Got it." Jackson pushed the door open and went into the room. "Hey, Harry."

Harry raised his head a few inches. "Hey, kid."

Kid? Harry hasn't called me that since Special Forces training. He's only two years older than me. Jackson walked to the bed and took Harry's hand. "Dr. Nicholson told me about your foot. I'm sorry about that. It should be me in that bed, not you. I wish you were going with us tonight."

"Me too, so I could watch your six. JJ, you have nothing to feel sorry about, you've always been faster than me. So unless you were dogging it, you would've always beat me to that foxhole. Just come back safe. I'll see you in the states. At least you'll finally put some meat on your skinny chicken legs and bony ass."

Jackson jerked on his baggy pants. "I do have skinny legs. They look better than your fur-covered woolly bear chest."

Harry rubbed his chest. "Yep, I love my fur coat. I'll miss you bugging me when I take off my shirt. You keep drivin' the women wild with your bare chest with only a few hairs in the center, Mr. Baby Face. Be careful, my friend. I'll see you in a couple of weeks."

"Bet on it, Harry. Just take it easy." Jackson waggled his finger at his friend. "Don't give the nurses any trouble."

"Look who's talking? The pot's calling the kettle black. You're in the hospital more than I am."

"Yep. Your last major injury was a splinter from the door to our quarters. Mine was shrapnel in my butt. I put in my own IV, and you whined like a baby."

"That splinter wasn't little."

"It was smaller than a toothpick. The doc popped it out in less than ten seconds. I spent a week on my stomach with stitches in my ass."

Harry's eyes crinkled at the corners. "Yeah, it was funny watching the nurse clean your wounds. You looked like a tomato when something rose."

"You had to bring that up."

Jackson gripped Harry's hand all the way to the ambulance. He released it when he didn't have a choice. Once the attendant shut the doors, Jackson stood in the roadway until the vehicle disappeared. Adjusting the rifle strap on his shoulder, he headed toward his quarters to await the final mission briefing with Colonel Johnson.

CHAPTER 4

January 27, 1972 – 1940 hours

Jackson donned his parachute and tightened the straps then grabbed the rest of his gear. At the doorway of his quarters, he paused, turned around, and secured the signed written orders inside his footlocker.

"Why'd you do that?" Bill asked, standing at the threshold.

"You need to ask after the POW camp? I will not let Charlie use the orders for propaganda. The only thing they'll be able to use is these." Jackson pulled his dog tags from under his shirt. "Go ahead. I'll meet you there."

"Yes, sir." Bill sprinted to the waiting olive green deuce and a half truck. He jumped in the open bed with Ty, Mikey, and Chief.

With the airfield only five-minutes by foot, Jackson tossed his jeep keys on his bunk. *I'll use the time to think.* He stood on the C-130 rear boarding ramp and looked across the vast expanse of the base. A strong feeling of déjà vu crossed his senses. *We shouldn't go. Something's wrong.* He shook his head to clear the errant thought. *It's only my imagination. Damn POW camp.* Turning on his heel, he climbed the ramp and sat on the port side bench next to Chief.

The C-130 accelerated down the runway. A sudden cross-wind sent it sideways on take-off. Jackson held onto a cargo strap to keep from being dumped from the bench on his head. Once the plane cleared the turbulence, it quickly reached the 30,000-foot jump altitude.

For thirty minutes, the men sucked one-hundred percent oxygen from a tank on the wall to purge the nitrogen from their bloodstream. They didn't want the bends. The green light flashed on at 2345 hours, and the men stoically stepped off into the darkness.

Cold air hit Jackson's face. It was too dark to see anything but the glowing hands of his altimeter. Freefall always gave him a rush. A natural high. His heart beat faster as adrenaline flowed into his bloodstream. He felt alive again. At 3,000 feet, he pulled the ripcord, his chute lines jerked then nothing but floating.

Their target LZ was a flooded rice paddy ten klicks north of Hanoi. Loud plops sounded as the men hit the ground. Jackson slid to a stop on his butt. He stood, slinging mud from his hands.

The men sunk their chutes in the muddy water to hide them from enemy patrols. They pulled baggy brown cotton pants and shirts over their fatigues to remain indistinguishable from the civilians. Completing the illusion, they wore cloths around their heads under floppy straw hats. With everyone covered head to toe in mud, the subdued lighting made for excellent cover.

As the blood-red sun peeked over the eastern horizon, Ty climbed a tree to scan for any unwanted eyes observing their activities. Mikey and Jackson patrolled the perimeter. Bill and Chief searched the riverbank for the two sampans needed for their entry into the city.

Jackson pointed at the river. "Put them in the water, guys."

"Thought the plan was to hunker down and go tomorrow, boss?" Chief waved at the sun. "It's almost noon."

"Remember, I changed the plan. And don't start the engines. I don't want local patrols on the riverbank to even look our way. We'll float with the current. It's slower but safer than using the engines."

Chief and Jackson piled into the first sampan. Ty, Bill, and Mikey in the second.

Jackson picked up a cane pole. "Might as well look the part." He dropped the bare hook into the water.

Chief adjusted the tiller. "Would be funny if you caught something, boss."

"Yeah, that would be a hungry fish."

After two hours, Jackson chunked his fishing pole aside. He was bored. "Want me to take over, Chief? With this slow-ass current, it'll take a while to get there."

"Nah, I got it."

Jackson pulled out his canteen. He gulped down a long drink then leaned back against the front bench. His M16 lay across his chest as he watched the riverbank for patrols.

The sun crossed the horizon to the west. Blue sky turned orange, red, gray, and finally black. The moon rose as the stars dotted the sky. Jackson checked his watch as the men hid the small boats in the rice paddies near the supports of the Long Bien Bridge. 0100 hours. They hiked in the shadows to 66 Nguyễn Thái Học Street, the former Catholic girls' school, now the Vietnam National Museum of Fine Arts.

32

Jackson stood at the corner of the building across from their objective. His men lined up behind him against the wall. "Don't see anyone around." He ran across the street and crouched behind a large bamboo tree with his right eye behind his rifle sights scanning the area.

One by one, his men followed.

"Belly crawl from here. It'll keep anyone from seeing us. Use your knives to make sure Charlie hasn't booby-trapped the lawn." Jackson pulled his KA-BAR out of the sheath.

"Why'd they paint the museum yellow, boss?" Chief whispered.

"Who cares? Made it easy to find."

The men squirmed along the ground in a line on their knees and elbows like worms. Their knives stuck out in front like barbed points. They stood a foot from the east wall.

"By the numbers. Just like we rehearsed it," Jackson said in a hushed tone. He kept his back to the wall of the three-story building, rifle out, watching their rear.

"Boss." Chief pulled on the door handle. "The side door's locked with a padlock in an eyebolt. Didn't the CIA guy say this door was broken?"

"Well, that's CIA intel for you. Wrong. Bill, get over here. You told me in the POW camp about picking the locks at your high school to swim laps in the pool. Too bad you couldn't pick the handcuffs the Cong used on us with that nail."

Bill pulled his lock picks out of his boot. "Knew these things would come in handy one day." He eyed his commanding officer. "Those locks weren't standard and rusted. Don't blame me for Chinese workmanship."

Seconds went by as Bill messed with the padlock.

Someone, a guard or passerby, could sound an alarm. Just as Jackson decided to pop smoke, Bill pulled off the lock and opened the door.

The men fanned out to their assigned locations. Bill and Mikey checked the first floor. Jackson and Chief bounded up the stairwell to the third. Ty stood guard on the second-floor stairwell door.

Jackson and Chief leapfrogged each other from room to room. Every gallery was dark. The statues made ghostly still shadows on the wall as moonlight streamed through the windows. Except for the ceiling fans, the only things moving on the floor was them. At the end of the hallway, they stopped and faced each other.

"Quiet as a tomb, boss." Chief wiped the sweat from his forehead.

"Nice choice of words. That's what worries me." Jackson drank a quick swig from his canteen. "Let's get back to the rendezvous point."

They met up with Ty, Bill, and Mikey in the stairwell at the second floor door.

"Anything?" Jackson pointed his M16 muzzle at the ground.

"Nothing. Not a guard in sight. No alarm system either. This'll be easy." Bill shouldered his M16 then pulled two cardboard tubes out of his pack.

Ty did the same.

"When is anything we do easy?" Jackson flipped his M16 across his back. He slipped his KA-BAR out of the sheath on his belt and pulled his service pistol from his holster.

"Well, there's always a first time," Bill said.

"Yeah, right. If we find anyone, no shooting unless we don't have a choice. We don't want to wind up in a firefight here. No cover in these open galleries. Okay, on three. One-two-three." Jackson eased the door open.

Chief stepped out with his back to the wall on the left side of the door, his Colt pistol in his right hand, combat knife in his left. Jackson matched him on the right. Ty and Bill came out between them. Bill flipped on his flashlight mounted on his pack strap.

Chief and Jackson led the way down the hallway. Mikey backed up on rear guard while Ty and Bill carried a cardboard tube in each hand.

Jackson spotted the small room with their objective on his right. "There it is. Bill, Ty, make quick work of this so we can get out of here."

"Roger." Bill popped the plastic cap off one cardboard tube, pulled out the painting, and unrolled it.

Ty removed the first painting from the wall and laid it face-down on the floor. He pulled a pair of pliers from his back pocket and carefully pried off the back. Bill held the forgery inside the frame as Ty secured the back with the staple gun from his pack.

Jackson checked his watch as he, Mikey, and Chief watched the hallway. *This took ten minutes back at camp.*

Bill tapped Jackson on the shoulder. "Done. All four paintings accounted for."

Jackson rechecked his watch. "Best time yet. Eight minutes. Let's double-time it out of here."

Outside the museum, the men took up defensive positions around the door.

A police siren echoed in the darkness. The men froze in place behind a small hedge as a spotlight lit the building ten feet from their location. Each man held his breath as the car continued along the road.

Jackson stepped out and looked both ways. "Close one. Looks like we did it. Let's get back to the river before anyone spots us."

Single file, leapfrogging each other from building to building, the men returned to the water.

"We do the same thing, float the seventy-five miles to the South China Sea. No engines to avoid the patrols." Jackson pushed his boat into the water with Chief beside him.

January 30, 1972 – 1645 hours

At the mouth of the river, the men beached their tiny fishing vessels, pulled off the civilian outerwear, and humped ten miles along the shoreline.

Chief ran up to the unmarked, black UH-1D hidden under a camouflage net. "Holy cow, boss. How did the CIA conceal a chopper inside territory controlled by North Vietnam?"

"Don't know and don't care. Get it uncovered so I can do my checks," Jackson glanced at his watch. "Ty, you, Bill, and Mikey set up a small perimeter. Once Chief's done, he'll join you. Eat your rations at your station. Sundown is at 1845. I'm going to wait until dark to take off. It'll be a lot harder to hit this bird with an RPG if Charlie can't see it."

Two hours later, as the rotors picked up speed, Jackson poked his head out of the pilot's door. "Let's go before something lands on us!"

The four men sprinted for the chopper and climbed aboard.

Bill stuck his head between the pilot and the co-pilot seat. "This thing is loud. I can't believe one of the local patrols didn't spot us."

"Me too. I'm not sticking around to push our luck. Sit down and strap in. It might get bumpy." Jackson pulled up on the cyclic and collective. The pitch of the rotors changed, and the bird lifted off. After a gentle turn on its Z-axis, he pointed the slick south along the coast for their rendezvous with CVA-43, the USS *Coral Sea* at Yankee Station.

January 31, 1972

After their last fuel stop at Pleiku, Jackson breathed a sigh of relief. They were only forty-nine miles from home.

A yellow flash crossed in front of the cockpit window from right to left and exploded. "Shit! RPG."

He pushed the stick to the left and jammed his left foot on the pedal in a hard bank to avoid the next one.

35

A second rocket hit the tail rotor.

The helicopter became a bucking bronco trying to throw its rider.

Jackson tightened his grip on the stick and collective to maintain control of his aircraft. Damage to the tail rotor and tailplanes made anything but a controlled crash impossible. The blue sky went orange-red when a third rocket hit under his seat. Smoke obscured his view. His ears rang. White-hot pain enveloped his body as shrapnel peppered the cockpit. He willed his arms and legs to move. If he let go, they were dead.

The numbered wheels of the altimeter rolled smaller and smaller. 600 feet. 500 feet. 400 feet. Jackson ignored the pain. He still had enough time to induce an auto-rotation by adjusting the pitch of the blades with the cyclic and collective. 300 feet. 200 feet. Treetops brushed the skids. A small clear area appeared between the trees. He wrenched the throttle to full power and yanked back on the stick. The ground came up to meet him, slammed against the chopper. More pain than Jackson could imagine grabbed his entire body. The fuselage slid sideways, rushing toward the trees at the edge of the clearing. There was nothing he could do. Jackson braced himself for another crash.

The aircraft slowed. Stopped without a collision.

He looked out the window. Cabbages. And mud.

"Oowww…" High and low pitched voices echoed from the passenger cabin.

Jackson glanced behind him as his men staggered like drunken sailors after an all-night binge.

Bill looked down into Jackson's eyes. "You still with us, sir?"

"Yeah, you know what to do."

"Yes, sir."

Chief shoved the sliding side door open. He hopped out and went into a crouch with his M16. Ty and Bill joined him. They took cover positions around the downed chopper. Bellies on the ground, rifles pointed downrange. Ready to lay down fire in case of attack.

The high-pitched squeal of abused metal sounded as someone pried open the half-melted, shrapnel-ridden door. Mikey's head appeared in the open doorway. "Time to get out, sir. So much for not needing my services."

"True." Jackson started to climb out but stopped when pain shot up his spine. "Shit!"

"Don't, sir. Let me get you out." Mikey pulled Jackson from the helicopter and laid him on the ground.

"How bad is it, Mikey?" Jackson felt cold mud ooze down the back of his collar and inside his boots. Lightning pulsed through his body with each beat of his heart.

"Bad. You have half the fuselage inside your body." Mikey slit the sides of Jackson's cotton tiger-striped shirt and pants then wrapped pressure bandages tightly over the deep lacerations to slow the bleeding.

Jackson caught the smell of alcohol as Mikey swabbed his right hip. When Mikey pulled out the morphine syrette, Jackson placed a hand on his arm. "Put it away."

"Colonel, you're in pain." Mikey waved the syrette in front of Jackson's face. "I need to give you this."

"No. I can't keep a clear head doped up on morphine. Charlie took out the tail rotor to bring us down in a remote location, so they're close by. We need to get moving to stay ahead of them. Help me up and give me my rifle."

"Sir! You have some pretty severe injuries. There's no way you can walk, let alone hold a rifle."

"Just get me up, damn it! That's an order. I'm walking whether you help me or not."

Mikey pulled Jackson to his feet and placed his left arm across his shoulders. "Hold on to me. Don't put any pressure on your right leg."

Ty grabbed Jackson's gear from the co-pilot's seat and slung the rifle across his back.

"Help me put on my pack." Jackson tried to pull his arm from Mikey's grasp.

"Across that shoulder? No way!" Mikey's hand tightened on Jackson's wrist.

Jackson gave him a hard stare. "You heard me, Roberts!"

"I'd do it if I was you, Sergeant." Bill dumped Jackson's pack upside down, spilling the contents onto the ground. Ty and Chief gathered everything and stuffed it in their packs.

"Yes, sir," Mikey mumbled, relinquishing the arm as Bill placed the harness gently on Jackson's shoulders.

The weight of the canvas bag caused Jackson's legs to buckle. He clenched his teeth until the sharp pain subsided. Bill buckled the waist belt as Mikey retook his position.

"I have the other side as a counterbalance, Sergeant." Bill grabbed Jackson's web belt. "Now I get it. By holding onto the pack straps, it's easier to distribute your weight between us. Good call, sir."

With one glance from Jackson, Chief took point. Ty went to rear guard. They headed south.

At the first rest stop, Mikey pulled out the morphine syrette. Bill yanked him aside with a hand on his collar. "Sergeant Roberts, I know you want to help the colonel. But he has to keep a clear head to maintain control of the situation. You know he takes his job seriously. He will not let you give it to him, and neither will I unless he relents to the pain. Even though we're in South Vietnam, someone shot us down. Remember how we wound up as POWs. I will not let that happen to him again. His pride dictates he walks to the base, not be carried like last time. Understood? Keep him hydrated when we stop for the night. He's in too much pain to eat anything."

"Yes, Captain. Understood." Mikey returned the medication to his bag.

"Thanks, Bill. I didn't want to explain it to him again," Jackson called from the ground.

February 3, 1972 – 1200 hours

After three days of hiking, sleeping in muddy ditches and the lucky find of a beat-up pickup, they arrived at base camp. They hid inside a bamboo thicket on the perimeter. Even there it wasn't safe. Charlie was everywhere. Yesterday's skirmish, even though a victory, almost became their last. Chief and Ty's rifles jammed. They used every hand grenade to keep Charlie at bay. Bill and Mikey tossed Jackson in a trench and lay on top of him. Firing over his back. They emptied every magazine. Only a round from the M79 grenade launcher saved their bacon. It landed on top of the enemy. All five men dropped in their tracks.

I wish the truck hadn't run out of gas. "Chief, check the area. Make sure there aren't any surprises." Jackson flipped the safety off the Colt pistol in his left hand. "We only have ten rounds of pistol ammo between us. I don't want to wind up in another scuffle before we get past the main gate."

"Yes, sir." Chief slid into the shadows. A short time later, a small whistle sounded. "All clear."

Bill and Mikey emerged from the brush onto the main road leading into camp with Jackson between them. They made their way to Chief's side as he drained the last swig from his canteen.

Chief pointed at a structure in the distance. "Look at that, Colonel."

"Wow. The base was mortared again while we were gone. Headquarters took a direct hit. It's nothing but a burned-out metal skeleton." Jackson glanced behind them as Ty came out on rear guard. "Now that everyone's here, let's go. I know you guys are hungry since we ran out of food yesterday."

Two steps inside the perimeter fence, Jackson lost control of his good leg. His weight sent him, Bill and Mikey hard to the ground on their knees.

Mickey pushed Jackson down on his back as he struggled to stand. "Not this time, Colonel. You have a high fever. We need to take you to the hospital."

"Get ready for your horsey ride, boss." Chief slung Jackson over his shoulder in a fireman's carry. He swatted Jackson's rear. "Hold on. It might get bumpy for a few minutes." In long strides, Chief ran toward the hospital. Jackson's head bounced up and down next to Chief's butt. His open mouth left a trail of vomit in their wake.

Inside the hospital lobby, Chief dumped Jackson into a wheelchair as Mikey went to the nurses' desk.

Jackson looked up at his men. "Find the temporary HQ, report to whoever's in charge, and turn over the paintings. I'm staying here."

Bill patted Jackson on the shoulder. "You'd better, or I'll have Chief sit on you. Let's go guys."

Seconds after they left, Jackson couldn't hold his body in the chair. He slid out into a heap on the floor. *I'm so hot.*

Alarm bells rang. "Dr. Nicholson, report to the lobby for an emergency." Jackson heard go out over the intercom.

Dr. Nicholson ran through the double doors into the front lobby and slid to a stop next to the wheelchair.

Jackson gazed up at Dr. Nicholson. "Hiya, Doc," he whispered.

"So much for not getting hurt, right Colonel MacKenzie," Dr. Nicholson said sarcastically. With the aid of two orderlies, he lifted Jackson onto a gurney. They pushed it down the hall at a run.

Jackson stared at the long string of fluorescent lights rushing by overhead. Inside the operating room, a nurse stuck a needle into the back of his hand as another one strapped an oxygen mask over his face. Then everything went black.

"What the hell!" Bill clasped both hands behind his head when an MP pointed an M16 at him in the doorway of the motor pool building. Ty,

Chief, and Mikey received the same treatment as a squad of MPs surrounded them.

Lt. Colonel Goodspeed leaned into Bill's face. "Don't say another word, any of you. Unless you want a bullet in your brains." He stepped back as the MPs handcuffed the four men and shoved them into chairs against the wall.

"Colonel, we're not going anywhere." Bill nodded at their watchers. "Could these guys please stop pointing guns at our heads?"

"No!" Goodspeed turned to his aide. "Call headquarters. I need to know what to do with these men." He paced back and forth across the motor pool until the call connected.

A young lieutenant waved the phone back and forth. "I have Colonel Tapper on the line, sir."

Goodspeed spoke into a box on a desk five feet away from Bill. "MacKenzie's men showed up today with the missing paintings, sir. MacKenzie's not with them. Neither is Russell."

A tinny voice came from the speakerphone. "That's strange. I know they went since JAG issued the warrants. Search the base. Those two may be hiding to avoid arrest. Good job on capturing the other four. There's a commendation in it for you. Secure those men at the base holding facility. I'll make the arrangements for their return to the states on my end."

An hour later, Goodspeed glared at Bill through the bars of the drunk tank. "Where's Lieutenant Colonel MacKenzie and Major Russell?"

"Major Russell didn't go. Colonel MacKenzie is at the hospital. He's probably in surgery to take the shitload of shrapnel out of his body." Bill's voice rumbled like subdued thunder.

The same question-and-answer session continued for the next forty-five minutes. Bill sat on the bench next to Chief. He refused to speak another word to the stupid officer.

An MP handed Goodspeed a piece of paper. He glanced over it and cleared his throat. "Captain Mason."

"Yeah. What do you want?" Bill crossed his arms over his chest.

"Headquarters has confirmed Major Russell is at the hospital in Da Nang."

"Good, I told you he didn't go with us."

Goodspeed shrugged. "My aide checked on Lieutenant Colonel MacKenzie's location. I've sent MPs to arrest him at the base hospital once he clears surgery." He waved the paper at Bill. "I have classified orders to put all of you on the next available aircraft bound for the states."

"You can't take the colonel out of the hospital. He's badly injured. It'll kill him," Mikey yelled across the cell.

"Right now, Sergeant Roberts, I don't care. You guys are traitors and don't deserve any more of my time or Dr. Nicholson's. I have my orders. If MacKenzie dies, he dies. So be it. Your ride to prison leaves in four hours." Goodspeed turned on his heel and left the room.

"Shit!" Bill slammed his fist into the wall.

Dr. Nicholson glanced up from writing notes at the desk when four soldiers burst into the recovery room. "Get out of here!"

Two men pointed M16s at Jackson lying unconscious on the bed. One man stood in front of the door, rifle held across his chest. The other one walked up to Jackson. Nicholson knew this man well. Staff Sgt. Reynolds had put more men in the hospital after bar fights than the rest of the base MPs combined. The man was brutal, heavy-handed, and obnoxious.

Reynolds did the unthinkable. He yanked the oxygen mask from Jackson's face and ripped out the four IV lines, one by one. With blood all over his hands, Reynolds wiped them on his pants.

Dr. Nicholson jumped between Reynolds and his patient. "What the hell are you doing? He needs the blood transfusion and fluids to raise his blood pressure."

"Get out of my way." Reynolds pointed his pistol at Dr. Nicholson's head and cocked the hammer. "Unless you want to join him in the grave. We have orders. MacKenzie's on his way stateside for trial."

"No, this man is my responsibility." Dr. Nicholson crossed his arms over his chest.

The MP from the door shoved Dr. Nicholson into the wall. He screwed his rifle barrel into Nicholson's ear. "Don't move. Tell your staff to back off."

Dr. Nicholson waved at his nurses and orderlies. "Do what they say. Someone call Goodspeed. I want to know why these guys are killing my patient."

Reynolds pulled the blanket off Jackson. "Shit, he's naked."

"Of course he is, Sergeant. I cut off his uniform in surgery." Dr. Nicholson's forehead furrowed. "Please don't do this. Any move could kill him if the shrapnel cuts open an artery. He's in serious condition."

41

"Don't care." Reynolds pointed at the male orderly in surgical scrubs. "You! Go get your fatigues and boots."

Sgt. Ross looked at Dr. Nicholson. "Sir?"

"Think about your answer." The MP pressed the rifle deeper into the doctor's ear.

Dr. Nicholson nodded to the orderly. "Do as he says, Sergeant."

Upon Ross' return, Reynolds manhandled Jackson into the clothing as he flopped around like a limp noodle. Instead of carrying Jackson on a stretcher, Reynolds dragged him outside by his arms. Two MPs pointed their M16s at Jackson's head while the other backed up on rear guard.

Dr. Nicholson walked behind the men. "You can't take Colonel MacKenzie. His injuries preclude him from going anywhere until he's stabilized. Take him back inside. That's an order."

"I don't take orders from you." Reynolds grasped Jackson's legs, the man on rear guard took his arms. They swung Jackson between them. "One-two," Reynolds called out. At "three," they let go. Jackson flew sideways into the back of a pickup. His body slid to a stop against the cab. Reynolds and company drove off with Jackson rolling around unsecured in the open bed.

"What did MacKenzie do to deserve this?" Nicholson walked back into the hospital. He had an objection letter to write. What happened was completely against regulations. Not even the President of the United States could override his medical orders.

Mikey flipped the handcuff on his left wrist back and forth with his finger. The MPs had secured the other end to the armrest. It was tight but not cutting off the circulation like the ones in the POW camp. *At least my fingers aren't asleep.* He glanced at Bill, Ty, and Chief. They were in the same boat. Locked down to their chairs in the seating area of the C-130 next to the cockpit bulkhead.

"Grab the other arm. Let's pull him up the ramp. I'm tired," said a winded male voice.

Oh no! Mikey looked in the direction of the sound. Two men were dragging Colonel MacKenzie up the cargo ramp on his back by his arms. His boot heels made dark streaks on the metal. His green uniform shirt was almost black across his right shoulder and down his chest. His pants looked the same. Sweat dripped from his forehead. Milky liquid dribbled from his mouth as his head lolled from side to side. "Captain Mason. Look. They didn't leave the colonel in the hospital."

Bill tried to stand, but the handcuff on his wrist prevented it. "I'll kill Goodspeed for this."

The two men dumped Jackson in the seat next to Mikey, handcuffed his left arm to the armrest, and latched the seatbelt. They walked away laughing.

"The great MacKenzie. Now he's buzzard fodder," said the man with Staff Sergeant stripes and the name tag, Reynolds.

"Stronzo!" Mikey clenched his right hand into a fist. He'd settle for getting his hands on Reynolds. Even though he'd never met the man, he knew his reputation. Reynolds loved to cause pain because he could get away with it. And the colonel just paid the price.

"Mikey, check on him. He's sucking air through an open mouth. His chest is heaving like my grandmother when her asthma acts up." Bill leaned forward in his seat. "Holy crap, there's blood dripping onto the floor. His eyes are so tightly closed, I see wrinkles at the corners."

Mikey tried to grab Jackson's collar to pull his head closer. He missed. Jackson's upper torso was leaning so far forward and to the left, he couldn't reach it. What he felt on the colonel's mangled shoulder scared him. Warm wetness. Blood. "I can't with the cuff on my arm." He threw his dog tags at the MPs to get their attention. "Guys, take him back to the hospital. Please. He's unconscious and contorted so much it's hard for him to breathe. The only thing keeping him in the seat is the seat belt."

"Shut up, Roberts," Reynolds yelled from the ramp.

"Listen, you assholes! Chapter one, regulation one in the manual states that casualties must be carefully handled. You just dragged Colonel MacKenzie in here by his arms. Number two states to stop life-threatening bleeding, open the airway, restore breathing, prevent or control shock, and protect the wounds from further contamination. You've broken all of those as well. That's just page one." Mikey became hoarse as he quoted the regulations page by page for the next six hours after the plane took off. He knew them by heart. They were the bible of all medics.

The MPs put in earplugs to drown out the noise.

While the C-130 was on the ground in Japan to take on fuel, the MPs escorted each man, in turn, to relieve themselves. Except for Jackson who remained slumped forward, unconscious, strapped into his seat.

Mikey stood to take his turn and dropped to his knees in front of his CO.

"Get up, Roberts." Reynolds poked Mikey in the back with his pistol.

"No!" Mikey placed his fingers on the carotid artery in Jackson's neck. *This isn't good. His heart's racing like a car in the Indy 500.* Running his checklist, he lifted Jackson's eyelids. *Eyes rolled back, pupils fixed.* He placed his palm on Jackson's forehead. *I could cook an egg it's so hot.* Unable to take the injustice anymore, he stood and faced his watcher. "Colonel MacKenzie needs medical care now, or he'll die in the next three to four hours."

"We have priority explicit orders to make sure all of you arrive together. I don't care if your traitorous friend is injured. I'll deliver a dead man if I have to. At least he won't give me any trouble like you are right now, Roberts." Arrogance oozed like slime from Reynolds' voice.

Mikey slammed his foot on the floor. "That's exactly what will happen if you don't take him to a hospital. You want that on your conscience?"

Reynolds jammed his pistol barrel between Mikey's eyes, finger on the trigger. "Do you want to join him, Roberts?"

Mikey stomped toward the head, his shoulders slumped in defeat. The metal snap of locks engaging caught his attention. A large square metal plate — a transport pallet had been secured in the cargo area. Folding cots were attached to it. One by one, nine men, either in wheelchairs or walking, boarded with their corresponding medical personnel.

After Mikey returned to his seat, the MPs sat in their chairs for takeoff.

"Stop ignoring me. Get a doctor over here before the colonel dies!" Mikey screamed at the MPs. *He kept me from torture in the camp. I can't repay that debt by saving his life. I'll never forgive myself. Bet they won't let us go to the funeral to honor him.*

Who's dying? All my patients are accounted for. What's going on over there? Once the plane took off for Hawaii, Dr. Franklin Howard, known to his friends as Frank, Major, United States Army, followed the noise. As he came around the cargo pallets separating the seating area from the cargo bay, he stopped, disturbed at the scene in front of him. A soldier slumped so far forward in his seat he looked like a pretzel. On his left wrist, a handcuff. His uniform so dark, it looked like it had been dunked in water.

Even from a distance, Frank could smell the iron in the air. Under the man's seat, a pool of black, crusted blood with fresh red blood dribbling down the chair frame. "Shit!" He ran to the MP with staff sergeant stripes on his sleeves. The man's uniform had the name tag Reynolds.

Frank pointed at the injured soldier. "Where are the medical personnel accompanying this man? He's almost dead already. Half his blood is on the deck under him."

Staff Sgt. Reynolds shrugged, his face hard and unfeeling. "MacKenzie's a prisoner. He doesn't have any."

"What! That's against the regulations!" Frank took a step to go around the man.

Reynolds sidestepped into his path. "You don't have clearance to be around those men."

"Get out of my way!" Frank pressed his height advantage over Reynolds. Six feet to five-ten. He breathed into man's nose. *Hope he likes garlic and anchovies.*

"No, sir."

"I'll have you up on charges, Sergeant." Frank clenched his fists at his side. He so wanted to bop the man on the head, but that went against his oath of do no harm.

"Don't think so, Doc. My orders are quite clear. If you want to see the traitor, then do it, but I ain't moving."

Frank climbed over a small stack of empty cargo pallets to get to the wounded man. He picked up the dog tags hanging from the soldier's neck to check the blood type and name. *O positive, MacKenzie, Jackson J.*

The staff sergeant in the next seat motioned for him to bend over. "The MPs pulled him out of the hospital. Colonel MacKenzie received several nasty shrapnel wounds four days ago. Dr. Nicholson probably removed the big stuff to stabilize his condition. Most of it's still embedded."

A colonel. Great. Wonder what he did to wind up here. Doesn't matter. He's my patient now. Frank glanced at the young man's name tag. "How do you know that, Sergeant Roberts?"

"I'm a medic, sir. The colonel was under my care until we arrived back at base camp. I checked his vitals as best I could before we took off. His pulse is weak and rapid. I'd estimate it at around 150-160. He's in hypovolemic shock from blood loss. His eyes are rolled back into his head. The pupils are fixed and dilated. And his forehead is hot and dry to the touch."

"Thank you, Sergeant Roberts, for the excellent report." Frank moved a few feet away to his next target. Back ramrod-straight, he stood in front of Reynolds. "Read my lips. This is a direct order. Take that cuff off now!"

Reynolds glanced at the gold oak leaves on the doctor's collar and yanked the cuff keys from the clip on his belt. "Whatever, sir. MacKenzie can't go anywhere. We're over the Pacific Ocean." He bent and unlocked the handcuff.

Finally. This man hasn't got a lot of time left. Frank waved over his two best medics, Sgt. Peters and Cpl. Tanner. Once they arrived, he unlatched the seatbelt.

MacKenzie, unconscious and limp, pitched forward. Frank and the medics caught him before he hit the floor.

Frank looped his elbows under MacKenzie's armpits while the medics grabbed his legs. Together, they carried the wounded man to the cargo area and laid him on a cot.

Frank examined his patient while his medics cut off the blood-soaked clothing and bandages. He confirmed Sgt. Roberts' rundown then glared at Reynolds through narrowed eyes. His medics waited for orders beside him. "Sergeant Peters, start two wide-open IV lines of fluids and plasma to raise his blood pressure. It's too low. Add a round of heavy antibiotics to the bags. We need to curb the infection present in the open wounds. Corporal Tanner, get him on a full face mask with one-hundred-percent oxygen. Then cover him with blankets to keep him warm. He's in shock."

The two men rushed around in a coordinated ballet. Smooth and practiced. Frank grabbed a morphine vial, injected a dose into the port on one IV line, and sat next to his patient. He turned to his medics. "Tanner, Peters, go help my staff take care of the other wounded men. My duty is clear. I need to stay with Colonel MacKenzie and monitor his vital signs. He's walking a fine edge between life and death."

The second the landing gear touched the runway in Hawaii, Reynolds and two MPs shoved Frank, Sgt. Peters and Cpl. Tanner away from MacKenzie's prone body.

"Get out of my way. That's an order. Medical protocol dictates I transfer Colonel MacKenzie to the hospital," Frank yelled at the men standing between him and his patient.

Staff Sgt. Reynolds chest bumped Frank. "No! He stays on the plane. I'm not losing my stripes for a traitor."

Frank wiped spittle from his face. "Sergeant Peters, Corporal Tanner. Put Colonel MacKenzie on a stretcher and take him to the ambulance."

As the two men picked up MacKenzie from the cot, three MPs pointed M16s at their heads.

Frank waved them off. "Sergeant Peters. Go to the hospital and grab as much O positive blood, plasma, saline and morphine you can cram into a transport container while they refuel the plane. Including the kitchen sink if you can swing it. I will not let a wounded soldier die on my watch." He

46

turned to Staff Sgt. Reynolds. "Since the cargo deck of a C-130 isn't a proper medical facility, could you at least let Sergeant Roberts help me take care of Colonel MacKenzie?"

Reynolds shook his head. "No can do. These guys are Green Berets. I don't want a scalpel in my back. You'll have to keep him alive all by yourself."

"Sergeant Reynolds, you made a hard job for two people almost impossible for me." Frank pointed at the colonel's bloody shoulder bandage. "If I can't get the bleeding stopped, Colonel MacKenzie will die before this plane gets halfway across the Pacific Ocean. He won't have enough blood left in his body to keep his heart beating. I hope you can live with yourself. You're nothing but an ignorant redneck. A wad of gum on the shoe of civilized people."

"Whatever, sir. He still stays on the plane. Deal with it." Reynolds flipped Dr. Howard his right middle finger.

"Asshole!" Frank bent over his patient to check his pulse. *It's barely palpable. I don't think I can save him. God help me. And him.*

Two hours into the flight to California, MacKenzie's breathing came in short, quick gasps. Frank pumped the blood pressure cuff around the colonel's left bicep. "Shit, I can't even get a reading." He put his stethoscope on MacKenzie's chest. "And he's tachycardic. His heart's racing over 210 beats a minute."

Frank grabbed a central line kit from the transport container and inserted the catheter under Jackson's left collarbone. He pulled a unit of blood from the cooler, attached it to the line, and squeezed the bag to force every drop into his patient. Pumping up the cuff, he rechecked the colonel's blood pressure. "Crap, no change." After three more bags, MacKenzie's breathing slowed. Frank checked the blood pressure again. "Finally, a reading, 90 systolic by palpation. Not good, but better. At least he's not as blue, and his heart slowed to 150." Dr. Howard inserted two more IV lines then hung a bag of plasma and saline wide open. Desperate, he went down on one knee next to the cot. "Colonel, keep fighting. It's taking every trick I know to keep you alive," he yelled in Jackson's ear.

The same routine continued for the next six hours.

Frank was met by the same excuse in San Diego. Orders. As they refueled the plane for the final leg of the journey, he stood toe-to-toe with

Reynolds. "Are you a robot? How can you let another soldier die? You're treating him like a piece of trash."

Reynolds walked over to MacKenzie, pulled a Colt service pistol from his holster, and racked a round into the chamber. He pressed the front sight between the colonel's closed eyes. "I can put him out of his misery if you want, Doc. That way, he doesn't suffer. It's what we do for dogs and horses. He's a traitor, and not even worth the price of a bullet, but I'm willing if you are. There are no deviations in our destination per orders from the Pentagon."

Frank pushed between Reynolds and his patient, the pistol muzzle against his chest. He glanced back at the colonel before returning his gaze to Reynolds. The muzzle had been pressed so hard into MacKenzie's forehead, a small circle impression remained. *He acts like a dictator. Must have little man syndrome. I bet his penis is the size of my pinkie. The colonel's defenseless.* "No, that's murder. If you do, I'll make sure you stand in front of a firing squad. You'll have to shoot me to get to him."

Reynolds holstered his pistol. "As you wish. I don't think you'll have to worry about it much longer." He turned and walked back to his post next to the other men.

"Dr. Howard," someone called from the front of the plane.

"Yes." Frank turned around.

The pilot stood in the cockpit doorway. "There's a delivery for you at the main gate from the San Diego Naval Medical Center. The note from Sergeant Peters says he figured you would need more supplies. This is like the last one. Do you want it?"

Peters, I'll put you in for a commendation and promotion for your quick thinking when I get a chance. "Yes, get it here, stat. I'm out of everything."

Eight hours later, the plane landed at Simmons Army Airfield. Frank stood in front of Reynolds when he approached to take MacKenzie off the plane. "Don't touch him. He's barely alive as it is. Get me an ambulance. Now!"

"There's one waiting at the edge of the airstrip. Your CO pulled a few strings. Not that I care. MacKenzie's a traitor. He deserves to die." Reynolds picked dirt from under his fingernails.

Frank leaned into Reynolds' face until their noses touched. "If I had the time, you would be scraping yourself off the deck." He pushed past the soldier as two men carried MacKenzie off the plane on a stretcher.

As Frank went down the ramp, he glanced at the green bus next to them. MacKenzie's men were climbing on board in handcuffs and leg irons.

Their shoulders slumped forward and heads hung low. The medic, Roberts, was last. He looked in Frank's direction.

"I'll do my best," Frank yelled. He'd heard the men over the engine noise. Wanting to know about their CO. Robert's voice the loudest of all. He couldn't leave his patient to tell them anything.

Roberts nodded and disappeared through the door.

Frank hopped into the ambulance. "Stick your foot in it, Sergeant. Colonel MacKenzie's barely breathing!" He squeezed blood into his patient. At his side, a medic bagged MacKenzie with a positive pressure mask attached to the oxygen bottle. Both men grabbed the gurney rails to keep from being dumped onto the floor as the ambulance slid sideways turning onto the asphalt road, lights, and siren screaming

Upon their arrival at the hospital, Frank rushed his patient into the surgical theater. Time was now the enemy. That golden hour slipped away hours ago. He had three possibilities. Death, brain damage, or a miracle.

CHAPTER 5

February 8, 1972

Jackson opened his eyes…nothing but a white blur. He slammed them shut, waited for a second, and forced both eyes back open. His vision cleared. White walls. White ceiling. *I'm in a hospital and wearing an open-backed gown with a brake line shoved up my penis.*

The melody from *Tie a Yellow Ribbon Round the Old Oak Tree* came from the FM radio on the table against the far wall.

Nice song. Jackson turned his head. Next to his bed sat a man wearing a white lab coat over green fatigues. Gold oak leaves stood out on his collar above the coat. He had an open *Time Magazine* with Henry Kissinger's picture on the cover propped on his crossed legs. *Bet he's my doctor. Reminds me of Clark Gable with the slicked-back brown hair and pencil mustache.* "Doc," he whispered.

The man lowered the magazine. "Good. You're awake. I'm Dr. Frank Howard." He checked Jackson's pulse at his wrist then placed a stethoscope on Jackson's chest. "Don't talk." Dr. Howard adjusted the valve on the wall next to the green line leading to the oxygen cannula under Jackson's nose. "Okay, I'm finished."

"What happened? Where am I? Other than in a hospital, I mean. Where are my men? Are they okay?"

Dr. Howard looped the stethoscope around his neck. He pulled a clipboard from a hook on the wall and wrote notes on the first page. "They're fine. You're the only one in the hospital. As to where they are, I'll get into that later. Please don't move your right arm or leg. I removed a pound of shrapnel from your body. The wound in your thigh went all the way to the bone and took over 150 sutures to close. The one in your shoulder is only slightly better at 125. You're on pain meds to maintain your comfort level. The wounds are infected, and you developed a high fever. To counter that, you're on heavy antibiotics. You'll be in the hospital for at least two weeks. Probably more."

I feel like a mummy in these bandages. Can't move anything on my right side at all. Not even my toes. Jackson swallowed to soothe his dry throat. "Okay. I know the hospital at my base camp, and this ain't it. You're not Dr. Nicholson, so where am I?"

50

"Colonel MacKenzie, you've been in the ICU for three days with a tube down your throat to help you breathe. That's the reason for your sore throat. You need to take it easy and not move around so much."

My nose itches. Bet I know why. Jackson reached up to scratch. His left arm stopped two inches above the bed rail as cold metal cut into his wrist. He glanced at his arm in surprise. "Why the handcuff? Am I under arrest or something?"

"Yes, you're under arrest, and I can't tell you why." Dr. Howard's jaw muscles bunched out as he ground his teeth together. "I'm merely your doctor. I don't understand it myself."

Even with his head buzzing, Jackson read the doctor like a book. "I like honesty, Doc. I'm sure this has something to do with our last mission. Are my men in the stockade?"

"Yes, and I do believe it has to do with your last mission."

"Then I wish I'd gone with my gut feeling. Now, where am I?"

"Home. Fort Bragg."

"Bragg, huh?" Jackson glanced out of the window. *Blue sky and fluffy white clouds. Where's the sidewalk? Oh yeah, the security ward is on the sixth floor.* His brain was foggy. The meds made it hard to concentrate.

"Yes, they yanked you out of the hospital against medical advice and tossed you on a plane." Dr. Howard shoved his hands in his lab coat pockets. "You were at death's door when we arrived at the hospital."

Jackson noted the doctor's disgusted tone and body language. "You must have something to do with me surviving or you wouldn't be here."

"You're perceptive, even pumped full of morphine and cephalosporin. You have a lucky leprechaun on your shoulder. No one will tell me why it was so important to damn near kill you getting you here in a hurry."

Thirsty, Jackson reached for the cup of water on his bedside table. The handcuff skipped across his wrist. He felt a sharp prick as it jerked the IV line from under his skin. Ruby-red blood ran like a flooded river from his forearm.

Dr. Howard grabbed the arm in a tight grip. With the other hand, he hit the bed buzzer repeatedly. "Someone get in here and help me!"

Six people dressed in white scrubs ran into the room.

Jackson sat still while Dr. Howard snugged a bandage around his forearm. "Gee, Doc, can you loosen it up? I want to keep my fingers."

"No." Dr. Howard laid Jackson's wrist across his chest. "Keep that where it is for a few minutes."

"Testy, aren't we." Jackson settled back in his pillows as everyone but the doctor and a nurse left the room.

Dr. Howard turned to the nurse. "Insert the line a little higher this time. I have a call to make." He stomped to the door. On the way out, he propped the door open. As the guard started to close it, Dr. Howard yanked it from his grasp. "It stays open, Corporal. I want to keep an eye on my patient. You damn guards are nothing but idiots."

Jackson watched the doctor pick up the phone at the nurses' station as his nurse put in a new IV line. This one near his elbow, away from the handcuff. *The doc's mad about something.*

Thirty minutes later, an older man dressed in an Army class A uniform approached Dr. Howard. Jackson squinted, but couldn't make out the rank on the shoulders. *Wonder who that is? Looks important with the CONARC patch. From the ribbons and overseas service bars, he's been in the army a while.*

Dr. Howard slammed his hand on the desk. "That stupid handcuff pulled out Colonel MacKenzie's IV line again. I poured over eight units of blood into the colonel during surgery to keep him alive. I don't need him losing more. That one small hole became a problem since he's on blood thinners to prevent blood clots due to his immobility. Are you trying to kill him? Sergeant Reynolds damn near succeeded."

What happened? Who's Reynolds? Maybe they'll say something. Jackson craned his head as far forward as he could without tipping himself out of the bed.

"No. Let me make a call. I don't have the authority to remove the handcuff. Only General Kowalski can do that." The man reached for the phone next to the patient monitors. A few minutes later, he hung up. "Okay, the general agrees to remove the handcuff. But the guard stays."

"As long as he stays outside the room, I don't care. I don't need any additional stress to my patient since some numskull ordered him flown nine thousand miles around the world while unconscious and nearly dead."

The officer bowed up. "Are you calling one of your superiors a numskull, Major Howard?"

Dr. Howard flashed an annoyed smile. "Yes, because it's the truth. I've already had this conversation with my commanding officer last night when I explained to him why I'm at Bragg, not Tripler. I sent him my report this morning. He agrees with me that anyone who gives an order that almost kills one of our own is an idiot. What are you going to do about it?"

"At the moment, nothing. I have my orders. Good day." The officer turned and walked away.

Wow, he's mad. Jackson leaned back in his bed before he caught an earful for stressing his body.

Dr. Howard came into the room pulling the guard by his shirtsleeve. "You heard him. Take it off. Now!"

The corporal glanced at Jackson as he held the key over the lock. Dr. Howard cleared his throat. The corporal removed the cuff, tucked it in his back pocket, and exited the room. The door closed slowly behind him.

He almost didn't follow the order. What's going on? Jackson shifted his gaze to Dr. Howard. "Doc?"

Dr. Howard lifted his head from writing notes on his clipboard. "Yes, Colonel MacKenzie."

"You've got some balls on you. Most staff corps officers I've run into don't push back like you do. From your reaction in the hall, my ride home wasn't pleasant, and the guys watched all of it."

"Yes, they did. You have a good medic in Roberts. He gave me an excellent rundown on your condition before I examined you."

I know that from large amounts of experience. Jackson pictured Mikey's face. Lips smushed together with his brown eyes narrowed and flashing. The kid was so open in his concern. "I agree. Mikey's a great medic. He kept me alive while we humped back to the base. Those guys are my friends. We escaped from a POW camp together."

"That explains why they wouldn't give up on getting my attention."

"Is anyone going to explain to me what exactly is going on?" Jackson reached up to scratch his nose. It itched. "And do I need the feeding tube now that I'm awake?"

"I don't know the answer to your first question." Dr. Howard's lips twitched in annoyance. "But in answer to the second one, yes. I know about your eating habits from Dr. Nicholson. Major Russell gave him a briefing once a week. If I were in Nicholson's shoes, I would've sent you home months ago. I'm surprised you didn't collapse from malnutrition in the field. Right now, all we're doing is maintaining your weight. Your body is burning off everything in the healing process. Since you need to gain over twenty-five pounds, it's in for the duration of your hospital stay unless I determine otherwise. With that huge gaping hole in your leg, at least you won't be jogging around the hospital."

Jackson rolled his eyes. A few seconds later, the comment soaked into his medicated brain. *Harry will never run with me again.* "Doc, could you do me a favor?"

"Sure, what do you need?"

"My executive officer, Major Harrison Russell, was hit during a mortar attack the day before we left on the mission. Dr. Nicholson was positive the orthopedic surgeon would remove Harry's foot once he arrived at Da Nang. Could you find out how Harry's doing and if he's stateside yet? We've been together for years. He's my best friend. Many a night, he would meet me with a candy bar in his hand at our quarters to keep me going."

"Sounds like something a best friend would do." Dr. Howard leaned on the bed rail. "Sure, I'll check on him. Major Russell won't be able to make a trip to see you until his leg heals up enough for a prosthetic. I'll contact his doctor and swap information with him about your injuries. Since Major Russell's your XO, I'm sure the army will talk to him shortly. I read in your records about one of your quirks."

Jackson cocked his head in curiosity. "What's that, Doc?"

"Milkshakes. You drank gallons of them while recovering from the POW camp when you wouldn't eat anything else. If the staff brings you a milkshake every day, will you drink it?"

Ice cream's better than bland hospital food any day. Jackson managed a couple of half head nods. Anything else made him dizzy. "Yep, I love ice cream. That was my mom's trick when I got sick and refused to eat. The guys surprised me with a milkshake two days before the mission. How Lieutenant Carter obtained a gallon of still-frozen ice cream at our base is a mystery. It's a rarity at a forward firebase since we don't have a lot of refrigeration capabilities." He chuckled softly. "If we did, Harry would've met me every night with one at our quarters, and I'd weigh a lot more."

"Good. I'll make sure the nurses bring one loaded with protein powder before you go to sleep."

Jackson smacked his lips. "As long as it's also loaded with a lot of ice cream, I'll drink it."

The levity caught Dr. Howard by surprise. As his laughter joined Jackson's, the door opened, and two officers walked inside. One of them the same older man Dr. Howard spoke with earlier. His rank stood out clearly. The eagles of a full Colonel. Gold single bars glinted in the overhead light on the much younger man. A second lieutenant. The solemn look on their faces changed the mood in the room to one of hostility and skepticism.

"Dr. Howard, could you leave the room for a few minutes? We need to speak with Lieutenant Colonel MacKenzie in private," the colonel stated, utterly professional.

Dr. Howard pointed at the door. "Your call, sir."

Jackson shook his head. "Stick right where you are, Doc." He glanced at the colonel's nametag. "With all due respect, Colonel Salem, I would prefer Dr. Howard stays after how well I was treated on the flight home."

The two officers outwardly bristled. They looked at each other, then Jackson and last at Dr. Howard.

"As you wish," Colonel Salem said in a flat tone. "You want a witness, given everything that has happened. I will say you shouldn't have been shipped home medically unstable. The records I received said the command staff wasn't informed about your medical status. There is a JAG investigation into criminal conduct by the guards. But first things first, I'm sure you want to know why you and your men are under arrest."

Jackson nodded. "Yes, sir. If it's about the mission, those orders came from the Pentagon. I forwarded my doubts up the chain of command after Colonel Johnson briefed me. I never heard back from General Thomas, so when Colonel Johnson gave us the green light, we went as scheduled. I don't understand any of this."

Colonel Salem waved the other officer behind him and stood next to the bed. "Understandable. Because you've been unconscious since you returned to the base, you don't know Colonel Johnson died during a mortar attack. The HQ took a direct hit. All they could find were body parts, and his blackened, half-melted dog tags. His aide is also missing, presumed dead."

Poor Colin. Good man. Talked about his wife all the time. Don't care about Johnson. The guy never liked me. Incapable of backing down from a challenge, Jackson returned the man's glare. "I was awake when we went through the main gate and remember seeing the HQ burned down. After my men dropped me off at the hospital, I sent them to report in. I didn't know about Colonel Johnson. As I stated before, we were under orders from the Pentagon for the mission."

"Your men told us the same thing. No one can find any written confirmation the orders ever existed."

Jackson's eyes narrowed into crinkled slits. *What the hell?* "But, they came by special courier in a locked briefcase. Those don't appear on our doorstep out of thin air as if by magic. It takes all kinds of forms to send one. There's a record of it somewhere. I left certified copies of the orders at the supply office and flight ops. That's the place to start looking."

"We already have. The North Vietnamese government is raising all kinds of hell about the museum." Colonel Salem pulled a document out of his pocket and handed it to Jackson. "Here's the propaganda statement they issued. As you can see, they have your names. They threatened to pull out of the peace talks unless the army arrested your unit for war crimes. That has the State Department running scared."

Jackson glanced at the paper. Their names jumped out. In bold print. *Don't like this one bit.* He returned his gaze to Colonel Salem. "How do they know we were in the building? We didn't come into contact with anyone. How do they know our names? Doesn't anyone wonder how Charlie has that information?"

"I'm not part of the investigation. My job is to inform you about your arrest and the charges against you. Nothing more. Since your unit was TDY with the 1st Cav, you're still under 5th Special Forces designation. The charges, however, are coming from a different command."

"If not the 5th or the 1st, then from where and who are they coming from, sir?"

"I don't have access to that information." Salem tapped the table with his finger. "All I have is you're being charged with Article 86, 106, 129, and 134 of the UCMJ. By who is classified above my clearance level."

"How can the convening authority be classified? Don't we have the right to confront our accusers?"

"I'm not a lawyer, either. JAG will assign one for your defense."

Jackson slammed his hand on his bed table. "We don't need a defense. Someone needs to get off their butts at the Pentagon and confirm the orders. Do you want me to fill out an after-action report?"

"I'm not part of the investigation. Tell your lawyer. As for an after-action report, that's up to you. If you want to lock yourself into a statement, by all means, write one out. Rumor has it, you're a rogue and let your men do whatever they want. That's why so much equipment disappeared around your base."

"I'm a what!" Jackson pounded the bed with his fist. "With all due respect, sir, I know about the missing equipment. Most of it was mine! As for my men, I expected military courtesy from the soldiers under my command at all times. I sure as hell enforced the regulations. It blows my mind why someone would call me a rogue! Except to sully my reputation and spotless record by suggesting I don't believe in military discipline. I went to West Point, not OCS."

The lieutenant stepped toward the bed. "You don't speak to a superior officer like that."

"OCS, right?" Jackson glared at the man. "Shut up, Lieutenant."

Salem held up his hand. "Step back, Cramer. Go ahead, MacKenzie."

Jackson returned his gaze to Salem. "Locking myself into a statement. That's rich. It's the truth. That's easy to say when you're not in my position. I'm flat on my back. My arm's full of tubes. I damn near died, and now you're telling me I'm charged with a crime! Why? Is it because some dumb ass can't find the orders? Or wants to hide them since they're now a political hot potato. And no one can explain to me how the North Vietnamese government has our names. There's a leak somewhere. Doesn't anyone care who or where it might be?"

"Since you're extremely medicated, MacKenzie—" Salem's irritation showed in his animated body language and rigid upright posture. "—I'll let the way you said that slide. You have a valid point. I can't do anything about it. I'm here to inform you about the charges, nothing more."

"Understood, sir." *Salem knows more than he's telling me. I'd better not get into a verbal fight with him. I'm already in enough hot water. I don't need that kind of stress.*

The two men left and Dr. Howard walked over to the bed. "Colonel?"

Jackson took a deep breath to calm down. "Yeah."

Dr. Howard leaned over the bed rail. "What was that all about?"

Shaking his head, Jackson met the doctor's gaze. "I have no idea, a warning, I think. I get the funny feeling the sky is about to fall and smash us flat. Then we'll be thrown under the bus and run over a few times for political expediency." He waved the propaganda report in front of his face. "What bothers me the most is the North Vietnamese government has our names and ranks. Since Harry's on that list, it was before the shelling. No one is investigating how they obtained the information or where the leak is, and there's nothing I can do about it."

"Colonel MacKenzie, you just told me everything I need to know about your character."

"How did you come to that conclusion so quickly? You don't know anything about me."

"Easy." Dr. Howard yanked the propaganda report from Jackson's hand and held it up. "They're worried about what our declared enemy thinks. You're concerned about a security leak. It tells me a lot. The fact they'd do this to a Medal of Honor recipient worries me about the direction our government is taking."

Jackson choked back a snicker. "The fact I have that particular award will be conveniently forgotten. So will any mention of us being POWs and neither one is a secret. Instead, the army will throw us to the wolves."

"You genuinely think that'll happen? Do you really think the United States Army would stoop that low?"

"Given what I just heard, yes. Those officers wouldn't give me any information on who brought the charges. The sixth amendment states we have the right to face our accusers. That's the convening authority. No one will tell me who it is. I've never heard of that happening before."

Dr. Howard picked up Jackson's wrist. "Well, your pulse is 120, and you need to sleep. I'll have the nurse give you a sedative. Don't try starting an argument with me that you won't win."

Jackson gave him a half-smile. *He's right. If no one makes me sleep, my mind won't quit. I'll wind up in the exact same place. Just as confused and even more tired.*

February 10, 1972

Jackson pressed the button on his bed buzzer several times. *What's taking them so long?*

Dr. Howard came into the room with a clipboard in his hand. "What do you need, Colonel?"

"Are you moonlighting as a nurse now?"

"Nah, I was on my way to your room when the light came on."

Jackson pushed a piece of paper across his bed table to the doctor. "Since you're here, can you help me with my after-action report? And take it by the main office?"

"Sure. What made you decide to file one?"

"It could make a difference to have my side on paper if someone investigates the case. Sure can't hurt to have the truth out there and might keep us from turning into sacrificial lambs led to slaughter."

Dr. Howard picked up the pen. "On one condition. You call me Frank, not Dr. Howard."

Jackson nodded. "Okay, if you insist. That goes both ways. Call me Jackson."

"Deal. Tell me what to say, and I'll write it out for you."

"Thanks, Frank." Jackson cleared his throat. "At the top, next to the subject line, write Vietnam National Museum of Fine Art - Operation Memphis - 72002001..."

Later that afternoon, after he got off shift at 1500 hours, Frank, dressed in fatigues and a lab coat with a stethoscope around his neck, delivered the document to the 5th Special Forces Group's main office.

A Sergeant First Class walked up to the desk. "What can I do for you, doctor? Are you thinking about joining us?"

Frank shook his head as he slid a manila folder across the counter and checked the man's nametag. "No. I have an after-action report from Colonel MacKenzie for you to file, Sergeant Collum."

"Okay. Is this for the mission I've heard so much about?"

"Yeah, that's the one. He told me to get a receipt and make sure you put this report in his file."

"How's the colonel doing?" Collum pointed at Jackson's picture on the far wall under the Medal of Honor banner. "He's a legend around here for saving those Navy Seals in '68."

"He's upset about everything, but healing nicely and still bed-ridden."

"Give it to me, I'll have Colonel Fox sign off on the receipt." Collum pointed at the door. "Can we go see him?"

"No." Frank placed his hands in his lab coat pockets. "He's under a no-visitor hold. Only people cleared by the 525th Military Intelligence Group can go into Colonel MacKenzie's room. Why?"

"A bunch of us wanted to come by and give him our support. We ran into a brick wall named Colonel Hammond."

"Yeah, I know. The guy's an ass. He's the commanding officer of the 525th. I've already butted heads with him over Colonel MacKenzie's care."

One general after another tramped into Jackson's room for the next week. One to three stars on their shoulders. Frank stopped counting at twelve. After each one, Jackson became more agitated. No one answered his questions. Everything came to a head when a four-star general, the Army Chief of Staff, General Windom, strolled in on day seven.

A few minutes later, Frank heard, "I'm a what? How am I a traitor? I nearly died for this country," in Jackson's raised voice through the open door.

The general's aide ran from the room.

Frank walked in to check on his patient. He ducked a full water pitcher thrown in his direction.

"Sedate him, doctor. MacKenzie's gone off his rocker," Windom yelled from behind an overturned chair.

"He'd listen to you, general, if you'd answer his questions." Frank went to Jackson's bed and grabbed his left arm. "Calm down, Colonel."

Jackson blinked. "What?" He looked at his hand and dropped the phone.

"I think it would be in your best interest, sir, if you didn't throw any more heavy objects at superior officers."

"Yeah, me too. But they won't listen, and it pissed me off. All they're concerned about is what the North Vietnamese government wants. Not about the security leak."

Both men looked up as the general disappeared around the doorjamb.

Frank yanked the blood pressure cuff off the wall, tightened it around Jackson's left bicep, and pumped air into the cuff. "Your blood pressure 160/110, and your pulse is 150." He hit Jackson's buzzer. When the nurse walked in, he turned to her. "Get me a sedative! Colonel MacKenzie's going to sleep for a while. I need his blood pressure and pulse to go down before he has a stroke."

After unloading the syringe into the IV line of his unhappy patient, Frank watched Jackson's eyelids droop lower and lower. "Stop fighting it. Go to sleep." He hit Jackson's buzzer.

A nurse came into the room. "Do you need something, Dr. Howard?"

"Yes." Frank finished writing notes on Jackson's chart. "No more visitors for Colonel MacKenzie without my permission. His medical condition is not stable. I don't care if it's the President of the United States. They see me first before coming into this room. Understood?"

"Yes, doctor. I will inform the staff."

"Good. I'm not about to have the colonel die of complications on my watch because the army's full of stupid officers. If you need me, I'll be right here in the colonel's room on my version of guard duty."

February 20, 1972

A baby-faced young man in an Army class A uniform entered Jackson's room carrying a briefcase.

Jackson laid the morning's copy of the *Fayetteville Observer* in his lap then adjusted the sling strap to keep the buckle from biting into his neck. "Good morning, Lieutenant. You must be special if Dr. Howard let you in here. He's chunked everyone else out on their ear. Who are you?"

The young man set the briefcase on the end table. "Second Lieutenant Matteo Moretti. I'm your assigned JAG lawyer."

Jackson's eyes narrowed into crinkled slits. "How old are you?"

"Twenty-four. I passed the bar last month and received my commission to pay for my law school loans."

"Have you ever tried a case before as a defense attorney?"

"Mock trials in law school, sir." Moretti's face lit up in a grin. "Won most of them."

"So, you've never been in a real courtroom before, Lieutenant?" Jackson pushed his body higher in his bed.

"No, sir."

"Why did they assign you to me? It's not standard procedure to assign a green attorney to a senior officer."

Moretti cringed, looked at his feet, and brushed the floor with his toes. "I know. But I'm your attorney for the duration."

"Okay." Jackson pointed at the briefcase. "Who's the convening authority?"

"I don't know. It's classified."

"Tell me the truth. The Army and State Department sold us out for political purposes, didn't they?"

Moretti stared at the ground. "Yes, sir."

"Moretti," Jackson thundered in his command voice. "Look at me and repeat that!"

The young man obeyed the order. "Yes, sir. They sold you out. I'm sorry. There's nothing I can do."

"What if I tell you where to find a copy of the official orders? That should be sufficient to get the charges dropped."

"Sorry, sir. It doesn't matter and irrelevant anyway. They won't let me submit anything to discovery, and the prosecution doesn't care. They've already decided you're guilty. I'd keep that to yourself at this juncture for an appeal."

What a wuss. I don't trust this guy. But he's right. Army procedure dictates our personal belongings shipped home with us. If I say another word, someone could open my footlocker and destroy everything. There would go any chance of JAG dropping the charges. Jackson cleared his throat. "Can you tell me who signed the charge sheet?"

Moretti remained silent and stared at the window.

Jackson climbed out of bed and backed the young man into the corner. His right leg wanted to collapse. He locked his knee, slid the leg forward, and pushed through the intense pain. *My reputation in 'Nam finally came in handy.* "You want to tell me what's really going on?"

Lt. Moretti's eyes widened. "The State Department threatened to deport my parents if I don't follow orders. They came here legally when I was five years old and have valid permanent resident status. I earned my citizenship in college before I went to law school. Last night, someone stuck a note on my front door with a knife and left a dead black cat on my doorstep. If I try to defend you, they'll kill my family. I'm sorry. I can't take that chance with my wife and one-year-old son."

"I understand, Lieutenant." Jackson lifted his left leg to return to his bed then turned back to Moretti. *A twenty-year career gives me an advantage. I know how the process of convening a court-martial. I brought a dozen men up on charges when I commanded the 5th Group.* "What about the Article 32 hearing?"

"The paperwork said all of you signed a waiver to stand before the judge. It's going directly to court-martial." Moretti reached into his briefcase and handed Jackson a copy of the documents.

Jackson glanced at the date next to his signature. "How in the hell did I sign this?" He waved the paper in front of his face. "I was in the ICU with a tube in my throat and unconscious. Moretti, this isn't my signature. I can't use my right arm, and I'm right-handed. What about my written request for a pretrial confinement hearing? I filed it the same day as the after-action report."

Moretti took a step back. "The convening authority has ordered all of you will remain in maximum security until the trial."

Shit! We're about to wind up in a deep, dark hole with no way out. "That's a direct violation of our rights to due process." Jackson sat on his bed. He didn't want to pitch forward onto his face. His right leg was on fire from too much movement. "JAG isn't going to acknowledge my complaints, are they?"

Moretti shuffled back and forth on his feet. "No, sir. They're going to convict you no matter what I do. I'm sorry." He grabbed his briefcase and exited the room without another word.

Jackson glared at the man's retreating back. *Our only chance is my testimony will convince JAG to start a real investigation. Then everyone will learn the reason behind the mission—including me.*

CHAPTER 6

February 22, 1972

Jackson looked from the TV to the door when Frank walked into his room with two members of the regular guard rotation, Cpl. Stevens and PFC Hanson. "Hey, Doc. What's up?"

Frank placed his hands behind his back and frowned. "I'm sorry. I lost my battle with Colonel Hammond's authority on this base. General Kowalski overrode my medical orders. These men are here to take you to the stockade."

"I knew that was coming." *But not this soon. Frank hasn't released me. My arm's still in a sling. They broke the regulations. Again. So much for rehab.* "They think I'm a traitor. Let's get it over with." Jackson stood with his hands out in front of him. He ground his teeth together as the handcuffs bit deep into his wrists. "Corporal Stevens, I'm not going to give you any problems."

Stevens bent down to snap on the leg irons.

Frank stepped between Jackson and Stevens. "That's where I draw the line, Corporal. His right leg is weak. Besides, he's leaving in a wheelchair." He stepped outside the room and returned with a wheelchair. "Sit."

Jackson eased his tired body into the chair. His leg throbbed with his pulse.

"Frank pushed Jackson through the hospital to the ambulance bay where a green box van sat idling with the rear doors open.

Stevens and Hanson, each holding an arm, helped Jackson climb into the back of the van and sit on the bench. Hanson hopped in and sat across from Jackson with his hand on his pistol.

Frank banged on the door with his fist. "Take care of yourself, Colonel MacKenzie."

Jackson peered around the doorframe to make eye contact with the doctor. "I'll do my best. Thanks for everything, Frank. Where you headed next?"

"Fort Campbell."

Corporal Stevens slammed the door shut.

The ride to the stockade was bumpy. The van hit pothole after pothole. Pain shot up Jackson's spine at every hard bounce. *This is a load of BS. Can't he drive on the paved part?*

After the van stopped and the doors swung open, PFC Hanson patted his pistol. "Get out!"

Jackson grabbed the doorframe with his left hand and eased his feet to the ground. His right leg and arm spasmed with even the slightest movement. *The meds are wearing off.* He limped through the open steel door with Stevens and Hanson following him. *Home, sweet home.*

In the central processing area, first stop the quartermaster's office where a clerk issued Jackson a plain olive drab prison uniform, underwear, boots, a blanket, pillow, and basic toiletries.

At the showers, Stevens, Hanson, and a staff sergeant surrounded Jackson. The staff sergeant pulled a nightstick from a ring on his belt. "Take off those scrubs."

Hampered by his injuries, Jackson sat on the bench and yanked at the pants with his good hand. He looked at a man standing in the corner five feet away. Squinting to focus through the pain, he made out colonel's eagles on the collar. His left shoulder had patch. A black/yellow checkerboard with a yellow lightning bolt splitting gray and blue. Intelligence. Might be with The Flying Eye. The name tag had seven letters, Hammond. *That jerk threatened Frank. Looks like a fat paper-pusher. What's someone from counter-intelligence doing here?*

"Stop delaying the inevitable. Are you trying to piss me off?"

Jackson glanced at the man's nametag. "No, Staff Sergeant Reynolds. It's hard with one hand."

Reynolds stuck a buck knife under the tail of Jackson's shirt.

Jackson knew better than to do anything but sit stock still. The man's hand might slip, and the knife would wind up in his gut. Reynold's excuse would be Jackson tried to fight back. No way would that happen. The ripping continued until all of his clothing fell to the ground. Even the sling.

"There, all nice and naked." Reynolds wiped the blade on his pants, folded the knife shut and stuck it in his pocket. "Stand up. Time for the cavity search."

Jackson pushed himself up, turned, and stared at the wall to take his mind off the humiliation. He stiffened. His breath came in short gasps. An image burst into his mind as Reynolds pulled on a latex surgical glove. *Toad.*

"If you don't relax, it'll only hurt more." Reynolds stuck his finger into Jackson's anus.

Jackson gritted his teeth as Reynolds thoroughly searched every orifice on his body. Gentle, not part of the vocabulary.

Reynolds shoved Jackson under a running showerhead and tossed a bar of lye soap at his feet. "Wash."

"It's c-c-co-o-old." Jackson levered himself down inch-by-inch to pick up the soap. He would never give the satisfaction of hearing his discomfort. *Oww...oww...oww...*

"Don't care. You don't deserve my hot water."

A minute later, another guard appeared with a fire hose. "Time for the chemical spray down for lice."

Jackson threw his left hand up to protect his face as the white foam covered his body and stung his eyes. After drying off and pulling on his underwear, fatigues, and socks, he slipped on his boots but let the laces hang. No way would his right arm move enough to tie them. And with the sling in pieces on the floor, he couldn't keep the stress off that shoulder. He stepped into the hallway and stopped at the door marked with a medical red cross.

Reynolds pushed him down the hall. "Keep going, traitor. You don't need a medical check. You left the hospital two hours ago. Next door." A few steps down the hall, the sign read, *Barber*.

Jackson limped into the room and glared at Reynolds. "What now?"

"Sit." Reynolds pointed at the chair.

"Why? My hair's regulation. It's shorter than yours." Jackson remained standing. He wasn't about to follow that ridiculous order.

Reynolds shoved Jackson into the chair. "Shave MacKenzie bald," he told the barber.

Jackson gritted his teeth as the razor scraped across his scalp. *Damn thing's dull as a butter knife.* His hair fell to the floor, speckled with drops of red.

"Get up." Reynolds jerked Jackson out of the chair by his collar.

Jackson wiped away the liquid running down his face. His palm turned red with blood. "Can I have a towel?"

"Why not? Don't need you messing up my hallway." Reynolds handed him a gray-colored dirty towel from the sink.

"Thanks." Jackson held the towel to his head as he walked to the main office.

The clerk wrote 16089 in black magic marker on the blank white tab on the right side of Jackson's shirt.

Jackson pointed at the number. "What's that?"

A hulking First Sergeant leaned into Jackson's face. His breath smelled like cigarette smoke and coffee with a hint of bourbon. "Your prisoner number. You are no longer Lieutenant Colonel MacKenzie. You will answer to 16089. Get used to it."

Reynolds and two other guards escorted Jackson to the same cell block as his men. The dingy white-painted concrete block room contained eight open-barred six-by-eight cells on one side. On the other side, a wall with four small windows, eight feet off the ground. At the end, a half-wall with a desk, video monitors, file cabinets, and chairs. Overhead, the fluorescent lights flickered in a random pattern.

Four guards jumped from their chairs as Jackson limped through the door. A man wearing staff sergeant stripes looked up from the desk.

One by one, his men poked their hands through the bars.

As Jackson passed each cell, he touched each one for a little comfort. He stopped at the last cell. The one nearest the guard area. Once Reynolds removed the handcuffs, Jackson stepped through the open door. The clang of the lock engaging behind him brought out an involuntary jump. A second later, his stomach churned. *Don't think tonight's gonna be fun.*

Right after putting the blanket, pillow, and shaving kit on his bunk, Jackson faced his men crowded against their cell bars. He felt lost. Haunted. Forsaken. But above all else. Betrayed by his country.

Bill grasped the bars of the cell next door. "How're you doing, Colonel?"

Jackson leaned against the bars to take the weight off his bad leg. "About as well as can be expected, I guess since they almost killed me getting me here. I can't use my right arm. My leg hurts something fierce. But enough about me. What were you guys told?"

"I think about the same as you, sir. Since you were unconscious in the ICU for several days, CID talked to us first. The army investigators can't find the orders. Colonel Johnson died in the mortar attack. The North is yelling about their museum, and our lawyer looks like a pimple-faced teenager. How'd they know our names?"

Jackson held onto a bar left-handed to stay upright as his good leg partially collapsed.

Bill grabbed Jackson's shirt to keep him from tipping backward.

"Thanks, Captain. You can let go. I have it now."

Bill released his hold. "You sure? You're pale as a ghost."

"Yeah, I think so. Did Colonel Salem speak with you?"

"Yes, sir. Right after we arrived. He questioned us separately in the interview room. The next day a Colonel from Intelligence asked the same questions. You know…the good cop, bad cop routine."

Par for the course. Trying to catch them in a lie. Hard to do since it's the truth. "I asked the same questions. Let me put it this way. We're on our own. After everything that's happened, trust no one with any information except us. Not even Lieutenant Moretti. That coward's more likely to hurt our case than help."

"Since you had flashbacks when the medical staff restricted you to your room in Da Nang, can you tolerate staying in that tiny cell? Your hospital room was a mansion compared to here." Chief's big, booming voice rang in the cell block.

Jackson stared at the window across from his cell. *Where's the genie in a bottle when you need him?* "Given how I already feel, I'm not going to deal with confinement very well."

"We'll get you through it, sir. We owe you that much for getting us out of the camp alive. Your blood is too high a price to pay for our protection," Mikey called from his cell.

"Thanks, Mikey, I appreciate it. I hope I'm wrong." Unable to remain standing, even using the bars as a crutch, Jackson limped to his bunk and sat down.

"Maybe your bad feelings are a side effect of the pain medication and the stress of the events in play." Ty forked his fingers through his hair.

Jackson cocked his head. *The mind-numbing drugs. Ty has a point. Something I didn't think about. My heart tells me no. I always trust my gut instincts. Well, except the last one. I should've listened to the stupid bird in my head.*

The room went quiet when a staff sergeant stood in front of Jackson's cell.

Jackson nodded to the man. "Sergeant."

The man quirked a small smile. "My name is Trotter, 16089. You will address me as Sergeant Trotter or sir. Your rank means nothing here."

"Yes, I know…Sergeant. But I will never call you sir. Live with it."

Trotter stiffened for a second then walked back to his desk.

Guess he thought better of saying anything. He might not like my reply.

At 1700 hours, a guard stood in front of each occupied cell. Staff Sgt. Trotter turned a key then hit a button on the wall that unlocked the cell doors.

Jackson remained sitting on his bunk. "What's going on, Bill?"

67

"Dinnertime," Bill said from the doorway of his cell.

"Okay." Jackson pushed his body out of his bunk. His right leg didn't want to move. He picked up his left foot and slid his right one. Once he stood behind Bill, Trotter opened the door that led into the hallway.

"All of you, march. Single file. No talking," Trotter ordered.

In the buffet line, Jackson looked around as he set his tray on the belt in front of Chief. Every prisoner glared at him. "Why are we separated from the others?"

"We're considered traitors, boss. No one wants to talk to us. Our first day here, several of them threatened to kill Mikey." Chief made a fist. "If one of them comes close, get behind me. You're a target as our CO."

"Got it." Jackson slid his tray along the belt. *That looks like meat, but it's a greenish-gray. No, thank you.*

Chief placed a full plate on Jackson's tray. The same meat, off-color carrots, lumpy gravy, and runny brownish mashed potatoes. At least they looked like mashed potatoes.

"I'm not hungry, Sergeant. My stomach's still upset from the morphine."

"You never are, boss. Consider me Major Russell's replacement."

Bile rose in Jackson's throat. *I can't eat that crap. It looks and smells like POW camp food. Maggots and bugs mixed with dog crap.*

Chief laid his hand on Jackson's shoulder. "Please try to eat something, sir."

"Okay." Jackson picked up a roll, a bowl of vanilla pudding, and a coffee cup. He tried to lift the tray one-handed but let go when the weight bent his wrist in the wrong direction.

"I'll carry the tray for you, sir."

"Thanks, Chief." Jackson limped to their assigned table and sat down. The first order of business. Relocate the gray prison food to the next table before he puked from the smell. His choices, the soft roll tasted good, the vanilla pudding even more so. The sugar gave him an instant jolt of energy. He scraped the sides clean of the thick, nearly white substance and drank two cups of coffee to wash it down.

The return to the cell block seemed like days instead of fifteen minutes. Jackson dragged his right leg and hopped forward on his left. He refused help from his men and slapped their hands away. No way would he show weakness in front of the guards. They would exploit it.

After Jackson's cell door clanged shut he removed his fatigue shirt and white t-shirt. He dried the sweat from his face and chest with his t-shirt. *I'm locked up. They can't gig me now.*

The angry red scars across his shoulder caught his eyes. A bolt of pain shot through his right arm when he flexed his hand. His right leg gave. He tipped backward into his bunk and saw stars when his head hit the wall. *Damn it!* After repositioning his body on the bunk, he propped his bad leg on a pillow.

Jackson massaged the tender area around the thigh wound. Frank only let him walk the five steps to the bathroom two days ago. *Why did I go to the mess? I wanted to be with the guys. My mistake.* Fire pulsed through his leg like a bayonet with a 220 cord attached. His right foot turned inward from the cramping. *Maybe I should take my meds. Bet the guards lost them.*

Jackson pushed the agony into the back of his mind. With each passing minute, the pain mounted on itself. His breaths came in short, quick gasps. He pressed his fingers on the artery in his neck. *190? I'd better ask or have a heart attack.* He clenched his left fist over his heart when the pressure made him lightheaded. It felt like a quivering muscle. *My chest hurts. Too late.* He willed himself up and limped to the bars. "Corporal Lewis, I need my meds. I can't take this anymore."

"Yes, sir. Lieutenant Baker instructed me to give you the medication if you asked." Lewis went to the lockbox on the wall. He returned to the bars with two white pills and a small Styrofoam cup of water.

Once the medication kicked in, his heart slowed to a normal rate. After a few hours of relative quiet, Jackson fell asleep.

He felt a hand on his shoulder. *Charlie found me!* In defense of his life, he opened his eyes, jumped up, and spun around. Extensive Special Forces training dictated muscle memory. First, he grabbed his right fist with the other hand. A half-second later, he squeezed with all of his strength to crush his victim's larynx.

"Colonel, wake up!"

That's Bill's voice. Wake up? I'm awake. Where are my men? It's too dark to see the squad. He squeezed his eyes shut then opened them. *When did the sun come up? Where am I?*

"Colonel, drop the guard...he's turning blue."

Guard? Jackson stared at the man in his grasp. *This is Toad.* He squeezed tighter then glanced up as several enemy soldiers came at him. *Oh crap.* He backed up with his captive as a shield and tripped over a

69

downed bamboo log. His head hit a wall. Stars circled his eyes. He squeezed them shut, opened them and looked at the man's back. The uniform was US Army olive green. Not tan. He released the guard.

The man collapsed to his hands and knees, gasping for air.

Oh shit. Jackson clasped his hands behind his neck and sat on his bunk.

Five guards burst into the cell, each with a nightstick raised above his head.

Jackson shielded his head with his arms as the blows fell onto his stomach, chest, and legs. A hand yanked him to the ground. Knees landed in his groin. "Ooowww…" he screamed, doubled in half.

Sgt. Hunter jerked Jackson to his feet, wrenched his hands behind his back and slapped the handcuffs on so tightly Jackson couldn't move his fingers.

Jackson tried to pull away to escape the pain, but the cuffs tightened more.

"Start walking, 16089." Sgt. Hunter pulled up on the chain between the handcuffs. "Unless you want a little more incentive."

Jackson limped out of the cell block with a guard on each side holding him up.

In the infirmary, Sgt. Hunter pushed Jackson into a chair and cuffed his left hand to a ring attached to the wall.

For thirty minutes, Jackson sat, head bowed, blood dripping from his nose and mouth onto the floor. As time ticked by, he lost his concentration to stay upright. "Aaww…" exited his mouth as he fell. His right shoulder hit the ground and popped. He couldn't bite back the otherworldly scream that slipped past his lips as he slid into the darkness.

"Colonel MacKenzie, can you open your eyes for me? Back off, all of you. He's semi-conscious. I don't need you beating the snot out of him again if he reacts violently when he wakes up."

Jackson cracked his right eye open. His left one was swollen shut. *There's an oxygen mask on my face.* He moved his left wrist. Tape pulled the hairs. *I have an IV in the back of my hand. Damn, I'm in a hospital bed.* "Yeah, I'm here."

"Good. I'm Dr. Wright," said an older, balding man in a white lab coat.

Three guards moved closer.

Dr. Wright stepped between them and Jackson. "Get out of my infirmary. All of you. I don't need you in my way. Not one word or I'll charge you with insubordination. Get out!" He pointed at the exit.

The three guards moved to the door, grumbling under their breath. The hinges squeaked as they shut the door behind them.

Three faces appeared in the window as Dr. Wright locked the door and dropped the key into his lab coat pocket.

Jackson focused his gaze on the doctor. "What happened?"

Dr. Wright sat in the chair next to the cot. "I was about to ask you that. Please don't move your right arm. Your shoulder's dislocated, and even the untrained eye of a moron can see it. That doesn't say much about the intelligence of the guards. Those numskulls weren't in any danger of you assaulting them. Given all the previous muscle damage, I'll need to sedate you to pop it back into place. If I don't, you'll be in extreme pain, and I want to avoid that. Once you're taken care of, Lieutenant Baker and I will have a long conversation about his men not following procedure. They should have laid you on a cot, not handcuffed your arm to the wall when you went into shock. Someone doesn't care about your welfare. I'm afraid this pattern of mistreatment will continue."

"I agree. Thanks for the help. As to what happened, we Special Forces guys receive training to kill anyone who touches us when we sleep. I guess a guard got stupid."

"That's a good enough explanation. Let's get you cleaned up and your shoulder back in place. The muscles injured by the shrapnel are weak. That's why it popped out so easily. I'll give you some valium to relax your body so you won't feel as much discomfort."

"Doc, I'm hurting so much, hurry up and get it over with."

Dr. Wright motioned to his medic, who brought over a bowl of water and a towel. As he cleaned the blood from Jackson's face and chest, the doctor injected medication into the IV line.

"Colonel." Dr. Wright gently slapped Jackson's cheek. "Can you hear me?"

Jackson nodded. "Yeah."

Dr. Wright slid the closed end of a sheet under Jackson's right armpit. The medic tied the ends together around his waist and leaned back on his heels.

"Stay on your back. Let us do the work. We'll be done soon." Dr. Wright looped a second sheet across the crook of Jackson's right elbow, bent at ninety degrees, hand pointed at the ceiling. He tied the ends

71

together around his waist and held onto the forearm. "Colonel, I'm going to lean back to pop your shoulder into place with counter-traction."

"Go ahead. You have me flying, so I'm not feeling much."

"Good. That's exactly how I want you right now."

In less than a minute—clunk—Jackson slammed his right eye shut as pain shot through his body.

"Colonel, you still awake?"

Jackson opened his eye when he felt hot breath on his face. "Are you done?"

"Yes. Your shoulder looks like a swollen black softball from the blood drainage into the surrounding tissue. I'll wrap ace bandages across your upper body to immobilize it to heal. Time for you to sleep." Dr. Wright injected a large, liquid-filled syringe into the port on Jackson's IV line.

Good. Jackson closed his eye as his body went numb and the lights went out.

February 23, 1972

Jackson cracked his right eye open. His left one refused to move. *Where am I?* The room smelled clean, antiseptic. His thoughts caught up. *The infirmary.* To get a better look, he raised his head. *No guards.* He groaned in pain. Unable to maintain the position, he dropped his head back to the pillow.

Only a large amount of morphine makes me feel this crappy. Well, that and getting my noggin pounded. Jackson reached to scratch his nose. *My head feels like it weighs a ton. Will this ever stop?* A flash caught his attention.

The on-duty medic laid his newspaper on the desk. "Colonel MacKenzie, I'm Sergeant Palmer. Do you want to sit up?"

"Yes. Can I have some water?" Jackson croaked.

"Sure." Sgt. Palmer stuffed several pillows behind Jackson's back. He placed a cup of water under Jackson's mouth and held the straw to his lips. Once Jackson emptied the cup, Palmer set it on the floor.

Jackson pulled on the feeding tube as it snaked away from his face. "Do I need this damn thing in my nose, Sergeant?"

Sgt. Palmer pushed the hand away. "According to Dr. Wright, yes, you do, sir. You're way too thin. All you ate last night was a roll and vanilla pudding."

"Last night the food looked like spoiled chunky milk mixed with rotting meat and smelled even worse. I didn't want to spend the night with my head in the toilet." Jackson tried to laugh. He went into a coughing fit instead.

"Easy, sir." Palmer slapped Jackson's back. Not hard, but with enough force ease the spasm. "Deep breaths."

When the hacking subsided, Jackson looked at Palmer. "Although I might've been better off if I did. At least I wouldn't have gotten beaten up."

Palmer adjusted the flow rate on Jackson's IV line. "I agree with you. I've seen the food in the prison mess. I wouldn't eat it either. But my body isn't bordering on malnutrition. Dr. Wright had a long talk with Dr. Howard last night. He's following Dr. Howard's recommendation about the feeding tube. It stays inserted while you're in the infirmary. When the next shift arrives, I'm supposed to get you a milkshake. Will you drink it?"

It's better than hospital food, despite the protein powder aftertaste. "Yeah, I'll drink it."

"Good. That way I don't have to make you."

"You think you've got the balls to do that, Sergeant?" Jackson gripped Palmer's forearm.

Palmer jerked his arm away. "On the other hand, I'm glad you'll drink it without the extra help. I don't want to wind in the bed next to you with a broken arm or a broken face."

Jackson quirked a small smile. *After yesterday, that's a given.* "Good thinking, Sergeant."

February 27, 1972

Upon his discharge from the infirmary, Jackson limped slowly back to the cellblock. Shirtless. His right arm strapped to his chest. *I'm not likely to cause a problem looking like George Foreman's last opponent. Why do I need three guards as an escort?*

With his normal gait racked up, it took forever to arrive at his cell. Jackson staggered inside and sat on his bunk. He stuffed a pillow behind his back to lean against the wall. The clang of the lock engaging echoed throughout the concrete room. *I know what's coming tonight. With my injuries and exhaustion, there's no way to prevent it.*

A guard walked to the front of Jackson's cell. He slapped his palm with his nightstick.

Jackson couldn't withhold a small snort. "Corporal Pendergast, relax. Not about to start a fight. I'm hurting. Please give me my medication. I'm sorry about what happened. That's Corporal Lewis' fault, not mine. I explained his mistake to Lieutenant Baker. No one has ever told you how they train us at the Special Warfare School."

Cpl. Pendergast looked at Staff Sgt. Trotter sitting at the desk. "Sergeant, what do I do?"

"Follow your standing orders. Give him the medication." Trotter pointed at a piece of paper taped to the wall.

"Yes, Sergeant." Pendergast pulled the medication from the lockbox. He handed Jackson two small white pills through the bars.

Jackson glanced at the sink in the corner of his cell. *My cup looks clean, but there's green fuzz on the spout. No way. I'm not drinking that water. I'll get worms or something.* He swallowed the pills dry and returned to his bunk.

Bill stood next to their adjoining cell wall. On the other side of his cell, Ty, Mikey, and Chief pressed their bodies against their bars.

"How're you feeling, Colonel?" Bill asked.

"Awful." Jackson flipped from one side to the other, trying to find a pain free position on his bunk.

"Well, you look like you feel. Have you seen your face or shoulder? They're bruised and swollen."

Jackson propped himself up on his elbow to look at his friend. "My entire body feels bruised. As much as I'd like to sleep, I don't think I'll get a lot of rest before it happens again."

Bill's eyes narrowed with a broad furrow between his eyebrows. "Didn't Dr. Wright get a psychiatrist to come talk to you?"

"I didn't ask, but he tried. Sergeant Palmer told me the doctor's request was denied. Hammond threatened to court-martial him if he didn't release me. So here I am."

"Why does a guy from Intelligence have any say in this?"

"Don't know. Wondered that myself."

"How can he deny you help, sir?"

"That's easy, say *no*." Jackson chewed a hangnail off his finger. "I probably wouldn't talk to a head doc, anyway. It's not like they understand what we went through. All they know is what they learn out of a book. It's not the same thing." *What am I saying? I don't believe that myself.*

"You need help, Colonel." Bill smacked the bars. "You need to talk to someone."

"I need time to think and reason it out, that's all."

"Right, sir." Bill rested his head against the bars. "You've been saying that for almost two years and it hasn't worked, has it? Did you eat in the infirmary?"

"No! They stuck me with another damn feeding tube. I hate those bloody things."

"Well, you might not like it, but at least they pushed something into you. I can't tell you gained two pounds."

Jackson arched an eyebrow. He was confused. "Who told you?"

"You did. At dinner your first night here."

"Oh yeah." *I forgot. Must be the meds. Or I'm losing my mind.* He leaned back against his pillow and counted the flyspecks on the ceiling—hundreds of them.

Bill held a copy of *Stars and Stripes* through the bars and waved it back and forth.

Jackson caught the movement in his peripheral vision and jerked to reality. He went to the bars and took the paper. "Thanks, buddy."

"You're welcome. Go sit down before you fall down." Bill returned to his bunk.

Jackson did the same. He spread the paper out on his bunk and read it front to back. *In combat, I never had time to think. Now, I have nothing but time.*

At 1700 hours, Bill poked his head into Jackson's open cell door. "You coming, Colonel?"

Jackson switched his gaze from the blue sky on the other side of the window to Bill. "No, I'm bowing out. There's no use in going, my stomach's upset from the medication. My shoulder and leg are throbbing. You guys go without me."

"You're never hungry, but I understand you're hurting. If they let me, I'll bring you something."

"Thanks. I appreciate it." Jackson leaned into his tattered pillow, massaging his leg. *I want to go home. Mom, Dad, I miss you so much. Wish you were here to help me.* He thought about all the fun times with his older brother. Building forts in the living room using chairs and their mother's bedsheets. She hated it when they got them dirty. Playing army in the front yard with their father using broomsticks and mop handles as rifles. The car was always a tank. Their dad let them win when they shot him. He could put together a pretty dynamic death scene. Suddenly that particular game didn't seem like fun since it happened for real in Korea.

"Colonel?"

Jackson glanced up at the bars. "Hey, Bill. Has it been an hour already?" *When did they open the door?*

"Yes, sir. Five minutes ago. Where were you? You had that million-mile stare they always talk about."

"It's not important. What's in your hands?"

"Your dinner." Bill set the pitcher on the floor, handed Jackson a bowl, and sat next to him.

Jackson stared into the bowl. *I know Bill. He talked Trotter's ear off. Unless I want a lecture, I'd better eat the chocolate pudding.* He picked up a spoonful and slid it between his lips. "Mmm." He shoveled the rest into his mouth and licked the sides clean. When he looked up, Bill presented him with a full white ceramic mug. *Coffee. I never turn down coffee.* He savored the warmth as it slid down his throat.

Bill winked. "I learned a long time ago how to keep you off my back. Stick a mug of your ultra-strong brew in your hand. It was hard to miss your grin when you sat at your desk doing paperwork or walked around camp with that beat-up Navy Seal mug. Hope you get it back one day. I know it was a birthday gift from your brother."

"Thanks." Jackson rubbed his eyes. "It's probably still sitting on my desk, and I'll never see it again."

"Your body looks like a Jackson Pollock painting." Bill held his hands up like a camera lens. "The multi-colored bruising on your shoulder with the pink shrapnel scars running through are in sharp contrast to the darker colors. The left side of your face is as colorful."

Jackson gave his friend a small grin. "Have you added art critic to your resume?"

"Nah. Saw one in a gallery once. It was pretty much the same colors as you. I wanted to see you smile. Drink your coffee, sir."

"Thank you for caring, my friend. I need the companionship right now. It helps calm my mind."

Staff Sgt. Trotter appeared at the cell door. "Sorry, Captain. I have no choice. Orders. Return to your cell."

Bill squeezed Jackson's good shoulder. "I'll be next door if you need me."

At 2200 hours, the guards dimmed the lights for the night.

Jackson didn't lie down. He sat in the same position and stared at the bars. Two hours later, he reached under his mattress. Dr. Wright hid six pills of a heavier pain medication that contained a mild sedative in Jackson's sock before the guards showed up that morning. He got lucky the men didn't search him. With a glance at the guard's locations, he popped one into his mouth and stretched out on his bunk.

The pain slowly subsided. Jackson drifted into sleep.

Four hours later, the meds wore off. The agony started anew and his heart sped up. Jackson opened his eyes. He listened for movement. Liquid dripped from his soaked shorts. Drool rolled off his chin. His limbs and body vibrated in uncontrolled tremors. *I hurt all over. My body's on fire. Make it stop.* "Go away! Biến đi…Xuống địa ngục. Leave me alone! Để tôi yên…Code of Conduct! Quy tắc ứng xử. . .Go to hell! Cút đi…No! Không…Đụ má mày…Dư mà nhiều, đi ăn cứt…Lồn bà già mày làm lòng…Hôn mông của tôi…"

Jackson fell off his bunk. His injured shoulder hit the floor first." Oowww…" He lay on his stomach on the cold cement for several minutes. As he rolled onto his back, he bit his lip as pain shot through his body. His stomach muscles strained from the difficulty of sitting up. He slowed each breath to gain control of his lungs. After rolling onto his good leg, he levered himself off the floor inch by inch. First onto his knees. Then with his left foot out, he rocked forward onto his toes, and stood with as little pressure on his right leg as possible. He limped over to Bill who stood next to the bars. "Did I wake you?"

"Yes. It's hard to miss the Vietnamese cuss words at the top of your voice. Nightmare?"

"Yeah. I don't know how much more of this I can take."

"You need help, sir." Bill's voice broke.

"Dr. Wright tried and got shot down." Jackson grabbed a cell bar to stay vertical. "The army isn't going to help me or they wouldn't have sent me back to 'Nam in the first place."

"True." Bill released an exasperated sigh. "How much of this can you take before you crack?"

"Don't know. I need to keep moving forward. That's all I can do."

"You need to talk about what's bothering you, sir."

"I can't tell you guys what happened when I was alone, let alone discuss that with a stranger. Just give me the time to sort it out."

Bill stuck his face next to the bars, eyes wide. "Colonel, you'll go completely looney tunes before you ever sort it out. You and I both know you can't do it alone. You're already cracking under the pressure and injured to go with it. Talk to us. Please. Tell us what they did to you."

Jackson inhaled deeply then released the breath slowly. *Even awake, the cell reminds me of Dung's torture chamber. Maybe I should tell Bill everything.* A split second later. "I can't. Not now. Maybe not ever."

"Then we'll watch over you and keep you sane until we get out of here."

"If we ever do, my friend. My gut says we don't have a snowball's chance in hell of proving our innocence. The army's stacked the deck against us. My heart hopes I'm wrong. I can't spend twenty years in this cell. I'm barely getting through it now."

CHAPTER 7

September 29, 1972

Jackson shuffled into a room wearing all-encompassing body restraints. Handcuffs attached to a wide leather belt. A chain attached the belt to the leg irons on his ankles. One guard as an escort, his hand gripped on the handle of his nightstick. The guard pushed him down into a chair next to a rough wooden table.

Where am I? I hear Dung's laughter. Jackson looked around the dingy hut with a thatched ceiling, walls and a dirt floor. All kinds of things hung on the walls. Rusty machetes, knives, leather straps, whips, bridles, cinches—farm implements. A car battery with wires and alligator clips sat on a counter. Next to it, a large bullet shaped object with an electric cord. He recognized it. An electroejaculator! It was used on bulls to make them – erect for mating. He shuddered. *Must be his private little hell-hole. I have to resist.*

The person next to the table kept flipping back and forth. Harry—Dung—Harry—Dung. It became only a blurred image the shape of a man in civilian clothes, leaning on the cane. "Shit! What have they done to you? Your eyes are sunk so deep into your skull I almost can't see them. In 'Nam, you were all tanned. Now you look like pasty bread dough."

Jackson blinked. *That's not Harry. Dung's screwing with my mind. Keep playing dead. Maybe he'll go away.*

Harry pulled on the sleeve of Jackson's prison uniform. "You're a walking skeleton. You've lost at least fifteen pounds since I last saw you. What did the prison barber do to you? Looks like he used his razor on a rock before shaving your head. Why are they weighing you down with ten pounds of chains and leather? And leg irons too! You're not in any condition to run away or put up a fight." He snapped his fingers in front of Jackson's face then leaned over until their noses touched. "Are you in there? Or a vegetable, incapable of a conscious thought, only existing as long as your heart keeps beating."

No...no...no. It's not Harry. I'm seeing things. Gotta fight.

"Those first few weeks at the rehab hospital, I needed a shrink. I couldn't shake the depression after I lost my foot." Harry placed his prosthetic left foot on the table in front of Jackson. "Now everything is in clear focus. I was the lucky one. Today, I would trade places with you. After the camp, you would be better off as an amputee than imprisoned without assistance."

Sounds like Harry's terrible sense of humor. Depressed. Imprisoned. Amputee. What does that mean? Jackson stared at the strange thing on the table. *Is that a sneaker-covered foot? Maybe I'm home?* He shook his head, trying to clear the fog from his brain.

Harry fished into his pocket and hopped to Jackson's side. He waved a candy bar under Jackson's nose. "You need to eat. Take this," he yelled in Jackson's ear.

Mmmmm. Chocolate. Harry! Jackson sucked in a deep lungful of air. The dingy gray hut faded away into a sterile all-white prison interview room. He looked at his clothes. Clean, but somewhat faded army fatigues. Not filthy tattered ones. And he smelled lye soap. Not body odor, death and mud. "Harry, you're really here? I'm not imagining you?"

"Yeah, you big, or shall I say little, ape, it's me. You need to eat something. You look like shit."

"Feel like it too." Jackson closed his hand around the proffered candy bar. "Is that yours, or did Captain Hook leave it here? No, Captain Hook has a hook, not a foot. Some wooden—no, plastic mannequin must be missing a foot."

"So you're still in there. I was starting to wonder." Harry squeezed Jackson's shoulder.

"Don't you think you'd better sit down? Since your foot's on the table and not on the floor."

Harry strapped on his prosthetic foot. "You're right, as always."

Jackson pointed at Harry's left leg with half a candy bar. "I'm sorry I never made it home to help you through this."

"Why should you be sorry? I made it home fine. You're the one they almost killed."

"Heard about that, huh?" Even with the intake of sugar, Jackson couldn't raise his voice much above a whisper.

Harry moved his chair to the other side of the table and sat next to Jackson. "Yeah, I couldn't believe it actually happened. Dr. Howard told me. It's taken me six months of complaining to my congressmen, the newspaper, and letter writing to get in here today. I don't understand why I had to twist so many arms. Or why Hammond has complete control over you, Ty, Chief and Bill. He's with intelligence. Not that he has any. Intel has nothing to do with JAG."

"No idea. Intel normally stays out of the light. They're afraid of melting. No one will give me a straight answer on who brought the charges. All they tell me is it's classified. How can that be classified? No one believes we had orders." Jackson jerked against the chain locking his hands to his waist. "You saw them!"

"I know." Harry laid his cane on the table. "I told everyone the orders were real. CID is under the impression I'll lie to protect you. JJ, you're as by the book as they come, and sure as hell not a flight risk. It doesn't make any sense to stick you in maximum-security and deny anyone access to you. I plan to testify at the court-martial, even though your lawyer told me not to come. Why does he not want the truth?"

Jackson counted to ten to regain his composure. "Someone threatened him. It's a frame-up job, pure and simple. The army's going to convict us. It doesn't matter what we say due to the heavy political pressure from North Vietnam. They had our names in a propaganda report, even yours, and you didn't go. No one cares the army has an intelligence leak."

"Except for you. Relax. You're getting worked up again. I don't want them to make you leave."

A guard looked into the room.

Jackson lowered his voice. "Yeah, and no one's listening."

"I'd ask how you're doing. But given how you look, not good."

"Yeah, not good. I've been a real pain in the ass to the guys. They're doing everything they can, but I can't take it here much longer. I hate to admit I've thought about making the pain stop forever. The only thing stopping me is the guys and how they'd take it." Jackson hung his head. "I feel so selfish. I always believed I was stronger than that."

Harry's eyes widened. "Do they know?"

Jackson shook his head. "No! Don't you tell them, or they'll never leave me alone. They fuss over me like I'm a child. I've been out of it lately, but I'm not a baby."

"Out of it? You walked in here on autopilot. No wonder they're fussing all over you."

"You win on that point. I don't remember the walk from my cell to here at all."

"Thought so." Harry rubbed his chin. "Now I know something's wrong. You're never this pliable. We always butt heads on everything at first until one of us convinces the other on the correct course of action."

"I can't take much more of this. I can't. If I don't find a way out, I will kill myself. It's that simple."

81

Harry grabbed Jackson's shoulders and shook them. "Fight. You have the strongest will of anyone I've ever met. JAG hasn't scheduled your court-martial yet. It's like they're waiting for something. Whoever is behind this intends to hijack the proceedings and convict you. No matter the information out there to the contrary. Don't wait for them to do it. Do what you did in the POW camp." He nodded at the corner.

Jackson glanced at the camera. *POW camp? Ahh...escape.* "Yeah."

"Get your head on straight. Find the evidence. Then JAG can have their so-called trial when you can present your case with a clear mind and a lawyer who isn't on the army payroll. Rumor has it the peace talks are getting close. Maybe that's what they are waiting on."

"Maybe. Charlie calls it talking while fighting, fighting while talking. How much hope is there for peace in that?" Jackson glanced at the door when a guard walked by. "Or maybe the army is waiting for me to go nutbar crazy. If they wait much longer, I will be. You know, boocoo dinky dau."

"Do like I said. Save yourself and figure the rest out later. Take care of yourself first."

"I'll try." *Harry's idea gives me a purpose. Something I'm sorely lacking. I'll do that rather than stare at the bars or pace across my cell. All day. Every day.*

"I wanted to tell you in person." Harry held up his left ring finger. "I'm engaged."

Jackson's eyes widened. *That's new. Harry's always shied away from that commitment.* "It's about time. Who's the lucky lady?"

"She works for a small newspaper in San Clemente, California. Her name is Gabrielle Banks. Everyone calls her Gabby. Boy, she is. She came to the VA when I was getting fitted for my prosthetic doing a piece on amputees. We hit it off on day one. Not long afterward, I moved in with her. You're my best friend, and I want you as my best man. I told her all about you. She wants to do a piece on you guys. You know, get off the fluff piece circuit. Dog shows and farmers markets."

Jackson opened his mouth, but Harry interrupted him.

"I told her it's not a good time. She knows I'm worried and wants to get how the army's treating you out into the public eye."

"How much time do we have left?"

Harry glanced at the wall clock. "About five minutes."

"It's not smart for her to write about me. Tell her to put in on hold for now. We need the guards to stop watching us, not add another rotation because my name's in a newspaper article. I'm flattered you want me as your best man. Don't wait for me. Go get married."

"Thanks. I wanted to tell you first. We'll stop off in Vegas on our way home."

"Good. Eat a steak for me."

"JJ, I'm—"

Sgt. Hunter walked in and grabbed Jackson's arm. "Time to go."

Not five minutes. Jackson shuffled ahead of his watcher, each foot moving twelve inches. *Damn chain.*

Harry gripped Jackson's arm at the door. "I'm sorry."

"Me too. Take care of yourself, Harry."

Sgt. Hunter pulled Jackson into the hall. "Move it, 16089."

In his cell, Jackson stood like a statue as Sgt. Hunter removed the body restraints. He went to his regular spot, grabbed his knees, and rocked in place. *I'm glad Harry's okay. The locking bolt reminds me of Dung's laughter. Makes my skin crawl.* He laid his head on his knees and wished he was someplace else. Anywhere but here.

September 30, 1972

Jackson awoke on the corner of his cell. His t-shirt ripped, holes in the knees of his pants. He could smell his body odor. Barnyard ripe. He had no idea where the time went. *Gotta concentrate. Escape. My purpose to exist. A reason to stay alive. I need to focus.*

Cpl. Stevens, Cpl. Lewis, and PFC. Hanson whispered to each other as they lounged against the wall.

Jackson caught a few words. Crazy, lunatic, crackers, traitor. And some big words he would have never thought one of those men knew, like *non-compos mentis*. The ruthless side of his personality. The one that made his reputation in 'Nam pushed its way out.

"Are you guys, men or mice?" Jackson pressed his face against the bars. "I think meek little mice. Not real soldiers. Just knuckleheads who didn't have the common sense to tell your recruiter *no*. None of you poor slobs would make it past the first hour of selection training when a battle-hardened First Sergeant jumps on your asses. You'd cry like tiny babies when someone yells in your ears. Bet you can't do a single Special Forces pushup."

Jackson dropped to the ground in a three-point stance. *Push, push, push. I did it and on my left arm, too. My right arm's even worse.* He sucked in air to catch his breath.

The guards fell all over themselves laughing.

Adrenaline dumped into Jackson's system as his anger mounted. He jumped to his feet and stalked across his cell like a caged tiger. "You think you're big men, huh? I think you're wearing women's panties under your uniforms. Mine's bigger." He cupped his crotch. "Realmente grande."

Cpl. Stevens bristled up like a rabid dog. "What did you say?"

"You know what I said, Corporal Stevens. I'm bigger than you ever will be, little man."

Stevens stuck a key into the lock to open the door.

"Stop!" Cpl. Lewis yelled. "Look at MacKenzie. He's not a piece of mindless protoplasm on the floor. He's a hooded cobra, ready to strike. I'd swear I saw that grin on Charles Mason."

Jackson clenched his fists. "Come on inside. I don't bite."

November 4, 1972

"Bill? Where am I?" Jackson felt his boots skip across a raised door threshold.

"Colonel? You're awake? Can you stand up and walk for me, so Chief and I don't have to carry you?" Bill pulled up on the waistband of Jackson's pants.

"Sure." Jackson moved his legs in step with Bill. "What month is it?"

Bill cocked his head. "November. Why?"

Jackson rubbed his head. "Did I just come back from the barber?"

"Yeah. How'd you know since you didn't even blink in the chair?"

"My head's bleeding."

"That damn asshole," Bill said with the force of an F-5 tornado. "He needs to sharpen his razor. I think he does that on purpose."

"Me too." Jackson glanced around. "Did the guard routine change?"

"Yesterday. There are three instead of five. You noticed?"

"Yes. Bet the army's trying to save money on manpower. Too many men still going to 'Nam as replacements."

Bill glanced at guards behind them. "True, but it still doesn't do us any good."

"Maybe. Let me go. I'll walk the rest of the way myself."

"You sure?" Bill pulled his arm from across Jackson's shoulder.

"Yes, leave me alone. I need to think."

The rest of the walk remained quiet.

Cpl. Stevens opened the cellblock door as PFC Hanson and Cpl. Lewis tapped their nightsticks against their legs.

Jackson, Bill, and Chief went into their cells, and the doors slid shut.

Jackson lay down on his bunk, crossed his arms behind his head, and stared at the ceiling. *Three guards. What can we do? I know. We take control of the guards and the keys. Fewer men make getting out an easier job. The stockade is laid out like a wagon wheel. The cell blocks are the spokes. Outside each exit door is a windowless corridor. Turn right, the hallway goes to the mess in the central hub. Left takes you to the outer doors and the parking lot. What can we use?* He raised his head and scanned the outside of his cell. In the guard's area stood a row of gray lockers. *The guards put civilian clothing in them. Great. That gives us something to wear other than prison issue. There's Corporal Lewis.* He waited until Lewis passed by and glanced at the wall calendar above the guard desk. *Christmas Eve's a Sunday. December 23rd is perfect. Minimal staff on a holiday weekend.*

November 23, 1972 – 1500 hours

Hoofbeats drummed in his ears. *Get over the bar, Firefly. Left turn, triple bar. Last jump. You cleared it by a mile, boy. Listen to the applause. We won another blue ribbon.*

"Colonel?"

Jackson dropped his hands from across his knees. He was sitting in the corner of his cell—again. And he didn't remember how he got there. "Huh? The door's open?" A tray slid next to his feet. He squinted at the blurry figure in the doorway. "Is that you, Bill?"

"Yes, sir. Today's Thanksgiving. The guards are letting us roam the cellblock. A reward for our good behavior. Got you some turkey. Sergeant Trotter brought a radio if you want to listen to the Dallas Cowboys football game." Bill pointed at the guard desk.

"It's not dog food today?"

"No, think recruit food."

"That good, huh?" Jackson picked up the fork. Five large bites later, he crawled to the toilet. His stomach rolled like the Atlantic in hurricane season. He heaved until only a tiny amount of blood-tinged liquid came out. "Bleh."

Mikey, Chief, and Ty ran for their doors.

Bill held up his hand. "Slow down. We don't want to overwhelm the colonel. He doesn't feel good. Sit in my cell if you want, but don't come in here."

The three men sat on the floor next to the bars.

Bill plopped down next to Jackson. "Easy, Colonel. I'm here." He snaked his arm across Jackson's back.

Covered head to toe in sweat, Jackson leaned against the toilet. The cold felt good on his aching head. "Turkey and mashed potatoes doesn't taste as good coming up as going down. But it was good the first time."

"I'm sorry, sir. I should've chosen something a little less rich."

Jackson wiped his mouth with his sleeve. "That's okay. At least you brought the coffee."

Bill picked up the cup from the tray and handed it to Jackson.

"Thanks." Jackson gulped it down to wash the bitter taste out of his mouth.

Two man-shaped shadows covered Jackson and Bill.

"I'm leaving, Sergeant Hunter." Bill reached for the tray.

"I'm not Sergeant Hunter," said a deep male voice.

Bill and Jackson looked up. Standing in the door, Dr. Wright and his medic, Sgt. Palmer.

"Hi, Doc. Didn't think you'd be dropping by today." Jackson dabbed the sweat off his face with his t-shirt.

"Duty day for me." Dr. Wright's eyes moved between the tray and Jackson. "Did you try to eat, Colonel?"

Jackson groaned and spat into the toilet.

Bill nodded. "Yeah. He puked it all up."

"Captain Mason." Dr. Wright sounded like a drill sergeant. "I guess you figured out a full Thanksgiving meal is too much for someone who hasn't eaten solid food for months."

"Yes, sir." Bill dropped his head. "The food was good for a change. My mistake. I'm sorry."

"It's the thought that counts." Jackson pointed at the white foam cup in Sgt. Palmer's hand. "Is that for me?"

"Yes, sir. Do you want it?" Palmer went down on one knee next to Jackson.

"Yeah, I'll drink it." Jackson made a blah face. "The ice cream tastes terrific. That protein powder aftertaste needs some help. Like more ice cream added."

"Yes, it does." Dr. Wright chuckled. "You're more talkative than normal. I'm going to insert the feeding tube whether you want it or not.

86

The question is, do you want to rest while we do it. I would recommend you sleep so your body and mind can relax."

"As tired as I am, drugged sleep is better than none at all. Sure, bring it on." Jackson's arm quivered with fatigue as he drank the shake. *I wish the doc brought some coffee to get the cardboard taste out of my mouth.*

"Captain Mason, can you and Sergeant Palmer get him comfortable on his bunk?"

Bill grabbed Jackson's outstretched left hand. Sgt. Palmer mirrored him with the other side. They pulled Jackson to his feet and helped him to his bunk. He sat and stretched out on his back.

With his thumb out like a hitchhiker, Bill pointed at Jackson. "How long will he be out?"

"About two hours." Dr. Wright put a stethoscope around his neck. "Why?"

Bill clutched Jackson's shoulder. "They're allowing us two hours in the library later. Do you want to go?"

Jackson nodded. "Sure." *It'll get me out of the cellblock to look around.*

Bill's eyes widened. "That's new. Most of the time, we have to drag him to the showers."

"Yeah, I know." Dr. Wright looped a blood pressure cuff around Jackson's arm.

"Relax, sir, I'll come back when you're done." Bill walked to his cell.

Palmer handed Dr. Wright a large, liquid-filled syringe.

Dr. Wright injected the contents into the puffed-up vein near Jackson's elbow. Everything went dark a few seconds later.

The wall clock read 1800 hours when Jackson opened his eyes. "Ohh…" *I hate this part. I feel so loopy.* He pushed his upper body into a sitting position on his bunk with his elbows.

"Look at me." Dr. Wright gripped Jackson's shoulder. "I need to check your pupil reaction."

"Okay." Jackson faced the fuzzy image of the doctor.

Dr. Wright flashed a penlight across Jackson's eyes. "They're slow, but returning to normal. How do you feel?"

Jackson shook his head to clear his medication-numbed brain. "Sleepy, but I'm here. That's all I can say for now."

"Here is good. It's better than you've been lately. I suspect this is a temporary reprieve for you. Your attitude and conscious level tends to change erratically."

Where did Dr. Wright learn his bedside manner? A barn. He sounds like my first riding instructor. Strict and demanding First Sergeant Goad. Jackson scratched his head. "I can't explain today. Maybe it's the open door and a little freedom for a change. Don't understand it myself. The days are blurring together."

Dr. Wright stuck his stethoscope in his lab coat pocket. "I'll take today as a good sign and leave it at that."

Bill stood in front of Ty, Chief and Mikey at the doorway to his cell. "Go save us a table. The colonel's my responsibility. We'll be along in a few minutes. Don't push. Let him do all the talking."

Ty, Mikey, and Chief followed their guard as Bill walked into Jackson's cell.

"The library, right, Bill?" Jackson stood from his bunk.

Bill cracked a small smile. "Yeah, the library."

Jackson turned slowly to face Dr. Wright. "If I go back into my shell tomorrow. Thanks."

"I hope you don't. I like you much better this way." Dr. Wright stuffed the blood pressure cuff in his medical bag.

"I like myself better this way too. Tomorrow is another day. I'll still be locked up, and they won't leave the doors open." Jackson exited his cell and walked beside Bill to the end of the cellblock. He gave Bill a thumbs down, clenched fist hand signal. Their hand sign for enemy. Then he put one finger on his arm.

Bill nodded in response.

Jackson smiled. *One guard as an escort. What are they thinking? Normally, it's two or three. I scare them.*

At the library, Bill chose the *Sports Illustrated* swimsuit edition and Jackson, *Horse and Rider* off the magazine rack. They sat at the table across from Mikey, Ty, and Chief.

Jackson glanced up from an article about training a cutting horse. Bill's face had a sweaty sheen. "Are those scantily clad women to your liking, Captain?"

Bill gazed over the top of the magazine. "Yes, sir. How'd you know?"

"You're drooling." *Not that I wouldn't after being here ten months.* Jackson scooted his chair closer to Bill. "How do you guys feel about escaping?" He caught Bill's raised eyebrows. "It's Harry's idea and I have a plan."

"We've already talked about it. Our problem was how to encourage you to come with us. The answer is yes," Bill whispered in Jackson's ear.

"Good. My plan is a simple sapper maneuver." Jackson checked out the other prisoners in the room. Five of them were looking in their direction. "But not here. Too many ears. Bill, I'll tell you after lights out. You relay it to Ty and so on. I want to thank all of you for being patient with me. If not for your support, I would've done something drastic months ago."

Bill rubbed the cross on his dog tag chain between his fingers. "By drastic, do you mean suicide?"

"That's exactly what I mean. I can't guarantee it won't come up again until we get out of here."

Mikey tipped his chair forward to lean across the table. "Colonel, we'll make sure you never get the chance. I guarantee that."

"Thanks, Mikey." Jackson flipped to the next page of his magazine as a guard walked by.

Two additional guards entered the library and stood on the other side of the room.

Jackson gave the cutoff signal by moving his hand, palm down horizontally across his throat. He didn't want any extra attention from the guards.

Chief launched into a lengthy dissertation about how the San Francisco 49ers used their defense to beat the Dallas Cowboys 31-10.

An hour later, the library closed for the evening.

Jackson, Bill, Ty, Chief, and Mikey stood when Cpl. Lewis, Cpl. Stevens and PFC Hanson surrounded the table with their nightsticks out. They walked to their cells like model prisoners. Jackson didn't want anything to change. His plan hinged on everything remaining status quo

CHAPTER 8

December 16, 1972 – 0700 hours

Jackson opened his eyes and stared at the ceiling. For several minutes, he stayed on his back. Blinking his eyes, he sat up. *What day is it? Why am I on the floor with a bloody nose, fat lip, and bruised knuckles? My legs won't work, and I peed on myself again. What's that smell? I crapped my pants too. Damn. I hate Toad and Pig for humiliating me like that.*

On hands and knees, he crawled to his bunk, climbed into it then levered his body into a sitting position. "Why can't they leave me alone for an hour? I want the faces to go away." He stared at his bloody knuckles and dropped his head into his hands. *I don't know what happened.*

"Colonel?"

Jackson looked at Bill standing next to their adjoining cell wall with his hands gripped on the bars. "Yeah. Lower your voice before you burst my eardrums. I can hear you."

Bill dropped his arms to his side. "Are you okay?"

"No! I'm not."

"Do you want to talk about it?"

"No!" Jackson pulled off his soiled clothing, wiped himself off with towel, and tossed everything into a corner of his cell. He put on clean underwear and a uniform then went to the sink to wash his hands. To ease the pain in his shredded knuckles, he wrapped them in wet washcloths. Unable to remain standing, he wobbled to his bunk, sat with his back against the wall and legs hanging off the edge.

Bill sat cross-legged on the floor next to the bars with his blanket.

"What are you doing, Bill?"

"Watching over you." Bill wrapped the blanket around his shoulders. "I won't leave you alone again."

Sunlight streamed through the barred window.

Where'd the time go? It was dark outside. I can't keep living like this. He pulled on the thin blanket he was sitting on. *Feels strong enough. What do I tie it to? The bars and lean forward after lights out. The army found my breaking point. Total betrayal, and never-ending pain. I have two options. Escaping or death. If I fail either, my destiny, a rubber room, encased in a straitjacket, a feeding tube in my nose, living the rest of my miserable life outside of reality.*

The hour hand of the wall clock pointed at nine when Dr. Wright walked into Jackson's cell. "What happened? Your hands and face are all chewed up. Did the guards beat you up again?"

Jackson stared through the doctor. *Why can't I just die?*

"Not going to answer me, huh? The last thing you need is an infection." Dr. Wright pulled a bottle and stack of cotton squares out of his medical bag.

The acrid smell of rubbing alcohol burned Jackson's nose and stung his knuckles. A thought came to him in that instant. He'd been thinking of doing the unthinkable. A mortal sin for a Catholic. He didn't want to die. It was difficult but he forced himself to say the words. "Doc, I need help. I can't go on like this." In those two sentences, he felt a weight lift. Just a little. He wanted to live. He wanted the pain to go away.

Dr. Wright wrapped Jackson's hands in a thick gauze cocoon. "Do you want to talk about last night?"

"No!" Jackson's eyes darted to Dr. Wright's face. "That's just as bad as reliving it. I can't do that again."

"But you do want help?"

"Yes." Jackson sucked in a deep breath. "I have to get out of this cell."

"Colonel, you know the procedure as well as I do. I don't want to bring a crowd of MPs in here to help me sedate you. If you overreact, it could get bad for all of us. Your emotions are too open and raw. As a fellow officer, I owe you this much. Will you cooperate with me?"

The world came crashing down. The stress enveloped him like a blanket. Jackson willed himself somewhere else. His cell became a grassy pasture under a cloudless bright blue sky. He walked up to his horse and climbed into the saddle. "Hi, Taco. Ready for today's ride. It's a beautiful day for practice. I want to win that blue ribbon tomorrow."

He guided Taco over the jumps set up across the field. "Up and over, boy. Dad's watching at the fence. Let's make him proud."

What hit my shoulder? Jackson pulled back on the reins.

Taco came to a stop, whinnied and shook his head.

Jackson looked around. Nothing. Only the wind blowing the grass. *Felt like a hand. But how? I'm alone.*

A weird sensation struck him—like a garden hose in his nose. *My face hurts.* He felt a sharp prick on his arm and looked around. *Did a bee sting me? Now I have a headache. What's that light ahead of me?*

Palmer flashed a penlight across Jackson's eyes. "Nothing, doctor. His pupils are fixed."

Jackson blinked away the white dots. The pasture became his cell. *What happened?*

"I can't leave him in a catatonic state. He'll die without care." Dr. Wright stepped to the bars.

"I'm still here, Doc," Jackson whispered.

Dr. Wright turned around. "Well, well, look who decided to join us."

Jackson reached up to his face. "How did Sergeant Palmer stick the tube in my nose without me knowing?"

Dr. Wright knelt to Jackson's eye level. "You zoned out for over ten minutes."

"I did?"

"Yeah, I thought you disappeared for good. Do you remember where you were?"

"Ahh…riding my horse. I was practicing for a big meet at the state fair."

"How old were you?"

"Twelve." Jackson cocked his head in confusion. "Why?"

"Because it tells me a lot about your mental status. I'll forward your request, but you know what Hammond will say."

"Yeah, denied." Jackson tried for a little mirth. "Probably in large red letters."

"You've given up, haven't you, Colonel?"

"Not totally, but I'm close. The army did what the Cong couldn't. Break me."

Dr. Wright placed both hands on Jackson's shoulders and locked eyes with him. "Have you thought about suicide?"

Jackson inclined his head, unable to maintain eye contact. *Last night nearly broke my spirit.* He had to say it. That one word. "Yes."

"That tips my hand. Once we finish here, I'll go file the paperwork. I don't have a choice. I have to follow protocol and admit you to the hospital for psychiatric care."

"You know what he'll say. The same thing the arrogant ass has for months. I must be a magician to look like a walking skeleton who's losing his mind."

Dr. Wright leaned back on his heels. "Yeah, I know. I'll go over his head all the way to the President, and if that fails, the press. I can't leave you like this any longer. It's pathetic I need to force the army to follow its own procedures. It might take a few days, but I will get you out of this cell. Promise me you won't try anything."

Jackson closed his eyes and relaxed. A piece of paper with his escape plan drawn on it appeared in his mind. *If we can't go when planned, maybe the doctor can give Hammond an ulcer. I'm out of options.* "Yeah, I'll keep fighting. At least until I have nothing else left."

"Good." Dr. Wright patted Jackson's shoulder. "That's all I ask. Will you drink the shake?"

Jackson reached for the container. "Yeah, I'm thirsty." *It's ice cream, even with the crappy protein powder added.* The cold, slightly melted, almost chocolate-flavored contents soothed his dry throat. "Is this because of what I told you?"

"Yes. I will hold you to your promise."

"I always keep my promises." Jackson forced a small smile. "As long as no one jumps in the middle of them. I promised Harry to help him through the loss of his foot. The army forced me to break that one."

"Dr. Howard told me about Major Russell. You had no control of the situation." Dr. Wright turned to Sgt. Palmer. "Take out the feeding tube, make him comfortable, and prepare a sedative. I'll be back in a few minutes to administer it."

The clang of the outside door echoed in the cell block. Dr. Wright motioned to Staff Sgt. Trotter to let him out. He met Bill in front of Jackson's open cell door. "Your colonel's in bad shape. From the cuts and abrasions, he had a terrible night."

Bill wrung his hands. "Yeah, he did, but he wouldn't tell me about it. The event turned violent. He kept running into the wall and pounding it with his fists."

That's what I did? Jackson thought for a second. *All I remember is trying to claw my way out of being buried alive.*

Dr. Wright pulled off his reading glasses. "That's not our only problem. Colonel MacKenzie's having suicidal thoughts."

"The colonel admitted that to you?" Bill exclaimed.

"Yes, but he asked for help. He doesn't want to die, or he wouldn't have said anything." Dr. Wright stroked his chin. "Your friend is on the fine edge of human endurance. It's only a matter of time before the acute strain on his body causes organ failure. Most men would've already crumbled under the pressure. It shows how much courage and strength of will he has to fight for so long. But he's in a lot of pain and losing the desire to keep going. It will take me a few days to admit him to the hospital since I have to go over Hammond's head. I need you to keep an eye on him at all times. His body might give out first. If it does, I'll force the issue and send him to the ICU, but keep him fighting."

"Will do, doctor." Bill's baritone voice rang in the quiet of the concrete room.

"I'll put him on suicide watch. It won't make a difference since the guards don't give a rat's ass. I'll sedate him, so he'll sleep for about four hours. I'll return at lights out to knock him out for the evening. That way, he doesn't suffer through another night like last night. It'll make it easier on his mind."

"Thanks, Doc. He'll thank you one of these days."

"He already has, several times. Colonel MacKenzie served this country with honor. It's the army who's failing him. Now, I have to force someone to listen to me." Dr. Wright walked back into the cell.

Jackson pushed his body up on his elbow. "I heard everything you told Bill."

"Good. I wanted you to hear it. Sergeant Palmer, give me the sedative."

"Bring it on. It's better than sleeping without it." *I won't dream.*

2100 hours

The world outside the windows—no moon, no stars, just black as coal. Jackson sat on his bunk wrapped in a blanket like a burrito, his lower jaw shaking, knocking his teeth together. The air felt like ice. At least to him. Everyone else looked comfortable. He leaned into the pillow behind his back with his feet hanging off the long edge.

Colonel Hammond strolled into the cell block and stopped in front of Jackson's cell. "Ahem!"

Jackson remained in the same position. He didn't have the strength to stand.

A vein in Hammond's forehead popped with his pulse. His face turned bright red. "Lieutenant Colonel MacKenzie, Dr. Wright delivered his recommendation concerning your release to the hospital for psychiatric care. My superiors have determined your problems are a smokescreen. Your court-martial is scheduled after the first of the year. You will be convicted no matter how much you try to fake your way out of it. I, therefore, deny his request."

Jackson's head lolled from side to side. He squinted at Hammond, trying to make his eyes focus. *I expected this. But not here.* His ears perked up at the roar of different voices in the cellblock.

94

"Did your mother have sex with a dog? Because you look like one." Chief yelled at the top of his voice.

Chief's giving Hammond hell.

"You're a son of a bitch, Hammond?"

I would never say that word in public. Mom hated it.

Mikey's voice echoed over the others. "You're nothing but a Punani, Hammond!"

Punani? That's from the Kama Sutra. It means vagina…oh…pussy.

"You're a bellend?

Where'd Mikey come up with that one? Dad said it once. It's British for penis head.

"And a wanker mixed with a gobshite."

Gobshite. That's Irish for stupid person. Well, it fits.

Bill threw his metal drinking cup at Hammond. It hit at his feet. "Hammond, you're an egotistical windbag. Your parents conceived you by laying an egg. A big one. You're a fat-ass slob."

I thought I had an imagination.

Hammond turned to the Staff Sgt. Trotter. His face looked like a rotten piece of fruit, winkled and reddish-black. "Write my statement word for word into the log, Sergeant."

"Yes, sir." Trotter caught Jackson's eyes as he signed the logbook.

Once Hammond exited the cell block, Trotter opened Jackson's cell then Bill's. "Dr. Wright asked me to let you stay with Colonel MacKenzie for a little while." He glanced at his watch. "I'll delay lights out for an hour." Turning on his heel, Trotter walked away.

Bill sat next to Jackson on his bunk. "Are you cold, sir?"

"F-f-frrreeezing." Jackson's body vibrated like an overworked washing machine.

Bill retrieved his blanket from his bunk. Mikey, Ty, and Chief poked theirs through the bars. Jackson wound up covered in a mound of thick, green wool army blankets. Bill sat on Jackson's bunk and placed his arm across Jackson's shoulders. With the support and warmth of Bill's body, Jackson dropped his head onto Bill's shoulder.

Bill pulled Jackson's body close to his. "You look terrible."

Jackson swallowed to soothe his sore throat. "Yeah. Hammond won't allow the doctor to put me in the hospital. You heard him. I'm making it up. I normally hate hospitals. I'd rather be there than here."

"Dr. Wright will do his best, but I agree after listening to Colonel Blow Hard."

"Me too. Dr. Wright has as much a chance as a snowball in July. If he manages to swing it before December 23rd, fine. We'll escape later. If he can't, then we go. I hate for you guys to stay in this hellhole if the doc pulls off a miracle."

"Don't worry about us." Bill patted Jackson's back. "Are you sure you'll be up to it?"

"You said that at the camp too." Jackson shuddered at the memory of that night. Toad damn near beat him to death as Dung watched. "I don't know, but I'll sure try."

"Don't give up on us, okay."

"I don't plan to, Bill."

"Do what you can and we'll take up the slack."

"As long as my body can hold out, so will I."

"Good." Bill cracked a smile. "Dr. Wright's coming by later to sedate you."

Jackson choked back a sarcastic snort. "He won't get a fight from me. I'm so tired it's better than the alternative. Once we escape, it won't be an option. I'll have to deal with my problems."

"Not I, *we*, Colonel."

"I have an idea on that. Not until we're outside the walls."

"Knowing you as well as I do, sir." Bill chuckled. "I should've figured as much. Rest. Do you want some coffee?"

"Yeah." Jackson perked up. "That would be great, but the mess already closed."

"The guards have a coffee maker. Let me see if they'll start a pot. It'll double as intel gathering." Bill pulled his arm from around Jackson's shoulders and raised it above his head.

"Trying to catch his attention?"

Bill nodded. "Yes, sir. Don't want my noggin knocked off by a nightstick. You learned that lesson months ago."

"True. I'm surprised it's still attached."

Trotter waved Bill to the desk. Ten minutes later Bill returned with a steaming cup. "The lockers have key locks. I can pick those in my sleep. The keys to the outer door are in the top desk drawer. Kinda stupid, but good for us. Someone wrote the lockbox combo on the desk calendar."

"Good job." Jackson held the mug against his chest, allowing it to cool. He tested the liquid with a small sip. *Marine Corps coffee. Excellent.* The coffee warmed the inside of his throat. Two gulps later, he handed Bill the empty mug. After one pot, Jackson had enough energy with a stomach full

96

of caffeine to hold his head erect. "Will they let the guys out or only you, Bill?"

Trotter released other men then paused in front of Jackson's cell "That was part of Dr. Wright's request, allow your friends a few minutes alone with you." He returned to his desk.

Ty, Mikey, and Chief sat cross-legged on the floor in front of Jackson's bunk.

Jackson bent forward to keep his voice from carrying. "We're still on, guys. As planned. If I stay any longer, I'll die in this filthy cell. The only way for me to live is to leave this never-ending purgatory. Hammond made that perfectly clear. I may need some help to walk out."

"You've always helped us, sir. Now it's our turn to help you. Don't worry. We'll pull it off, promise." Ty ran his hand nervously through his dark curly hair.

"Thanks, guys." Jackson turned to Chief. "Don't even think about tossing me over your shoulder again. I will not leave like a sack of potatoes. It's inelegant and embarrassing. The last time I looked like a dead body covered in blood and bandages, not an army officer."

CHAPTER 9

December 23, 1972

Jackson rolled onto his side. *I want to throw up.* He pulled his knees to his chest to ease the pain. *Feels like someone chucked my stomach in a blender.* A burning pain erupted in his throat. He threw off his blanket, stumbled to the toilet and heaved until he threw up blood. *What time is it?* He glanced at the wall clock. 0900 hours *I'm so hot.* He stuck his head under the sink faucet to cool his cooking brain. Wet and miserable, Jackson sat in the corner, hugged his knees, and rocked.

At 2000 hours Chief and Ty pulled Jackson to his feet. "Time for your shower, boss."

"Let me go! Leave me alone." Jackson dug his heels into the concrete and wrenched his arm free to swing at Chief. He missed wide and ran face-first into the wall. *Why change the routine? It would look strange if I cooperated. The guards would notice. That could cause a kink in my plan.* The two men retook hold of his arms and continued their trek to the showers.

Bill and Mikey carried their shaving kits, towels, and fresh clothes. Their job, watch the guards.

Chief pinched his nose. "You stink, boss. Take off your clothes and get in the shower."

"Make me." Jackson clenched his fists.

"Your choice." Chief sent Jackson under the running water fully-clothed with one push.

I need a shower. I smell like body odor, sour sweat, and rank urine. I ought to be used to this by now.

Ty reached for the buttons on Jackson's shirt. "Time to get undressed."

"Leave me alone." Jackson shoved Ty's hand away. "That's an order! I can do it myself." To get away from Ty, he sat on the floor.

"Then take off those stinky wet clothes and stop acting like you're five years old."

Touché. Jackson stood, took off his shirt, pants, and underwear, balled them up, and threw them at Ty.

Ty ducked as the wet garments flew over his head.

Jackson chunked his boots outside the stall, lathered up his body, and quickly rinsed off. *Ouch, I hate lye soap. The barber scraped my scalp yesterday. Asshole.* His threadbare towel didn't help soak up the water. He pulled on his fresh underwear, uniform and boots then sat on the bench.

"Get up, boss." Chief held up a toothbrush.

"No."

Chief yanked Jackson to his feet then held him down next to the sink. "Open up. Don't make us do this the hard way."

Jackson shook his head.

Ty pinched Jackson's nose closed. When he opened his mouth to breathe, Mikey brushed his teeth.

Jackson spat on Mikey's leg to get the nasty-tasting cheap prison toothpaste out of his mouth. *Gotta keep up the illusion.* He gripped Mikey's hand with his teeth. Not hard. Just touched the skin.

Mikey jerked his hand back and massaged it.

He did good. I even believed it.

Jackson sat still as Bill shaved him. He didn't want his carotid artery cut. Bill had the steadiest hands. Ty's shook so bad he looked like a horror movie. Mikey wouldn't after the POW camp.

Jackson waited for his cue as his men carried him through the cell block doorway. At the click of the lock turning after the guard shut the door, he fell to the ground in convulsions. He jerked across the floor from one wall to the other, drooling bubbles out of his mouth. *Thank goodness for the cheap toothpaste.*

Chief and Ty dropped to his side as their watchers went down with them.

Cpl. Stevens, all five-foot-five and 120 pounds, bent over Jackson's head.

Jackson grabbed him by the neck in a chokehold. He squeezed just enough to render the guy unconscious. He didn't want the sorry excuse for a human dead.

At the same time, Ty and Chief dispatched PFC Hanson and Cpl. Pendergast.

Bill and Mikey stood watch on the door. In case someone surprised them.

Jackson unlocked his arm to release Steven's limp body. He sat on the floor to regain control of his lungs while Mikey and Bill dragged Stevens into his cell. They removed Stevens' uniform, tied him to the bunk, and stuffed a dirty sock in his mouth.

Chief and Ty repeated the same operation with their unconscious subjects. They returned, helped Jackson up, walked him to the guard desk, and sat him in a chair.

Bill picked the locks. He retrieved the civilian clothing, money, and car keys from the lockers.

Because of the large black P on the back of their shirts, identifying them as prisoners, the men changed into the guards' uniforms. They left their prison-issued ones inside the lockers.

"I thought you were convulsing for real, Colonel." Mikey stuffed a wad of clothes into a pillowcase.

"I think we all did." Bill helped Jackson into a shirt too big on his thin frame.

"It was supposed to look real, or they wouldn't fall for it." Jackson rubbed his painful lower back. *Hope that's not my appendix or we're in trouble.*

Mikey covered Jackson's shoulders with a green wool army blanket. "When was the last time you took a dump?"

"Getting a bit personal there, Mikey?"

"Professional question, sir." Mikey pointed at the wall calendar. "When?"

Jackson thought for a moment. "To tell you the truth, I don't remember. Why?"

"Your backache may be a blockage in your bowels."

"Well, we can't do anything about that right now, can we? What else might it be, just to clear the next question?" *I already know, I want Mikey to confirm.*

"Your liver could be failing, sir."

"Which means what?" Jackson scowled. *That's worse than my appendix.*

Mikey looked Jackson in the eyes. "We find a hospital as soon as we're far enough away the army can't scoop us up and bring you back here. Because that'll kill you quick."

"Then we'll deal with it later. Who has the keys?" Jackson tried to stand, but his legs wouldn't cooperate. When Chief took a step toward him, he held up his hand. "I'm walking."

"Okay, boss." Chief pulled Jackson's right arm across his shoulders. "Ty, get the other side. Colonel, move your legs. We'll take your weight."

"Get that door open, Bill. The clock's ticking," Jackson called out.

"Easy as pie with a key." Bill pushed the door open. Chief and Ty turned sideways with Jackson between them and went through the opening. Bill came next, with Mikey last carrying the overstuffed pillowcase over his shoulder. They turned left and headed toward the parking lot.

Jackson sucked in a breath of fresh air outside the building. He felt something cold on his face. White particles floated in the air. "Hey, it's snowing. Bill, find us a car. Make sure it has a full gas tank. I don't want to stop until we're across the state line."

"Yes, sir." Bill ran into the parking lot. A low whistle pierced the air in less than two minutes. "Found one. Let's make tracks."

Chief jumped into the driver's seat of a black four-door '69 AMC Ambassador with Bill riding shotgun. Ty and Mikey sat in the back seat with Jackson ensconced between them wrapped in a blanket and padded with pillows.

Jackson pointed over the front seat. "Chief, use the Longstreet gate. It's a twenty-four-hour gate. The guards have to deal with the public all day. Since it's snowing, I hope they'll pass us through without checking IDs, or this will be a brief escape attempt."

Luck was on their side. As a result of having a visible gate pass on the front window, the sentry raised the crossbar and waved them through without a second glance.

Jackson tossed the map Ty gave him into the front seat. "Chief, head west. Take highway 401 until it meets with I-20. Drive the speed limit so the cops don't look our way. Let's put a few hundred miles under the tires before the shift change. We'll change into civilian clothes when we need gas."

Chief glanced at Jackson in the back seat. "Where are we going, boss?"

"San Diego."

December 24, 1972

"I'm gonna throw up." Jackson doubled over with his arms wrapped around his stomach.

Mikey laid his palm on Jackson's forehead. "Chief, find the closest hospital. The colonel can't travel any farther. He's burning up."

Chief turned off the highway at the exit titled Cairo, Mississippi, near the Alabama state line.

"Why are we taking this exit?" Ty leaned over the front seat.

Bill turned around. "We're better off using a local doctor than a big city hospital where the staff will ask too many questions about the colonel's terrible condition and call the cops."

At the town limits, Bill pointed. "There's a sign for the doctor. Follow the directions, Sergeant."

A few minutes later, Chief stopped in front of a large, one-story white house.

Bill peered out his window. "It's dark inside. Everyone's gone home. It's Christmas Eve."

Mikey and Bill helped Jackson out of the back seat and assisted him up the steps to the porch. Ty and Chief hid the car around the corner. Bill picked the lock and pushed the front door aside as Mikey held Jackson upright. Bill retook Jackson's arm. They carried Jackson into the small clinic and sat him in a chair.

Jackson pulled the blanket around his body, dropped his head into his hands and shivered. He couldn't sit up straight. The muscle spasms in his back twisted his body in a dozen different directions.

"Don't turn on the lights, Mikey. We don't want to alert anyone we're in the house," Bill whispered. "The last thing we need is for someone to call the police. It wouldn't take long for Hammond to show up at the jail with a squad of hulking MPs."

"Yeah, and a few hours later, the colonel will be on a cold slab in the morgue from organ failure," Mikey said in a hushed tone.

"I'm not that far gone." Jackson glanced up at the slight bang of a drawer.

Bill put his finger to his lips as he stood at Jackson's side. His other hand on the colonel's back.

"If you're looking for drugs for your strung-out friend, you're looking in the wrong place," a disembodied male voice said from around the corner.

Jackson eyeballed the white-haired man standing in the doorway. "I'm not high or stoned, mister, and I'm not on drugs."

Mikey stood up from his search. "Sir, this has nothing to do with drugs. I need IV set-ups, saline bags, and an enema bag or two."

Jackson glared at Mikey. "You planning to stick something up my butt, Sergeant Roberts?"

"Yes, sir. If your bowels are impacted, it's the only way to get the crap out, so to speak."

The man walked over to Jackson but turned to speak with Mikey. "Do you have medical training, son?"

"Yes, sir, army medic."

"My son's an army medic like you, young man. Turn on the lights so I can take a look at your friend. The switch is on the wall next to you."

"Yes, sir." Mikey slapped the switch.

"I'm Dr. Curtis Rose." The man rubbed Jackson's shoulder. "Look at me, mister."

Jackson locked his eyes on the doctor's brown ones. *I just want to catch a break.*

"You're jaundiced. Does your back hurt?"

"Yes, sir."

Dr. Rose squeezed Jackson's shoulder. "What's your name, son?"

"Jackson MacKenzie. My mom called me JJ."

"Okay, I'll call you Jackson since I'm not your mother. When did you have your last bowel movement?"

"To tell you the truth." Jackson shook his head. "I don't remember. All the days have run together. At least five days. I think."

"Given the fact you're not old and haven't had a bowel movement for five days, I agree with your friend with impaction. But your gaunt appearance tells me that's not the only thing wrong with you."

"I may not be old, but I sure feel like it."

Mikey moved to the doctor's side. "No, sir. It isn't. He's been rail-thin since we escaped from a POW camp almost two years ago. He hasn't been eating properly. He's also suffering from depression and...PTSD."

Jackson gave Mikey a piercing stare through narrowed eyes at those four distinct letters.

Dr. Rose's eyes widened. "PTSD, huh? I heard on the radio five men escaped from the Fort Bragg stockade yesterday. Would that be you, and if it is, where are the other two?"

"Behind you." Chief popped his head around the corner. He entered the room with Ty at his hip. "And, yes, that would be us. The army was killin' the colonel by not putting him in the hospital. Escaping was our only option to keep him alive."

"Your face is flushed." Dr. Rose placed his palm on Jackson's forehead. "And you have a high fever. I want to check something. I'm going to stick my hand under your shirt. It might be a little cold."

"Go ahead," Jackson whispered. He jerked as the doctor hit the sore spot. "You're right, Doc, your hand feels like an ice cube. Warm it up next time."

Dr. Rose removed his hand and stood up straight. "It's hard to tell with you all hunched over, but you may have appendicitis."

"Doctor, we'll leave. Give us three hours to vacate the area before you call anyone."

"I'm not going to turn you in, Jackson. I would be in violation of my medical oath to let you leave. You're not in any shape to travel. I can't believe the army didn't put you in the hospital."

Mikey spoke up. "Believe it, sir. Dr. Wright tried everything short of breaking Colonel MacKenzie out himself. Last week he started showing signs of organ failure. We had two choices. Escape to get the colonel medical treatment or watch him die in his cell. What would you have done?"

"The same as you, young man. Move your friend to my treatment bed. Take off his clothes and stick this IV line in his arm wide open." Dr. Rose pulled an IV set-up and saline bag out of a cabinet and handed the items to Mikey.

Carefully, Mikey and Bill wrapped their arms around Jackson's shoulders, lifted him from the chair, and walked him to the bed. After Jackson sat on the thin foam mattress, Bill removed his boots and pants while Mikey helped him off with his shirt. Slowly while supporting Jackson's head, Mikey eased him down onto his back.

Dr. Rose bent over Jackson's torso. "Those were some nasty wounds on your shoulder and thigh. They look recent."

"Yes, sir. It happened about a year ago." Jackson pulled his knees to his chest to ease the pain in his back. "Owwww!" he shrieked.

"What's wrong?" Dr. Rose clasped Jackson's face with both hands.

"My back feels like someone shoved a white-hot poker in it, and I ate a bowlful of glass!"

"Lie still." Dr. Rose pressed his hand along Jackson's abdomen. "I don't think it's your appendix. Your liver and spleen are swollen. The impaction started an infection. That's why you have a high fever and turned yellow. Once your intestines have emptied, you should feel better. Just be warned, it might take two enemas to clean out your gut. Then I'll start a large dose of antibiotics through the IV line to get the infection under control." He nodded to Mikey and left the room.

Mikey looked down sheepishly. "Sir, the underwear has to come off too. I'm sorry."

Jackson felt his ears burn as he slipped off the nearly gray prison-issue briefs.

"Here, sir." Mikey pulled a thick quilted gray blanket over Jackson's body. "This will keep you warm."

And maintain what's left of my dignity.

Dr. Rose walked back into the clinic as Mikey started the IV line. "First try with his veins collapsed from dehydration. Nice touch, young man."

"Thank you, sir. I've had lots of practice on the colonel. I know how to stick him when they roll on me."

Humor was all he had left. It helped with the pain. A little bit. Jackson sneered at his friend. "Traitor."

"Mikey, the portable toilet chair is the bathroom." Dr. Rose pointed down the hall. "After you hang the bag, bring it in here."

"What's the chair for, Doc?" Jackson examined the IV line taped to his left forearm.

"You know what it's for. There's no way we'll make it to the bathroom in time carrying you. This is the only way to keep from making a mess."

"I know." Jackson watched Mikey park the chair next to the bed. "But that doesn't mean I have to like it."

Mikey folded the blanket down to Jackson's knees. "Colonel, turn onto your side and keep your knees against your chest so we can insert the tube."

Taking in a deep breath, Jackson wrapped his arms around his knees. He tensed as the cold, vaseline covered rubber tube entered his rectum. *This feels so weird.* He concentrated on his father's last Christmas at home to pass the time at the clock ticked. Dad gave him and Jim a .22 caliber Remington model 550 rifle. They spent all winter break at the range plinking targets until neither of them missed a shot.

The first enema took over an hour to work. The second, ten minutes. His butt was raw after Mikey scrubbed it clean with a cloth diaper. At least he felt better without the bomb of glass shards going off in his gut.

Mickey gripped Jackson's shoulder. "I'm sorry for the shock, sir. Please don't kick me in the groin when I put in the Foley catheter."

Jackson released a single, sarcastic bark. "Don't worry, I knew that was coming. I can't stand, so making it to the bathroom to pee is out of the question. Not that I even need to because I don't."

Mikey inserted the catheter and tucked the blanket around Jackson.

Dr. Rose returned. In his hands, a tray with syringes and a white cloth mound. "Put these on him, Mikey." He held up a pair of white boxers. "I don't need him under any more stress because he's embarrassed about being naked in front of everybody."

Jackson started to sit up.

"Lie still, sir." Mikey pushed Jackson down onto his back. "Let me do it. If one of those lines gets jerked out, it'll hurt, and you're already hurting too much." He eased the shorts up Jackson's legs, taped the collection tube to his thigh, and propped him up with pillows.

Dr. Rose tightened a rubber strap around Jackson's bicep.

Jackson bit his lip as the doctor slipped a needle into a vein in his forearm. Even the little prick sent a shockwave up his spine. He watched the blood trickle into the test tube. *I'm still alive.*

Dr. Rose held the tube up to the light. "It's a little dark. Probably from the infection and some congestion in your lungs." He placed it on the tray.

Mikey handed Dr. Rose another empty syringe. "Here's one for the urine sample."

"Put it away. Jackson's dangerously dehydrated. I need to wait. The small amount coming out of his bladder right now has the viscosity of light vegetable oil. Its dark brown color makes it unusable for testing." Dr. Rose picked up three filled syringes from the tray and injected them into Jackson's IV line.

"What are you putting into me, Doc?" Jackson squinted in the overhead light.

"You can't lie still. Antibiotics, pain medication, and valium."

Mikey covered Jackson with another thick warm blanket. "How's your back, sir?"

Jackson leaned into the pillows. "Better now the little gremlins running around in my guts aren't trying to extract my organs with a plastic knife."

Dr. Rose inserted a feeding tube into Jackson's nose and another IV line near his elbow.

"What's that for, Doc?" Jackson asked.

"More fluids and a glucose solution. Your blood sugar's low. Stop fighting the medication and go to sleep."

Dr. Rose walked over to Bill, Chief, and Ty standing next to the wall. "I know you guys are concerned. Thank you for staying out of our way instead of hovering like three little ticks. You have an extremely sick friend. He's not stable and will need constant, intense care for the next week to ten days before you can take him anywhere. His emaciated appearance concerns me the most. Dr. Wright is correct to worry about organ failure due to the impaction and malnutrition. From Mikey's description of Jackson's PTSD issues, I'll have to sedate him to avoid problems."

Bill rubbed the back of his neck. "Yeah, you will. Colonel MacKenzie can be dangerous if left uncontrolled in a nightmare. He has five combat tours under his belt. Also, he understands what's happening to him since he's gone through the combat medic's course. The man has an iron will. You found out the standard sedative dose isn't enough because he fights it. The only way he'll sleep is for you to give him enough to knock out a horse."

"Got it. You've mentioned the names of two doctors, Dr. Howard and Dr. Wright, who've treated him recently. Did I catch the names right?"

"Correct on both." Bill leaned against the wall. "If you contact them, be careful what you say. They were vocal about the lack of medical care. I can see the army watching them because he's so sick."

"As I said earlier, my son's an army medic. Jerry received his honorable discharge two days ago. He should be home today." Dr. Rose pointed at the ceramic Christmas tree on the counter. "Merry Christmas. I'll have him contact one of those doctors. It shouldn't raise any suspicions if a former army medic calls them. At least I hope it doesn't."

"Thanks. We appreciate your help. As soon as we can scrape up the money, we'll pay for his care."

"I don't care about the money. All I want is for Jackson to get better. This is my house. I have several extra rooms. Go crash out. Mikey and I will watch him overnight."

Bill fiddled with his dog tag chain. "We can split the watches with you."

"I'd rather someone with medical training do that. The only other one besides Mikey and me is Jackson. He's not qualified to watch himself while he's asleep. That leaves the two of us to monitor him."

They're talking about me like I'm not even here. "I'mmm not asslleep," Jackson called from the bed. But he was close to it. He fought to stay awake and hear what they were saying about him.

Chief held up his hand. "I'm cross-trained as a medic. I rarely use it since Mikey's the best, and the colonel tended to take over when needed. He even started his own IVs after being wounded in combat."

"Started IVs on himself, huh?" Dr. Rose raised an eyebrow. "Well, that's one way to stay in a battle. Okay, you joined the rotation, Chief, is it?"

"Yes, sir. My name's Dakota Blackwater. Everyone calls me Chief."

"Okay, now that's settled, let's move him into my overnight room and make him comfortable with lots of extra blankets to keep him warm." Dr. Rose pointed at the tray on the table. "Mikey, prepare another sedative, his eyes are still open."

Jackson watched Mikey hand Dr. Rose another syringe. "I don't need whatever's inn that thinnngg."

Dr. Rose stuck the needle into the port on Jackson's IV line. "Time to follow orders. Goodnight, Jackson."

"G-g-g-oodnight." Jackson drifted off into the darkness

CHAPTER 10

December 25, 1972

During the beginning of his shift, Curtis Rose heard the front door open. He stepped out to see his son emerge from the dark entry hall into the living room dressed in regular clothing. Jeans, a maroon Mississippi State sweatshirt, leather bomber jacket and sneakers. His brown hair remained in a short crew cut.

It's like a dream. Curtis forced himself to walk, not run to the young man. The boy was all he had after his wife died. He'd felt so alone. What kept him going was his practice in their house. He hugged his son. "It's good to see you, Jerry. You look great."

"So do you, Dad." Jerry dropped his green army duffle bag on the floor. "Did you hear about the big escape? They're Special Forces commandos and real badasses. No one knows where they went."

"Yeah, I heard about it." *And know the truth.* "Come with me. I have a patient in the house." Curtis led his son to Jackson's room.

"Who's that?" Jerry pointed at Jackson asleep in the bed.

"I need your confidence on this. Please be quiet and don't call the sheriff. The men you talked about are in the house." Jerry's mouth opened, but Curtis held up a hand. "They're not armed, at least they haven't been around me, and he's—" he pointed at Jackson— "the not sick CO, except he's very sick. The army refused to put him in the hospital for several months. Their two choices, escape to save his life or watch him die. They chose to escape."

"There are medical procedures in place to prevent that from happening. What's wrong with him?"

"You have medical training, son. Go take a look. I have him sedated, so he shouldn't wake up. Make sure to tuck the blankets around him since he gets cold rather easily. Then come back, tell me what you find, and I'll let you know if you're right."

"Got it, Dad." Jerry walked to the bed, pulled the blankets down to Jackson's knees, pressed on his abdomen, and pulled up the blankets. He continued the exam by palpating the sides of Jackson's neck, lifting his eyelids, checking the flow on the IV line then he laid his palm on Jackson's forehead.

Curtis was impressed with Jerry's professionalism. The army trained his son more extensively than he realized. Now he understood how Mikey anticipated his needs in the clinic. He shook his head as Jerry stuffed the blankets around Jackson. His patient looked like a gray wrapped burrito. Jerry still had a joker streak.

Jerry moved back to Curtis' side. His eyes flashed with anger of untold horrors only a combat solider could imagine. Men like Jackson and his friends. "Dad, your patient is skinny to the point of being malnourished. He has several fresh but healed deep lacerations. With his skin flushed and warm to the touch, he has a fever. His skin stands up when pinched, and his neck veins are flat, so he's dehydrated. I felt two masses in his abdomen, probably his liver and spleen since his entire body has turned yellow from jaundice. So you're right, he's sick."

"Good rundown." Curtis picked up an antibiotic filled syringe from the dresser. It was time to give Jackson another dose. "The bowel obstruction started an infection. That's why his liver and spleen are enlarged, and the reason for the high fever. I won't know about liver damage until I get a blood sample to the lab. Even after running five bags of fluids into him, he only began producing urine in the last two hours that isn't dark brown. So I'm concerned about his kidney function. It took a long time for him to get this rundown." He picked up IV line and injected the contents of the syringe into the port.

"Yeah, it's easy to see he's sick, even for someone without medical training. I still can't believe the army would leave him like that."

"But they did," a husky voice said.

Curtis and Jerry turned to look at Bill standing in the doorway wearing boxer shorts, an off-white t-shirt with 16085 stenciled on the front. A two-day growth of facial hair darkened his face.

"The army forced our hand. Colonel Hammond denied every request to transfer him to the hospital. That asshole isn't qualified to make medical decisions. But no one with any authority overruled him. So here we are with the colonel nearly dead again."

Jerry's eyes widened. "Again?"

"Yes, again." Bill pulled his t-shirt down over his shorts. "I've been watching you for several minutes. You saw the scars. Those are from our last mission. I will not go into all the sordid details, but do you know how horrifying it is to see a friend pulled by his arms up a C-130 cargo ramp and handcuffed to a seat? Even worse, he nearly died from the neglect."

Curtis pointed at the living room. "Jerry, is there any way you could find a contact number for Dr. Franklin Howard or Dr. Samuel Wright? I want to speak to one of them about Jackson's treatment since they're more familiar with his medical condition. Just be careful what you say. Captain Mason thinks the army will be watching them."

"Sure, Dad. I can ask my buddy to look up the numbers on the base computer." Jerry paused when Bill shot him a hard stare. "I'll be careful. Is there anything I can say to be cryptic about it?"

"Hmm." Bill tapped his upper lip "Say something about weight. The doctors were always on the colonel's ass about the subject."

"Okay, got it. I'll go make the call." Jerry took a step to leave.

Curtis grabbed his son's arm. "Jerry, it's Christmas Day."

Jerry spun around to face his father. "I know. Spaddy told me he'd be working today."

"Thanks, kid. I appreciate it. Colonel MacKenzie will too." Bill scratched his head.

"Bill, I have a turkey in the refrigerator. The potatoes and canned stuff are in the pantry. Do you mind fixing dinner tonight? I need to stay with Jackson."

"Hell no, Doc. We'll take care of everything. We haven't had a decent meal since Thanksgiving. The food in 'Nam sucked. The pig slop in the stockade tasted like what they fed us in the POW camp. It reminded me of dog food, except I wouldn't feed it to my dog if I had one."

"I'll show you." Curtis looked at his son. "Jerry, keep an eye on Jackson. The sedative will wear off soon. I want someone in the room when he wakes up. After you call your buddy, could you run a blood and urine sample to the lab for me?"

Jerry mocked his father's earlier tone. "Sure, Dad, but it's Christmas Day."

Curtis chuckled. "Brat."

Bill pointed at Jerry. "Don't ever change, sir. Enjoy your son while he's here. I've always wanted a family. The army's BS killed that dream. At least for now."

Jerry stuck his hands in his back pockets. "Go show him the kitchen, Dad. I'll watch over your patient." He peered at Bill. "What do you guys call him?"

A grin spread across Bill's face. "Most of us, *Colonel* or *sir*, just like you would, Sergeant Rose. Major Russell calls him JJ, and his name is

Jackson. He'll answer to any of them. Only his best friend calls him JJ, so if I were you, I'd call him Colonel."

Curtis shook his head. "Army guys."

Am I dead? Sure feels like it. Jackson opened his eyes and blinked a few times. Confused, he slammed them shut. *Where am I?* He eased one eyelid open then the other. *Oh yeah...Dr. Rose...I'm at his house.* A shadow fell across his face. *Who put a wet cloth on my head? What's in my ear?* He reached up, but a hand pushed his arm down to the bed.

"Hold on, sir. Let me finish taking your temperature. I'll be done in a few seconds," said a male voice he didn't recognize.

"Who are you?" Jackson squinted at the blurry image hovering over him.

"Jerry Rose, sir. I'm Dr. Rose's son. I was a medic in 'Nam. Take it easy, Colonel. You're safe. Do you want to sit up?"

"Yeah, my nose is clogged."

Jerry helped Jackson into a sitting position and stuffed two pillows behind his back to keep him upright.

Jackson swallowed to soothe his dry throat. "Is there any water around here, Jerry?"

"Yes, sir." Jerry filled a cup with a straw in it from a pitcher on the table. He turned and leaned over the bed.

"Thank you." Jackson grabbed the cup in both hands, angled the straw into his mouth, and sucked out every drop of water. Now his mouth didn't feel like a dry cotton ball. He handed the cup back to Jerry and settled into his pillows.

"No problem, sir. Glad to help. Lie back and relax. My dad will be back in a few minutes."

"Just got out of the army, huh? Bet your dad's glad you're home safe."

Jerry grinned from one ear to the other. "He is. I can tell."

"Good morning, Jackson." Dr. Rose walked up to Jerry's shoulder.

"Dad, his temperature is 104."

"Thanks, son." Dr. Rose picked up a syringe from the tray on the dresser.

Jackson watched Dr. Rose bend over the side of his bed, out of view. "What are you doing?"

"Since Bill told me you're a medic, you should know. But, Mr. Curious, I'm getting a urine sample out of the collection bag."

"Okay, I'll have a talk with him later about keeping military secrets. Where are the guys?"

"Fixing Christmas dinner." Dr. Rose straightened with a syringe filled with yellow liquid. "Well, everyone but you is getting a turkey dinner. All you get is what's going into your nose."

"They get turkey and all the fixings, I get a feeding tube." Jackson rolled his eyes. "Doesn't seem fair now, does it?"

"I'm glad you have a sense of humor. I've had patients scream at me from that bed when I give them news they don't want to hear."

"Doc?" Jackson fought the urge to shit in his shorts.

"Do you need to go?"

"Yeah." *At least the guys aren't watching this time.*

"Good. I was hoping your bowels would start functioning properly so we wouldn't have to give you another enema." Dr. Rose glanced at his son. "Jerry, could you help me get him to the chair?"

"Sure, Dad." Jerry went around the end to the bed to the other side.

Careful of the feeding tube and IV lines, the two men pulled Jackson's arms across their shoulders and lifted him up. Jerry jerked the shorts down as they moved Jackson to the toilet and sat him on the seat. The shorts came to a rest on Jackson's ankles.

Jackson relaxed against the chair back releasing lots of gas and a little runny waste. "Ahhh..." He felt semi-normal. Not an over expanded balloon. "I'm done." He tried to stand but his legs wouldn't cooperate.

Dr. Rose held him up as Jerry wiped his backside with a disposable cloth then pulled up the shorts.

A bit embarrassed, Jackson tasted metal in his mouth. "It's been a long time since I couldn't wipe my own ass...except for last night."

Jerry and Dr. Rose shook their heads. They helped Jackson into a sitting position in the bed, propped up on a mound of pillows, and covered up to his armpits with two thick blankets.

Chief popped his head in the door "Hey, boss. You're awake? You feeling any better?"

"A little," Jackson whispered. "What are you doing? You're wearing an apron with five pounds of flour all over you."

"Makin' biscuits like my mom taught me." Chief squared his shoulders and puffed out his chest. "She always added a tablespoon of sugar to the dough. I wish you could have one."

Jackson settled back into his pillows. "Me too, Chief. Me too."

113

"No solid food for a few days, Jackson. Right now your system is entirely out of whack. Don't even attempt to stand up. You'll fall on your face." Dr. Rose injected the contents of two syringes into the port on Jackson's IV line.

"Give me a few days, and I promise to try one, okay?" Jackson said to Chief then peered at Dr. Rose with his best command stare. "I guess I'm stuck in bed until further notice, huh, Doc? Can I have some coffee?"

"Coffee, I will okay as long as you drink water with it. You need fluids to help with the dehydration."

Jackson smiled at his friend who stood in the doorway. "Sergeant."

Chief snapped a sharp salute. "Got it. Fresh, hot coffee comin' up."

"Terrific." *Coffee makes any bad day better.*

Intent on his task, Jerry left the room to run the samples to the hospital in Collinsville. The most important thing came first. He dialed the number of Brooke Army Medical Center at Fort Sam Houston. Once he slipped past the switchboard operator, a familiar voice answered.

"Triage area, Sergeant Jacob Spade."

"Spaddy, it's Jerry."

"Hey, Jer. Are you glad to be home? How's your dad?"

"Great. We have a big turkey dinner planned tonight with a few friends." Jerry picked up a pen next to a notepad. "Could you do me a favor?"

"Sure. Shoot."

"Look up two doctors I met in 'Nam and give me their phone numbers. I want to ask them some questions."

"No problem. Give me their names."

"Dr. Franklin Howard and Dr. Samuel Wright." Jerry crossed his fingers Spaddy wouldn't connect Dr. Wright to Colonel MacKenzie.

The staccato punching of keys rang across the receiver, then Spaddy's voice returned. "Dr. Wright is assigned to Womack Army Medical Center. His office number is 910-555- 0100. Dr. Howard is stationed at Blanchfield. His number is 270-555-0199. The computer doesn't show Dr. Wright on duty today. It shows Dr. Howard on duty until 1000 hours."

Jerry wrote down the numbers then looked at his watch. 0930 hours. "Thanks, Spaddy. I owe you one."

"Eat a lot of turkey and pumpkin pie for me, Jer. Merry Christmas."

"I will. The pumpkin pie smells wonderful. Merry Christmas to you." Jerry hung up the handset, and his finger hovered over the dial. *Who should I call? Dr. Howard. I used up my luck with Spaddy.* He punched the number and waited. Someone picked up the phone after the third ring.

"Blanchfield Army hospital, Dr. Howard speaking," said a baritone voice.

"Sir, this is Sergeant Jerry Rose. I'm a combat medic. You treated a shrapnel injury to my right shoulder. I lost a bunch of weight while I was in the hospital."

"Sorry, doesn't ring a bell, Sergeant."

Jerry racked his brain for an idea given his limited knowledge of the colonel. He remembered the write-up in Stars and Stripes. "I was in a helicopter crash about eleven months ago. An RPG hit the tail rotor."

Thump. Ten seconds ticked by—the sound of footsteps—a door shutting—the crinkle of silence across a static-filled phone line—then Dr. Howard's voice returned. "Sorry about the delay. Yes, I remember you, Sergeant. I'll call you back after I check my records for the specifics. Do you mind waiting for a day or so?"

"No, sir. I didn't expect to get you today. I was going to leave a message on your answering machine."

"Thank you, Sergeant Rose. Can you give me your phone number?"

"Sure. 769-555-0115. It's my dad's number. He's the town doctor. I'm staying with him until I can get my own place. I have to run some samples to the hospital lab. Dad might pick up if you call back today."

"I understand. Does he know who I am?"

"Yes. Thank you, sir." Jerry set the phone on the cradle.

The obnoxious clang of the telephone echoed in the house. Curtis ran from Jackson's room into the living room. *Might be Mrs. Yost about her sciatica again. Don't want Jerry getting an earful from a crotchety old woman after a few hours at home.* He beat Jerry to the phone on the end table and picked up the handset. "Hello."

"Is this Sergeant Rose?" asked a concerned male voice.

"No, I'm his father, Dr. Curtis Rose. Who's this?"

"Dr. Frank Howard. Your son called me. Did I catch his hint correctly? Is Jackson MacKenzie at your house?"

There's more here than a doctor/patient relationship. "Yes."

"How's Jackson doing?"

Jackson? They're on a first-name basis. Probably friends. I hate to break it to him this way. "Fighting for his life. Hold on a second." Curtis cupped the mouthpiece with his hand. "Jerry, go keep an eye on Jackson." *This may take some time.*

"Sure, Dad." Jerry walked toward the bedroom.

Curtis put the phone to his ear. "I'm back."

"What exactly is wrong with him? Sam was worried about organ failure."

Sam? Oh yeah, Dr. Wright's first name is Samuel. "I don't know yet. Jerry took the blood and urine samples to the hospital two hours ago. It'll be a day or two before the test results come back. Upon his arrival at my clinic, the waste inside Jackson's bowels looked like black concrete. We gave him two enemas to remove the impaction. His liver and spleen are inflamed. He's dehydrated, malnourished, weak, has a 104-degree fever, and his blood pressure is erratic. I have him on a feeding tube, IV fluids, antibiotics, and pain medication."

"Sounds good. That's what I would do. What else? Jackson can be a difficult patient."

Exhausted after a long night, Curtis sat in a recliner. *Difficult. Hah. More like impossible.* "Tell me about it. Earlier, your friend surprised me by drinking two pots of black coffee. It's amazing it didn't come back up. I wasn't going to let him have the second pot, but it's hard when he turns on the charm. I hope he has the strength of will to keep fighting."

"Jackson Joseph MacKenzie will fight until he doesn't have the strength left to fight anymore. I know how much he loves coffee. Give him all he wants. It can't hurt, and it helps with his attitude. He loves ice cream. It's second behind coffee. Give him vanilla or chocolate milkshakes. Take good care of him. Jackson's been through hell these last eleven months."

"Yeah, Mikey and Bill told me about it. I want to clear up one question since Mikey and Jerry explained the medical regulations to me. How did he wind up on the plane?"

Dr. Howard released a long sigh. "Of all the things you could ask about that one thing still bothers me. How? I have no idea. If I hadn't boarded that C-130, Jackson would've bled to death before the plane was halfway to Hawaii. He went into V-fib during surgery. It took two rounds of epinephrine and four hits with the defibrillator stabilize his heart rhythm. I had to pump eight additional units of blood into his body to keep him alive. Since Colonel Hammond and I butted heads for days over his extended care, General Kowalski forced my hand by ordering his release to the stockade with no access to rehab."

"Anything else I should know?" Curtis switched the phone to his other ear.

"No. I think that's it, medically. Wait, there's one more thing. It has nothing to do with his medical status. The army wants this kept out of the press. It's not a secret, just forgotten about."

"What's that?"

"Treat him with the respect due a man who's earned the Medal of Honor," Frank said.

Curtis shook his head. "You're kidding?"

"The army awarded it to him in '71."

"Do you know what for?" Curtis' curiosity piqued about the man under his care.

"I do. But that's his story to tell, not mine. Jackson's tight-lipped about it. His response to me, he was only doing his job. Jackson's a certified master of understatement. He told me the wounds were minor. I believed him until I read his medical records. Minor, my ass. He was shot three times. One round collapsed his left lung, one went through his left bicep, and you could drive a golf ball through the one in his left thigh. He refuses to consider himself a hero and will not say anything about the POW camp. Period. If you want to know anything about that, ask his men. I'll tell Sam his star patient is in good hands. Call me when his test results come back. If you need anything special for him, let me know, and I'll get it."

"I'll take good care of him, Dr. Howard." *He needs some reassurance.* "Do you want to talk to him?"

"Is Jackson awake and coherent enough to talk to me?"

Curtis glanced at the room. Chief was leaning against the doorjamb motioning with his hands. With Jackson the only one in the room, Chief was talking to him. "I think so. Give me a minute to get him a phone. I removed it last night so it wouldn't wake him up." Leaving the handset off the hook, Curtis grabbed the spare phone from the shelf and attached the cord to the wall socket in Jackson's room. Both men stopped their conversation as he placed the green princess phone on the nightstand and handed the receiver to Jackson. Curtis waved at Chief, and they left the room.

Chief pointed down the hall. "I'll be in the kitchen if you need me."

Curtis nodded. He went into the living room, hung up the phone then turned to his son. "Dr. Howard wanted to talk to Jackson. Jerry, here's the kicker. What's the highest award for bravery in any branch of the service?"

"That's easy, Dad." Jerry looked at Jackson's room. "Don't tell me he has the Medal of Honor, and the army treated him like shit before throwing him out like yesterday's garbage."

"Aptly put, and yes, that's how I understood what Dr. Howard told me. Treat him with respect, Jerry. We'll figure it all out later. Our job is to get him better."

"Hello," Jackson said into the receiver. "Who is this?"

"Frank Howard. I'd say Merry Christmas, but it hasn't been much of a happy year for you."

Jackson choked as his dry throat closed up for a second. "No, it hasn't, but at least I'm still alive. I guess Dr. Wright told you everything."

"Yeah, most of it. I'm glad you didn't get the chance to follow through with the idea. Sam did everything he could. Everyone took Hammond's word over Sam's, and no one I've spoken with can figure out why. He doesn't have any medical training."

"A rock has more medical training than Hammond. He reminds me of a tall, walking gnome with his bulbous pointed head, red Rudolph nose, and pot belly."

Frank howled across the phone line. "You say the darndest things. Sam told me about the big show."

"Yeah, Hammond acted like a pompous ass. It pissed him off when I didn't come to attention. It was all I could do to concentrate on what he was saying. I felt like a sick popsicle that night." Jackson couldn't hold the bitterness out of his voice.

"That happened in December. The army doesn't heat those cell blocks to save money. You're so thin, you don't have any extra padding to keep you warm. Hammond knows you're sick. It's impossible to ignore two doctors writing dozens of letters about your welfare. I think his instructions are coming from somewhere else."

"Me too. I have an idea about it. Hammond's superiors were waiting for me to go crazy or kill myself, whichever came first. If I committed suicide, it would take care of the problem without the need to terminate me with extreme prejudice. I'm the only one, besides Colonel Johnson, who knew every detail of the mission plan."

"How long have you been thinking about this?" Frank asked.

"A little while now, when I've been thinking rationally, which hasn't been much lately. I'm the key to the whole thing. That's why they stuck us in maximum security. It gave Hammond more latitude. Moretti never made an appearance after the hospital, and my only visitor was Harry. Whoever's involved let Dr. Wright keep me barely alive to maintain appearances in case the press got involved." Jackson yawned over the phone. "Sorry, Frank."

"Sounds like something right out of the CIA playbook. I'll stay in touch with Dr. Rose. Do everything he says while you're under his care. I agree with keeping you on a strict diet because of your stomach problems."

"I know, he explained it to me." Jackson scratched his nose. The tape holding the feeding tube in place made it itch. "I have to live with it because I don't have another choice, do I, Frank? Maybe next year, I can eat Christmas dinner at the table like everyone else."

"Sam told me about Captain Mason's little faux pas on Thanksgiving. The next time we meet, I don't want to see a rail-thin twig with skinny chicken legs."

"Funny. I'll try my best. I promise to listen to Dr. Rose. He's been so good to us. I wish we could pay him for saving my life."

"Don't worry about that right now. I'll pay Dr. Rose for his services. You can pay me back someday. I know you'll be good for it. Get well, snake-eater."

"Thanks, Frank. I'd better get off now. Dr. Rose might need his phone for a patient or something. Goodbye." Jackson set the handset in the cradle and smiled at Chief, relaxing against the doorframe. "Could you ask the doc to come in here, Sergeant?"

"Sure, boss." Chief turned and disappeared from the doorway.

Jackson grabbed the phone base off the nightstand and placed it in his lap.

Dr. Rose walked into the room. "Chief said you wanted to see me?"

Jackson held up the handset. "Yeah. I hate to run up your long-distance bill, but I need to make a phone call."

"To whom, may I ask?"

"A friend of my dad's who's known me since I was a baby. I'll need a place to sort everything out. Uncle Jason will keep me safe until my head's screwed back on straight."

"Make any calls you like and don't worry about the bill. I'd rather you have a safe place to go than hide out in a sleazy, roach-infested motel room." Dr. Rose pulled the clipboard from the wall and wrote on the first page. "What about your friend, Harry? Wouldn't he like to know how you're doing?"

"Thanks, Doc." Jackson shook his head. "It's too dangerous to call Harry. Everyone knows he's my best friend. I'm sure the army is watching him. I'll have Uncle Jason contact Harry through other means. Marines love to stick it to the army. The Sergeant Major should have fun letting Harry know what's going on."

"Marines, huh? Wait till I'm done." Dr. Rose changed the nearly empty bags on the feeding tube and IV lines. He put his stethoscope on Jackson's chest and adjusted the valve on the large green O2 tank counter-clockwise. After he pulled the green tube from the wall hook, he placed the cannula around Jackson's head and under his nose, then stood against the wall. "I'm sticking around for this call. Your body is under extreme stress from the infection. Any aggravation could send your medical condition into a downward spiral. I don't want to find you not breathing in that bed."

"And the oxygen? I'm a medic, remember."

"Same reason. I heard some rattling in your lungs, and your skin has a slight blue tinge."

"Blue? Not a good color for me." Jackson took a semi-deep breath as he dialed the number. Each rotation of the dial helped to relax his mind. *The last time I saw Uncle Jason was R and R stateside after my first deployment to 'Nam. I wish I hadn't taken my ex-wife. All she did was bug Aunt Rachel about her out-of-date clothes. I hope Uncle Jason will help me like he did Dad. If he refuses, I'm sunk. I don't want to burden my godparents with my problems.*

"Hello," a gruff voice said on the other end.

I don't know how to say this so Uncle Jason will understand. Jackson remained quiet as static filled the line.

"Hello, is anyone there?" The same voice came across even more abrasive.

"Sergeant Major Nichols," Jackson whispered into the receiver.

"Retired, mister. Who is this? This better not be a sales call trying to sell me a condo in Jamaica on Christmas Day."

That's the Marine Corps attitude I remember from my childhood. Jackson cleared his throat to help his voice. "Not a sales call, Sergeant Major. It's Jackson MacKenzie."

Jason's voice changed to one of solicitude. "Jackson? How are you, squirt? I heard you're in trouble."

Jackson flashed a brief smile at his parents' nickname for him. "In more ways than you can imagine."

"How can I help you, kid?"

"It's kinda complicated, sir."

"You don't sir me. I sir you. Like I said, how can I help you?" Jason said.

"You helped Dad after the war." Jackson sucked in a deep breath. "Can you help me?"

"Nightmares? That was your father's problem after World War II."

"Yeah, from the POW camp where I nearly died. I'm sure you've heard about our last mission."

"All I know is what I've seen on TV. I need to know what's going on before I agree to anything. I'm sorry, even though you're Colonel MacKenzie's youngest son, I don't need trouble coming my way if you're the one who screwed the pooch."

He'll do anything to protect Dad. Jackson ran his tongue over his front teeth. "What do you want to know first?"

"Tell me about the escape. Let's start there."

Jackson shifted his body into a more comfortable position. He grunted in pain when he banged his head on the wall. His breaths came in short, wheezing pants.

"You okay there, Jackson?"

Relax. Jackson licked his dry lips. "No, I'm not. It's Christmas Day, and I'm flat on my back. I'm so sick I feel like a Mack truck ran over me. I have constant nightmares, and the army refused to help me."

"There are regulations in place to prevent that. What's really going on?"

"They ignored the regulations."

"Fine." Jason let out an exasperated sigh. "The news said you're armed and dangerous?"

"Hardly. You know all the guards carry in the cell blocks are nightsticks." Jackson rubbed his head. *They hurt, too.*

"How sick are you?"

"I'm jaundiced from head to toe. I have a high fever, an infection in my gut. I'm too weak to get out of bed. My kidneys nearly shut down. I have a feeding tube in my nose. The doc has me on oxygen since he's afraid of pneumonia. Sure smells good in the house, like Christmas at home when I was little, but I can't have any. Hell, I can't even sit up in this bloody bed. I have pillows propping me up because I'll tip over without them. Dr.

Rose has to sedate me because of the nightmares." Jackson forced himself to say it. The army was his only home. "I have no place to go, sir."

"There you go with the *sir* again."

"Just showing the respect due."

"Okay, duly noted. You're a Lieutenant Colonel and earned the Medal of Honor like your dad. It should be the other way around."

"I haven't gotten any respect lately. My life's been a living hell." Jackson massaged his sore throat. "My depression was so bad a couple of weeks ago I wanted kill myself."

"What about now?"

"I just want to feel better. My body hurts so much. I want the pain to stop."

"How long until the doctor will let you leave?"

"I have no idea! Depends on a lot of things." *My chest hurts.* "Uuugg-hhhhh…" Jackson placed his hand over his heart. He couldn't catch his breath.

"Like what?" Jason pressed the phone harder to his ear. Several seconds of silence went by. "Jackson, are you there?"

A faint thump came across the staticky line. "Jackson, are you okay? You're shivering. Are you cold?" said a voice, distant and concerned. The sound of hurried footsteps across a creaky floor—several clunks—the rustling of clothing—then silence. Minutes ticked by before the same voice responded. "Hello, who am I talking to?"

Jason matched the abrasive tone with one of his own. "Retired Marine Corps Sergeant Major Jason Nichols. Now that I answered your question, who are you?"

"Dr. Curtis Rose."

"Okay, now that we've introduced ourselves, how's Jackson?"

"Terrible. Exactly what I was afraid of happened. He stressed himself out trying to convince you that he's telling the truth. It sent him into shock. I gave him a sedative. He's sleeping now."

"How long are you going to keep him?" Jason paced across the living room, back and forth, stretching the phone cord to its limit.

"Before I answer, are you going to help him once I do, if I do? He has a long road ahead of him. I want him some place safe."

"Jackson's my old CO's son. I respected his father and would follow him anywhere. Colonel MacKenzie saved my life when he died in Korea.

He took a bullet meant for me. If Jackson needs help, then, yes, I'll help him. I would be disrespecting the memory of his father if I didn't."

Dr. Rose's voice softened. "Good enough. Jackson's extremely sick. Letting him leave will depend on several things. First, how his liver and kidney function tests come back. If those organs are failing, then he's going to a hospital critical care unit because he won't live much longer. He's in bad shape physically."

"And if the tests come back okay, then you'll release him?"

"Not for several weeks. I will not let him leave my house until he's gained at least five pounds. Conservatively, I'd say a month, barring any setbacks on his part. Since you haven't seen your friend lately, let me describe him to you. Jackson looks like a bony skeleton with loose skin attached. His thighs are the size of my upper arms from muscle loss. His face is a skull with skin stretched over it and his eyes are sunken hollows. He looks bad and feels even worse."

"Sounds like the guys who survived Bataan. How much does he weigh?" Jason asked.

"Don't know. Haven't had a chance to put him on a scale. Maybe 120-125, if that. It's hard to tell since he's so skinny. I've already spoken with Dr. Howard at Fort Campbell. I suggest you call him. Be careful what you say. He was vocal about Jackson's lack of treatment and suspicious of everyone. If you want information about the POW camp, ask his men. Jackson won't talk, but they will. I've heard several stories and can't believe he survived. The rest, Dr. Howard can tell you."

"I understand. Take good care of him. I'll contact Dr. Howard. I need more background on the issues I'll be dealing with. I don't want to start more problems than I'm fixing. When he wakes up, tell him I believe they're innocent and to call me when they're on their way to San Diego. If he needs anything, please contact me." Jason picked up a photograph of a grinning ten-year-old Jackson standing next to him from the fireplace mantle. "One more thing, since Jackson mentioned Christmas, tell him I promise he'll have a great Christmas next year to make up for this one."

"I will. He's a bit bummed he can't eat with us tonight. I sedated him so he'll sleep through dinner. I don't need any more stress causing another decline in his medical status." Dr. Rose's tone, barbed of a reprimand.

Jason accepted his dressing down gracefully. "Goodbye, Dr. Rose."

Mangus Malone reached across his desk when the phone rang. He picked up the handset and put it to his ear. "Hello."

"General Malone. It's Sergeant Major Nichols."

Mangus chuckled. "Merry Christmas, Jason. I retired the same time you did, so please call me Manny like I've asked you for years. What's up?"

"Jackson called me earlier tonight."

Mangus sat up straight in his chair. That meant his godson was in trouble. The kid would never contact him first. "Jackson called you? How is he or, more to the point, where is he?"

"I don't know where he is, but the rumors about Jackson's ill health are true. They escaped to save his life because the army refused to give him medical treatment."

Mangus' fear mounted at the ominous tone in Jason's voice. "How sick is he?"

"Damn near on his deathbed and until the test results come back, it's up in the air on whether or not Jackson's in organ failure. If he is, then Dr. Rose will put him in the hospital because he's dying, the army be damned. If the tests are negative, then the doc isn't releasing him until he's back on his feet. Jackson needs help with his nightmares."

"Then let's hope for the best. I promised James to watch out for his son when he died in my arms in Korea. I intend to keep that promise. The army and the US government can go to hell for all I care. They hurt him, and Jackson gave the army everything he had. They'll have to come through me to get to him. Anything else?"

"Yes, Dr. Rose suggested we contact Dr. Howard at Fort Campbell to get the full scoop on what happened to Jackson. But do it on the QT so we don't raise any suspicions."

"Hmmm…" Mangus thought for a moment. "Are you up for a trip to Fort Campbell?"

Jason chuckled. "I take it, sir, you have a plan."

"Yes. I'd rather talk to Dr. Howard in person to get a better feel for what's going on and make the army do a little saluting to boot. You game?"

"Yes, sir. I'm ready to see the United States Army polish their butts for a retired Marine Corps Lieutenant General."

"Great. I'll catch a flight out of Billings tomorrow morning and arrange a flight for you from San Diego. We'll meet at the motel right off the base, stay the night and go to Fort Campbell the next day. I'll tell the base commanding officer I'm on a layover with some time to kill. Actually, I visited Jackson when the army reassigned him to the 101st Airborne after he graduated from West Point. It surprised the command staff when I showed up wanting to see a brand spanking new, wet-behind-the-ears Army Second Lieutenant. My appearance turned a few heads and earned him a lot more respect I wish he had now."

"Yes, sir." Jason let out a short laugh. "Second Lieutenant Jackson Joseph MacKenzie was never wet-behind-the-ears as a veteran of Korea and Colonel James MacKenzie's son."

"True." Mangus smiled at the memory of his baby-faced godson standing next to him in the main office. "His captain thought he was until I set him straight. I'll see you tomorrow night, Jason."

After hanging up the phone, Mangus picked up the picture on his desk of him standing next to James, holding Jackson on the day of his christening. "I promise to get him the best care possible so he will feel no more pain. I will find whoever hurt your son. They will pay...Marine Corps style."

CHAPTER 11

December 26, 1972

Beep–beep–beep…Curtis rolled over and slapped the alarm clock. *Seven o'clock already? That's a quick four hours. I'm glad Jackson started breathing better after we propped him up. His immune system is compromised, he caught a cold, and his nose stopped up. I should have thought about that with the feeding tube in his throat. My fault. I almost lost him.*

After the short trip down the hall, Curtis stood in the doorway to Jackson's room. *Good, he's asleep, his breathing's steady, and he's not blue. Jerry's so intent on watching Jackson he doesn't know I'm here. My son will make an excellent doctor one day.* He walked up behind Jerry and gripped his shoulder. "How is he?"

Jerry craned his head up to look at his father. "Quiet. The crisis has passed. The fluid in his lungs has cleared a little, and his fever is down to 101. He's hydrated and putting out urine by the gallon. A good sign his kidneys are functioning properly. His liver isn't as palpable and his spleen is shrinking."

"Excellent rundown. We'll see tomorrow when the test results come back on how his organs are functioning."

"Yeah. Hope it's good news. It'll be a shame for him to go through this only to die."

"I agree." Curtis pointed at the open door. "Go get some sleep."

Jerry stood from his chair and stretched. "Not sleepy, Dad. I need some coffee and a shower."

Curtis sat in the vacated chair. "Me too." *I'll have to snag a cup before Jackson wakes up and drinks it all.*

Inspiration hit as Jerry watched steam rise from the stainless steel percolator in the kitchen. He ran to the bedrooms and woke up Chief and Bill. "I have an idea."

Bill looked at his watch. "Do you know what time it is? 0800 hours. Since we're AWOL, we can sleep in."

126

Jerry sighed, his shoulders slumped in defeat. "Sorry to bother you, Captain."

Bill shook his head. "It's okay. You were excited. What's your idea?"

"I have a 1961 blue Ford Econoline van in the garage. It doesn't run because the engine blew out before I left for 'Nam. Since it's worthless, why don't we swap motors with your car? That way, you can drive to San Diego in a vehicle that's not reported stolen. It's big enough for all of you to stretch out. It'll be more comfortable for the colonel to sleep on the floor than on the ground or cramped up in the back seat of a car."

Bill turned to Chief. "What do you think?"

"Great idea." Chief jumped out of bed. "Grab the keys and meet me in the garage, Jerry. First order of business, check out the engine in your van."

Jerry couldn't contain his grin as he pushed the door all the way open. "Come with me."

December 27, 1972

Chief pulled his head from under the hood of the Ambassador. "I love the 390 cubic inch engine in this car. It has 315-horsepower. It's far superior to the 144 cubic inch 6-cylinder with 90 horsepower in Jerry's van. It'll give the van a lot more giddy-up by quadrupling the horsepower. A lot like my cherry red baby back home. Hand me a half-inch wrench."

Bill slapped the tool in Chief's waiting hand. "Sounds great. Will you have any problems changing the engine?"

"No, it's pretty straightforward. There's one thing I dread. Jerry's van is a cabover. The engine's in the passenger compartment between the driver and front passenger seat. That makes it a lot harder because of the limited room to move around. I'll make Mikey stick his tiny hands where my big ones won't fit."

After hours of busting knuckles on the rusted, nearly frozen bolts inside the Ambassador's engine compartment, Chief, and Bill looped a chain around the motor. They jerked it out with a cherry picker Jerry borrowed from a friend.

Chief sat on the floor and started taking the engine apart.

Bill leaned over Chief's shoulder. "Well, what do you think?"

"Damn thing needs a complete overhaul. Once that's done, it'll get us to San Diego."

"Great. While you're doing that, we'll strip the interior out of the van."

At five past 1400 hours, the men headed into the house for lunch. Chief and Bill bypassed the kitchen and went to Jackson's room. Dr. Rose was sitting in a chair next to Jackson's bed.

Bill knocked on the doorframe. "Hey, Doc, since the colonel's asleep, can we borrow you for a minute?"

Dr. Rose craned his head around. "What do you need, Bill?"

Chief and Bill stuck out their hands.

Dr. Rose's eyes widened. "What happened? Your hands look like they've been through a meat grinder."

"Big hands, box wrenches, and small openings don't mix well. Mikey refused," Chief said.

"Go grab Jerry in the kitchen. Tell him to come watch Jackson then meet me in the clinic so I can clean those cuts and abrasions. I have enough work to do with Jackson. Don't need the two of you getting sick from an infection."

Chief sucked the dried blood off his bruised knuckles. "That's for sure."

My nose itches. Feel better too. Jackson opened his eyes when Dr. Rose come in. The man had a distinctive walk. He dragged his left heel instead of picking it up. "Doc, take this damn tube out of my nose!"

Dr. Rose turned from hanging a bag of IV fluids above the bed. "You're not ready yet."

Jackson picked at the tape holding the tube to his face. "Yes, I am. Take the thing out, or I'll do it myself."

"Don't touch that. You'll tear up your throat." Dr. Rose pushed Jackson's hand away.

"Then take it out."

"Soldiers. Now I know where my son gets his new stubborn streak. I'll be back. Don't touch anything." Dr. Rose disappeared around the doorjamb.

Don't touch. Jackson tested how much force it would take to remove the tube. "Ouch!" *Nope, shouldn't do that.* He heard familiar footsteps and dropped his hand to his side.

Dr. Rose walked into the room with a plate in one hand and a small yellow bucket in the other. "If the egg stays down, I'll take the tube out temporarily."

Jackson raised an eyebrow. "Temporarily?"

"You heard me."

"What's the bucket for?" *I can eat a simple egg.*

"You know what it's for, Mr. Smartass."

Slowly, Jackson ate a piece of egg white. His throat burned. He tried to hold it. The taste overwhelmed his tongue, and he retched into the bucket.

Dr. Rose copied Jackson's earlier smug expression. "Do I need to say I told you so? You should see your face. It's lime green."

Jackson spit into the bucket to get the terrible taste out of his mouth. *Gotta push the doctor's buttons. He's too uptight.* "You win. How about getting out of bed?"

Dr. Rose exhaled, his lips twitched with amusement. "You couldn't make it to the toilet chair this morning on your own, so you already know the answer. You're being difficult on purpose to amuse yourself."

Jackson gave the doctor a small smirk. "Maybe."

Dr. Rose leaned against the doorframe, shaking his head. "Were you this bratty as a child?"

"Maybe, but you know my dad was a career Marine officer."

"True. But I have a son…I bet you got away with a lot batting those baby blues and blaming it on your older brother."

Jackson rolled his eyes. The doctor had him pegged. *I did get away with almost everything by blaming it all on Jim. He took the flack to protect me. I miss our fights.* "Maybe."

Dr. Rose twirled the reading glasses in his hand by one temple. "Did you learn your lesson? Will you listen to me now?"

"Yeah, I'll follow orders." Jackson jutted out his chin. "I had to try."

"Of course you did. Let's get back to business. Your stomach and intestines need to heal from the impaction. The stuff going into you is basically pre-digested to make it easier for your system to accept. I know that sounds gross, but it's the best way I can describe it."

"I wish there was a better way. I'd rather eat my shoes than have this thing in my nose."

Dr. Rose rocked back and forth on his heels. "I'll make you a deal. Once you can hold down something in your stomach, I'll take the feeding tube out during the day and remove the IV lines since you're doing so well hydrating yourself."

"Okay, what's the catch?" Jackson tapped his head. "Even after three days, I've learned you're not this agreeable."

"You eat everything I bring you, no questions asked. We'll start with a little at first, several times a day. I know there will be things your stomach can't handle. Accept the fact it will be a hit and miss process. The bucket will be your friend for a while. Unfortunately, you'll be on a limited diet for the rest of your life. The other side of the coin is, once you're up to a good weight, you'll have to watch how much you eat. If you don't burn it off, you'll gain too much due to the muscle loss. But that's far in the future at this point."

"Duly noted. You said temporarily." Jackson touched his nose.

"The tube goes back in while you're sleeping to push calories into you 24/7. You want to get out of your bed, right?"

Jackson snapped to sitting attention and threw a salute. "Yes, sir."

"I know you want to go to the bathroom under your own power. It gets funky smelling in here at times." Dr. Rose pinched his nose. "The tube stays until you gain a few pounds. Then you can take a bath instead of us giving you a sponge bath."

"Cute. I want my butt to stop waving in the wind, wear pajamas, and have a private moment in the bathroom. Sitting in a bathtub full of hot water would be so wonderful. It's cold in your house."

Dr. Rose rolled his eyes. "It's not cold. I set the heater at eighty degrees two days ago. You don't have enough meat on your bones to keep you warm. I intend to do something about it. Right now, you are a little squirt."

Jackson yanked the diaper off the toilet chair arm and waved it in the air. "At least I'm not squirting out of certain places, or you'd have a big mess to clean up and me with it."

"Funny. I'm glad you're not." Dr. Rose's face remained a stone mask.

"Nice comeback. You said it with a straight face. Me too."

0800 hours – Screaming Eagle Motel – Oak Grove, KY

Mangus called the Ft. Campbell main line from his room. "I need the hospital switchboard."

"Yes, sir," replied a young female voice. Keys clicked in the background then crackly silence.

"Blanchfield Army Hospital, how may I direct your call?" asked an older female voice.

"Scheduling." Mangus leaned against the dresser as rings echoed in the receiver.

"Scheduling. Sergeant Bayles speaking. How can I help you?"

"All I need is some information. What time does Dr. Howard go off duty today?"

"1630 hours, sir."

"1630, thanks."

"Do you want to leave a message?"

"No." Mangus shook his head. "I'll catch him at his office this afternoon. Goodbye."

Jason looked at his watch when Mangus hung up the phone. "I heard, 1630 hours. How about we hit Fort Campbell at 1300 hours? We can drive around for a couple of hours, then go find Dr. Howard."

"Good plan." Mangus turned on the TV. "Know much about soap operas?"

1300 hours – Fort Campbell

Mangus glanced over the crossbar at the jump towers in the distance as Jason stopped at the guard shack and rolled down his window. *Now the fun begins.*

An MP in green fatigues with sergeant stripes and a black helmet walked up to the 1972 gray Chevy Impala. "Passes."

Mangus pulled his retired Marine Corps ID card of his wallet. "Hand him this, Jason."

"Yes, sir." With a smile, Jason stuck his hand outside the window with the card gripped between his fingers.

The guard grabbed it, glanced at the front then snapped to attention.

Mangus leaned forward in the passenger seat. "At ease, Sergeant."

The MP stuck his head in the window. "What can I do for you, General Malone?"

"We want to take a look at the base." Mangus arched an eyebrow. "Is it a problem?"

"No, sir. I have to call the main office first."

"I know the procedure. Call away, Sergeant." Mangus leaned back with his arms crossed. "This ought to get interesting."

1310 hours

A green Ford sedan bearing the flag of an Army Brigadier General parked next to the guard shack.

Jason climbed out of the driver's seat and opened the door for Mangus. They leaned on the hood as a man in an Army class A uniform strolled up to them. He came to attention in front of Mangus.

His attention looks like a sloppy parade rest. That's the army for you. "At ease." Mangus squinted at the name tag. "General Baskin."

General Baskin placed his arms behind his back. "Thank you, General Malone. I can have a full escort assigned to you."

"Don't need it. Sergeant Major Nichols will drive me around the base." Mangus huffed. "We're Marines, not Army. We can read a map and don't need anyone to show us around. Good day." He marched back to the front passenger door.

Jason opened the door.

Mangus climbed into the car. "Does he look pissed off to you?"

"Yes, sir." Jason glanced over his shoulder. "I've never seen a general's face turn purple like an eggplant or heard one sputter that much before. I'd swear he doesn't know how to take your brush off."

"Good. Close the door and let's go." *I got a little revenge.*

1600 hours

Jason pulled into the second row of the hospital parking lot. Mangus threw open his door and climbed out before Jason put the car in park. He walked to the hospital, back straight, chest out, and chin tucked in. At the front door, he stopped the first person to cross his path, a young man wearing the rank of PFC. "Where's Dr. Howard's office?"

The PFC looked like a deer in headlights. "T-t-third floor, room 312."

"Thanks." Mangus shouldered his way past the young man with Jason at his side. They went to the elevators, and Mangus pushed the button. He patted his foot until the car arrived and the arrow pointed up. The elevator was jerky and slow. Two floors took forever. This didn't help Mangus' mood.

A man in a white lab coat, army dress uniform pants, and Corfam shoes walked past the elevator as the doors opened. Mangus and Jason filed in behind him. When he pushed open the door to room 312, Mangus cleared his throat. "Dr. Howard?"

The man spun around. "Yes."

"Is there any place we can talk in private?"

"First…" Dr. Howard looked Mangus and Jason up and down. "Who are you?"

"Lieutenant General Mangus Malone, Marine Corps, retired." Mangus pointed at Jason. "This is Sergeant Major Jason Nichols, Marine Corps, retired."

Dr. Howard snapped to attention. "Sir."

"At ease, Major. Now, where can we talk in private?"

"My office, General." Dr. Howard pointed at his name on a brass plaque next to 312.

"No! Not within army ears." Mangus pulled a faded color picture of a grinning young Second Lieutenant Jackson MacKenzie out of his coat pocket, palming it where only Dr. Howard could see it.

Dr. Howard's eyes widened. "Are you hungry, sir? There's a nice restaurant nearby. It serves an excellent lunch and dinner menu?"

"Sounds good. The meal is my treat. I want to thank you for saving a good friend in Vietnam. Since I'm retired, it took me a long time to track you down."

"I accept your offer. Being a bachelor, I was going home to a frozen TV dinner and whatever's on television tonight. My car's in the parking lot if you need a ride?"

"Not necessary. We have a rental car." Mangus pointed at the elevators. "How about we follow you?"

"Yes, sir."

Fifteen minutes later, Jason pulled beside the doctor's green US Army sedan at a restaurant two miles from the main gate. "Dr. Howard's already out of his car, sir."

Mangus' forehead puckered. "He's suspicious of us. Doesn't matter. He'll come around. Let's see what the good doctor has to say."

Jason and Mangus walked shoulder to shoulder to the front of the restaurant. Mangus pulled the picture out again. Once they stood next to Dr. Howard at the doors, Mangus handed him the photograph. "That was taken at Fort Campbell. Before you ask, Jackson's my godson. Dr. Rose gave us your name."

Dr. Howard looked at the photograph and handed it back. "I recognize the jump towers. How'd Dr. Rose know to call you?"

"He didn't. Colonel MacKenzie did." Jason pointed at the gold oak leaves on Dr. Howard's collar. "I will not disrespect his rank since the kid earned it. Jackson was the youngest and quite a bratty kid. His father called him little squirt."

"Interesting, but it fits what I've seen of his personality. Colonel MacKenzie felt betrayed by the army when I saw him earlier this year. Let's go in, General Malone." Dr. Howard opened the door leading into the building. "We don't want to draw any unwanted attention by standing here."

"Right." As the senior officer present, Mangus took the lead to the waiting area. A hostess directed them to a table near the back. Mangus didn't look at the menu. "Give us three of the daily specials." He looked at Dr. Howard. "Have you heard anything about Jackson's test results?"

"Yes. Jerry Rose left a message on my answering machine this afternoon. Colonel MacKenzie's test results are normal. Now they're working on putting a few pounds on his skinny ass frame."

"That's good news. Dr. Rose said it would take a month."

"A month would be the bare minimum in my opinion. Did Dr. Rose explain the issues about Jackson's diet?" Frank turned over his coffee mug when the waitress returned with the pot.

Jason spoke after taking a drink from his mug. "He mentioned something about getting him to eat, but nothing about that. Dr. Rose wanted off the phone. Jackson collapsed, trying to convince me he was telling the truth."

Dr. Howard's eyes narrowed. Anger rolled off his squared shoulders. "Makes sense. If Colonel MacKenzie felt you were questioning his honesty, he's so sick the stress probably sent him into shock."

"Yeah, that's what Dr. Rose said. Shock."

Mangus slapped his hand on the table to divert Dr. Howard's attention from Jason. "What's this about his diet?"

Dr. Howard stiffened. "Okay, business first. I can do that. Excuse me if I get informal here. Colonel MacKenzie insisted I call him Jackson. It's better not to use his rank or last name in public around here. Because of the POW camp, Jackson's having a hard time tolerating some foods. His diet might be limited for the rest of his life. We'll see how it goes once he's on solid food. It's entirely up to him on what he can eat. He'll have to figure it out one step at a time."

"Okay, we'll wait to find out when he arrives in San Diego since it's an evolving process." Mangus' tone turned blunt as their meals arrived. "What happened to him, Dr. Howard? From the beginning."

Dr. Howard explained about the last eleven months of Jackson's life as they ate.

"Hammond! Why's someone from fracking intelligence involved in this?" Mangus latched onto the only thing he could, his plate. "I sent a request via the commandant of the Marine Corps to visit Jackson about seven months ago. It came back stamped *denied* in red block letters. There was a note attached on army letterhead with Hammond's signature. It said this is an internal army matter. Therefore, assistance from the Marine

Corps is not required. Request denied. I stayed out of the matter for Jackson's sake. Do you know what I want to do to Hammond?"

"What, sir?" Dr. Howard grabbed Mangus' arm. "Please don't throw the plate across the restaurant."

Jason's fork hit the table with a metallic thwack. "Bet the same as me, sir. Turn him upside down by his ankles in front of the 1st Marines and let him suffer."

"Exactly. No one should treat a Medal of Honor recipient with such disrespect and lack of assistance when needed." Mangus leaned back in his chair. "Let me go, Major."

Dr. Howard released his grip. "General, I have to ask. How are you going to help Jackson with his nightmares?"

"I own a cattle ranch in Montana. We're going to take him to the wide-open spaces, far away from anything to remind him of the army. There isn't a military base for five hundred miles in any direction. I'm going to work the crap out of him. He'll go to bed tired every night, and getting my hard-headed godson to talk will be easier when he's exhausted."

"Good plan. Now that I know more about Jackson, his eating habits make sense. It may have been the food in the chow hall making him sick rather than him refusing to eat. A field mess isn't known for having anything but grease, starch, or processed foods, and by the same token, neither is a prison mess. I don't think he can tolerate any of them."

Mangus tapped a finger on his empty plate. "I know how bad the food in the mess hall can be, doctor. Jason and I have eaten our fair share of K-rations, shit-on-a-shingle, lumpy gravy, burned mystery meat, and Jackson's favorite, powdered eggs."

"Me too, General." Dr. Howard shoved his empty plate away. "I think army cooks learn from the Marine Corps. I have to warn you, Jackson's mind may not return to normal considering how long he's been under extreme stress. There lies the problem. Even if the army does clear him, his career is over. They'll medically retire him. If that happens, you may need professional help if he tries something drastic. You'll have to watch him for the rest of his life."

Mangus stabbed his fork at Dr. Howard. "I'll do everything in my power to help him through this. Jackson Joseph MacKenzie is the embodiment of his father. Not only physically but also in leadership ability, bravery, guts, and sheer tenacity. He never gave up. That's his father to a T. Jackson's his mirror image. Every time I see him, I think about his father, our friendship, and my promise. Jackson adored his father and copied everything he did. James was his hero. They were inseparable before and after World War II. I've known the young man since the day he was born. My godson will bounce back. I will get him the help he needs, no matter the cost. Anything else?"

"Yes. Dr. Rose is giving Jackson sedatives so he can sleep. Right now rest is the most important thing. Once you get him into a controlled environment, he needs to stop. They're highly addictive. In his broken state he could start depending on them and make things worse. He needs to talk about what's bothering him. It's the only way to put his demons behind him. Do you have any ideas?"

Mangus drummed his fingers on the table. "Yeah, I do. Several Marines who survived the Bataan death march are friends of mine. I've already asked one of them to give me a hand if I need more help. I figured if Jackson could talk to someone who went through the same thing, he might open up."

"Good idea. It could work when and if he's willing to talk, but it'll take time to get him to that point. I have to ask about his men. They won't leave him, and he won't leave them."

"I have plenty of room, so no problem there. They are welcome to stay with Jackson, and he'll do more talking with them around."

Dr. Howard handed Mangus a piece of paper with a phone number written on it. "You need to contact Major Russell. He's Jackson's best friend and the man who stayed on his ass in 'Nam. I don't know if you know this. Jackson volunteered to go home after the mission to help Harry through the loss of his foot. If anyone can get Jackson to talk, it's Harry Russell. Be discreet. Just like you were careful contacting me, the army will be watching him."

"I know." Mangus patted his left leg. "Major Russell needs to visit the VA for his prosthesis fittings, right?"

"Yeah. Why?"

"Use his doctor at the VA to relay messages. They're government employees. Not military doctors. We'll use sealed envelopes with special markings."

Dr. Howard's face lit up. "Excellent idea. I call the VA all the time on consults. Please keep me informed about Jackson's progress. I'll call you instead of the other way around. That way I can call from a different phone. Eventually, I'll want to examine him to make sure he's okay, health-wise."

Mangus held up his empty mug when the waitress walked up with the coffee pot. "Jackson trusts you, or he wouldn't have mentioned your name.

If you hadn't suggested it first, I would have insisted you give him a physical once his head's on straight. You and Dr. Wright kept him alive, and I thank you for it."

"No need to thank me, sir. I did my job. Jackson's gone through too much pain and suffering for one lifetime. He deserves peace and happiness. I know his army career meant everything to him. He needs to find something else to hold on to. I hope your ranch will give him the stability he needs. Maybe soon the army will figure out its mistake."

"My thoughts exactly." Mangus held out his hand across the table. Dr. Howard took it in a tight grip. "I like your spunk. Jackson found a good friend."

Dr. Howard dropped his hand and cleared his throat. "If that's the case, call me Frank."

"Okay." Mangus admired the doctor. The man was a straight shooter.

Frank poured sugar and cream into his coffee mug. "General, you said Jackson acts like his dad. Did his father drink a lot of strong black coffee?"

"Yes. James always had a coffee cup in his hand. The mess at Pendleton kept a special pot just for him." Mangus picked up his mug. "Jackson followed his father's example when he was twelve years old. James gave him a pony before we left for the Pacific campaign. That damn kid spent every waking moment with Scout when he wasn't in school until James returned to the states. Kimberly told me it was all she could do to get him to come home, eat dinner, and do his chores. Then Jackson would jump on his bike and go back to the barn to do his homework. I think Scout helped him deal with his father's absence."

Frank stirred his coffee. "Now everything makes sense."

Mangus glanced at the inside of Frank's mug. The liquid was light tan. "Typical army guy. Looks like sweet milk. Not Marine coffee."

"You mean mud." Frank took a sip from his mug. "You're probably right about why Jackson spent so much time with his pony. He was afraid his dad wouldn't return from the war. As a seven-year-old kid, it was his way of dealing with the pressure. It's a good thing his mother didn't make him come home. Now that I know more of Jackson's history, your ranch is the best place for him. It will give him a stable platform to get his life back in order."

"I agree." Mangus tapped the table. "And he will. You can bet on it."

CHAPTER 12

December 28, 1972

Dr. Rose walked into Jackson's room and handed him a copy of the *Cairo Times*. "Read this."

"Why?" Jackson unfolded the newspaper. "Ahh, we made the front page the day after Christmas. They used the guy's processing picture. Mine is from my promotion in '68. I guess the army didn't want to use a picture of me looking like a stick figure."

"I noticed that. Check out the article."

Jackson flipped to the next page. "The press release details how I lured the guards into a false sense of security." He laid the paper in his lap. "I must be a chameleon to pull off being yellow from head to toe, even my eyes, right, Doc?"

"Yeah, it amused me too. If the army ever catches you and charges you with the escape, please contact me. I'll set them straight that it was to save your life."

Jackson's heart sped up at the thought of being in a prison cell again. *This room has a door. It's open. I can leave any time I want.* "No one will ever lock me up again if I have anything to say about it." The words hung in the air like a dark cloud filled with lightning and wind. Jackson hadn't meant to sound so grim. "But if that ever happens, I'll send them your way." *Don't want to talk about this.* He cleared his throat. "Are the guys still working on the van?"

"Yep. They pulled the engine out of the car yesterday. Chief's overhauling it. They need an interior to make the van more comfortable. The damned thing was Jerry's love machine in high school, so there aren't any seats in the back."

Jackson quirked an eyebrow. "Had a lot of girlfriends, did he?"

"More than I could count. They fell all over him as I bet they fell all over you in high school."

"Maybe." Jackson laid a finger on his lips.

Dr. Rose chuckled. "Yeah, maybe, my ass. You had to beat them off with a stick with your blond hair, baby blues, and the cute little dimples in your cheeks. I bet it drove your poor mother crazy."

Jackson went back to drinking his coffee.

"If you want another pot this evening, behave yourself, or I might not let you have it."

Unable to resist the challenge, Jackson gave him a pitiful look, wide puppy dog eyes with a huge frown.

Dr. Rose gripped his chest. His slightly overweight body giggled in time to his laughter.

"Didn't know Santa Claus moonlights as a doctor?" Jackson flipped the newspaper in front of his face and peeked over the top.

"Someone is getting coal in their stocking next year. I see those mischievous blue eyes looking at me."

Coal? Jackson wadded up the front page and launched it at the doctor's head. Except with his throwing arm weak, it took a wicked curve and bounced off Dr. Rose's chest.

Instinctively, Dr. Rose retaliated. He picked up the ball and threw it back. His aim a little truer. It hit Jackson in the head.

Only little children throw wadded up newspapers. Did the power go out? It's dark. Jackson felt hands on his shoulders, shaking him.

"Breathe, Jackson. You're laughing so hard your face is turning blue."

Breathe? Jackson opened his mouth. As the oxygen entered his lungs, he felt hot breath on his face, and the lights turned on. "Hiya, Doc. Do I still get my coffee?"

Dr. Rose shook his head. "You may be a grown man, Jackson. But you're still a little boy playing army instead of living it. Since you're behaving, for the most part, yes, you can have your coffee later this afternoon. You already drank the entire pot I made an hour ago. Read your paper." He handed Jackson the wadded up ball. "Minus the front page."

Jackson pitched the ball into the trash can like a basketball. "Nice, three points. Got a pencil?"

"What do you want a pencil for?"

"Crossword puzzle. I need something to write with." Jackson pointed at the folded newspaper in his lap.

Pulling the pencil from behind the clip on Jackson's chart hanging on the wall, Dr. Rose handed it to him. "Sure, let me know if you need me to sharpen it later."

Jackson took the implement, touched the tip to his tongue, and put lead to paper. *I understand the doctor's reluctance. The pencil has a sharp point.*

"I'll leave you alone for a few minutes. If you need anything, yell out. Taking care of you has created a huge dent in my on-hand supplies. The medical supply company delivered my order this morning. I need to put everything away while I have the time."

"Do what you need to do, I'm not going anywhere," Jackson called out with his head down, scanning the paper. *What's a six-letter word for marine mollusk?*

"Hey, Chief, you going to get off your butt and help us?" Mikey yelled from the roof of the van, a roll of duct tape and butcher paper in his hands.

"Unless you plan on fixin' this engine, no. I have a lot of work to do. The colonel can't walk, and without a motor, we're stuck if the army finds us. You do your job, Mikey, and I'll do mine." Chief threw a dirty cloth in Mikey's direction and went back to work.

"Whatever." Mikey returned to his task of masking off the van windows, bumpers, and other reflective surfaces.

Jerry walked in with two paper sacks in his hands. "I hope I bought enough. All I could afford was cheap canned spray paint."

Bill stopped sanding the right fender and stood up. "What color did you get?" He looked in the sacks. "Blue?"

"Yeah, since the van's blue, I thought it would be better to use the same color."

"Let's see." Bill sprayed a sample on a piece of paper and held it up. "Well, it's kinda the same color. We'll make it work."

Right after the men finished lunch, Jerry opened the garage windows. "This stuff will kill us if we breathe too much of it. We don't want to wind up patients of my father. He'll never let me live it down."

"You gonna help now, Chief?" Mikey poked his friend in the shoulder. "That way, we'll get done faster."

Chief stood and towered over Mikey. A cheeky smile crossed his face. "Yeah. I bought some beer last night. Let's have fun." He pushed a red ice chest from behind a cabinet.

"Sounds good to me." Mikey grabbed a spray can then pulled a beer out of the ice chest. The first thing he planned to paint wasn't the van. Chief was his first target, even if he got a black eye in the process. Within minutes the painting party began.

During the early evening, the men stumbled into the house and took showers to remove the coating of grease, grime, and blue automotive spray paint.

Mikey wobbled into what he thought was the colonel's room. There were three openings instead of one. "Hiya, Colonel."

Jackson set the crossword puzzle in his lap and stuck the pencil behind his ear. "Guess you drew the short straw today to give me a progress report, Sergeant Roberts."

"Yes, sssir. Weee painted the van today. It lookkss good."

Jackson waved his hand in front of his face. "I bet it's blue from the paint in your hair. How much beer did Chief bring to the party?"

"Two cases. The goodd stuff too."

"I can see that. Are the other guys as drunk as you?"

Mikey giggled. "Yep."

"You're dismissed. Go sleep it off before you fall on your face."

"Yes, sssir." Mikey stumbled out the door. *Where's my room? Doesn't matter.* He found the living room and flopped onto the couch face-first. *This'll do.*

December 29, 1972

"Still working on your project?"

Jackson looked up at Dr. Rose from the crossword puzzle in his lap. "Yeah. Is something wrong?"

"No. It's lunchtime. You've improved more than I expected in the last couple of days." Dr. Rose held up a plate and a bucket. "Want to try again with the eggs? If you can hold them down, I'll take out the tube until you go to sleep tonight. The catch is, you don't throw up."

Jackson nodded. *I want this tube out so bad.* "Yeah, I was ready yesterday."

Dr. Rose shook his head. "Not really."

Jackson grabbed both eggs and shoved them into his mouth. He chewed, chewed, chewed, and swallowed. *Nothing. No nasty taste. Needs salt.*

"You're ambitious today."

"Yep, I'm a Green Beret, so it's in my nature." Jackson covered his mouth as he belched rather loudly.

Dr. Rose held up the bucket.

"Don't need it." Jackson pushed the bucket away. "How about letting me get out of bed?"

"No way. I'll take out the feeding tube and IV lines. But not that. You need a solid foundation to build a brick wall. You're not there yet. Let's take one step at a time. We need to go forward, not backward. Deal?"

"Deal." Jackson tugged on his ear. "Do I get my coffee?"

"What's new?" Dr. Rose patted his stomach. "Where do you put all that coffee?"

"Haven't you heard? We special ops guys have a second stomach implanted for that purpose to keep us awake."

"Then maybe I should take it out before it floods in here."

Jackson ducked his head and laughed softly. "Good one, Doc."

December 30, 1972

*One line left, what's a ten letter word for...*Jackson felt a tap on his shoulder. "Huh?"

"You really can tune everyone out. Ready to try something different?" Dr. Rose pointed at the bowl in Jackson's lap.

"Yes. As for your first question, I learned how to ignore the world in the POW camp. It was the only way to escape the pain. What time is it?"

"One o'clock."

"You mean thirteen hundred hours, right, Doc?"

"Geez, soldiers. You're as bad as my son, maybe worse." Dr. Rose grabbed the bowl. "Do you want this or not?"

Jackson pushed the doctor's hand away. He thumped the standing straight up spoon with a finger. "You sure this gray-colored substance is oatmeal? Looks like lumpy wallpaper paste."

"Wallpaper paste? No arguments or the tube goes back in."

"Okay. It was a joke." Jackson ate one spoonful, savored the nutty flavor and swallowed. "It's not bad but needs some milk and sugar added."

"Sure, but no extras until I test you first." Dr. Rose tapped his head. "Remember the deal."

"Okay, okay. No milk or sugar yet." Jackson ate the rest of the oatmeal. After setting the empty bowl on the bedside table, he fixed his gaze on Dr. Rose. "Can I have a cup of coffee?"

"You are the most persistent, pig-headed, and incredibly stubborn patient I have treated in my life. I'll give you a pass today because those qualities kept you alive."

Jerry popped his head around the doorjamb. "Dad, I'm headed to the salvage yard."

Dr. Rose looked at his son. "Jerry, are you taking anyone with you? Some of the parts you guys want are heavy."

"Yeah, Mikey. He's close to my age, and we look a lot alike. I can pass him off as my brother. We're going to tell them we're fixing up the van to pick up girls. The other guys are too old for that excuse to work."

Jackson and Dr. Rose looked at each other. "Good idea," they said in unison.

2000 hours

Jackson sat up in his bed when Dr. Rose came in shaking the thermometer in his hand. "It's check-up time, right?"

Dr. Rose nodded. "Yes, you know the drill."

"Yeah, temperature, blood pressure, heart, and pulse." Jackson opened his mouth and lifted his arm for the blood pressure cuff. He jumped when Dr. Rose placed the stethoscope on his chest. "It's cold."

"Hush, I'm listening to your lungs."

Jackson drummed his fingers on the blanket as the doctor wrote down the readings. "Well?"

"Everything is normal. Your lungs are finally clear. Feel like getting out of bed?"

"Are you kidding?"

Dr. Rose leaned outside the room into the hall. "Jerry, can you help me for a few minutes."

Thirty seconds later, Jerry stuck his head through the open door. "What do you need, Dad?"

"Help me get Jackson to the bathroom so he can take a bath."

Jerry walked to the bed. "You know the routine, sir. Just like getting to the toilet chair."

"Yeah." Jackson looped his right arm across Jerry's shoulders, placed his feet on the floor, and stood. Dr. Rose pulled Jackson's left arm over his shoulders. Together, they walked to the bathroom. As they went through the door, Jerry flipped on the switch to the overhead heater. Jerry and Dr. Rose eased Jackson down until he sat on the edge of the tub.

Jackson pulled off his blue flannel pajamas as Jerry turned on the water. "Can I stay in here? It's warm."

"No. This is my only bathroom. You'll get in the way lying on the floor." Dr. Rose shut a cabinet door.

143

"And you call me a joker." Jackson swung his legs into the tub. Dr. Rose and Jerry held onto his arms as he eased his butt into the warm water.

Dr. Rose handed Jackson a bar of soap. "Take your time."

"This is so nice." Jackson washed every part of his body. *I love feeling clean.* As he pulled his head from under the running faucet, a hand patted him on the shoulder.

"Take this." Jerry held out a silver handle.

"I haven't used a razor in months. The guys were afraid I would cut my throat."

Dr. Rose handed Jackson a can of shaving cream. "Trust works both ways." He stuck a small suction cup mirror to the tile in front of Jackson.

"Thank you." Jackson lathered up his face, eased the razor under his chin, and paused. *Don't think about it. One stroke at a time.* Each pass across his cheeks and chin were slow to keep from nicking his skin. With his face stubble-free, he handed the razor back to Jerry. He slapped the water and watched the waves rebound on the sides of the tub. It helped him to relax.

"Ready to get out?"

"Huh?" Jackson looked in the direction of Dr. Rose's voice. "Uhh...yeah. The water's cold."

Dr. Rose draped a towel over Jackson's shoulders. "You've been in there for an hour. You look like a prune."

Jerry climbed into the tub with bare feet and rolled up jeans. "Give me your hands."

Jackson grasped Jerry's hands and pushed up with his legs as Jerry pulled until he leaned into Jerry's chest.

"Put your arms around my neck."

Jackson grasped his hands together behind Jerry's head.

"Now put your feet on mine."

Jackson placed his feet on top of Jerry's and let his muscles do the work. No way did he have the strength to climb out of the tub.

"Lift your right leg when I pick up my left."

Jackson did the best he could. His legs shook but worked.

"Good. Step down. Do the same with your left. Good, we're out." Jerry maneuvered Jackson to the toilet. "Now, sit down."

"No, let me stand." Jackson grabbed the fresh underwear off the countertop. "I can dress myself. I'm not a baby." He stuck one leg into the hole, lost his balance, and tipped forward.

"Whoa!" Jerry grabbed him around the waist. "Why don't you sit down before you're face-first in the toilet?"

"Okay. Maybe I should rest my legs." Jackson sat on the toilet lid.

"Wise decision." Dr. Rose held out a red flannel pajama shirt and pants. "Put these on. I'll let you do it now you're sitting down."

Jackson slipped on the pants and buttoned the shirt.

Jerry stood in front of him. "Give me your hands."

"Only to pull me up. I'm walking to my room."

"Are you sure after almost breaking your nose?" Dr. Rose patted his foot.

"Yeah. It's hard to explain. But I can do it."

"I know why. You're prideful, pig-headed and stubborn. Go ahead. Prove me wrong."

"Thanks, Doc."

Jerry grabbed Jackson's extended hands. "When I say three, rock forward. One…two…three."

Jackson pushed as Jerry pulled and stood. He locked his knees to remain upright.

Dr. Rose laid a white terry cloth robe across Jackson's shoulders then held open the door.

Jackson put one hand on the wall to maintain his balance. He took baby steps as Jerry and Dr. Rose stayed on either side of him. *I've got this.* At his bed, Jackson climbed under the thick quilted blanket. "Got ya, Doc. Point for me."

December 31, 1972

"Open your eyes, Jackson. I know you've been up stretching your legs. You smacked the wall fifteen minutes ago."

Jackson rubbed his eyes. "Can't I have a relaxing day in bed?"

"Right, that's why you're sweating. Don't push so hard. For my peace of mind, let's go to the clinic." Dr. Rose pointed at the door with his clipboard.

"Only if you let me walk by myself. I feel a lot better this morning."

"I can tell. Now get up."

"Okay, okay." Jackson pushed himself out of bed, followed the doctor, and sat on the exam table. He bit his tongue as Dr. Rose took blood, had him pee in a cup then checked his heart, lungs, and reflexes. His body felt like a painful boil. After being stuck with needles since Christmas Eve, he was ready for a break.

Dr. Rose walked Jackson back to his room and sat on the bed next to him. "You can move around the house. Make sure to let me know so I can watch you. I don't want to find you sprawled out on the floor with a broken leg. We need to keep moving forward, not backward."

Jackson grabbed his crossword puzzle from the nightstand. "Thanks. Do you know a six-letter word for plant root growth?"

"No." Dr. Rose left the room.

Jackson plumped up the pillow behind his back, sat cross-legged, and leaned against the headboard. *What time is it?* He glanced at the clock from the completed puzzle. *Noon. Time for a change of scenery.* He peeked around the doorframe of the clinic. "Is it okay if I watch TV?"

Dr. Rose looked up from writing notes at his desk. "Sure. Don't overdo it. The remote is on the table next to the couch. There's a blanket on the back."

"Roger." Jackson sat on the couch, curled his legs under his body, and wrapped the blanket around his shoulders. He turned on the TV. As he flipped through the channels a familiar logo made him stop. "Hey, Doc!" he yelled over the television.

Dr. Rose ran into the living room. "Is there something wrong?"

Jackson pointed at the TV. "It's New Year's Eve."

"Yes, it is. If you're asking to stay up, I was already going to let you. I thought we could celebrate the fact you're still alive. And please call me Curtis."

"Okay. Can I have popcorn?"

Curtis cocked his head. "Why?"

"Oklahoma is playing Penn State tonight in the Sugar Bowl. How's this for an idea? We watch the game together, and I always eat popcorn with football. The Sooners are Chief's favorite team. That makes it kinda special."

"Sure, why not? I don't know about the popcorn, but we can give it a shot. The guys will love it. They keep bugging me about giving you more freedom."

"Then I bet you were testing me for dinner tonight when you gave me chicken and pie earlier."

"Exactly. That way you can eat with us and the football game is a great idea. No beer for you. Your stomach can't handle it."

Jackson looked down at his hands. *Learned that lesson the hard way.* "Don't want any, sir. I don't drink, not even beer."

"Okay. Do you want a soda tonight?"

"Nah, never been much of a soda drinker." Jackson picked up his coffee cup from the side table. "I'd rather have coffee instead."

"Sounds good. I'm going to the clinic to finish my paperwork."

Jackson hit the remote to change the channels. As the screen stopped scrolling, he recognized the actor. John Wayne. The Eagle, Globe, and Anchor was on the pocket of his utility uniform. *Nice.*

Curtis came in with half a peanut butter sandwich. "What are you watching? Looks like a war movie."

"*The Sands of Iwo Jima.* Sergeant Striker reminds me of my dad."

Footsteps echoed in the entry hall after the front door opened.

"Mikey, why don't you..." said Chief's deep baritone voice.

Jackson turned and smiled at his friends. "Hey, guys. Do you want to watch a football game with me tonight?"

"Which game?" Chief sat on the back of the couch.

"The Sugar Bowl."

"Hell, yeah. The Sooners are playing."

Mikey jumped two feet in the air. "It'll be nice doing something normal with you for a change."

"Great. Go take a shower and get ready for dinner." Jackson held his nose. "There's a sweaty funk in the air."

As *The Sands of Iwo Jima* ended, the title of the next movie splashed on the screen, *The Horse Soldiers.* Jackson leaned back under his blanket to watch the film.

During the confederate railroad depot battle scene, Curtis stood in front of the television. "Are you going to eat in the kitchen or stay here?"

Jackson leaned sideways to look around him. "Stay here. I love John Wayne."

"Hmmm. Okay, I'll bring you a plate. We'll have dinner and a movie together. Everyone can eat off their laps."

"Terrific." Jackson rubbed his stomach. "I'm starving."

A few minutes later, Curtis stuck the plate under Jackson's nose. "Take this."

"Mmm...real food." Jackson inhaled deeply then ate every bite of skinless roasted chicken, potatoes, and pumpkin pie filling. He used the roll to sop up the juices and held out the empty plate. "Got any more pie, Doc?"

"As much as you want. It's incredible you can eat that much considering where you started a few days ago."

"You should see me when I don't look like a stick. I can eat more than Chief."

Curtis scratched his head. "I believe it."

Right before the game started, Chief walked into the house wearing an Oklahoma sweatshirt and carrying a large ice chest.

Bill clapped his hands then rubbed them together. "Someone came prepared. Toss me one, Chief. Feels like squad party time."

Jackson picked up his coffee mug. "As long as you guys don't wind up trashed like the other night. I thought Mikey was about to puke all over me." A crimson flash caught his eyes. "Why are you wearing an Alabama sweatshirt, Jerry?"

"Don't have a Penn State one." Jerry patted his chest. "Hand me a beer, Chief."

"Wearing that trash from the SEC, get it yourself, kid." Chief popped open a beer can then threw the tab at Jerry.

Everyone piled around the TV. The popcorn bowls made the rounds as the teams kicked off. Jackson placed two kernels in his mouth and swallowed. His stomach remained quiet. He filled a small bowl and settled down to enjoy the game.

Three hours later, the gun sounded. Chief sang *Boomer Sooner* at the top of his voice. His team won, 14-0.

Jackson smiled. His croaky voice wasn't up to singing yet. He changed the channel to the show hosted by Three Dog Night. At midnight when the ball dropped in Times Square, everyone clinked their glasses together.

"Good riddance. This painful year is gone," Chief yelled over the fireworks on TV.

"Hear, hear!" the group echoed.

"And the colonel lived through it," Mikey added.

Jackson winked at his friends. "You got that right, Mikey."

January 18, 1973

Jackson turned on the TV to watch the evening news. He settled back on the couch wrapped in his blanket to stay warm. The house was cold, no matter what Curtis said.

The screen flickered as the tube warmed up with a greenish tint. Music played in the background as an older man with salt and pepper hair in a dark blue suit looked at the camera. Behind him, a composite picture of

Jackson and his men. The same photographs from the *Cairo Times*. "Good evening. Lieutenant Colonel Jackson MacKenzie, Captain William Mason, First Lieutenant Tyler Carter, First Sergeant Dakota Blackwater, and Staff Sergeant Michael Roberts are still at large. These men are considered armed and dangerous."

Jackson shook his head. "Armed with what? I'm dangerous as a baby right now. Unless my weapon is explosive farts then they might be right."

The news anchor held up a piece of paper. "According to the experts, their escape from custody proves their guilt. North Vietnam has threatened to pull out of the peace talks unless they are captured immediately. The VFW, DAV, and American Legion have all issued a directive to their members, if these men are seen, to call the police immediately. All three groups stated they are a disgrace to the country as traitors and should be shot on sight."

Now other veterans are against us. What else can go wrong with my life?

"Colonel MacKenzie's parents must be embarrassed to have a traitor in the family. His father, Colonel James MacKenzie, is a highly decorated Marine Corps veteran of World War II and Korea. His mother, Kimberly, served as a nurse in the US Army before meeting her husband then rejoined for two years during the Korean War. We are attempting to locate them in San Diego to obtain an interview and get their reactions to raising such a dishonor to the American people."

Reactions? They're dead. So is my older brother. Jim died in 'Nam. What are they going to do? Take a news crew to Arlington and stand over their graves with a microphone and camera.

"If anyone sees these men, please call the authorities. As soon as we find Mr. and Mrs. MacKenzie, we will…"

Jackson turned off the TV. He didn't want to hear the lies. He wanted to be a kid again. No worries, only being with his dad, mom, and older brother. His thoughts locked on the last day he spent with his father at home.

At 0700 hours, their father, James, walked into the kitchen wearing a short-sleeve gray shirt and jeans. He looked strange not wearing the uniform of a Marine Colonel. It was the fabric of his being.

Dad leaned between Jackson and Jim at the table. He held out three tickets in his hand. "Want to go to a San Diego Padres game?"

Jackson and Jim stared at their father then Jim reacted. "Dad, it's a school day."

Dad smiled. "I know, but I leave for Korea tomorrow. I want to spend time with you boys. Grab your mitts, and let's go. The game starts in two hours."

"Yes, sir!" Jackson downed the rest of his milk, ran to his bedroom, and grabbed his baseball glove from the dresser. He didn't care who the Padres played. All that mattered. He was with his dad behind home plate.

For three hours, they watched the game, ate hot dogs, popcorn, and pounds of peanuts. Jackson even caught a foul ball in his mitt.

On the way home, Dad pulled their 1940 black Studebaker Champion into the A&W drive-in and rolled down his window. He pushed the button and spoke into the speaker. "Three large root beer floats."

"Great, ice cream." Jackson licked his lips.

Dad turned to look at Jackson and Jim in the back seat. "Take care of your mother while I'm gone."

"Yes, Dad," Jackson and Jim echoed together.

The waitress arrived with a tray and clipped it to the window. She handed two frosted mugs to Dad. He passed them to Jackson and Jim. "Don't tell your mother. She'll kill me for spoiling your dinner."

Jackson smiled. "Never, Dad."

"Jackson, are you in there?" said a disembodied male voice.

The image of the car faded away to the living room, lit by a lamp. "Huh?" Jackson looked at Curtis shaking his shoulder. "Yeah, Doc."

Curtis looped his arm across Jackson's shoulders. "You okay?"

"Yeah." Jackson nodded. He wanted to hide in the past. He willed his eyes to stay open in the present. That was the MacKenzie way. Fight to the end.

Curtis pointed at the door. "Want something to eat?"

Jackson thought for a second. His stomach told him yes. Tonight he only wanted one thing. "Yeah. Do you have an A&W in town? I want a root beer float." *It'll be like being with Dad and Jim again.*

January 20, 1973

Jackson climbed off the exam table after Curtis checked his blood pressure, heart, and lungs. "Can I go now?" *I'm bored. Nothing but game shows or soaps on TV.*

"No." Curtis pointed at the white Detecto medical scale. "Let me check your weight."

"Okay." *Maybe he'll get these check-ups out of his system.* Jackson hopped on the black platform.

Curtis slid the upper weight back and forth across the bar several times.

"How much?" Jackson rolled his shoulders to loosen his stiff neck. "I'm going stir-crazy cooped up in the house."

"Yes, I know after you bugged Jerry for two hours yesterday about getting you some real clothes in your command voice. A direct order? Really, Jackson? That's why I sent him to Goodwill with enough money to buy you a week's worth."

"Yeah, no more pajamas." Jackson hugged his body with both arms. "And I'm finally warm."

"You're wearing a t-shirt, thermal shirt, and a sweatshirt. That's three layers, in addition to the blue jeans. I hope you're warm, or you're dead because there's no blood pumping in your body," Curtis said as the pointer balanced level in the trig loop. "That number can't be right? Maybe it's the clothes. Get off. Let me check the calibration."

"Sure. Want me to strip?"

"Yes, down to your t-shirt and underwear."

Jackson pulled off his clothes and laid them on a chair. *I'm cold.* He hopped back and forth and ran in place to stay warm.

Curtis removed the test weight from the platform. "Get on."

Jackson climbed on the scale, waited a few seconds then poked Curtis in the shoulder. "How much?"

"Six pounds," Curtis said, shaking his head. "My turn to keep my end of the bargain."

"Yep." Jackson stepped off the scale. He dressed, picked up his coffee cup, and headed to the living room to grab the crossword book Chief brought him.

In the hall, Jerry handed Jackson a piece of paper. "Take this."

"What is it?" Jackson flipped the paper around to see the writing on the other side.

Jerry pointed at his signature next to the notary seal. "A bill of sale to prove ownership of the van if you get stopped by the cops."

Chief, Ty, Bill, and Mikey came up behind Jerry with smiles on their faces.

Jackson knitted his brows. "You guys look guilty. What's going on?"

"We finished the repairs this morning, boss." Chief tucked a dirty towel in his back pocket. "When do you want to leave?"

Jackson walked into Curtis' office and ran his finger along the checkerboard of the wall calendar. "Is five days from now good for you guys?"

All four men nodded.

"Five days, it is." Jackson circled January 25th with a red pen. "Let's get busy."

CHAPTER 13

January 23, 1973

In the late evening, Jackson stretched out on his bed, cupped his hands behind his head, and stared at the ceiling.

Curtis forgot to give me a sedative. I'm going to test myself. He closed his eyes and thought about parents, his brother, his beloved horse, Taco. And for a while, it worked. The nightmares stayed away. Then blackness pulled at him. Warred with his thoughts. Pain tried to savage him until he couldn't feel his own heartbeat. Flashes of explosions backlit his mind as screams of dying men echoed in his ears. Faceless soldiers ran about covered in blood.

"Medic! Medic!" Jackson's eyes flew open. Nothing but darkness. On shaking arms, he pushed his face out of the pillow and listened. He always listened for footsteps.

The house remained quiet. *Why am I alone?* As his eyes adjusted to the dim light, he glanced at the door. *Mikey closed it again. That's why no one heard me scream.*

Jackson sat on the edge of the bed. His chest heaved like the bellows of an accordion. The room spun as his vision faded in and out. To ease his breathing, he grabbed a paper bag off his nightstand. As his senses kicked in, he felt himself shivering. *I'm cold.* Sweat dribbled down his back He touched his pajamas. *I'm soaking wet.* He put on a fresh set and his robe. *I have to pee.* He headed to the bathroom.

On the return trip, he stopped. *There's the wet bar.*

No, it's not the answer.

Another voice, his own, darker, bloodthirsty overrode his logical side. *Why not? It sure couldn't hurt.*

On autopilot, Jackson went into the living room. He pulled a new fifth of Jack Daniels out of the cabinet. Glass and bottle clutched in one hand, he switched on the TV, lowered the volume, and settled into a recliner.

With a twist, the seal broke, then off came the cap. Jackson poured a full glass. He sipped the brown liquid. *If I drink enough to take the edge off, maybe my mind will pause. I want to sleep and find some inner peace.*

His devil side wanted more than sips. It wanted a quick buzz. Up came the glass, down his throat went the whiskey in two gulps. The alcohol tore up his delicate stomach. He didn't care. His expiation for screwing up.

"What am I doing? ...Getting drunk." The next glass disappeared even quicker. *What will Murphy throw at me now? My career's gone. A whisper fallen silent in the wind. Doc says it's extreme depression and PTSD. What does he know? What now?*

Nothing made sense anymore. *My dreams. My life. All gone. Honor and duty aren't simple, meaningless words. Not to me. I gave my blood, sweat, tears, and nearly my life freely. Even though dumped like yesterday's garbage, I would jump to serve in an instant.*

He pictured his father's face. A man full of life and love. *I patterned my life in his courageous example. Korea. The last time I saw him. Dad's face lit up the 1st Division camp like a Christmas tree when I showed up wearing corporal stripes. My mentor, idol, hero, father, all rolled into one man. He died too young.*

"Dad, I wish you were here to tell me what to do." A tear ran down Jackson's cheek.

"Stand tall, son. You always make me proud," said a male voice from nowhere and everywhere. Not quite his father's, but not unlike it either.

Jackson shook his head. "Who said that? Dad?"

No. It wasn't his dad. It was the booze added to his tortured mind.

Dad, Mom, Jim. Everyone's gone. There's a black shroud around my heart. Permanently branded into my memory. Every time I lift the veil, a thick, black ooze pours over my soul. Why did my life go so wrong? What do I have to live for? Nothing!

"Don't quit, my little squirt," said a birdlike, faint female voice.

Jackson looked around the empty room. "Mom, is that you?" His voice meek, quiet, childlike.

It wasn't his mother. She was gone too.

The room was illuminated by a faint green glow from the television. On the screen, a late-night news program showing a fierce, bloody firefight with the caption, "Hue."

I fought there too. Sorrow flooded him for the soldiers, forsaken and despised by the American people for answering the call to serve. Young men like his friends. They kept dying for no reason other than duty, honor, and the government that sent them to war.

I'm supposed to be watching their backs. That was my job. I'm one of those soldiers. I understand the mud, the blood, the dying, the killing, and the pain. I'm wasting away like a sick child instead of dying an honorable death. I don't know what kept me going after the POW camp.

"Your father and I did, son. We supported your spirit," said the birdlike voice. This time it came from all corners of the room.

Jackson jerked his head up. Of course no one was there. "Mom? Dad? I'm drunk. My mind's playing tricks." He looked at his unadorned left ring finger. *My wife divorced me. Carolyn lied in court...claimed I abandoned her. I was listed MIA for over six months when the judge signed the decree. Typical rubber-stamping. Major somebody from JAG visited me. I could barely hold my head up. He wanted me to sign paperwork. Asshole.*

Then a Navy chaplain handed me a telegram about Jim. He died during a covert Seal mission into Laos. I called the priest some nasty names. He was only doing his job. I made it worse. Don't remember anything else. My nurse stuck a needle into my IV line.

My family's gone. My men are all I have left. They hated me. In a POW camp, survival breeds a need for companionship. Our pact joined us in life and death. Now we are friends forever.

Bare feet planted against the footrest, Jackson pressed his body into the worn-out cushions of the recliner. Something sharp poked through his pajamas. "Ouch!" He felt behind him. A cold metal point met his fingertips. "My luck, I picked the one with a loose spring." He stuffed a throw pillow behind his back.

Jackson refilled the glass, drained it, and poured yet another round. *My head feels like it's full of bees.* He emptied the glass again. *I lost our freedom. I didn't listen to my gut. This is my fault. Who knows where this road will take us?*

Setting the empty glass on the table, Jackson glanced around the room. His gaze paused at the picture of Jerry and Curtis on the fireplace mantle. *This is their home. Home. Don't have one. The home of my soul is gone. I can't ever go there again. The bond formed, forged in blood, the fog of combat and death was jerked away from me. I can't see my wartime friends. I can't check on Harry. It'll put his freedom in jeopardy.*

Jackson smacked his head with his empty glass. "Dad, make the horror movie stop."

"Relax son, let it come. It'll help. Trust me," murmured the male voice.

This time he didn't even look. His dad wasn't there. He'd conjured up the voice from his own memory. He loved hearing it even as he knew it wasn't real. "Okay, I'll try." Jackson squeezed his eyes shut as his heart beat like a trip-hammer. *Battles. Screaming. Dying men. Sweat. Pain.*

Blood. Artillery booming in the distance. The whirl of helicopter rotors filling the air. Faces of men dying. Blown apart bodies. Medic! Machine-gun fire. Planes flying overhead. The whistle of falling bombs. Explosions. The sliced open throats of the enemy as their blood dripped down his blade. Car batteries and wires. An oak tree. Large knife. Staring at a blood-coated ceiling as he lay naked on a table. A ten-foot bullwhip. Colonel Dung. Pig. Toad. He wiped the sweat from his eyes. "I can't do this, Dad. I can't look at their faces anymore."

"Yes, you can. Don't give up. Close your eyes."

"No!" Jackson refilled his glass then glanced out the window at the pitch-black night. A dark caricature of himself stared back at him. Eyes nothing but empty holes sunk into his skull. His skin, the pallor of a white sheet. He looked dead.

"Jackson, honey, think about what you're doing," said the faint whisper of his mother's voice.

"Mom, come back to me." Jackson shook his head. "I remember how Dad acted after he returned from the Pacific. I was ten. I thought I'd done something wrong."

"Listen to your heart. Let what happened be your guide."

"I know you're not here, Mom. It's my messed-up head and the crap in my stomach making it worse." Jackson concentrated on the memory. A week before the Medal of Honor ceremony, his dad couldn't stop saying *I love you*, with an unopened bottle of Jim Beam in his hand. He kissed Jackson and Jim on the forehead, rubbed their heads, and left the house with the bottle. *Now I understand why.* He came back two days later, standing straight and proud like a Marine. But his face and hands looked like he went through a twelve round heavyweight title fight. He'd gone to see Uncle Jason to get his head back on straight.

Time stood still as Jackson stared through the amber liquid in his glass at the images of war playing out on the television. *Was that a gunshot? Who brought a loaded gun to the Nha Trang BOQ? Jackson stepped out of his room. Silence echoed across the building's lower level. Another officer stepped out of the room to his right. Jackson turned left and opened the door. He made the sign of the cross over his chest, mumbled, "In the name of the Father, Son, and the Holy Spirit," pulled the crucifix from under his shirt, and kissed it. Major Fletcher went through Special Forces selection with him. Harry short-sheeted his bed, poured green dye in his boots, and chocolate syrup in his helmet. He loved the pranks. Fletcher was a tightly wound spring. It surprised everyone he didn't ring out.*

The room looked like a murder movie. Only the bumbling detective was missing. Blood spray on the ceiling, floor, and dripping down walls. Brain matter and skull fragments stuck to every piece of furniture. Slumped across the bed, Fletcher's body with the top of his head missing. A Colt service pistol in his hand. On the front sight, a pink chunk from Fletcher's upper lip. Jackson looked in Fletcher's open mouth at the large hole in the back of his throat.

He bent over to read the note. Block handwriting, neat and perfect. Fletcher wanted to die instead of going through a court-martial for his stupidity. A few weeks earlier, he led his company into an ambush that would have been clear to even the greenest butter bar. Fifty men died because he let the alcohol consume his life in the fog of war. Jackson squeezed his eyes shut at the wake-up call. He set the glass down with a thud.

Alcohol isn't the answer.

He blinked...once, twice. The scene of horror faded, retreated into the past. Once again it was a living room lit by a lamp and a television.

His legacy awaited. The United States Army had stripped his entire life away. It couldn't take his friends or their future together. Only in death could that happen. *I will not leave them inside a bottle.* Jackson carried the full glass and the bottle to the sink. He put the bottle in the cabinet then poured the whiskey in the glass down the drain. *My life is mine to command. The passage of time, hard work, and determination will dictate a way. A direction to survive. I will follow Dad's heroic example. I will not fail him*

"No, you won't, son. I know it. Sergeant Major Nichols will provide the support and guidance you need," said the male voice as it faded into nothing.

"I hope so, Dad." Jackson stopped mid-turn at a familiar figure in the doorway. "How long have you been there, Curtis?"

"Long enough to watch you debate with yourself. I'm relieved you made the right decision. I understand who you were talking too. I've seen my parents a few times when I was drunk." Curtis pointed at a picture on the wall.

"Maybe, but it felt so real, like they were standing beside me with their hands on my shoulders. But you're right unless I've gone off the deep end."

"Nope, been there myself after my dad died. Angels always walk with us. I'm sorry, Jackson. We were so busy with the guy who fell off his roof it slipped my mind to give you a sedative. Did you have a nightmare?"

Jackson inclined his head. "Yeah. Don't worry about it. My mistake. I've made a lot of them."

"Somehow, you making mistakes isn't how I picture you. If you make any at all, it's very few. What mistake are you talking about?"

"Not following my instincts and declining the mission."

Curtis relaxed against the doorframe. "Hindsight is always 20/20. You did nothing more than follow orders like any good soldier."

Jackson hitched his hip against the counter. "True, but it still doesn't change how I feel. It's hard to spend my entire life pointed in one direction. To follow in the footsteps of my father and serve my country with honor, only to have it upended for following my orders. It stinks. We did nothing wrong!"

"Jackson, your anger is natural and well deserved."

"I know. I just want this to end."

"Me too. You deserve recognition as a brave soldier. A man of honor. Not a war criminal and a traitor. But you need more help than I can give you."

"True. It's hard to admit that until it's staring you in the face. I don't know how to describe what I'm feeling. I still don't. Until things change, I don't know how to fix my problems. Without any stability, my nightmares won't go away, only get worse. I can't keep doing this."

Curtis tapped his head with his finger. "You know what that tells me?"

Jackson rinsed his glass in the sink, set it on the counter, and leaned against the bar. "What's that?"

"Given enough time and support, you will find your way home."

"Yeah, I hope so. I'm ready for a good night's sleep without the drugs. I feel so tired the next day it's like I didn't sleep at all."

"The sedatives you are on will only induce unconsciousness. You need to dream to get real rest. Unfortunately, instead of a nice, relaxing dream, you go into a nightmare. Only when you face your demons will you find the peace you seek."

Jackson cocked his head. "Never thought of it that way."

Curtis pulled an orange pill bottle from his pocket. "Do you want something to sleep for a few hours?"

"Nah, I'd better stay up to burn off the alcohol in my system."

"Since you brought it up, how do you feel?"

158

"Stupid." Jackson massaged his pounding temples. "I'm buzzed, and my stomach is tearing me up."

"That's because you poured half a bottle of whiskey into your touchy stomach. Let's get you something to eat. Then I'll give you something to settle your stomach." Curtis rapped the cabinet door with his knuckles. "I hope you learned your lesson about drinking?"

"Oh, I did. I feel like an absolute idiot right now."

"As long as you realize your mistake, that's all I ask."

Jackson pointed at his chest. "Oh, I do. I sure do."

"Good. I won't insist on giving you a sedative because you're right about burning off the alcohol. It might depress your breathing, but you need to rest. You have a long trip ahead of you."

"Yeah, I do. Thanks."

The two men sat at the table, talking, drinking coffee, and eating peanut butter sandwiches. With each passing minute, Jackson felt the heavy weight lift from his heart. As the sun rose, he hopped on the treadmill in Jerry's little workout area. He walked until the foul odor from his armpits wafted under his nose. *Yuk. I smell like a brewery mixed with a gym locker and a gas station bathroom.*

Jackson stood in the shower for thirty minutes to soothe his aching muscles before everyone hogged the hot water. He dressed and went to the kitchen. The refrigerator was full, so he pulled out a skillet, scrambled two dozen eggs, cooked two pounds of bacon, and toasted a loaf of bread.

Time for everyone to get up. Jackson grabbed a large cowbell off a shelf. He walked down the hallway, slinging it from side to side.

Mikey, Ty, Bill, Jerry, and Chief stumbled out into the hall. They crouched into defensive positions next to the wall with their hair stuck up in every direction.

"Breakfast's ready, guys!" Jackson felt the remaining tension ebb from his body and smiled. He turned on his heel in military precision and walked to the kitchen with a ramrod-straight back. "Come on. They're still a bit shell-shocked," he whispered to Curtis leaning against the doorjamb.

"Yeah." Curtis followed him into the kitchen.

Jackson picked up a plate from the counter. "You'd better hurry up or I'll eat it all."

Jackson ran a hand over his head. *I'm getting a little shaggy.* He looked up from the TV when the front door opened. "Where are you going?"

Mikey jingled a set of car keys. "The store to buy lunch meat and stuff for the trip. We'll be back in an hour."

"Is Jerry going?"

"No, just me and Ty. Chief and Bill are checking over the van again. You need something, Colonel?"

"I'll have Jerry take care of it." Jackson flipped a two-fingered salute to his forehead. "Off you go. Get the job done, Sergeant Roberts."

Mikey snapped to attention. "Yes, sir." He grabbed the door handle then pulled it shut behind him.

Jackson walked into the clinic. "Jerry, you busy?"

Jerry slipped the last saline bag into the cabinet. "No. I'm at your disposal."

"Good, grab your hair clippers and give me a haircut."

"Colonel, your hair is only an inch long. Isn't it more of an advantage to let it grow out?"

Jackson stood eye-to-eye with Jerry as his command attitude surfaced. "You heard me, Sergeant Rose. Do I have to make it a direct order?"

Jerry stepped back. "No, sir. I'll do it."

"Good." Jackson draped a towel around his neck and sat in a chair. "Make it high and tight."

Jerry put a guard on the clippers and ran it over the top of Jackson's head, then changed to the smallest one for the sides. "Done, sir."

"That was quick." Jackson ran his hands along the sides of his head. *Feels right.*

"Yeah, it doesn't take long when you have less hair than a guy a month into basic training."

"Funny." Jackson stood and checked the haircut in the clinic mirror. "Not bad." *Harry does a better job. The sides are perfect. Jerry needed to use the #2, not the #3 guard for the top. It's too long but will do for now.*

Jerry handed Jackson a crimson ball cap. "Here."

"What's this for?" Jackson shook his head at the logo. The University of Oklahoma.

"To hide your face in public and keep your head warm, sir."

"It's not like anyone will recognize me. I don't look anything like the picture in the press release. It's from my promotion ceremony to Lieutenant Colonel."

"Yeah, I saw it. You look great, fit, tan, and happy." Jerry pointed at the skeleton hanging in the corner. "Not walking death."

Chief came up behind Jerry, wiping his hands on a towel. He grabbed the cap out of Jackson's hand and shoved it over his ears. "Now you look good, boss."

Jackson adjusted the cap so it fit right. "I guess so since I'm wearing the colors of your favorite team on my head."

"All battles are fought by scared men who'd rather be someplace else..." came from the TV in a low drawl as Jackson shoved a handful of popcorn in his mouth.

Curtis strolled into the living room. "What movie is that? Sounds like a true statement."

Jackson swallowed before answering. *"In Harm's Way* with John Wayne and I can confirm that it is. What do you need?"

"Dinner will be ready in an hour. Why don't you call Jason to let him know you're leaving in the morning?"

"Good idea." Jackson turned off the TV, walked over to the phone and picked up the handset. Still disillusioned about what happened the last time, he paused before dialing the number. *Stop acting like a baby.* Each rotation of the dial helped him concentrate. He drew a breath as the ringing stopped.

"Hello," said the gruff, familiar voice.

"I'm not selling a condo in Jamaica."

"It's good to hear your voice. You sound a lot better than the last time we spoke. How're you doing, squirt?" Compassion filled Jason's voice.

Jackson relaxed at the use of his nickname. "Much better. We're heading to San Diego tomorrow. Since we're in Mississippi, expect us in about four days. We're stopping at night to avoid the cops."

"How're you guys getting out here?"

"Road trip in a van the doctor's son gave us. Chief changed out the engine. Now it runs like a top. It should make the two-thousand miles, or we're in trouble."

"Do you guys have any money?" Jason asked.

"About four hundred dollars." Jackson fingered the roll of cash in his front pocket. "We sold the stolen car to a scrapyard. We should have enough for gas, barring any unforeseen complications. We stocked the ice chest with food. That way, we don't have to go into any restaurants and take a chance on getting recognized."

"What are you going to eat? Dr. Howard said you're on a strict diet at the moment."

"Peanut butter sandwiches. Lots of peanut butter sandwiches, hard-boiled eggs, and cold pre-cooked oatmeal. Since we have limited space, so is the menu."

"Understood. Could you give the phone to Dr. Rose for a few minutes?"

"Sure." Jackson handed the handset to Curtis. "Jason wants to talk to you."

Curtis put the phone to his ear. "Hello, Jason."

Jackson didn't return to the couch. He trusted Curtis and Jason. After what happened to him, he hated secrets.

"Hold on a minute." Curtis laid the handset on his shoulder. "Go sit down, Jackson. This is a private conversation." He stretched the ultra-long phone cord around the corner.

Unable to curtail his curiosity, Jackson inched his head through the doorframe to hear one side of the conversation.

"—he prefers the milkshakes from Dairy Queen. Make sure he gets nothing with a lot of grease in it, like shortening, margarine, or lard. Even biscuits and pie crusts are out. No processed meats like bacon, ham, or sausage as they contain large amounts of salt. Skinless chicken, turkey, and pork with the fat trimmed off are excellent. He can eat red meat as long as it doesn't contain a lot of fat. Lower fat milk is okay and about any vegetable. You can use a little butter for flavoring. We've learned this the hard way over the last month. Jackson's doing well physically. He's been walking on a treadmill and using a light barbell for his arms every day. Hold on. I have two prying ears." Curtis picked up a stained yellow plastic bucket from the corner and held it out. "Why don't you go wash this? It's dirty from last night's little event with the hamburgers."

Jackson went to the kitchen with the bucket. *Little event? I puked my guts up.* He washed the bucket and set it outside the kitchen door. *Won't need it again.* He returned to the living room and sat on the couch next to Chief.

Chief elbowed him in the ribs. "Everything okay, boss?"

"Yeah. Not used to being overridden by a civilian." Jackson turned on the TV, picked up his popcorn bowl, and went back to his movie.

As the credits rolled across the screen, Jackson felt a tap on his shoulder. "Huh?"

"I guess you found something to do." Curtis waved the handset. "Jason wants you."

"About time." Jackson stuck the receiver to his ear. "Sergeant Major, may I ask what you wanted to know?"

"I hear the command tone in your voice. You sound like your father when he gave me an order. But sure, I'll tell you. I needed to know about your medical status. The only word you know is okay. Please accept my apology for what happened on Christmas Day. It's my fault you collapsed. I didn't understand the extent of your illness until Dr. Rose explained to me."

"It's okay. There's no way for you to have known."

"Not true. I heard it in your voice and blame myself for questioning your honesty. Your father was the bravest man I've ever met. I was afraid if you screwed up, it would come back on him. Dr. Rose said the press release about your family tore you up. It was obviously an attempt to draw you out. Once the media found out your dad received the Medal of Honor, they dropped the story. The Commandant told the Secretary of the Army and the Chief of Staff to knock it off about the MacKenzie family. Rumor has it he did it at a meeting of the Joint Chiefs. I'm positive the ears of an army head or two were chewed off for the mistake."

"I wish I could've seen that." Jackson smiled at the picture in his head. The Commandant with Hammond's huge ears between his teeth, shaking and growling like a wolf on the hunt.

Jason chuckled. "Me too, kid. You have friends who believe in you. They will be there to back you up when the time comes."

"What happened to rank, Sergeant Major?"

"I've known you since the day you were born. Forget the formalities crap. Call me Uncle Jason like you always have and I'll call you Jackson."

"I will if you will, Uncle Jason."

"That's much better. You guys obey the speed limit. I don't want to see you again as a blurb on the news. We'll have a hot meal waiting. I'm sure you'll be tired of peanut butter and oatmeal by the time you get here."

"Thank you so much. Tell Aunt Rachel I can't wait to eat her cooking. Goodbye, sir." Jackson hung up. *Got you, Uncle Jason.*

Curtis extended his head around the doorjamb. "Dinner's ready."

Excellent company and full stomachs made for a rambunctious evening. Within minutes of everyone sitting in the living room after dinner, Jackson stood. "Okay guys, all bets are off. It's time for my fun." He pulled a paper ball out of a sack at his feet and launched it at Chief.

Chief picked up the ball and bounced it off Jackson's head. Paper balls went flying across the living room.

"Point for me. I hit Chief where it counts." Jackson jumped onto the seat of the recliner, throwing arm cocked and ready.

Chief jerked both hands across his midsection. "That was my crotch, boss, and I'm not wearing a cup."

Ty and Mikey looked at each other, then at Bill with a beer can his hand. Next came the wrestling match with everyone tickling Bill, who sounded like a cross between a baby pig and laughing hyena on the floor.

Curtis kept yelling over the mayhem. "Easy with Jackson, guys, don't break him."

The subsequent laughter rocked the house for several hours.

At 2200 hours, Curtis stood from the couch. "Everyone go to bed before Jackson collapses from exhaustion." He handed Jackson a sleeping pill. "I don't want a repeat of last night."

Jackson threw, "I agree," over his shoulder as he stumbled to his bedroom.

January 25, 1973

Jackson swung the cowbell in the hall. He stuck his upper torso into a bedroom and hit the light switch. "Everybody up."

"What the hell is that noise?" Bill stuck his head under his pillow.

Really? Jackson rang the bell even harder. "I said, get up, Captain. We need to hit the road."

Mikey rubbed his eyes. "Colonel, deep-six the cowbell, please."

"No, get up. That's an order. I've already walked on the treadmill, taken a shower, and eaten breakfast. The sun will be up soon."

Chief swung his legs over the edge of his bed. "What time is it, boss?"

Earlier than reveille. Jackson smiled. "0400 hours."

Bill sat up. The blankets fell into his lap. "The sun doesn't come up for another three hours."

Jackson leaned against the doorjamb. "Yeah, but Ty will take two of those in the shower. Get up, unless you want another serenade with the bell."

"I don't take that long." Ty hopped out of the upper bunk and pulled on his sweatpants.

Chief threw a wadded up sock at Ty. "Yes, you do."

Jackson tapped his watch. "The clock's ticking, guys."

The top curve of the sun peeked over the horizon as the men assembled on the porch.

"You were saying, Lieutenant?" Jackson pointed at the orange-tinted eastern sky.

Ty ran both hands through his dark curly hair. "Not my fault. Chief used all the hot water. I had to wait for the tank to catch up."

"Next time, you get a cold shower. I will push you in myself for a little revenge."

Curtis walked out the front door. "You are a hard taskmaster, Jackson. I thought a herd of noisy bulls was wrecking my house this morning." He grabbed Jackson by the shoulders at arm's length. "Please take care of yourself. Do your best to stay out of trouble. I never want you again as a patient, ever."

Jackson flashed a smile. "I agree. I was horrible to you and Jerry. Once I get everything sorted out, I promise to come back for a visit. That day, I will wear my uniform as a United States Army officer, complete with the Medal of Honor. I need to repay you adequately for saving my life."

Curtis' face lit up. "You'd better try hard."

Unable to leave yet, Jackson enveloped the doctor in a hug. He patted him on the shoulder and turned to follow the others. From the front passenger seat, he winked at Curtis as he shut the door. His hand remained stuck through the open window waving as the van backed out of the driveway.

CHAPTER 14

January 28, 1973

Jackson glanced around as the van came to a stop at the I-5 Oceanside exit ramp. Chief missed the exit to Highway 76. The area looked different. Built-up with houses, businesses, and traffic. "Well, things have changed since the last time I was here."

Chief revved the engine. "Which way, boss?"

"Right. We need to get off this road. It takes us to the main gate at Pendleton."

"Got it." Chief turned onto Harbor Drive.

Jackson didn't want to admit he should have bought a map. It took him thirty minutes to find the right road. The direct route to Jason's house was now a parking lot with a fast food joint in the center. Chief made several U-turns, rights, and lefts before Jackson found the street into the residential area. Even then, it still looked different. Jason's neighborhood the last time he visited was only five houses on three-acre lots in an open field. Now it contained dozens of houses and winding streets. At the end of Infantry Drive, Jackson pointed at the one-story stucco house with a two-car garage and a workshop in the back. It hadn't changed one bit. Not even the color. Desert tan. "That's it, Chief. Park in the street. You guys stay here."

"Do you want us to stay out of sight?" Mikey called out from the back seat.

Jackson popped his head into the open door. "Yes. We're still a story on the news. The army keeps posting our pictures on TV."

"You got it, boss." Chief climbed out of the driver's seat into the back of the van.

Jackson shut the door and walked toward the house.

"Get off me. Your knee is in my groin," Mikey yelled in a high-pitched soprano voice.

"Oh, hush Jayhawk lover," Chief matched Mikey's volume with his growling bass tones.

Can't they be quiet for once? Jackson walked up the sidewalk, climbed the steps, and rang the doorbell. He patted his foot like a jackhammer until the door opened. In the opening stood the stocky, barrel-chested, five-foot-eleven-inch, crew cut, brown-haired form of Jason Nichols. In a flash, Jackson stood up straight, tucked in his chin, and looked him square in the eyes. "Hello, Sergeant Major Nichols."

Jason's stance changed into a Marine Corps drill instructor, hands on hips, gruff voice with a hint of annoyance. "What did you call me?"

I feel like a new recruit. Can't hold his stare down. "Okay, okay, Uncle Jason."

"Much better. Now, where are the rest of you?"

Jackson pointed behind him. "In the van. With all the press coverage, five guys standing on your doorstep might draw a lot of unwanted attention. It was better for me to come to the door alone."

Jason nodded at the street. "Making sure it was safe, right?"

"Yes, sir…I mean yes, Uncle Jason. It's been a long trip. I'm sorry, we haven't showered or changed clothes in three days, so we're pretty ripe." Jackson saw Rachel standing behind Jason with her arms crossed. Her shimmering long blond hair always reminded him of honey in the summer. But her attitude and posture matched Jason's. Marine Corps all the way. *She's unhappy about something. Probably how I look.*

"Okay, let's remedy that situation. First, park that van in the driveway. I don't want my neighbors calling the cops because they don't recognize the blue rattletrap in front of my house. Then double-time your men inside so all of you can get cleaned up for dinner."

Maybe I should use Jason's rank. He's giving me an order…Nah, better not. This is his house. "Yes, Uncle Jason." Jackson walked to the van and stuck his head through the open passenger side window. His friends looked up at him from the floor. "I see you guys got situated. Chief, park in the driveway. Everyone else, out." He opened the door, grabbed his small bag from the floorboard, and slammed the door shut.

The sliding door opened. Ty, Bill and Mikey climbed out, faded green canvas bags in their hands that matched Jackson's…worn-out Army surplus. It was all they could afford.

Chief pulled the van into the driveway and got out with the same bag.

Single-file, they followed Jackson into the house.

Jason and Rachel met them in the living room.

Mikey, Ty, Chief, and Bill stood off to one side of the room in a staring contest with Jason.

This is awkward. I'd better introduce them. Jackson pointed at Chief. "Uncle Jason, this is—"

Jason held up his hand. "Hold on a minute. Someone's here waiting for you."

"Who?" Two massive arms went around Jackson's shoulders. He spun around. His eyes widened. The large body pulled him close. Jackson returned the hug. *Uncle Manny! He and Aunt Sara never forgot me. Aunt Sara always sent me cookies and soft toilet paper in her care packages. Uncle Manny pulled strings to call me wherever I was posted. I should have written them more.* For a long moment, they stood. Unable to stand the tight quarters any longer, Jackson pressed his elbows out to break the hold.

Mangus released him and stood back at arm's length. "Hey there, Jackson."

"Hi, General Malone." Jackson came to attention, his thumbs along the seams of his jeans.

"Huh?"

This is hard. I've been in the Army for twenty years and he's a general. Jackson forced his body to relax. "Hi, Uncle Manny."

"That's better." Mangus sniffed the air. "You're right. You guys need showers."

"Yes, we do." Jackson wrinkled his nose at his foul body odor. A 'Nam outdoor latrine over a slit trench came to mind.

Chief held out his hand. "I'm Dakota Blackwater, but call me Chief."

Mangus shook Chief's hand. "I know who you are, Sergeant. Jackson told me all about you at the Medal of Honor ceremony. It's an honor to finally meet you."

Mikey, Ty, and Bill stepped forward and introduced themselves to Mangus, Jason, and Rachel.

"Follow me, guys." Jackson picked his bag up off the floor. "The bathroom's this way."

"Jackson." Mangus squeezed Jackson's shoulder. "Stay here. Let the others go first."

The four men stood like statues.

Chief raised an eyebrow. "Boss?"

Jackson inclined his head at Jason. "Go ahead. Get cleaned up. I'll be along in a few minutes."

Jason waved the men forward. They turned to catch Jackson's eyes before proceeding. He saluted. His friends nodded and followed Jason to the back of the house.

Mangus smiled. "Your men are loyal. They maintain a military decorum I wouldn't expect in your situation. I like them. They'd make excellent Marines. Now, are you okay, kid?"

"Thanks, Uncle Manny. They're my friends, and, no, I'm not." Jackson wiped his runny nose on his shirtsleeve. "The army screwed me up good. I can't sleep without taking sedatives, and that's not the answer. I turn into a mindless psychopath when I'm having a nightmare. There lies the rub and the need for the pills. If something bothers me, I've gotten into a bad habit of rolling in on myself to come to grips with it."

"I agree with your assessment. Here's the plan." Mangus jiggled the car keys in his hand. "Tomorrow, we're driving to my ranch. We will screw your head back on straight or as straight as we can get it. Everything will be hard in the beginning. I truly believe, together, we'll guide you through this." He pointed at Jackson. "If your sorry ass had been under my command, I would've sent you home no matter how much you complained. Then made you go through a full evaluation. The way you look tells me everything I need to know."

Jackson rubbed the back of his neck. "Yeah. When I volunteered for another tour, maybe I had a death wish after the camp. With Jim gone, I didn't see a reason to go home. Now I understand what a mistake I made."

"Well, you realize it now. That's a step in the right direction. We have a lot more steps to take."

"Just how do you intend to screw my head back on, sir? I have some pretty severe mood swings, from happy to leave-me-alone-or-I'll-knock-your-head-off depression."

Mangus seized both of Jackson's shoulders. "Look at me. A lot of hard work, talking, open spaces, working out, and eating Sara's good home cooking. I'll put you to work on the ranch once you're ready. I have one of my best horses already picked out for you."

Uncle Manny found my happy place when the pressure gets too much. I spent so many hours reliving every meet, practice, and playtime with Firefly, Taco, and Scout. "Let's leave now!"

"Tomorrow, kid." Mangus pointed at the couch. "Sit down. I'm sixty-seven years old. My back is killing me after the non-stop drive from Montana."

"Sure, Uncle Manny. Those old war wounds bothering you?" Jackson sat next to his godfather.

"Yes, they are. Getting shot in the ass will do that to you."

Better not say anything, been there.

169

Once Jackson disappeared around the corner to take a shower, Mangus patted the vacated space on the couch. "Captain Mason, tell me how Jackson reacted on the way here."

"Yes, sir." Bill sat down and faced Mangus. "He stayed almost mute until we hit Dallas then loosened up and started a round of slug bug. We couldn't shut him up after that. I think he hated leaving the one place he felt safe. It bothers him to be called a screw-up. He always went by the book. Someone told me he had perfect scores on all his evals. I've always heard that's impossible. At least for the rest of us. For him, that's a rumor I can believe is true. When the news crucified his family, it threw him for a loop."

"I would feel the same way in his shoes. His family, especially his father, meant everything to him." Mangus placed a hand on Bill's shoulder. "Those rumors are true. I've seen his scores. I heard the same scuttlebutt through the Marine Corps grapevine. The MacKenzie name is a legend in the Corps. I called in a few favors and obtained a copy of his service record up to his last promotion."

"Wow. Anything else you want to divulge, sir? Other than knowing Colonel MacKenzie graduated from West Point, he's tight-lipped about his past."

"Tell me about it. He's independent like his mother. Jackson refused the automatic appointment from his dad's Medal of Honor. He didn't want to go to Annapolis. His family name casts a big shadow in the Corps. He wanted to avoid any preferential treatment. That's why he enlisted in the army during the Korean War. The kid wanted to earn his appointment to West Point on his own merits."

Bill cocked his head. "That's where he gets the stubborn streak. Anything else, sir?"

Mangus sat up straight like a proud father. "Sure. General Walker called the academy superintendent from Korea to recommend Jackson's admittance to West Point. I heard he talked for an hour about Jackson's intelligence. When Sergeant MacKenzie arrived on orientation day, the command staff sent him to a psychologist for an IQ test. And that damned eighteen-year-old kid scored 172. That puts him in the genius level range. He joined MENSA and double-majored in military science and mechanical engineering, graduating at the top of his class with a perfect 4.0 GPA. Jackson could have been anything he wanted in life but chose the path of a career soldier. I know one language, English. Jackson speaks four. He learned Spanish in high school then German and Russian at the academy."

Bill held up five fingers. "Five, sir. He learned Vietnamese in the POW camp. I knew the colonel was smart, just not that smart. When did he go to flight school?"

"He did that entirely on his own as a Second Lieutenant during his off-hours while with the 101st. After General Daly learned Jackson had a private pilot's license, he sent him to helicopter school. Jackson puffed up like a peacock on graduation day when I pinned those aviator wings on his chest. General Daly was impressed by his initiative. Jackson's hard-driving nature to become the best pointed him toward the Special Forces. With the engineering background I heard after explosives training at Special Warfare School, he perfected the art of blowing things up."

Bill grinned. "Yes, I can say for a fact, Colonel MacKenzie can make extremely large things disappear in a hurry with a few pounds of C-4."

Jackson walked into the room, a dimpled grin on his face. "My ears are burning. Someone must be talking about me."

"Right on point as always, sir," Bill said.

"I get no respect." Jackson shook his head. He peeked up when Mangus, Bill, and Mikey laughed. "What?"

"You should patent the pouting look, Jackson. It's spot on." Mangus' hazel eyes crinkled at the corners.

"Why me?"

"Because you walked right into it, kid."

While waiting for dinner, Jackson couldn't shake the feeling of confinement. Everyone kept watching him. Like they were waiting for him to explode. He went outside to sit on the porch steps. Footsteps marked the approach of someone behind him. "Hey, Uncle Manny. I know that walk."

"Is something wrong?"

Jackson squinted into the setting sun at Mangus. "No, sir, just thinking."

"Do you mind if I sit with you?" Mangus pointed at the step.

Jackson shook his head. "Hmm…no…go ahead."

Mangus sat next to Jackson. "We're worried about you, son."

Jackson gripped his dog tags tightly. "I'm tired of feeling sorry for myself and retreating when I can't handle the pressure. It never happened to me before they locked me up. Uncle Manny, it scares the living shit out of me."

"The army caused your uncertainty." Magnus squeezed Jackson's shoulder. "JAG should have pulled you out of that cell when the nightmares started. It was a mistake for them not to consider the year you spent as a POW under extreme torture. Medical regulations dictate you either be in the hospital or restricted quarters, seeing a psychiatrist."

"Yes, sir." Jackson stared at the horizon. "Look what going by the book got me. Dumped into a hole, shit on and I'm nearly out of my mind. The Medal of Honor, don't even get me started." He slapped his hand on the concrete. "What has that gotten me? Nothing! I should've canceled the mission and came home with Harry."

"You know the regulations as well as I do. If you refused the mission, and the brass wanted to go that route, you could be in the same boat, up on charges. Given your exemplary record, as someone who has commanded entire divisions, I would not make such a rash decision." Mangus let out a sarcastic snicker. "But this is the army we're talking about here. For the Pentagon brass not to listen to their expert in small unit tactics is extremely short-sighted. Whoever cleared your return to active duty in a combat zone did you a disservice. You should not have gone back to Vietnam. Period!"

"I know. I wanted everyone to leave me alone about the camp." Jackson dropped his head into his hands. "I thought I could handle it. I was so wrong."

"The fact you admit that tells me a lot. It's those who refuse to acknowledge they need help who are dangerous to everyone around them. I'd trust you with a weapon even now."

Jackson looked at his godfather. "I'm not sure I would, sir."

"Open up your ears and listen to me, Jackson. You understand you need help. I trust you. Promise me one thing." Mangus tipped his closed fist to his mouth. "No Jack Daniels."

"Ahh...Dr. Rose told Uncle Jason about that too," Jackson said.

"Yes, but he said you walked away when you realized it wasn't the answer to end your pain."

"Just my life, if I let it. Besides, it tore up my stomach. I hate being so sick I want to puke my guts up." Jackson stuck out his tongue. "Bleh. The aftertaste is horrible."

Mangus chuckled. "You're headed in the right direction. Don't give up. We'll follow the path of recovery together. You'll be standing tall like a Marine at the end just like your dad. Do you feel better now you've vented a little? I know you're hurting."

Jackson grinned. "Yes, sir."

"Then let's get up off these steps, you skinny kid, and find the coffee."

"Yes, sir." Jackson extended his hand. "Help me up. My legs stiffened up sitting on the porch."

Mangus stood, grasped Jackson's hand, and pulled him to his feet. "So did mine, but I'm old. Your problem is you have skinny, untoned twigs as legs." He threw his arm around Jackson's shoulders, and they walked into the house together.

Odors drifted across the living room under the breeze of the ceiling fan.

Jackson sniffed the air. "Something smells great."

Rachel Nichols stood in the doorway. "Dinner's ready."

Jason picked up a handbell from the shelf above the fireplace. He marched across the living room, ringing it.

Jackson saw Bill, Mikey, Ty, and Chief with fire in their eyes. *Uh-oh. The cowbell.* "I didn't tell him."

Chief popped his knuckles. "Right, boss. Then, who?"

Only one suspect. Jackson grinned. "Curtis."

Everyone made their way into the dining room. The table was covered in bowls of food and a giant turkey. Jackson sat next to Mangus. Jason and Rachel sat across from them. Bill, Ty, Chief and Mikey grabbed the remaining chairs.

Jackson filled his plate with lean turkey breast, corn, and a baked potato then placed two rolls on top. After a second helping, he grabbed another roll, wiped the plate clean, and shoved the roll in his mouth.

Rachel pointed at the shiny plate. "I guess I don't have to wash that one, do I, Jackson?"

"No, ma'am," Jackson mumbled, covering his mouth with his hand, trying desperately to keep it closed. The half-eaten roll almost fell from between his lips. After swallowing the mouthful, he gulped his coffee to wash it down.

"You look like Bugs Bunny with those cheeks." Rachel's sweet, joyful laughter lit up the room. She sounded like a mother robin in song to her nest of babies.

Jackson smiled. The pain of his past melted away for a brief moment, replaced by the hope things would turn out for the better. He patted his almost full stomach. "It was terrific, Aunt Rachel."

"I guess so since you ate enough for a sumo wrestler. Want some dessert?"

Jackson grinned. "Yes, ma'am." *Aunt Rachel's desserts taste extra-special. I remember when Mom and Dad left Jim and me with her when they went out for the evening. They wanted to spend a few hours away from us. We drove them nuts.*

The food disappeared then everyone leaned back in their chairs.

Jackson carried the leftovers into the kitchen.

Rachel joined him as he ran hot water into the sink and added dish soap. She pulled a dishtowel out of the cabinet. "You wash, I'll dry. You're such a gentleman. I know your mother's house rules."

"Yes, ma'am." Jackson handed her a clean plate.

With the last dish placed in the cabinet, Rachel handed Jackson a stack of small dessert plates. After he sat at the table, Rachel set a large baking pan and a half-gallon tub of vanilla ice cream in front of him. She laid her hand on his shoulder as she lit the candles stuck in the dessert. "You didn't get to celebrate your birthday last month. Make a wish."

For the army to admit they are wrong.

"Happy..."

Mangus waved at everyone to stop singing.

Jackson looked at his godfather. "I'm not going to have a melt-down. They can sing if they want."

"That's okay. I'm worried about my ears. I've heard Jason sing. Blow out the candles, son."

Jackson sucked in a big breath. But with thirty-eight candles and his limited endurance, not all of them went out. His men chipped in until every tiny flame disappeared.

Once the laughter subsided, Jackson scooped out an enormous portion onto a dish. He loved sweet potato casserole with pecans. On top, he placed a baseball-sized mound of ice cream. As he ate, everyone else spooned out smaller amounts. His blood sugar spiking, Jackson bounced in his chair as he ate another plateful. *It's been a long time since I tasted something that fantastic.*

Mangus stood without a word and left the room.

Jackson leaned back in his chair to relax, then an armload of wrapped presents dropped in front of him. The pile obscured the view of the other side of the room. He looked up into his godfather's smiling face.

"What about the guys? Don't they get anything?" Jackson smacked the table with his hand.

"Jackson," Mangus started.

"Colonel, they're your family." Bill said as the other three nodded in agreement. "It's for your birthday, not ours. It doesn't bother us that we don't get anything."

I will repay their loyalty by getting our honor restored. "Thanks guys." Jackson examined the gifts stacked up to his chin. "I hope one of these boxes contains something to wear. All I have is used clothes and underwear from a second-hand shop. Not that I can complain, but wearing someone else's underwear, even washed and bleached, is a little gross."

"Yes, sir," Chief, Ty, Mikey, and Bill said in unison.

Mangus pulled out his chair and sat down. "Have at it, kid."

Jackson yanked the paper off the first box. He pulled out a dark tan shearling sheepskin coat, size forty-two long. Stuffed in the pockets, a stocking cap and matching lined gloves. "Uncle Manny, I love the coat. You bought the right size too. I needed the stocking hat since my ears get cold." He tried on the coat. "It's a little big across my shoulders. But will fit in a month or two after Aunt Sara stuffs me full of her special desserts and large, country meals. I'm so looking forward to fresh farm-raised eggs and homemade pancakes."

Mangus smiled. "Yep, I know, and she will too. I may have to put you on a diet when she finishes with you."

After hanging the coat on his chair, Jackson grabbed another package. Once the paper hit the floor, he opened the large cardboard box. He pulled out a smaller box and studied the picture on the side. "Is this a new type of coffee maker? Never heard of Mr. Coffee."

Mangus balanced his cup on his knee. "Yes, I bought one for Sara last year. It's better than a percolator. The coffee doesn't taste burnt. I thought you could use a pot in the bunkhouse."

"Great. What about these?" Jackson held up a red metal can in each hand.

"You needed the coffee to go with it. Those three-pound cans should last, what do you think, about a week?"

"Yeah, a week, give or take. What about this?" Jackson set the cans aside and pulled a large white ceramic mug embossed with the Special Forces patch out of the box.

"The way you drink coffee, a twelve-ounce one is too small. That one holds twenty-four. A friend made it special for you."

"Thanks. It's heavy too." Jackson raised the mug like a barbell. He opened the next package and thumbed through the clothing. Five pairs of jeans, a brown leather belt and five different-colored flannel shirts. He stood and held a pair of jeans against his legs. *They're the right length, but way too big in the waist.* Paper flew as he tore open another gift. Dark brown cowboy boots. "Thanks, Uncle Jason. The color will fit right in with the cow shit."

Jason slapped his knee. "Funny, kid."

Jackson picked up a round hat box, unbuckled the strap, and pulled off the lid. A felt Stetson cowboy hat that matched his new boots. He set the boots on the floor then placed the hat on his head.

"Trying for the John Wayne look, boss? It's pulled low over your eyes," Chief drawled in a decent imitation of the actor.

"Uh-huh." Jackson thumped the brim up with his fingers. Ripping the paper off the next box, he pulled out six plastic packages. T-shirts, socks, underwear and a new duffle bag. "This is great. Love the new bag, Uncle Jason. Mine wouldn't hold all my new clothes."

"You're welcome." Jason winked at him.

Jackson pulled the full-leg, brown leather western riding chaps out of the last box. A sign of good times to come. He stood and held them up to his legs. "Nice."

"You really think you'll need those, boss?" Chief said.

Bill, Ty, and Mikey almost fell out of their chairs holding their stomachs.

I'll get them good. Jackson laid the chaps on the table. He wadded the wrapping paper into balls then picked one up and cocked his arm.

Jason grasped Jackson's arm with a Marine drill instructor glare. "Don't even think about it." He picked up the paper and carried it to the kitchen. A few minutes later, he returned and handed new shaving kits to Ty, Bill, Mikey, and Chief. "See. We didn't forget your friends."

Jackson shook his head as Jason handed him one. He gathered up his new stuff and carried it his bedroom.

On the return trip, Rachel grabbed him on one side, Jason the other. They smashed him in the middle like a sandwich.

Rachel kissed him on the forehead. "Happy birthday, my little squirt."

Jackson shuffled back and forth on his feet. "Thanks, Aunt Rachel."

It didn't end there. Once they let him go, his godfather's massive arms went around Jackson's back. "This is kinda appropriate, don't you think? You look like a gray-haired bear with a high and tight," he mumbled into Mangus' shirt.

The embrace went on for almost two minutes.

Mangus stepped back. "Bear, huh?"

"Yeah." It meant so much to know he wasn't alone anymore. "Thanks, everyone."

For five minutes, the room stayed quiet as everyone drank their coffee.

Mangus stood. "Do you guys want to hear about Jackson's childhood misadventures with his older brother?"

"Yes, sir," Mikey, Ty, Chief, and Bill echoed together.

Jackson glared at Mangus. "Don't you dare, Uncle Manny?"

Mangus cleared his throat. "Well, there was this day when Jackson was twelve. He and Jim went out on a camping trip …"

Minutes later, Jackson couldn't take the embellishment any longer. "If you're going to tell the story, tell it the right way. Jim and I …"

Everyone had a great time. It was well past 2200 hours by the time they went to bed.

Jackson picked up the phone on the way to his bedroom. "Hello, Curtis. Sorry for calling so late. We made it safely to San Diego. Tomorrow, we're heading to Montana…"

CHAPTER 15

January 29, 1973 — 0600 hours

Jackson and Mangus climbed into the Double M Ranch red Ford Bronco. A large Marine Corps Eagle, Globe, and Anchor sticker obscured the center of the rear window.

Jackson looked at Mangus from the passenger seat. "How do you plan to bluff your way past the cops if we get stopped?"

Mangus stuck the key in the ignition. "That's easy. Lies and deception. It works for those army assholes. Why not retired Marine generals?"

"What will you tell them?" Jackson set his cowboy hat on the dashboard and reclined his seat all the way back.

"That you're my son. It's not a lie. You're my godson, right?"

Jackson loved seeing his godfather so normal instead of the uptight, squared away Marine. "Yep. Sure am…Dad." He pointed at the blue van in the street. "What about the guys?"

Mangus started the SUV. "Ask harder questions. That one's even easier. They are employees of the Double M. My status as a retired three-star general should give me a lot of leeway. Think positive. It's not going to happen because I won't let it."

"We'll see. I hope you're right." Jackson rolled his eyes. "Murphy always finds me."

"Not this time." Mangus pulled a red plaid car blanket from the back seat and tossed it in Jackson's lap. "Get comfortable. It's a long drive."

Jackson waved at Rachel and Jason on the porch. "Why isn't Uncle Jason coming with us?"

"Rachel bought a bunch of flowers at the nursery. Jason promised to plant them in the flowerbed." Mangus held up his wedding ring. "She has him wrapped around her finger. I bought him a plane ticket. He'll meet us at the ranch in a few days."

Mangus passed the blue van on I-15 to become the lead car of their little convoy. He drove under the speed limit. As a result, they arrived in Logan, Utah, over fourteen hours later.

"This travel court looks like crap. You sure you want us to stay there?" Jackson said as they pulled into the horseshoe of the Driftwood Motel. Peeling red paint littered the ground around the one-story structure. Inside the bent-over chain-link fence, the frozen water in the swimming pool was algae green.

"This is my operation, Lieutenant Colonel MacKenzie. Keep your mouth shut."

Jackson scowled but followed orders.

Thirty minutes later, Jackson opened the door and threw his bag on the full-size bed.

Mangus dropped his small duffle on the floor next to the dresser.

Jackson looked around the room and took off his coat. *It's eighty degrees in here.* The off-white paint had water marks from the ceiling to the floor. The green shag carpet had a worn path from the bed to the bathroom. "At least the heater works. It's way overpriced at fifty bucks a night, and you paid for two rooms."

"Don't want you sleeping in the van or scrunched up in the back seat of my Bronco with your current health problems." Mangus stuck his hand into his coat pocket. "Like I said, this is my operation, and I'll run it how I please."

Chief walked into the room through the adjoining door. "Your room looks like ours, boss."

Jackson examined a white stain on the dresser. *Eww. Is that semen? Gross.* "Yeah, like shit."

Mangus handed Jackson a key attached to a red plastic rectangle. "I'm headed to the restaurant next door to grab some food. You guys stay here. It's too dangerous. Your faces have been plastered all over the news for the last two months. Not that anyone would recognize Jackson. He looks like a holocaust survivor." He opened the door and closed it behind him.

Jackson shoved on his coat and pulled his cowboy hat over his eyes. *I need some space.*

"Where are you going, boss? The general said to stay here."

"Outside. Leave me alone for a while. I need to burn off some energy before I explode." Jackson wandered around the motel on the covered walkway for the next hour with his collar up next to his ears and hands in his pockets. He saw Mangus go into their room with plastic bags but kept going. *Why can't I shake this? I'm a man. A soldier. Not a child afraid of the dark.*

As he passed the door to their room, Mangus stuck his head out. "Come in and eat before the food gets cold."

"Yes, sir." Jackson rolled his head to loosen his shoulders. *I am kinda hungry.*

January 30, 1973

Late in the afternoon, as the sun disappeared behind the trees, the small convoy arrived at the Double M ranch.

Jackson tossed the car blanket in the back seat. "We're finally here."

Mangus shoved the gear shift into park. He placed a hand on Jackson's shoulder. "You feel okay? I don't want you getting sick again. Last night was interesting. I've never seen anyone puke that much into a toilet for half the night. The words coming out of your mouth in five different languages were colorful."

"Yeah, I'm fine." Jackson opened his door and looked at his godfather. "It was the mashed potatoes. They tasted funny. Like the cook used spoiled milk and rotten potatoes."

The bunkhouse was sturdy, windproof, and warm. Hand-built by the original ranch owner from trees over one hundred years old using rough-hewn boards and interlocking construction. The gaps chinked with Portland cement. Five bunks on each side, headboards against the wall. All lined up identically. A small end table stood next to each bunk. Over each one, a shelf jutted out from the wall. The single-shower bathroom was in the corner adjacent to the foreman's room. Next to the bathroom wall, a rustic, old-west style water-stained wooden dresser that still smelled of cedar. In the open space between the dresser and the front door was a card table surrounded by four folding chairs.

Jackson pushed his way inside. "Excuse me, Chief." He tossed his bag on the bunk at the far end on the right side next to the corner wall, directly under the window.

Chief claimed the bunk directly across the aisle. Bill chose the one next to Jackson. Mikey and Ty next to Chief. Once they made up their beds and turned up the heat, the men walked to the two-story white farmhouse for dinner. Everyone but Jackson went inside. He stood on the covered wrap-around porch and watched the snow fall.

Chief craned his head around the doorframe. "You coming in, boss?"

Jackson stuck his hands into his coat pockets. "In a few minutes. I need to stretch my legs so I don't go off on you again. Sorry about the rest stop this morning. My mind was somewhere else. I needed to pee."

Mangus walked outside after thirty minutes. "Get your butt in the house before Sara corners you for a lecture. You know her rules."

"Yeah." Jackson followed his godfather into the house, hung his coat on the chair next to Mangus, and sat at the dining table.

Sara glared at Jackson for a second then nodded to Mangus.

The food looked and smelled delicious, but Jackson wasn't hungry. His stomach churned. It was still upset after last night. *Maybe I got food poisoning.* He carried his plate into the kitchen. As he scraped it into the trash, his coat appeared in front of his face. He looked at the impenetrable countenance of his godfather.

Mangus pointed at the kitchen door. "Come with me."

Jackson shoved his arms through the sleeves. He walked beside his godfather to the main barn.

"You first." Mangus opened the door.

Something's up. His curiosity aroused, Jackson entered the building. The second he walked in front of the first row of six stalls, the head of a big chestnut quarter horse with a blaze shot over the door of stall number three.

Jackson petted the horse. "The name on the door says Bandit, but he looks like Firefly." He peeked over the stall door. "And he has four socks."

"Yep. That's how I knew he was perfect for you. I hope you like him."

"I don't like him, Uncle Manny, I love him. Thank you so much." Jackson pulled a handful of peppermints out of his pocket. He got them to settle his stomach. Feeding them to the horse meant so much more. Seconds later, his entire arm was wet with slobber as Bandit looked for more.

Mangus leaned on the wall. "I see you raided the candy jar in the house. Did you leave us any?"

"A few." Jackson wiped his sticky hands on his jeans.

"I'll tell Sara to buy a few more bags. We'll be needing them."

"Yes, sir." As Jackson stepped back to leave, Bandit shoved his head into Jackson's chest. Jackson was in the middle of a turn and off balance, so Bandit almost knocked him to the ground. To stay upright, he grabbed the animal around the neck. Bandit laid his head on Jackson's shoulder. At that simple interaction, Jackson felt the tension slip away. "Let's go find me a saddle."

Mangus unbuttoned his coat. "Lead the way. You know where everything is."

Jackson opened the door to the tack room and went inside. It held a dozen western saddles on racks. One had a piece of paper attached to the horn with *Jackson* written on it in large block letters. A saddlecloth, matching bridle, breast collar, and rope lay on the shelf attached under the frame. "You already bought one for me."

"Yep. You have long legs, and Bandit's the size of a Mack truck. Nothing I had on hand fit him."

Jackson rummaged through several items stacked in the corner. "Found a rifle scabbard. I'll need it when I go out chasing cows."

Mangus shook his head.

"Why'd you do that?"

"You know exactly why I did. Let's go to the bunkhouse. I'm cold."

An hour later, Jackson gulped down the last swig of coffee from his mug. He glanced at Ty, Chief, Bill and Mikey. They looked comfortable sitting in folding chairs around him. He hoped they would like the ranch. The half-open door to the foreman's room caught his eye. "What's in there, Uncle Manny?"

Mangus leaned back in his chair. "Take a look."

"Okay." Jackson strolled over and stuck his head inside.

Next to the window, an electric treadmill. In the center of the room, a weight bench with an empty barbell and a stack of weights of different sizes lined against the wall. In the corner on the other side, a heavy bag with a speed bag a few feet away.

Jackson tried to bob and weave as he double jabbed the heavy bag. He slipped and almost fell on his face. Instead of punching, he watched the bag swing back and forth on the chain. *Oops. I'm glad no one saw that.* For the next ten minutes, he inspected every piece of equipment then returned to his bunk. *Tomorrow will start a new chapter in my life. In the morning, I'll get back on the weights and use the heavy bag to work my way back into shape. I look like a flabby mess.*

"General, how cold does it get in Montana?" Bill poked Ty in the chest. "Ty doesn't do cold. He's a rich-kid city boy."

Mangus chewed on a toothpick with his chair tipped back on two legs. "Think of a freezer full of dry ice. The coldest I've ever heard was minus seventy degrees near Helena."

Ty shivered. "You're kidding, right?"

Jackson rolled his eyes, popped a sleeping pill into his mouth, and went to bed. *I have to face my demons. But not tonight. All I want to do is sleep. The pain will start soon enough, come tomorrow. I can't avoid it any longer. Gotta stop the sedatives cold turkey and let it happen.*

January 31, 1973

A pack of wolves started howling and wouldn't shut up

182

Jackson sat up in bed. *Sounds like they're on the prowl tonight. It's keeping me awake.* He made his bunk, slipped on his sneakers and crept to the foreman's room.

After walking a mile on the treadmill and stretching to keep from getting stiff, Jackson sat on the weight bench. He pressed a set of four on his back and squatted four times with the same empty bar. In light of his limited endurance, he tired quickly. He stuck his head around the door into the main room. *Good. They're sound asleep.*

Jackson tiptoed to the dresser, pulled out his clothes, and swiped his boots from the top. He jumped into the shower. Clean and dressed, he grabbed his coat and cowboy hat from the rack. He opened the door and slogged through the snow in the early morning darkness.

Inside the barn, Jackson snagged the lead rope from a peg on the wall and clipped it to Bandit's halter. The horse followed him outside the stall. With a quick flip and tie, Jackson secured Bandit to a ring on the wall.

Time for the stinky job. Jackson retrieved a pitchfork from the tack room and tossed the soiled bedding into the wheelbarrow parked next to the stall door. Next, he snatched the hay hook from the wall, pulled a bale of fresh straw to the stall and spread it around with his feet and the rake. He parked the wheelbarrow next to the door and picked up the bucket with his grooming supplies.

Jackson petted Bandit's blaze. "Are you my buddy?"

Bandit whined and bobbed his head.

"All righty then." He pulled out the rubber curry comb and started at the neck. With each stroke he felt his anxiety lift. His stomach felt better. Just the simple act of caring for his horse calmed his mind. The passage of time slowed as he loosened the caked mud, dirt, sweat and old hair from Bandit's coat. The horse leaned into the brush, enjoying his massage.

"You like that, huh?" Jackson stopped when his hand cramped.

Bandit stomped his front foot.

"Really, oh impatient one." Jackson worked his way around the horse with the curry comb. He told Bandit about the war. The things he could. Battles. Lost friends. Bad days when nothing went right. The POW camp he didn't want to think about. Not yet. Those memories haunted him even awake. He dropped the curry comb into the bucket and picked up the soft brush.

"Jackson, stand up," Mangus said in a commanding tone.

"Huh?" Jackson stuck his head up above the horse's back. A few feet away stood Mangus, Mikey, Bill, Ty and Chief. Their faces had the same look. Concern. "Something wrong?"

Mikey played with his robe tie. "You left without telling us. We were worried. It's snowing outside."

"Yes, it is. I'm okay. Really. But I didn't sneak out. You guys are the ones who didn't wake up as the wolves prowled around, making all kinds of noise."

Mikey glanced at his friends. "What noise?"

Jackson looked at his godfather, who winked at him.

"Are you guys deaf from artillery fire? I even heard those mangy things last night, and I'm deaf as a post." Mangus put his hands around his mouth and howled like a wolf. "Ou...ooo...who...oh...oll!"

He's in a good mood. Jackson cleared his throat. "Uncle Manny, how about letting me ride Bandit in the north pasture today?"

"Now you're trying to provoke a reaction out of me. Don't push your luck. Not until you're on a solid footing for a few days. I want Dr. Wells to clear you before you ever put a foot in a stirrup. You have to show me you're not going to fall off."

"I won't fall off. You know that."

"Wrong. I don't think you can climb onto that animal at the moment. I don't need Bandit trampling you because you can't stay in the saddle. This is as much interaction you'll have with him until you build up the strength in your legs." Mangus pointed his finger at Jackson. "Understood?"

Even though he understood the reason for the decision, Jackson's anger spiked. He came to attention. "Yes, sir! Completely understood!"

Mangus walked to the other side of the horse. "Jackson, until you get your mind straight and temper under control, we have to limit your activities to keep you safe. What just happened is a prime example of that."

Jackson dropped his defensive posture. "I lost my cool. I'm sorry."

Mangus petted Bandit's neck. "I know. Don't keep saying you're sorry. You'll wind up with laryngitis. For a while, you'll say and do things completely out of character for you. It'll be the tortured part of your mind trying to vent."

"Yeah." Jackson still couldn't believe this really happened. "Like the filthy mouth and chunking food across the room like a five-year-old throwing a tantrum I don't remember doing."

"Yes, things like that. We'll work it out together and screw your head on straight, I promise."

"Thanks. I'd better thank you now before I become that other person again."

Mangus dropped his hand to his side. "Why don't you finish up with your horse? Sara will have breakfast ready in an hour."

Jackson pushed Bandit's wet nose out of his face. "Yes, sir." He glanced at his watch. "Why don't you guys go take a shower? I still have work to do here."

Mikey spoke up. "I'm curious about what you're doing. Since there's only one shower in the bunkhouse, I'll go last. If that's okay with you, sir?"

"Fine by me. You can't help if you don't know what you're doing."

"That's okay. I'll watch and ask questions."

"Sure?" Jackson shook his head. *Mikey's too obvious. He'll never make a good liar.*

"I know that look. Don't be too hard on the young man. I'll see you at breakfast," Mangus whispered to Jackson.

Bill, Ty, and Chief followed Mangus as he walked toward the barn door.

"Have fun, Mikey," Bill yelled over his shoulder.

Jackson went back to brushing his horse. "You stayed behind to keep an eye on me, right?"

Unable to maintain eye contact, Mikey stared at his feet and brushed the dirt with his toes. "Yes, sir. You were leaning with all your weight on that horse."

"My legs are tired. I know what I'm doing, you don't. Besides, I've almost finished. All I need to do is run the cloth over him and clean out his hooves."

Mikey perked up. "Do you want me to do his feet?"

Jackson peeked over Bandit's back. "Have you ever picked up a horse's hoof before?"

"No, sir."

"Then I'd better do it. You have to know what you're doing so he doesn't kick you."

Mikey looked at Bandit's hooves and the steel shoes. "Yes, sir. Getting kicked by a thirteen-hundred-pound horse would not be good."

"Right, my ranch life greenhorn." Jackson pointed at Mikey's feet with the brush. "Neither does having your feet stepped on. That's why you wear boots in the barn, not worn-out sneakers. You don't want to wind up with broken toes."

For his next task, Jackson ran a large cloth over Bandit to give his glistening coat an extra shine. His spirit felt as if it was shining like Bandit's coat. At least for now. He stuffed the cloth into the bucket. That left cleaning the mud, straw, and embedded manure out of Bandit's hooves. Jackson pulled the hoof pick out of his bucket. Leaning into the horse's right shoulder, he slid his hand down to the ankle and picked up the hoof, clicking his tongue. Each bit of mud got a name as he scooped it out. Toad…Pig…Dung. It was a way to put those—he couldn't call them men—scum where they belonged. In the trash.

Mikey's eyes widened. "You're right. My noggin would go flying if I tried that."

"Told you. Stay quiet and let me finish. I don't want him to trample me if he spooks from your voice."

Bandit was well-schooled, responded to his touch. The job went quickly. Jackson wiped the pick with a towel and returned the bucket to the tack room. He pulled a red blanket from a wall hook, threw it over Bandit's back, and buckled the belly strap. Done with his chores, Jackson led Bandit into the stall. He secured the door with the snap clip. *This horse is smart. I saw him pulling the clip with his teeth. He'll open the door at the first opportunity. He reads my mind, and I read his. I feel connected.*

With a glance over the door as Bandit ambled to his oat filled feed bucket, Jackson turned to his friend. *Now the naïve Mikey will get a little schooling in ranch life.* He rocked backward as a sharp pain shot through his right hip.

Mikey pointed at Jackson's leg. "Something wrong, sir?"

"No, my leg's cramping a little." Jackson massaged his thigh. "Don't worry about it. Could you do me a favor? I'll tell you what to do."

Mikey gave an energetic nod. "Sure."

"We need to dump the wheelbarrow and bring it back."

"Where to?" Mikey wrinkled his nose.

"The compost pile. It's on the backside of the barn. Follow me." Jackson led the way along the well-worn path. He looked over his shoulder then bit his tongue. No way would he laugh at his friend. Mikey's face was green. The smell of the manure, horse pee and used bedding floated in the breeze. Totally disgusting. He breathed through his mouth to keep from retching.

Mikey pinched his nose with one hand and tipped over the wheelbarrow with the other.

First lesson learned.

"Uncle Manny, what's your latest count, cattle, and horses?" Jackson eased his right leg across the chair next to him. The cramps started out as an irritant. Now every muscle in his thigh felt stretched to a breaking point on both ends. He grabbed his coffee cup on the dining room table. *Maybe the caffeine will help.*

Mangus ticked off the numbers on his fingers. "Last check, 2,211 on the cattle and twenty-five horses. Why?"

"Just thinking about how to streamline operations. When we get the chance, can I look at the roster?"

"There's the man I know. We can go over it after lunch."

Boots hitting the ground echoed in the house. Jackson turned to look behind him. "Hi, guys. Take a seat. Breakfast will be ready in a few minutes."

Mikcy laid his palm on Jackson's back. "Still cramping, sir."

"Yeah, a little. Don't go grab your medic kit. I'm worried more about tomorrow than this. I have to come face-to-face with my demons. I can't keep putting it off by taking sedatives, and you know what?" *This is hard to say.* "It scares me."

Bill, Ty, Mikey, and Chief gathered around Jackson's chair.

"You? Scared? I've never seen you uneasy about anything." Chief said.

"Yes, I'm scared." Jackson pointed at his chest. "I would be stupid or ignorant if I weren't. Only an idiot or a fool doesn't admit to being scared. Fear is a bizarre thing. Sometimes it can put you on your toes, ready for anything, or throw you into a hole with your mind unwilling to come out. It's all dependent on the person and the situation."

"You'll come out on top. We all know it, sir." Mikey tapped the tabletop with his finger.

"Thanks. I sure hope so."

Sara stepped into the dining room. "It's ready. Go into the kitchen and fill your plates."

Jackson pushed back his chair to stand.

Sara stomped her foot. "No, you stay put. I'll bring you a plate."

"Thank you, Aunt Sara. I appreciate it." Jackson draped his napkin across his lap. *I'd rather get my own food. I can't tell her no. She cares and I almost can't walk.*

Mikey, Ty, Bill, and Chief ran into the kitchen.

187

Mangus strolled up to Sara, kissed her cheek, and disappeared through the doorway.

Everyone returned a few minutes later with full plates.

Mangus had one in each hand. He placed a plate at the head of the table and the other in the space to his left.

"Here you go, honey." Sara set a plate with a bowl of oatmeal, two pieces of toast, and a mound of scrambled eggs in front of Jackson. She placed two drinking glasses next to the plate—one water, the other fresh milk with foam on top.

Jackson picked up his coffee cup.

Sara stopped him with a hand on his arm. "Drink the water first. You're dehydrated. You can't live on coffee."

"Yes, ma'am." Jackson drained the glass while she glared at him. Then he made a sandwich using the toast with eggs as filler. He poured the milk over the oatmeal, making it into a soupy, almost drinkable porridge before adding several spoonsful of sugar.

Sara sat next to Mangus and nodded.

Mangus picked up his fork. "Okay guys, dig in."

Ty spoke between bites of his breakfast. "General Malone, do you have an accountant?"

Mangus shook his head. "No. I do all the books for the ranch. Why?"

"I have a business degree from The Citadel, sir. I won't take to ranch life well. I've never been around horses or cows. I can take care of your ranch books and personal finances."

"It's okay with me. I hate doing the books. If you want to keep the numbers straight, I appreciate the help. I'm always afraid I'll stick a decimal point in the wrong place and we'll wind up broke."

Ty grinned like a Cheshire cat. "Consider me your new accountant. All I need is an air-conditioned and heated office."

Chief jumped in next. "I'm a good mechanic, sir. I can keep your equipment running in tip-top shape."

"That would be great." Mangus wiped his mouth with a napkin. "You'll have plenty to do. We break things all the time around here."

Jackson smiled over the rim of his coffee cup. *Uncle Manny's impressed. He didn't have to ask. My men are volunteering all on their own.*

"I'm not sure what I'll be good at, General." Mikey shrugged. "I'm pretty much just a medic. And as the colonel will attest, I've never been on a ranch before."

Mangus raised an eyebrow. "I thought you came from a farm in Kansas."

"I did, sir. A wheat farm. We use tractors to take care of the fields and didn't have any livestock, except a few chickens and the family dog."

"Well, we don't have much use for a medic around here, barring a few cuts, sprains, and the occasional step on or kick by a horse. How about I check with Dr. Wells in town? Jackson told me you wanted to go to medical school after the army. It would be a good place to get your feet wet. You can brief him on what to look for since he's keeping an eye on Jackson for Dr. Howard."

Mikey nearly jumped out of his chair. "Thank you, sir. I'd like that."

Jackson sighed. "Another doctor on the payroll."

"Oh, hush up. It's your fault." Mangus picked up his coffee cup. "How about you, Bill? I need a truck driver. My last guy quit. He didn't like the snow. Can you drive a large truck and pull a cattle trailer? We make feed runs for the horses about every other day and the cattle several times a month. Since I have a standing order at the store in town, I need someone to pick up the food for the ranch twice a week."

Bill's face lit up. "You have your man, sir. I paid for college driving delivery trucks and pulling trailers."

Mangus nodded to each man. "Great. I'll pay you in cash, including Mikey. Dr. Wells does mostly a barter business. Is it a deal?"

"Deal, sir," the men echoed together.

Jackson massaged his thigh. *I know my job. It'll wait until I get over my problems.* He craned his head around when a hand landed on his shoulder. "Need something, Aunt Sara?"

"I ran a hot bath for you." Sara ruffled Jackson's hair. "Why don't you go soak for a while to work that painful cramp out? We'll take care of the dishes."

"Yes, ma'am. Thank you, ma'am."

"And stop the *ma'am*, Jackson." Sara's voice rang with annoyance. "I helped your mother change your messy diapers. It's Aunt Sara or Sara, you bratty kid."

"Yes, Aunt Sara." Jackson pushed himself up from the chair, shaking his head. *It's not the first time she's scolded me for the same thing.*

"Guess you have your orders, sir." Ty leaned back in his chair.

"Hush up, or you'll wind up on compost pile duty. Ask Mikey." Jackson limped to the bathroom, removed his clothes, climbed into the tub, then leaned back, stretching out his legs. He closed his eyes, relaxing as the water warmed his body, making time stand still. A gentle shake on his shoulder woke him up.

"Jackson, you fell asleep, and the water's cold. Do you want me to run more hot water into the tub?" said Sara as her apron rustled.

"No, I'll get out now. My leg doesn't hurt like before. I'll stretch it good on the bathroom floor," Jackson mumbled.

"Okay. Do you need help getting out of the tub?"

"No, I can do it, but thanks anyway." Jackson's eyes widened. *I'm naked in front of my godmother!* He sat up straight and placed his hands between his legs. "Aunt Sara, could you please leave."

"Bratty kid. You don't have anything I haven't seen before." A small titter escaped Sara's lips. "Only now much bigger."

"Aunt Sara," Jackson whined.

Sara left the room and shut the door, soft laughter trailing behind her.

Jackson stood and looped an extra-long bath towel around his waist. Using the towel bar to maintain his balance, he climbed out of the tub and sat on the floor. He grabbed his right foot, pulled back, and held the stretch until his thigh rebelled. *Without pushing myself, I will never find out the limits of my body. But today, it was a little too much from a standing start behind the line.*

Unable to stand without help, Jackson grabbed the towel bar for leverage and pulled himself up. He gingerly tested his leg. *It hurts, but not as much.* He gave in to a long, leisurely stretch of his limbs. His joints popped like firecrackers. *I feel better after my short nap. The sleeping pill wore off hours ago. I slept without a nightmare. How? Something to think about.*

Jackson limped into the living room.

Mangus laid his newspaper in his lap and peered at him over his reading glasses. "Jason's plane lands in Billings at 1800 hours. My foreman's picking him up. How's your leg?"

Jackson rubbed his thigh. "It's loosening up the more I move around. I've been parked on my butt too much the last few days."

"Now you see why I said no riding. All you did was muck the stall and brush the horse this morning. Think about what could happen if you cramped up on Bandit's back."

"I'd be unable to control the horse and fall off," Jackson admitted somewhat sheepishly. "I get it, Uncle Manny."

"Good. Then no more arguments about riding."

"Yes, sir, for now."

Jackson limped into the bunkhouse whistling a snappy tune. *Things are looking up.* He picked up the pot to fill his mug next to his new Mr. Coffee.

Mikey leaned on the dresser. "How are you feeling, sir?"

"Pretty good." Jackson thought about falling asleep in the house. "Got a question for you."

"What?"

"I fell asleep in the tub and nothing happened. No nightmare. Why?"

Mikey shook his head. "Out of my expertise, sir."

"Mine too. I still want your opinion."

"Exhaustion maybe." Mikey motioned like he was driving a car. "We've been on the road a lot. The ranch and seeing your godfather and godmother. Family can cure lots of ills and uplift spirits."

"Could be. I hope so." Jackson thought about those things. He could feel his demons lurking just under the surface. "I don't think it's over, my friend."

Mikey shuffled his feet. "Me neither, sir. I'm no expert. I have a hard time with what happened in the camp myself. And I wasn't tortured like you."

"Then we'll get through it together, little brother."

"Yes, we will."

Jackson walked across the room and pulled his coat from the rack.

"Where are you going, sir?" Mikey sidestepped in front of the door before Jackson could grab the handle.

"The barn. Horses crap a lot when you leave them in their stalls. I'm going to turn him out to graze and clean the stall again. I need something to do."

With a glance at the other men, who shook their heads, Mikey shrugged like a timid ten-year-old. "Want some company, sir?"

Jackson nodded. "Sure."

Mikey discovered how much horses crap and pee as Jackson leaned on the stall door. "Get the pile over there too. The big lump in the corner."

Mikey pointed at the back of the stall. "Which one? There are like a dozen."

"All of them. If we don't get the floor clean and dry, Bandit could contract thrush. Keep shoveling. You wanted to learn."

CHAPTER 16

February 1, 1973

Jackson stared at the blood-coated thatched roof ceiling. He was strapped completely immobile to a rough wooden table. The room was dark, lit by candles. He couldn't see the walls, only shadows.

Dung leaned into Jackson's face. His hot breath stunk of nasty fish. "Tell me where the next operation is planned."

"MacKenzie, Jackson J. Lieutenant Colonel United States Army, 5th Special Forces Group. O748528, 7 December 1934."

Toad held up a thin bamboo sliver. He lowered it out of Jackson's view.

Pain went up his arm as Toad shoved the sliver under the fingernail of Jackson's right index finger. He ground his teeth together. No way would he scream.

Dung's pitted face reappeared. "Tell me what I want."

"Xuống địa ngục. MacKenzie, Jackson J. Lieutenant Colonel, United States Army, 5th Special Forces Group. O748528, 7 December 1934."

"You've learned *go to hell* in my language. Not impressed." Dung waved at Toad.

More pain than Jackson could imagine. Like burning white phosphorus shot through his body as Toad shoved slivers under the other four fingernails. Pig did the same thing to the fingers of the other hand.

An ear-splitting wolf howl broke through. Jackson opened his eyes. The ceiling was made of rough-hewn lumber, not thatch. There was no blood on the ceiling.

The bunkhouse. He was at the ranch, not in 'Nam.

"Colonel, are you okay?" Bill called from his bunk.

Jackson sat up and squeezed his eyes shut. *Why can't I take command of my dreams in a place as open as the Double M? We're out in the middle of nowhere.* He counted to ten and opened his eyes.

Mikey patted Jackson's arm. "Colonel, do you want to talk about it?"

Jackson pulled away from the physical contact. His nerves were too raw. "No!" He glared at the four men standing in front of him. "Get out of my way." When they didn't move, he bulldozed a path through the living barricade toward the old foreman's room.

Why me? I followed the code. Did everything right. Kept our secrets. Jackson laced up his sneakers then grabbed the boxing gloves off the shelf. He put on the gloves—swing, slap. Right hand, left hand. Repeatedly. One swing missed, the rough canvas scraped his shoulder, taking off skin. *Ouch!* Spun around, he hit the ground so hard his head bounced several times.

Shaking away the stars, Jackson stood, wiped the blood from his nose, sweat from his eyes. One punch, then two. Another swing missed. He stumbled. The bag arced wide on the chain. Eighty pounds of sand hit him in the stomach. Back to the ground he went, face first.

Need to catch my breath. Hope I didn't break a rib. He stared at the rough unpolished floorboards. *Gotta watch that stupid bag so it doesn't knock me down.*

He grunted, pushed himself to his feet. For the next hour, he threw punches at the bag. His hands felt like one-hundred-pound weights on the ends of his forearms.

Jerking off the gloves, he threw them across the room.

Jackson glanced at the door as he limped to the treadmill. Four heads, one stacked on the other, craned around the door frame. Chief on top, Bill at the bottom. Ty and Mikey in the middle. *They want to come in. They're afraid I'll swing at them. And I would.*

Run. Gotta run. Helps slow my mind. Have to burn off my aggression. Jackson shuffled, step by slow step on the treadmill until his legs cramped from exhaustion. When he climbed off and found his path blocked, the vile smell of his sweat-soaked clothes hit his over-stimulated brain. Wrinkling his nose, he shouldered his way through the human blockade, skulked to the bathroom, and locked the door.

Jackson turned on the water to warm it up. He hated cold showers. *I can concentrate better here than in my crappy cell. Something's making a difference.*

The spraying water helped him collect his thoughts as it warmed every muscle to the bone. He needed to take his focus off POW camp. That experience almost put him in the grave. He had to find balance to maintain his sanity or what was left of it. His internal clock stopped as Jackson tried to pick up the pieces of his life. *What the hell? The water feels like snow. I'd better get out and put on some clothes.*

Time marched on as he shaved and brushed his teeth.

"Do you think we need to call Dr. Wells? The colonel has a crazy look in his eyes. We may need to sedate him," said Mikey's concerned voice on the other side of the door.

"No. I don't want to go that route yet. It'll make things worse. If he turns violent, let's try to talk him down. Only if that doesn't work do we pin him to the floor while you knock him out. Make sure to have something strong ready...just in case," Mangus replied.

I can hear everything. The door isn't soundproof. Jackson glanced at his watch. *It's only been thirty minutes since I turned on the water. Can't they give me enough time to pee, crap, shave, and take a shower?*

Someone knocked on the door like a machine gun.

Jackson pulled on his pants, threw on his shirt, and jammed his feet into his boots. *Click, click* crossed his ears. *Bill's busy with his lock picks.* He braced his foot behind him. The door swung open, and he pushed through the crowd.

Mangus grabbed Jackson's shoulder. "Are you okay? Do you want to talk about it?"

"No! Sir!" Jackson pulled away and stalked to his bunk. *Why do they keep asking the same question? Are they trying to piss me off more?* With a flip of the quilt and a few tucks, he followed the rules set forth on his first day at basic training. His bunk now military tight, he walked to the front door.

Jackson reached for his coat. A wall of violence almost came crashing down. Chief blocked his path. This brought out a deadly glare and guttural growl low in his throat. His troubled soul wanted out of the bunkhouse. They would not stop him.

"Let him go, Chief." Mangus' command voice rang in the room. "Ill-focused anger won't remedy the situation."

Chief stepped aside.

Jackson shoved on his coat. He stomped off toward the barn, hunched over with his hands in his pockets.

Two sets of footsteps crunched the snow behind him.

Jackson turned Bandit into the pasture, mucked the stall then filled the water and food buckets. He saw Mangus and Jason watching him from the other end of the barn. *My legs are shaking. I'll go lean on the fence before I face-plant myself in a pile of manure.*

Bandit stopped mid-buck and trotted up to him, looking for a treat. As the horse nibbled the candy from his palm, Jackson petted his neck with the other hand. Bandit shoved his head into Jackson's chest. In return, he laid his head on Bandit's neck. *He knows I'm hurting.* "Help me," Jackson whispered to him.

Bandit rubbed his head up and down Jackson's chest.

Jackson led the horse back inside. As he brushed him until his red coat glistened, he tried to tell him the nightmare. He couldn't. It still hurt too much. Too fresh. Too painful. He put Bandit back in his stall. As he left the barn, Mangus and Jason blocked his path.

"Jackson," Mangus said in a low tone.

Jackson bobbed his head once. *No one will force me to talk.* Out of respect, he looked his godfather in the eyes.

"You need to tell us what's bothering you."

"No." Jackson shook his head to emphasize his point. He pushed his shoulder between the men.

Jason anticipated the maneuver.

Jackson countered. His reaction born of intense training as he ducked under the grab. He came up in a fighting stance, arms raised, fists balled up, ready to swing.

Mangus and Jason stepped aside.

Jackson glared at them as he walked past. *Can't believe I did that.* The pain in his hip went from annoying to gut-twisting nausea by the second. "Ouch," he repeated with each step through gritted teeth. He stopped at the bunkhouse door, punched the wall then jerked the door open. It slammed back against the hinges with a loud bang.

Jackson pulled off his coat and hung it on the rack. He limped to his bunk and lay down, his hands behind his head.

Mikey stood beside Jackson's bunk. "Colonel."

Jackson clenched his teeth to keep a word from slipping out.

"Do you want to go to breakfast?" Mikey pointed at the door.

"No! I want everyone to leave me alone." Jackson slammed his hand on his bunk. "Can't you figure that out by now?"

The door opened inch by inch. Mangus extended his head through the opening. "It's clear." He eased through the opening with Jason behind him.

Jason shut the door then followed Mangus over to Ty, Bill, Chief, and Mikey standing next to the bathroom.

Mikey tugged on Mangus' sleeve. "The colonel doesn't want to eat breakfast, sir."

"That's okay, son. The only word we'll get out of him, for the time being, is *no*, like a reluctant child. One of you stays here. The rest of us will go eat breakfast. We'll bring a plate back for Jackson and the volunteer. I know him pretty well. And rank has its privileges."

"I'll keep an eye on him, sir," Mikey said.

Jackson ignored the conversation. He propped his right foot on a pillow to ease the discomfort in his hip.

"Let's go, guys." Mangus held open the door while everyone left single file.

Jackson glanced at Mangus and caught his eyes. Mangus nodded and disappeared through the door. It closed slowly behind him.

Mikey sat on Bill's bunk. "Colonel, is your leg still hurting?"

He saw me trip on the threshold. I can't deny it. "Yes."

"Can I look at it, sir?"

"Go ahead, if you'll leave me alone afterward." Jackson huffed through gritted teeth.

Mikey flexed Jackson's ankle then his knee. "Any pain there, sir?"

"No."

"Okay." Mikey pressed on the right side of Jackson's groin.

Jackson jerked as pain shot through his body. "Owww! Stop!"

Mikey stepped back. "You've strained your hip flexor, sir. Nothing major. You need to stay off it as much as possible for a couple of days. Do you want my heating pad? It'll help. I can stretch your leg out for you later. I have some over-the-counter pain medication in my bag. Do you want one?"

Whatever. Maybe I'll stop hurting. "Yes."

"Lift your butt, sir." Mikey slipped a heating pad under Jackson's bad hip and offered him a small pill with a Styrofoam cup of water.

Jackson stuck the tablet on his tongue then flipped his head back to wash it down with the water. He crumpled the empty cup, threw it on the floor, and returned his gaze to the wall.

An hour later, everyone returned.

Mikey stopped Mangus at the door. "Colonel MacKenzie's limp is nothing serious. Just a bad strain. Since his leg's propped up to take off the stress, let him eat in his bunk."

Mangus sat straddle-legged on the chair next to Jackson's bunk. He crossed his arms on the back, and rested his chin on his forearms. "Are you going to eat breakfast?"

Jackson nodded and stuffed his extra pillow behind his back.

Mikey grabbed a pillow from another bunk and added it to the pile.

Mangus placed the plate and bowl on Jackson's lap and a glass of milk on his table.

Mikey brought over a fresh cup of coffee.

At the first bite of eggs, a switch turned on. Jackson's stomach rumbled. His chaotic mind said, "I'm hungry." At that point, he shoveled the eggs into his mouth and wiped the plate clean with the toast. He scraped every last remnant of oatmeal out of the bowl, drank the entire glass of milk and half the coffee without stopping. With the mug still warm, he placed it against his chest and leaned into the pillows. *I'm so tired. I want this to end.*

Mangus set the dishes on the floor. "Do you want to talk, Jackson?"

"No."

"I'm only going to get a one-word answer out of you, aren't I?"

Jackson rotated his eyes to meet his godfather's. "Yes."

Mangus tipped the chair forward on two legs to hold the stare down. "Okay. I'll give you time to think. Once I determine leaving you alone isn't the answer, you will talk to me. Jason and I will be watching you. Once you're ready, we'll be there for you. Is that understood?"

"Yes, sir." Jackson broke first.

"Okay, now we have that settled." Mangus eased his chair back on four legs. "Mikey thinks the reason you're having problems with your legs is you don't have enough muscle tone for stability in your joints. I know you need to vent your frustrations. You're pushing too hard. Stay off the treadmill for a couple of days. That way, you can walk to the barn. Bandit's keeping you grounded. I will not take him away from you. Let someone help you clean the stall and brush the horse. Understood?"

"Yes, sir," Jackson whispered. *Maybe everybody will leave me alone now.*

February 8, 1973

Bandit's coat reflected the light of the barn like a mirror. Jackson dropped the body brush into his bucket. His blurred reflection scowled back at him. He clipped a lead rope to Bandit's halter. The horse refused to walk into his stall. Instead, he placed his head on Jackson's chest and shoved until Jackson sat on the bench next to the stall.

What's this crazy horse doing? Jackson pulled a handful of peppermints out of his pocket.

Bandit ignored the treats. He whinnied in Jackson's face, stomped his front feet and nuzzled Jackson's hair.

Maybe he feels how much I wanted to die this morning? He shook away the thought of the razor blade against his wrist.

Bandit went into his stall and stuck his head into the feed bucket.

Mangus shut the door, put in the pin, and sat next to Jackson. He waved over Jason, who mirrored him on the other side.

Jackson dropped his head into his hands. *I don't want to die but I can't go on like this.*

Mangus eased his arm across Jackson's shoulders. "I guess your horse told you it's time. Are you ready to tell us what's bothering you?"

"Yes, sir." Jackson lifted his head. "Where do I start?"

"The beginning always works for me, son."

"Yes, sir." Jackson crossed his arms and braced his elbows on his knees. "Colonel Dung wanted information on our current and future operations. Hell, we'd been there three months already. I couldn't have told them anything recent, even if I wanted to. I kept preaching the code of conduct to every prisoner in camp. That pissed Dung off royally. He wanted to break my spirit as an example to everyone. I was the senior officer, so everyone turned to me for leadership. That stuck a big ass target on my back. Dung found out I was the temporary commanding officer of the 5th Special Forces Group. Made my life a living hell." He stopped to take a breath. His shoulder muscles bunched up under his shirt then his body shook under pressure.

Mangus rubbed Jackson's back. "Go at your own pace."

The images kept rolling faster and faster. Almost too fast. Bandit bobbed his head over the stall door and whinnied as if telling him to keep going. Jackson willed his mouth to open. "Toad took me to a hut and beat the crap out of me for hours. He beat my head so much my eyes nearly swelled shut. I could barely see. Every time I'd pass out, they would dump water on me to wake me up. When a simple beating didn't work, he and Pig got nasty. They forced me on my knees and tied my arms behind my back. Toad looped a rope around a pole above my head. He pulled my arms up...and kept pulling." Burning agony hit as his arms spasmed uncontrollably. "It hurt so much when my elbows bent in the wrong direction. My shoulders felt like they would pop out. I think it was only about twenty-four hours. It felt like days before they cut me down."

Mangus pulled Jackson tight to his body. "I know it's hard. Dung can't hurt you again. Please keep talking, and we'll get through it." He rubbed the top of Jackson's head.

"Dad used to do that when I had a hard time telling him something."

"I know. He told me the little trick the first summer you stayed with me at the ranch. He knew you'd miss your mother."

"Thanks. It helps. I still wouldn't talk. Toad untied me. Felt like a million knives sawing through my arms as the circulation came back. I passed out and woke up on my stomach. Toad tied my left arm above my head between two boards nailed to the table with my forearm hanging off the edge. Dung bent over me. I hacked up the crap in my nose and spit in his face. That pissed the living shit out of him. Toad beat my kidneys into mush." Jackson arched up. "Ohhhh…my back hurts."

Mangus rubbed around Jackson's waist. "Easy. Does this help? Take your time."

Jackson bit his upper lip to keep it from quivering. "Yeah, a little. I know everything's okay down there. My mind doesn't want to cooperate." *Normally, I would fight to the death. Today, I want to run away.* To curb the impulse, he locked his butt to the bench. "I wanted to curl into a ball and die. All I could do was take the pain. I sure wasn't going to scream or beg them to stop. Pig leaned on my left arm. The bastard weighed nearly three hundred pounds. It broke rather loudly. Then everything went black."

"It's okay. You're doing well. Don't stop. Tell us what happened next."

"I woke up outside with my arms tied to a metal pole hung from a tree. My toes barely touched the ground. The strain on my left arm sent this ungodly pain through my body. Toad ripped off my shirt as Colonel Dung stood in front of me. The asshole asked if I was repentant. I spat at him and told him off in English and Vietnamese. Everyone laughed at him."

Mangus massaged between Jackson's shoulder blades. "Slow your breathing before you hyperventilate and pass out."

"Okay." Jackson sucked in a breath down to his hips. The pulsating in his ears lessened as he released the air through pursed lips.

"Good." Mangus pulled him close to his shoulder. "The Vietnamese hate losing face. You dishonored him. He made you pay for your insolence. The fact you did it in two languages impresses the hell out of me, son."

Jackson looked at his godfather. "I said those things on purpose to get everyone to laugh at him. I even saw his men smiling. Dung strutted around like a pompous ass all the time because he had the power over us with guns and guards. I put him in his place with just my words. However off-color, disgusting, and vulgar they were, I made a point. It embarrassed him so much he turned red. The bastard hated the smile on my face."

"I know that smile. You tried it on me when you wanted to ride in the north pasture."

"Yeah. That's the one. It didn't work." Jackson shuddered as a massive amount of adrenaline dumped into his body. He clenched his hands. To avoid exploding, he opened the valve. "I damned near bit my tongue in half on the first hit. I didn't scream. That's what Dung wanted. I passed out after about ten minutes. Pig dumped water on me." He sniffed to clear his stuffed-up nose. "I couldn't be unconscious while they whipped the living shit out of me."

Mangus handed Jackson a handkerchief. "Take this."

Jackson saw Bandit's head extended over the stall door. Giving him reassurance in his big brown eyes. *I'm ready to move forward.* "I woke up on my stomach in a pile of filthy straw with wet, bloody rags on my back. My arm splinted with sticks. The hut smelled like rotting meat. When I rolled on my side, I came face-to-face with a dead American prisoner. His eyes stared at me. They were blue like mine, but all clouded over. Toad and Pig beat him to death before they punished me." The same face, translucent, ghostly, half-rotted hovered in midair. Jackson shook his head. He squeezed his eyes shut. *Go away. Leave me alone.*

"Relax, son. You're tensing up."

Stop acting like a child. Monsters don't exist. Jackson opened his eyes. The face was gone. "I c-c-can't forget those eyes. They stared into my soul. His body looked like a swelled up sweaty balloon. The room smelled so bad I puked until I threw up blood and passed out. I woke up face-planted in my vomit. The other guy's body had exploded. The skin was falling off. There was a thick milky liquid oozing everywhere. I crawled into the corner to pee. It came out blood. I thought I was a dead man. Then Toad came in. It was the only day I wanted to go back to my little metal box. I didn't have to look at the dead guy anymore." Two clouded blue eyes floated in his vision. Jackson twisted his head from side to side. "Go away. Stop staring at me."

Mangus gripped Jackson's shoulder. "We understand. It's called survivor's guilt. Jason has it. I have it. So did your dad. He couldn't shake the memory of Iwo Jima. He'd wake me up on the troop ship screaming about eyes watching him."

"Is that the nightmare Dad went to see Uncle Jason about?"

Jason patted Jackson's knee. "One of them. The men he lost on Iwo tore him up good. The machine-gun fire from Suribachi shredded his entire company. Most of those men survived Guadalcanal with him. You think you're weak, don't you?"

200

"Yeah." Jackson looked at Jason. "How'd you know?"

"Your dad called himself a wussy marshmallow for breaking. One thing's for certain. Your dad wasn't a coward, and neither are you. If the Army or the Marine Corps has a poster child for bravery, it's you and Colonel MacKenzie. Are you ready to continue? I'd rather listen than throw you into a boxing ring. I had to beat some sense into your dad."

Jackson's eyes widened. "That's why his face was so chewed up."

"Yes. He was a much better football player than a boxer. I was the 1st Division champ, and he didn't know when to duck."

A shrill neigh broke the silence. Jackson knew Bandit was listening. His ears were flicked forward. Maybe understanding the despondency in a way only an animal can. The smell of dashed hopes and dreams. It was the kick he needed to continue. "I have to get it off my chest or I never will. Two days after the whipping, I developed a high fever. Dung wouldn't let me die. At least not yet. The camp medic gave Mikey the supplies. I spent days on my stomach with my head in Harry's lap as Mikey cleaned the wounds with alcohol. Chief sat on my legs. Bill and Ty held my arms down. They almost couldn't control me. Mikey stuck a leather strap between my teeth. I bit through it several times."

Jackson paused as the muscles in his butt contracted at the memory. "Don't get me started on the dull ass needles. It felt like a bayonet when Mikey gave me the antibiotics. I had to gut out the pain with no medication."

Mangus pressed his hand on Jackson's chest. "Slow your breathing. I can feel your heart racing through your shirt. The last thing I need is for you to pass out or have a heart attack."

Jackson inhaled deeply, held it for several seconds, and exhaled. His mind slowed to a crawl. "Dung wanted me to go through the excruciating agony as it healed. Luckily, my arm did without too many problems since I didn't use it. Every guard made it a point to lay a hand, rifle, or stick hard across my healing back or bang the splint to make me jump." His voice softened. "Mind games to impress on me who had the power." The walls of Jackson's internal defenses broke down. He couldn't hold back his despair any longer. It welled up like a spring.

Mangus turned to Jason. "Go make sure no one walks in on us."

"Yes, sir." Jason went to the door, locked it, and returned to the bench, sitting at Jackson's side.

Mangus grabbed Jackson in a tight hug. "Just let it out. It doesn't make you any less of a man. I've seen a lot of Marines cry. Most men would've crumbled after what you endured, and you're still standing. I wouldn't have survived as well as you if I did at all. That says a lot about your courage."

Like a cork shooting from an agitated champagne bottle, Jackson succumbed to his bubbling emotions. He wrapped both arms around his godfather's neck. As if a small child, he buried his face into Mangus' coat and allowed the tears to free his soul. *I'm so lost.*

Mangus held on tightly until Jackson pushed away an arm's length.

"They loved the rope trick. Each time was as painful as the first. There's nothing like feeling your shoulders and elbows dislocate as they pull your arms back. Toad used manacles too small for my wrists. My hands turned black from the lack of circulation. It was as bad as the ropes when the feeling came back."

Mangus glanced at his hands. "My wrists are bigger than yours!"

"Yeah. They remind me of bear paws." Jackson wiped his runny nose with the handkerchief.

"We need to put something else to bed. At least around us."

"You want to see the scars."

"I think it would be best if we did. That way, you don't have to worry about it later on."

"Okay." Jackson unbuttoned his shirt and pulled his t-shirt over his head.

Mangus placed a gentle hand on Jackson's shoulder. "Stand up so we can see them, please." He turned to Jason. "This is taking every last bit of his courage. I don't want him to freeze up. He may never push through and try again."

Both men drew a sharp intake of breath behind Jackson.

"How did he survive? His back looks like a crisscrossed piece of leather." Mangus gripped Jackson's arm. "I'm going to touch your back. Is that okay?"

"Yeah." Jackson flinched when Mangus touched the hard scar tissue. But his sense of humor slipped out. "You won't catch me without a shirt on since the scars go down to my thighs. Women would run away in a hurry. I won't get a lot of dates once they see my back."

"I didn't know the scars were that bad. I'm sorry for pushing you so hard."

"I needed you to push me. I needed to swallow my pride. It took a little while to sink into my hard head." Jackson turned to grab his clothes. *I'm cold.*

Mangus pointed at the scars on Jackson's chest. "Are those from your last mission?"

Jackson pulled his t-shirt over his head. "Yeah, they're nasty too. I won't be running around at the beach in swim trunks." His mood turned from semi light-hearted to serious. "I talked about this nightmare. That's four days out of almost a year. We didn't banish much."

"We started the process. I know we're still tip-toeing though a boulder-strewn minefield. If we have to do the same thing with each one, so be it. It'll take a while, but we'll get there. Now we understand a little better about what you went through. If you feel up to it, let's go eat breakfast. If not, I'll bring it to you," Mangus said in a level tone.

After he slipped on his shirt and coat, Jackson paused. He felt a small change in his heart at a few simple words. "Let's go to the house. I'm hungry."

Mangus draped his arm around Jackson's shoulders. This time, he didn't flinch. "Good. Sara will be happy to see you in the house. You've taken the first step on a long road. We'll keep taking them until you reach the finish line. The first step is always the hardest."

Jackson nodded. "Yeah, hope they get easier."

Bandit neighed as if in agreement.

CHAPTER 17

February 9, 1973

Jackson awoke face-down next to his bunk, soaked in sweat, his knuckles skinned up and blood dripping from his nose. He saw his friends watching him from their bunks. Each one poised to say something but didn't. *They know better.*

He rolled over, sat up, and dropped his head into his hands. *Another damn nightmare. I hate Dung. This needs to stop before I hurt someone.*

Slowly he wiped the blood from his swelling nose. *Or myself even more.* He ran his tongue over his front teeth. *At least I didn't chip a tooth. What time is it?* The wall clock yielded an answer. 0400 hours. *Might as well get up.*

For an hour he pounded the heavy bag. He showered, dressed and put on his coat then paused with his hand on the door knob.

"Sir?" Mikey said.

Jackson turned to his friends a few feet away. "Stay here." He opened the door and closed it behind him.

Bandit's happy whinny greeted him as he walked in the barn. He fed the horse peppermints then did his chores in a daze. The image of Dung's sneer and Toad's nasty BO smell were hard to shake. So was the rack when they tried to make him taller than six foot one.

Mangus and Jason came in as Jackson led Bandit into his stall. Bandit nuzzled Jackson's hair. Lipping it. And it tickled. He couldn't bring himself to laugh. Not yet. He latched the door shut and sat on the bench.

Mangus and Jason sat on either side of him.

Mangus pulled off his coat and laid it across the bench next to his leg. He placed his hand on Jackson's shoulder. "Only if you want to?"

"I need to do this," Jackson admitted softly. Swallowing his pride the day before gave him immense relief. He might as well continue.

"Go at your own pace."

Jackson hugged his knees to his chest. He picked the easiest memory. He couldn't talk about the rack. Toad ratcheted the spool tied to his feet as Pig did his arms. The only clear thing he remembered. Agony. "When the NVA captured us, we were on a seek-and-destroy mission in support of the 101st Airborne. Our assignment was to take out NVA platoons advancing on the firebases. About halfway there, a mayday call came from two downed Navy F-4 Phantoms. The forward air controller asked us for assistance. Our position was less than two miles from their last known location. I sent the other helicopter back to base and we went looking for the air crews. We found them quickly since they didn't lose their emergency transponders. As we lifted off, the chopper took a rocket hit to the tail rotor. There wasn't anything Captain Nelson could do, even with me helping on the controls. We crashed in a flooded rice paddy. Five men died on impact."

Mangus squeezed Jackson's shoulder. "You're doing fine."

Jackson massaged the small scar above his right eyebrow. "I clobbered my head on the instrument panel when we hit the ground. It knocked me so silly I barely escaped before the chopper blew. The next thing I knew, I'm flat on my back, looking up at my men, and surrounded by the enemy. With the blood running in my eyes, I couldn't see much. I puked up my lunch. The world kept spinning around me."

"Concussion?"

"Yeah. A doozy. I had two options. Surrender or be mowed down by automatic fire. I'd already lost too many men. I ordered my men to drop their weapons. I spoke just enough Vietnamese to get by. Boy, I learned the language after that. I had lots of practice at getting it wrong."

Mangus rubbed Jackson's back. "I'm not going to leave you."

"Thanks. You don't know how much that means to me. Harry and Chief helped me up. I was so dizzy I couldn't see straight. If either one of them had let go, I would've face-planted in the mud. Mikey tied a bandage around my head to stop the bleeding."

"Good ol' Mikey. I owe that kid more than he'll ever know."

"Tell me about it." Jackson chewed his lower lip. "The North thought all pilots were CIA because of Air America. Luckily, Charlie never found out I was a pilot, or they might've killed me on the spot. My cracked noggin made me a problem. I'm sure these guys shot us down. They had RPGs. The two Navy pilots wound up standing next to me. One did something stupid. He tried to pull away as two soldiers tied his hands behind his back. The NVA Lieutenant inspected the idiot's flight suit and pointed his pistol at the man's head." He shuddered like an overworked engine.

Mangus squeezed Jackson's shoulder. "You okay?"

Two faces floated like apparitions in his vision. *Go away.* Jackson squeezed his eyes shut. He cracked one open, then the other. Nothing.

"Yeah, I think so. Charlie put the other Navy pilot with his partner. Damn them if they didn't lock eyes with me. Then the lieutenant executed them. It surprised me because of the conversion of F-4s into Wild Weasels. The Russians wanted information on how those planes locked onto the SAM missile sites. My failure burned those faces into my eyeballs."

Mangus got very still. "Jackson." His voice lowered, a whisper of his normal commanding tone.

Jackson leaned forward to hear him. "Yes."

"I've never admitted this to anyone." Mangus refused to look Jackson in the eyes. "Your dad visits me the same way on the day he died every year. His eyes haunted my soul as his life faded away in my arms. You're almost his mirror image. It's like seeing him beside me. I promised him that day I would protect you at all costs. It bothers me that I failed him so badly."

In a role reversal, Jackson pulled Mangus tight to comfort him. "Don't feel guilty about anything. I could've stopped this a long time ago if I admitted to myself that I had a problem. Do you want me to stop?"

"No." Mangus blew his nose into a handkerchief. "I'm here for you, and you're trying to ease my anxiety. That's what makes you special. Keep going. I need to hear this. Listening to you will help us both."

"Okay." Jackson stared off into space for a few seconds. "They marched us for three days. By the time we arrived at the camp, I couldn't stand. I felt like someone pounded a rusty railroad spike through my head. Harry and Bill held me up in front of Dung. He knew we were Green Berets from our uniform patches. Then that asshole spotted my rank. Dung ordered his guards to take me to a hut in the back. They tossed the guys into the open pit next to the main barracks. Toad and Pig beat me to a pulp. After the first couple of hours, my brain went numb. I don't remember much, except puking on Dung's shoes."

"You really did that?" Jason exclaimed.

"Yep. The bastard strutted around like an uptight banty rooster all the time. He always wore highly polished riding boots. I loved to spit or puke on them. It pissed him off every time they had me in for interrogation. All I would give them was my name, rank, and service number. I challenged and bad-mouthed Dung constantly. The prick beat me regularly to return the favor."

Jason rubbed his chin. "That's a tried and true tactic for getting information. Pain."

"Yeah…Dung kept me separated from the guys to soften me up and give them an incentive to talk. I spent so much time in the same sweatbox

I should have hung pictures to make it homier. And I received the smallest amount of what they called food to break me faster." Jackson slapped his hand over his mouth. His cheeks puffed out as he swallowed the bitter bile that burned his throat.

"What's wrong?" Mangus asked.

"I remembered my last meal in the camp. One cup of maggot-filled rancid rice. It smelled like the compost pile in July."

Mangus rubbed his lips. "Ewww. Did you eat it?"

"No!" Jackson's entire body tensed. When his muscles unlocked, he trembled violently.

"Go at your own pace. We have all the time in the world." Mangus slipped his arm across Jackson's shoulders.

Bandit shook his head over the stall door. His mane flopped back and forth. He neighed. Shrill and loud. As if he felt Jackson's uneasiness.

Jackson looked at Bandit. The horse blinked and bobbed his head. Giving him the will to keep moving forward. He sucked in a large lungful of air. *This is hard.* "Toad strapped me to a table. He pulled off my clothes and looked me up and down like a piece of meat. When his eyes stopped at my groin, he licked his lips. A bad feeling hit the pit of my stomach. He pulled out an electric cattle prod and poked my penis until I peed on myself. Pig untied me and flipped me onto my stomach. I cringed when a hand probed my ass. I was sure they were going to rape me when Pig pulled open my butt cheeks. Toad poked me right in the hole with the cattle prod until runny shit ran all over the table. Toad laughed his head off as Pig played with my penis saying I was so small." His voice rose several octaves. "And I'm not small."

"That's a humiliation tactic."

"I know, and it worked. Toad attached my balls to a car battery with alligator clips." Jackson wiggled like a bug on a hotplate. "Felt like my lower body was cooking in a blast furnace, and my damn dick would fall off."

Mangus and Jason stood and walked around the barn.

Bet their balls retracted. Jackson rubbed the back of his neck. *I'd have to walk it off too.*

Minutes later, Mangus and Jason returned to the bench.

Jackson shrugged. "At least mine still works."

"No way could I have taken that as well as you obviously did." Mangus' hand slipped down to cup his balls.

207

"Don't sell yourself short, Uncle Manny. You survived Guadalcanal, Iwo Jima, and Okinawa."

"True. But I never went through this. Keep going, son."

This will always haunt me. "Pig liked to point a pistol at my head and pull the trigger to see me flinch. There were times I hurt so much." Jackson swallowed hard, almost unable to say it. "I w-w-wished Pig loaded that damn gun. So he'd put a bullet in my brain to end my misery."

Mangus drew a sharp breath. "Kid...don't dwell on that. You were under extreme stress and pain. It's okay."

Jackson grabbed hold of the next memory. He needed a release. "Toad tied a rope around my ankles and hung me from that same damn oak tree. He covered me with red ants and spun me around while the ants stung me. My skin was on fire. The motion sickness made me puke upside down then I passed out."

One little tickle, bite, then another. Jackson squirmed on the bench, scratching at his body. He couldn't fight the perception of bugs crawling all over him.

Mangus grabbed his wrists. "Jackson, stop that!"

Jackson stared at the blood all over his fingernails. *What am I doing?* "Okay."

"Don't make me find a rope." Mangus released Jackson's arms. "I woke up covered by red fire ants in a foxhole at Guadalcanal. I know how much that hurts." He absent-mindedly scratched his shoulder. "I spent a week in sickbay. I had an allergic reaction and swelled up like a balloon. Your dad laughed his head off at me."

"I know. He said you were pink from head to toe when the docs covered you in lotion." Jackson chuckled. "Pink isn't a good color for you."

"No, Marines don't do pink. Do you want to stop? We can start again tomorrow after you get some sleep."

"No. I need to keep going. It's the only way to make it stop." Jackson glanced at Bandit for reassurance. The horse met his gaze and hung his head low over his stall door. The emotion in the barn was thick as molasses. *He feels my pain.*

Jason wiped his face with a handkerchief. He looked as distraught as Mangus.

Jackson concentrated on pushing his thoughts back onto the right track. "I woke up soaking wet on my belly. Dung appeared in front of me demanding information. I puked on his boots. That bastard went bananas. Toad and Pig beat the crap out of me. My head swelled up so large it looked like a black and blue watermelon. My face was covered with golf ball sized welts for a week."

Mangus shook his head. "Geez. What kept you sane?"

"Not sure I am...heard it's overrated. I never saw our chopper pilot again. He disappeared after we arrived at the camp. Dung probably killed him out of spite since I refused to talk. Our job was to rescue those Navy guys. Not get them killed. Their faces will haunt me forever."

Mangus gripped Jackson's shoulder. "I'm so sorry. That would cause anyone to have nightmares. I know it's hard, but you're doing well. What about the escape? I read the first report the army made public, but it's vague. Can you tell us what happened?"

Jackson looked at the ground. *My reputation for being ice cold under pressure is shot. I have nothing to lose. Sure couldn't hurt.* "Well, for the first few months, I spent most of my time tied up in a sweatbox at night. They would kick the sides to wake me. My normal response was *go to hell* or *xuống địa ngục*."

Jason slapped his hand on the bench. "I would've said something stronger than that."

"If you curse like Dad, I'm sure of it. Toad and Pig's comprehension of our language was limited. They understood *go to hell*. Anything else would have gone over their heads."

"Makes sense. Still..."

"I know. More is better. After six months, Toad and Pig stopped separating me from the guys. I refused to walk. Part of it was an act. But I was getting weak. Why not let them carry me everywhere since it was so important to beat the shit out of me. At night, the guards stuck our feet into foot traps, cuffed our wrists together, and tied nooses around our necks. Every two hours, they jerked on the ropes." Jackson reached to his throat when the rough hemp rope cutting into his neck shot through his brain. "We couldn't stand up. We had to shit and pee on ourselves." Unable to sit any longer, he stood.

Mangus stood with him. "Jackson, please sit down."

Jackson stuck his hands into his pockets. "I'm not going anywhere. I need to burn off some energy. I'm okay."

"Glad to hear it. This ranch is a big place. You and Jim made it a habit of finding places to hide where Sara and I couldn't find you."

"That's what made it fun." Jackson paced back and forth in front of them. "Two months before we escaped, they stopped putting those damn contraptions on our feet. That's when I planned the escape. It all came together when Bill found an old rusty nail in the dirt next to the kitchen. Chief pounded it flat on a rock with his boot heel. During the day, we took turns sawing the ropes on the bamboo fence poles while the others stood guard. Once we could squeeze through, I created a diversion."

Mangus raised his eyebrows. "What did you do?"

Jackson slowed his steps. "On the way to a beating session, I slipped in the mud during a thunderstorm. Right in front of Dung's pet. An American raccoon. Leave it to a psychopath with a Napoleon complex to want a thief as a pet. When the cage fell off the stand, it broke. Toad chased the damn thing. So did the rest of the internal guards. That gave us the chance to sneak past the perimeter guards. We slipped into the jungle, hidden by the downpour."

Mangus patted the empty space next to him. "Sit down before you collapse. You're dragging your feet. Not picking them up. You don't want to fall and break something."

"Okay." Jackson's butt hit the bench with a loud slap. "I was so sick I could barely put one foot in front of the other. The guys took turns helping me walk. We survived on anything we could find to eat. Berries, figs, uncooked frogs, bugs, even a couple of weird colored snakes. We evaded the patrols by hiding in flooded rice paddies. Chief made a bamboo float tied together with pieces of our shirts to help us cross the Ben Hai River. We humped until we came across a long-range patrol. They called in a dust-off to take us to the closest hospital."

Mangus leaned forward to make eye contact with Jackson. "I don't have enough pull with the army to sneak a copy of your medical report out of the Pentagon. They threw a classified label on the entire event. Are you okay with telling me?"

"Yeah. No one thought I'd pull through the first night. My gut was full of parasites. I had dysentery, malaria." Jackson rubbed his boot tops. *The doctors smeared pink goo on my legs. Like Uncle Manny!* "This nasty ass green fungus all over my feet. A broken left collarbone. Badly infected cuts everywhere. A half dozen broken ribs. I was on the fine line of being too far gone to survive the malnutrition. Since it could've gone either way, it surprises me that I lived. I felt so horrible. They stuck me with tubes and wires to keep me alive. The nurses shaved off my hair since it was full of lice." *My head itches.* He violently scratched his head.

Mangus grabbed Jackson's wrists.

"Let me go." Jackson tried to jerk his hands from his godfather's grasp.

"Not until you control yourself."

"Okay." Jackson rolled his head to relax his shoulder muscles.

"Better." Mangus released his vise-like grip. "You have blood running down your face." He pulled a handkerchief from his pocket and pressed it against Jackson's head. "Here, hold this."

"Yes, sir." Jackson held the cloth. "Is it okay if I finish?"

"Do you feel up to it?"

"Yeah." Jackson pulled away the bloody cloth. "Has it stopped?"

Mangus peered at the top of Jackson's head. "Yes. Thank goodness they're not deep. Sara will kill us both when she sees scratches on your scalp."

"Yeah, I'll get another lecture." Jackson chuckled. "I overheard the doctors talking the first night about my chances. They didn't know I was awake. Or maybe that was their terrible bedside manner. What a way to boost someone's morale." He cocked his head. "But now I think about it, maybe that was their point. Make me mad by saying my chances were slim to none so I wouldn't give up. Even if that was their plan, I surprised them the next morning. I could see it in their faces when they came by on their rounds. I was still alive. Not a cold, lifeless corpse." Unable to maintain his composure any longer, Jackson buried his head in Mangus' chest and wrapped his arms around Mangus' back. Time meant nothing as he cried in the silence of the barn.

"Jason, take care of the door." Mangus draped his coat around Jackson's shoulders.

Jackson felt the crushing weight lift from his heart as he pushed away from Mangus' warm chest. "You wanted to know." He wiped his runny nose on his sleeve.

Mangus massaged his neck. "Yes, we did. How do you feel? Sara will give you one hell of a lecture about that snot covered shirt."

"Yeah." Jackson wiped his nose again. "It'll go along with the one about my head. I feel better. Not great. But a little better."

"Better is good. Today was another step forward for you. As long as you tell us what you're feeling, we'll get there together. You're already dealing much better with everything. Bill told me in your cell the nightmares started when you fell asleep. Now, you're sleeping for several hours before they happen and getting a lot more rest. Given enough time, they'll go away or at least diminish."

"Sure hope it's soon." Jackson glanced up as Bandit stuck his head out of his stall and neighed.

"He wants you."

Jackson stood and handed Mangus his coat. "Thanks." He walked to the stall door. Bandit gently laid his head on Jackson's chest. This helped lift his spirit. He placed a handful of mints from his pocket under Bandit's soft muzzle.

Mangus gripped Jackson's shoulder. "Ready for breakfast? Bandit's had his."

"Yes, sir, I'm starving." Jackson grabbed his hat and coat from the peg on the wall.

"Great. So am I." Mangus' face lit up. "Let's go make my wife happy."

Jackson put on his hat. His spine straightened. A confidence he hadn't felt in years surged through him. He was once again that young Special Forces soldier, ready to take on all the odds.

Jason placed a hand on Jackson's arm. "Your dad's proud of you for standing tall. Remember that."

"I know. I feel him." Jackson tapped the center of his chest. "Here." He pushed the door open and three men left the barn, in step, headed for the house.

Right after lunch, Jackson turned Bandit out into the pasture. He watched from the fence with a pocket full of peppermints. The horse trotted over and nuzzled the hand containing treats. He rammed his head full-force into Jackson's chest, peppermint slobber dripping from his mouth.

Jackson nearly fell off the fence rail. Chuckling, he jumped off and cleaned his sticky hands on his jeans. In the mood to have a little fun, he walked along the fence with the horse mirroring his movements.

"Ahem!"

Jackson slid to a stop. Mangus stood a few feet away. "Come on over. It's okay. I feel a lot better."

Bandit flicked his ears forward and snorted as Mangus strolled up.

Mangus leaned on the fence. "So I noticed. Bandit wants to play. Why don't you give it a try? Please don't fall down and get stepped on."

I want to ride, but Uncle Manny said no. Playing with Bandit will have to do. For now. Jackson scrambled over the fence. Bandit laid his head on Jackson's shoulder, confirmation of a permanent partnership and total trust between the two living beings.

Jackson started at a slow jog, the horse trotting along beside him. He reversed course with Bandit chasing him. After a few minutes, they stopped, facing each other. Bandit stuck his head in Jackson's chest.

Jackson stroked the animal's neck, laying his head between the horses' ears. He felt some of the black ooze slide away from his spirit and the veil lifted. Light peeked through the opening.

"What's going on?" Chief asked as he, Ty, Bill and Mikey walked up behind Mangus.

"Bandit has bonded with him. Jackson did this with his academy horse. Firefly would do anything he asked. It's a good thing because if he's ever thrown, Bandit won't leave him."

Jackson jogged to the fence with Bandit on his heels. They stopped in front of his friends on the other side. Bandit placed his head on Jackson's shoulder, eyeing the group watching them.

"Why don't you take him in? I'm cold, so I know you are." Mangus flipped the collar of his sheepskin coat up around his ears.

"Not really, but okay, if that's what you want." Winded, Jackson's words came between short pants. After a deep breath, he walked to the barn door. The horse followed him, off lead. As he led Bandit into the stall, the chilly air seeped into his sweaty clothes. He pulled the blanket from a wall hook, threw it over Bandit's back and buckled the straps.

"Are you okay?" asked Mangus.

Jackson peered over Bandit's back at his godfather on the other side. "Yeah. I don't want him to get cold."

"Good. I was worried when you didn't come out of the barn."

"Sorry." Jackson shut the stall door.

Bandit poked his head over the top, stomped his front feet and flipped his head back and forth.

"I'm only a treat dispenser." Jackson produced another piece of candy from his pocket and held it out in his open palm.

Mangus petted the horse. "He likes you. I don't think it's the treats, kid."

"I like him too. What about riding?"

Mangus pointed his finger at Jackson. "Don't push your luck. When the doctor and I agree you're ready. You're not ready."

Crap. Caught at my own game.

Bill stopped Mangus and Jason when they exited the barn. He waited until Jackson went into the bunkhouse before saying anything. He didn't want his friend mad at him for butting in. "Can I talk to you, sir?"

Mangus cocked his head. "Sure."

Bill gathered up his courage. *The general told us about his friends tortured at Bataan. A few techniques remind me of those used on Jackson.* "I need to talk about a few things. The guards in the POW camp did some...*How do I say this*...uhh...awful stuff to Jackson."

"Keep going, Bill. I need to know."

General Malone and Jason served in two wars. They understand how much the human body can take before the mind breaks completely. "Has he told you anything?"

Mangus shook his head. "Yes, but what do you want to talk about."

Bill rubbed the back of his neck. "Dung beat Jackson constantly. He'd disappear then reappear beaten to a pulpy, swollen mound of flesh. We were always being dragged into the square to witness punishment. Dung liked to show us what refusal to cooperate would get us. His favorite was outright execution. Toad would tie Dung's target of the day to a telephone pole and blow his head off with a shotgun then leave the body to rot. One day it was Jackson tied to that pole."

Mangus' eyes flashed like a lightning storm. "What?"

Unable to take the pressure, Bill crawled into himself. *Please stop looking at me like that. I can't breathe.*

"Bill, you're acting like Jackson." Mangus gripped Bill's shoulder. "Tell me something. Do you have PTSD?"

"Yes, sir. I'm sure I do." Bill tugged his collar away from his throat so he could breathe. "It's not as bad as Jackson's. I have bad dreams and flashbacks every once in a while. I'm dealing with it."

"You sound like him too. Bill, if you need help, ask. We're willing to listen." Mangus dropped his arm to his side. "Sorry for interrupting. Keep going if you want."

"Thanks, I need to talk. It bothers me Dung forced us to watch this. Since Dung couldn't execute the camp's senior ranking prisoner while he was unconscious, Toad dumped a bucket of water on Jackson's head. That wart-faced asshole was the bane of Jackson's existence as Dung's senior interrogator. His blubber butt buddy Pig wasn't too far behind as his shadow. Dung stood in front of Jackson when he opened his eyes."

"What happened?" Mangus asked.

"Jackson told him off in English and Vietnamese. At the same time. And it wasn't nice. Think about what you'd never call your mother or your wife for a better picture. He questioned Dung's parentage. Said his parents were brother and sister. Then he called Dung's mother and father buck-toothed hillbilly kissin' cousins. What an American way to call his family inbred."

Mangus raised an eyebrow. "You're kidding?"

A hunting hawk on the horizon caught Bill's attention. He watched it dive to the ground and catch a mouse. *That's what I feel like, trapped, and dinner.* He returned his gaze to Mangus. "No, sir. I don't think Dung understood the reference. Next, he compared Colonel Dung's father to a dog, saying he and his wife did it doggy style. He said Dung's mother had great pussy, and his father wasn't his father, but the farmer down the road. He told Dung to *di đâu di đó di ăn cứt chó.*"

"What's that mean?"

"You go somewhere else, you dog shit eater whore."

"It fits. What happened next."

"Toad punched Jackson in the gut and the chest. Then Toad pulled out the shotgun, shoved it in Jackson's ear and pulled the trigger. It went click. I flinched. Jackson didn't. He was unconscious." Bill dropped his head. He thought Jackson died from internal injuries. That his heart burst.

"Bill, look at me," Mangus commanded.

Bill forced his head up. "Yes, sir."

"I know this is hard. Can you keep going?"

"Yes, sir. Toad cut Jackson down and dragged him away. A couple of days later, we saw him again. Toad dumped him in the sweatbox next to Dung's quarters. Jackson was a little too crucial to Dung's career and the North Vietnamese war effort to kill. They wanted information out of him."

"I would be a whimpering blob of jelly on the floor. Did they leave him alone for a while?"

Bill sighed. *The words are hard to say.* "No. Toad still took him in for interrogation several days a week. Jackson was always covered in deep infected cuts and bruises. Toad shoved him to the ground to burst open the scabs, so the pus and blood oozed out. That's why he didn't want anyone to touch him. Too many painful run-ins with the guards."

Mangus nodded. "He's pushed through that. He let us see the scars on his back."

"He did? I didn't know."

"What about his left arm? Jackson said Toad broke it but not much else. I heard through the grapevine the army almost retired him because of it."

Bill chewed on his lower lip. This he didn't want to talk about. He talked around it. "Toad broke it good. The bones weren't straight since the camp medic didn't set them properly. After we escaped, the orthopedic

215

surgeon didn't want to mess with it. He'd have to re-break the arm to fix the problem. Dr. McKay didn't want to attempt such an invasive surgery with Jackson already dealing with so many health problems."

"Did he ever tell you about what they did to him alone?"

Bill kicked a rock at the barn wall. "No. We asked him several times. Jackson told us to…well, he was more civil with us than CID."

"When did CID talk to him?"

"The hospital."

Mangus groaned. "What happened?"

"CID debriefed me and Major Russell first. We told them everything we knew. They kept harping on what happened to Jackson. Asking what Dung and Toad did to him all those months in that hut in the back of camp. We didn't know. Things went sideways when CID interviewed him. They got what they deserved when the lead investigator ordered him to talk. Jackson exploded into a rage. He threw things from his bedside table at them and cursed like a sailor. The stress caused his blood pressure and heart rate to spike. His doctors forced the investigators to back off. When he wouldn't calm down, they sedated him to stabilize his medical condition."

"The same thing happened in Korea when I told him about his dad." Mangus blew his nose into a handkerchief. "A nurse stuck something in his IV as the doctor reamed me a new one. Jackson was still in serious condition. The bullet came within inches of his heart. My bad news made things worse. But he didn't throw things at me. He gripped his dad's dog tags so tight, his knuckles turned white. The tags left a deep cut in his palm."

A wolf howled in the distance. Bill glanced toward the sound, as did Mangus and Jason. "Those damned CID guys were in too much of a rush to finish their stupid ass reports. They should've waited a few days for him to get stronger. When the docs told us what happened, Major Russell and I went to check on him. I couldn't understand why the doctors even allowed them in the room. Jackson looked like shit. The nurses propped him up on a half dozen pillows. He was too weak to sit up and couldn't breathe lying down. Why would you interview someone with an oxygen mask on his face, a feeding tube in his nose, and IVs stuck in his arms to keep him alive? Once the boneheads finished debriefing us, they left without getting a statement from him. The investigators didn't want the doctors on their case if his condition crashed again. Somehow, he fell through the cracks of the medical bureaucracy. That's why the problem's popped up now."

"Poor kid." Jason glanced at Mangus, who nodded in agreement

Mangus gripped Bill's shoulder. "Thanks. He's told me a lot. But that tells me more. And it helps you too.

"Yes, sir." Bill pulled the St. Michael's medal on his dog tag chain from under his shirt and rubbed it between his fingers. A survival gift from Jackson. He gave the unit matching engraved ones to wear for luck.

"I have a question. How'd Jackson finagle his release from the hospital before he was ready?"

"Ahhh…He intimidated his doctor into signing the release papers by standing toe-to-toe with him. As he towered over the poor guy, he gave him that patented icy cold glare he gave you. Jackson gained a reputation in 'Nam for his ability to kill without remorse. It's not at all accurate. He hates to kill, but to think about it can put you on a cold slab in a body bag headed for Arlington. The doctor backed down. It scared the living crap out of him."

"Yeah, Jackson's evil glare doesn't work on me. I do know when that hard-headed kid wants something, he doesn't back down."

Bill inhaled for a count of three to slow his thoughts then exhaled. His lips twitched in repressed laughter at watching this play out in front of him. *Jackson's a master technician of strong-arm diplomacy. Not even Teddy Roosevelt can hold a candle to him.* "Yes, sir. They did compromise. The negotiation process wound up pretty one-sided. I'm sure you know which side did all the talking. To escape the hospital, Jackson agreed to a month-long leave in Hawaii. He threw in one caveat. Hotel reservations and leave paperwork for us to stay with him. It was the first time I received an all-expenses-paid vacation from the army. He took it easy for about a week, lounging on the beach until he was bored out of his skull. Then he ran around the island, and I don't mean like a tourist."

"I know my godson. I'm sure it has something to do with horses."

A picture of Jackson in the lobby of the Hilton with a bag of peppermints in his hand flashed into Bill's thoughts. "Come to think of it. He told me about a horse ranch on the north side of Oahu. I didn't put it together until now why he did so well in Hawaii. He gained over half the weight the doctor requested eating lots of fresh fruits and vegetables in the local restaurants. I think Jackson unconsciously knew about his stomach. He stayed away from anything fried and, thank goodness, the SPAM." Bill's face screwed into one of disgust. *The pink ham-colored substance makes me want to puke.* "I can't eat that crap. It looks and smells like canned dog food. He didn't throw up again until he returned to 'Nam and lost most of the weight he gained."

Mangus nodded. "Thanks for the info. It tells me a lot."

"No. Thank you. For listening. I needed to talk."

March 8, 1973

Jackson opened his eyes at 0500 hours. *What the hell? I slept all night. No nightmare.* He stretched his limbs then climbed out of his bunk. *Good, everyone's asleep.* Slow and easy, he padded in the darkness to the bathroom and exited as softly. He started with the weights and shifted to the bag. As he wrapped his hands, the door opened.

Chief peeked around the corner. "You had a quiet night, boss."

Jackson's lips twitched. The air felt cool on his front teeth. "Yep. It's nice to wake up to silence and dry shorts." He nodded at the bag as Chief helped him slip on the gloves. "Want to hold it?"

"Yes, sir."

For twenty minutes, Jackson honed his technique. A picture of improving power and grace. Words and grunts of exertion between the loud slaps of leather on canvas. He felt like a boxer instead of a free-swinging maniac.

The smell of sweaty leather permeated the room as Jackson removed his gloves. He winked at his friends in the open door then climbed on the treadmill for his morning run.

Mangus and Jason pushed through the crowd into the room.

Bill nodded to Mangus then herded Ty, Chief and Mikey into the main living area.

Mangus stood next to the treadmill. "You didn't have a nightmare last night?"

"No, sir." Jackson panted, quickening his pace. "Slept like a rock. My demons are still there. They'll make fewer visits now I've put a lot of things to bed."

"Yes, you have since you're talking to us. Just to let you know, I spoke with Dr. Howard about your improvement. He took it on himself to speak with a psychiatrist friend about your case. It shocked him that you're doing it without drugs. I'll call the good doctor back this evening about your first quiet night."

"They depend on drugs way too much. And I wouldn't take them anyway."

"I know." Mangus rubbed his hands together. "After breakfast, I'll ask Dr. Wells to come check you out. If he gives you the green light, then you have it from me."

Jackson eyeballed his godfather. "You were waiting for me to calm down first?"

"Yes." Mangus pointed at Jackson. "I was afraid you might do something rash if you had trouble coping. You needed to gain some strength and muscle first. Finish up with your workout. I'll see you at breakfast."

Sweat running into his eyes, Jackson flipped his head. He flashed a grin as Mangus wiped his face with a towel.

Mangus nodded to Jason. "Let's go back to the house."

"Yes, sir." Jason turned on his heel.

Mangus followed him out of the room.

Four heads popped around the doorframe.

"Looking good, sir." Mikey clapped like a seal wanting a fish.

Bill patted the doorjamb. "I'll start a pot of coffee for you."

"I already took my shower. The tank will be hot when you finish." Ty pulled the towel from around his neck.

Chief winked then ducked back from the doorframe.

All the extra encouragement had an up side. Jackson finished three miles at a reasonably fast pace. Less than an eight-minute mile. Full of energy, he hopped off the treadmill like a tightly wound spring, propelling himself almost two feet in the air. On the downward arc, he grabbed a towel off the wall to dry his sweaty face. Still feeling on top of the world, he pulled a set of clean clothing out of the dresser. At the bathroom door, Chief handed him a protein shake. "Do you know how bad those things taste?"

Chief gave him a cheesy smile. "Don't care, boss. Drink it anyway."

Jackson drank the entire glass, grimacing at the aftertaste. *The chocolate makes it more palatable. The crap still tastes like cardboard.* Today, with a new attitude and outlook on life, he took a Special Forces shower. A quick and efficient use of water. In and out in less than ten minutes. *Why waste my time if I don't need to?* He whistled the theme to *Bonanza* as he sashayed to the barn for his morning chores

At 1000 hours, Jackson fidgeted in a living room chair as Dr. Wells placed the stethoscope on his chest and checked his blood pressure.

"Someone's excited this morning," Dr. Wells said in the backwoods country accent of a Montana native. "Your pulse is 120."

"Hurry up. I've got things to do." Jackson tapped his foot on the floor. *This medical stuff's ridiculous. I feel great.*

Dr. Wells slipped his stethoscope into his lab coat pocket. "Your heart sounds good, your lungs are clear, and your blood pressure is excellent. Mikey gave me a copy of Dr. Rose's last exam. One more thing, go to the bathroom and get on the scale. I want to check your weight."

"Awww, Doc. Why?"

"Either get on the scale, or I say no." Dr. Wells crossed his arms. "Which is it?"

"I'm going, I'm going." Jackson walked to the bathroom his friends behind him. He climbed on the scale. "Well?"

Dr. Wells bent to check the reading. "Excellent. You've gained eleven pounds since you left Mississippi." He squeezed Jackson's bicep. "And most of it's muscle in your arms and chest. You have your clearance to ride."

"Woohoo!" Jackson jumped off the scale. He spotted Sara's face in the crowd at the doorway. He kissed her cheek then bulldozed his way through the blockade. His excitement grew exponentially as he sprinted to the barn. Feeling more like a kid than a grown man who'd been through so many painful horrors.

As Jackson threw the saddle over Bandit's back, the barn door squeaked. Footsteps signaled the approach of several people. He glanced under Bandit's bridled head at his friends. "Did I leave you guys in the dirt? You're a little slow today." After cinching the saddle, he tied a coiled rope to the horn. He turned when a hand fell on his shoulder.

"Here." Mangus handed Jackson a 30-30-lever action Winchester rifle. "Take this for your protection."

Jackson cocked the lever to insert a round in the chamber. He slipped the rifle into the scabbard. *Nice.*

Ty, Bill, Mikey, and Chief's eyes shifted between him and the gun.

"I'm okay, guys. Really. I'm not about to do something stupid."

Mangus came over to stand with the men. "You've heard the wolves, right? It's winter, and they're hungry. The pack will go after anything they find, including cattle and riders on horses."

Mikey patted his legs. "What about the chaps, sir?"

Jackson smiled at the naïve question. "I'm riding, not herding cattle. The chaps are to protect your legs from brush and thorny vegetation. I'm only going to the pasture."

Before leading the horse to the adjoining paddock, Jackson buttoned his coat. He slipped on his gloves, pulled his stocking hat over his ears, and placed his cowboy hat on top. *There's two feet of snow on the ground. I don't intend to go far. It's too cold. All I want is to see how well Bandit responds to me.*

A large audience stood on the other side of the fence. Even Sara. She had a brilliant smile of pure love lighting her face.

In one fluid, practiced motion, Jackson grabbed the reins and mounted his horse. The weight of the world lifted from his shoulders as his right foot slipped into the stirrup. He queued Bandit into a walk using his voice and legs. He put the horse through his paces. First a trot then a full gallop across the field. They finished with several lazy figure eights. Bandit backed up at his command. Snow shot up in the air from Bandit's hooves. *I have to teach Bandit the piaffe, pirouette, and half-pass. He's more sure-footed than Firefly. He'd make an excellent dressage horse. Maybe better than Firefly.*

Mangus walked up to Bandit as Jackson dismounted. "Want to be my stock manager? I need a second foreman to help out Cruthers."

"Yes, sir!" Jackson held onto Bandit's bridle when he bucked. The horse was wound up. He wanted to run. And Jackson wanted the wind in his face. "It'll give me the opportunity to perfect my roping skills. I'm a little rusty."

"A little rusty? They're probably downright corroded. The job is yours."

"Great." Jackson grabbed his rope off the horn. "I'll get right to work."

CHAPTER 18

March 30, 1972

Jackson stopped Bandit on the hill overlooking the ranch and looked across the rolling pastures split by barbed wire fences. The yellow-orange sun hovered just above the trees to the west. He was tired. It had been a long day and an even longer night. Yesterday had been a reminder of his past. Flashbacks had kept him from falling asleep the night before. Battles. Lost friends. Dung.

The Vietnam War, at least for American troops was over. A bitter stalemate with a staggering loss of life. All for nothing.

"The war's over, Bandit. I'm frustrated. Angry. They wouldn't let us win. Protesters spit on the soldiers coming home. Soldiers who served this country with honor and courage. It's not fair. None of this is fair."

Bandit bobbed his head.

"I thought you'd agree. The American public is fickle."

Jackson turned Bandit back the way they had come and rode down the hill.

After putting Bandit in his stall, he headed to the bunkhouse. He walked through the door and immediately tripped. Only his hand on a support beam kept him from running headfirst into the wall.

Two dresser drawers sat on the floor in front of the door. Mikey stood on the other side of them looking guilty.

"What are you doing, Mikey? What is all this?"

"Packing. Dr. Wells invited me to come stay at his house. Hope you don't mind?" Mikey clipped his green army surplus duffle bag closed. "You're getting better every day."

Jackson bit down on his emotions. He didn't want his friends to know the demons still hovered in the distance. Mikey had a right to his own life. It took effort, but he forced a smile and exuberance in his voice. "No, that's great. You can jumpstart your dream. Get your ass in gear. Go."

"Yes, sir." Mikey slung the bag over his shoulder and ran out the door.

"What a knucklehead." Jackson put the drawers back where they belonged. It cut a little that Mikey was leaving. But his friend deserved to find his path in life. Mikey would be a great doctor one day.

222

After a restless night troubled by dreams of Vietnam, Jackson got out of bed. He saw Ty and Bill packing their duffle bags. *Them too?* Jackson leaned against the wall with his arms crossed. It helped control his sudden sadness. "Mikey's leaving to train with the doctor, I understand and fully support. Where are you two going?"

Ty pointed at his bunk. "We need privacy."

"No." Jackson refused to allow himself to feel sad about this newest loss. He decided to rag his friends instead. "You're tired of Chief and me being on your backs about the mess. We can't stand the dirty underwear and clothing all over the place. The bathroom looks like a hair factory." He wiped his finger across the dresser and held it up. "See, hair. Both of you are slobs. I can't believe you guys were ever in the army. If you'd clean up after yourselves, we'd shut up."

"That's okay. I found a nice little two-bedroom house in Beaver Creek." Bill picked up his clothes from the floor, sniffed them, and stuffed everything into his bag.

"How are you going to pay for it?" Jackson brushed his filthy hand on his jeans.

"With what the general pays us. Ty's family's sending him money via their lawyers to help out. Thank goodness for the post office. They make it easy to set up dead drops. The intelligence guys are stupid."

Ty wiggled his eyebrows. "I have to maintain my image."

"As what? A hippie. You need a haircut." Jackson turned around. He didn't want to see Ty sulk. His dark curly hair looked like a fuzzy mop. "What about you, Chief?"

"No way." Chief kicked back on his bunk. "Staying at your side is a matter of honor. I owe you my life."

"It's okay if you want to go."

"Nope. I have more privacy here than I ever had in the army or at home. You're the best roommate I could ever ask for...now that you don't wake me up screaming or cursing in Vietnamese anymore. You're neat, quiet, and always have a book in your hand. The general pays me good. Sara feeds me excellent meals. I can't ask for more."

Jackson tipped his cowboy hat to his friend. "Thanks buddy. That means a lot coming from you."

Every time Jackson saw the news reports about the POWs returning home during Operation Homecoming, he would hang his head. Sadness would wash over him. Desolation knocked him in the head. But he refused to cry. He'd done enough crying.

On May 24th, 1973, during the evening news broadcast, Jackson felt someone had kicked him in the gut. The President was holding a party for the repatriated POWs. And he wasn't invited.

Jackson went into the kitchen and stared out the window at the world beyond. All he could see were visions of Dung, Toad and Pig. And objects. The rack. The oak tree. His metal box. A bull whip. Even farm implements gave him the shivers from time to time. His demons still lurked under the surface. Just not as strong.

"Are you okay?" Mangus asked.

Jackson shook himself to reality. He faced the man he respected the most in his life. "Yeah, I guess. At least the government made an effort to get them home. If that same government would admit they were wrong about us, everything would be great. We know that's not going to happen, is it? Not with what they keep saying about me."

Mangus tapped his folded newspaper on the countertop. "Maybe someday it will. I know it's hard to take after how you came home. Keep moving forward. We'll finish the journey together. You've fought hard to get this far. Be happy for those men."

"I'm happy for them. I wish I was one of them. Not AWOL with my honor and reputation gone. It hurts so much when they call me a traitor. Then to see those men being honored as heroes. It hurts even more. I went through the same crap and nearly died. The army refuses to address the issue. Don't get me started on the Medal of Honor. Has that helped me? No! It's as much a secret as being a POW."

"All you're doing is getting upset." Mangus glanced at the window. "Why don't you go play with Bandit?"

Jackson looked at Bandit grazing in the pasture. He grabbed a bag of peppermints off the shelf. After he walked up to the fence, Bandit trotted over and rammed his head into Jackson's chest, knocking him off balance. Jackson grabbed his buddy around the neck. The touch made him feel better. His melancholy faded into the dark box of his demons.

Bandit stomped his front feet.

Jackson fed Bandit a few treats and a handful to himself. His enthusiasm, passion and zest for life returned. He felt like a wound-up bunny.

To burn off the energy, he played with Bandit in their version of tag. He'd slap Bandit's nose or hindquarters when he galloped past. Bandit nosed him in the back or used his head to flip Jackson's legs out from under him as he ran across the pasture.

Jackson bent over with his hands on his knees, sucking in deep breaths. He looked at Mangus in the kitchen window. "This could've gone in the wrong direction if Uncle Manny didn't get my mind on something else."

June 9, 1973

Another big red horse entered Jackson's life. Secretariat. Caught up in the excitement of a possible Triple Crown champion, Jackson bought all three national magazines with Secretariat on the cover. *Time*, *Newsweek*, and *Sports Illustrated*.

His first set wore out with the covers falling off. The second set wound up dog-eared, then he secured them in his battered footlocker for safekeeping.

While Jackson waited for the Belmont Stakes to start, he couldn't sit still. He walked around the living room waving the newspaper with Secretariat's picture in the sports section. "Anyone betting on Sham?"

Ty shook his head. "Nope, but I like Private Smiles. Sounds like Mikey."

"That horse has never won a race. Ain't gonna happen." Jackson threw popcorn at Ty.

"Hey, why not. But I'm not going to make waves. Secretariat's my pick." Mikey pulled a cookie out of the package on the end table next to the couch.

"Same here, Secretariat." Chief grabbed another beer can.

"What about you, Bill?" Ty leaned back in the recliner with his hands behind his head.

"Secretariat all the way. Sorry, but you're outvoted, Ty." Bill popped the tab off his beer can.

Jackson couldn't resist. "Okay, Ty. Make you a deal. If your horse wins, I clean your nasty house."

Ty clapped his hands together. "Sounds good."

"Let me finish. If Secretariat wins, you shine my boots for six months."

"Deal." Ty held out his hand.

Jackson slapped his palm.

Once the broadcast started, Jackson stood the entire time. He jumped up and down as Secretariat ran down the final stretch. "Go, go, go!" he screamed at the television screen over Chic Anderson's track call. "Secretariat is widening now! He is moving like a tremendous machine." At the point Secretariat crossed the finish line thirty-one lengths in front of the next horse as the ninth Triple Crown champion, Jackson grabbed his hat and rifle.

Mangus blocked his route to the front door. "Is something wrong, Jackson?"

"No, sir." Jackson hopped back and forth. He had a new mission. Nothing could stop him now. "Just have some extra training for Bandit in the south pasture."

"What kind of training?"

"It's a surprise." Jackson grabbed his cowboy hat and headed to the barn.

CHAPTER 19

June 15, 1973

Jackson loved his new life. Being a cowboy gave him a freedom he never had in the army. The ability to go anywhere at any time. No orders. No rank. His only responsibilities were to his godparents and friends. He could do his job without someone looking over his shoulder.

After a long day of chasing cattle, he walked into the house and sat at the table to read the newspaper. He looked up at Sara standing in the kitchen doorway. "What are you doing, Aunt Sara?"

"Comparing you to the picture I took in January." Sara waved the small photo in her hand.

"Why?"

"I wanted to see how much you've changed."

"Okay." Jackson cocked his head. "But that doesn't answer my question?"

"Well, in this picture, you look a lot older than thirty-eight. Your eyes are haunted and sunk into your face. Today, they are clear and bright." Sara picked up a framed photograph from the counter. "This is from your graduation from Special Forces selection when you were a twenty-six-year-old Captain."

"Still not understanding, Aunt Sara."

"Now that you eat like your horse instead of an infant and gained over twenty-five pounds, you look more like you did in this picture. Jackson, I'd swear you're ten years younger. Your clothes fit now instead of looking like you're wearing potato sacks." Sara giggled. "And your upper body is so muscled up you look like this guy." She produced a picture of the bodybuilder, Frank Zane, from her apron pocket.

"Are you drooling, Aunt Sara? What would Uncle Manny think?" Jackson leaned on his elbows and rested his chin on his palms.

"Oh hush up. Can't an old woman dream a little? You look so much like your dad did at your age. Kim loved to watch him walk around the house without a shirt. He worked out almost as much as you."

"Yeah, I remember Dad in the garage with the weights."

Sara looked at the framed picture. "You know, in this, you don't look twenty-six either. You look like a baby-faced teenager."

"Let me see that picture." Jackson held out his hand.

Sara handed it over. "I want that back."

"Yes, Aunt Sara." Jackson stared at the picture for several seconds. "You're right. That's why Harry called me *kid* during Special Forces training. He said I fudged my age on my enlistment papers. He couldn't believe I was old enough to have served in the Korean War to earn all those medals."

"Yeah. Mangus was so proud when he saw you at Pendleton right before you reported to West Point. You had sergeant stripes on your sleeves with a Combat Infantry badge, Paratrooper wings, a Distinguished Service Medal, Soldiers Medal, and two Purple Hearts on your dress uniform. He said you were a real hero for taking command of your platoon."

"All I did was my job." *Why does everyone make a big deal out of nothing?*

June 30, 1973

Mangus opened the front door after the doorbell rang. "Nice to see you again, Dr. Howard. How was your flight?"

"Better than the long drive from Billings. I told you to call me Frank. Thanks for the invite to check on Jackson." Frank carried his army duffle bag into the house.

The two men walked into the living room and sat on the couch. Mangus handed Frank the last report from Dr. Wells.

"Wow, Jackson's pushing 160 pounds now. Blood pressure 110/70. His liver and kidney function tests are normal. Excellent."

Mangus and Frank looked up when someone knocked on the front door.

Sara led Harry Russell and his wife Gabby into the living room.

Frank pointed at the infant in Harry's arms. "Does Jackson know?"

Harry's eyes twinkled. "Nope."

At 1601 hours, Mangus glanced at his watch. "Jackson's never late on Saturdays. He always stops by the house to give me the weekly report."

Harry handed the baby to his wife. "Do you think something's wrong?"

"Don't know. Other than an occasional nightmare, he's been doing good." Mangus pointed at the door. "Let's go."

Their first stop, the bunkhouse. It was empty.

Mangus doubled-timed to the barn. His worry mounted with each passing minute.

Harry and Frank ran to keep up with him.

Bandit was in his stall, brushed and fed.

"Well, he's around here somewhere." Mangus headed to the workshop. Empty. Jackson's beat-up work truck was parked out front. "Where in the hell is he?" *I hope his demons didn't pop up. Nobody's heard a gunshot. That kid knows all the hiding places. He wouldn't want to leave a mess for us to clean up.*

Mangus stopped his foreman, Larry, walking toward the barn. "Have you seen Jackson?"

Larry pointed over Mangus' shoulder. "Yes, sir. He's in the foaling barn with Lady."

Mangus rolled his eyes. "I'm an idiot." Not breaking stride, he led the way to the smallest barn on the ranch. Before Mangus walked through the wide-open door, he turned, put a finger to his lips, and entered the building. Twenty feet away stood the object of his search, draped over the stall door on crossed arms. Due to the heat, Jackson had dressed down, wearing a white t-shirt with a towel tucked into the back pocket of his jeans. Walking up behind him, Mangus leaned on the rail. "How are things going?"

"Take a look for yourself." Jackson pointed at the chestnut mare on the stall floor. "The front feet are showing, so it should be soon. I came to check on her before I headed to the house. Lady was restless when I walked in, so I stayed. Sorry if I worried you."

Mangus patted Jackson's shoulder. "No, it's okay. You made the right call. I'm letting you run the stock operation. It was my mistake. I didn't think about Lady foaling today. By the way, you have some long overdue visitors who've traveled over a thousand miles to see you."

"Who? Where?"

"Behind you, JJ."

Jackson spun around at the familiar voice. He closed the distance in three long strides and grabbed Harry in a bear hug. He refused to let go until Harry kicked him in the shin. Wiggling his toes to get rid of the numb feeling, he turned to Frank and extended his hand.

Frank brushed the hand aside. His arms enveloped Jackson like a vise. Patting him on the back and swaying back and forth.

"It's good to see you too." Jackson raised his elbows to pry himself out of the man's grasp.

Frank backed up. "You look terrific, Jackson."

"Thanks. I could take on the world right now. It's much nicer than when we met."

"What's going on over there?" Frank pointed at the stall.

"Come take a look." Jackson waved them over to the stall door. "Lady's about to drop her foal."

Mangus, Frank, and Harry crowded around him as the foal's feet came out, the nose, then the head and neck.

Jackson went into the stall, pulled the towel from his pocket, and wiped the membrane off the foal's muzzle. This allowed the baby to breathe without obstruction. A grunting noise caught his attention. The mare was straining to push out the foal. Jackson grabbed the front feet, and gently pulled with each contraction. He rotated the foal from side to side until it slid out onto the ground. The foal plopped onto its side. A small whinny escaped his mouth. Jackson checked the foal's breathing and levered him onto his belly. His hand brushed the bump between the hind legs. "It's a colt, Uncle Manny." He exited the stall, drying his hands on the towel.

"Good. With Lucky Cheyenne as his father, he'll bring a good price when we sell him."

Lady scrambled to her feet and started licking her foal clean.

Jackson leaned against the stall door as his friends stood next to him. *What a great day.*

Harry pointed at the colt. "How long until he stands?"

"Say…thirty minutes or so."

The barn went silent as the colt stuck out his front legs and pushed up with his hind legs. His legs splayed out from under him, and he fell down.

"Come on, boy, one more time. I know how it feels." Jackson knocked on the stall door with his knuckles.

The colt stumbled to his feet and stayed up on wobbly legs. Lady sidled up next to him. He pushed his nose under her belly and latched onto a teat.

"He's eating. Let's give them some peace and quiet." Jackson grabbed his shirt from a wall hook and exited the barn.

Mangus, Frank, and Harry followed him outside.

Harry spoke up first. "That was incredible."

230

"A new life always is. I've delivered a few babies but never seen a horse give birth before." Frank pointed at Jackson. "I guess you have since you knew what to do."

"Yep, not my first time." Jackson flipped the shirt over his shoulder then glanced at his watch. "The guys are probably here by now. I need to shower and change clothes. Are you guys going to join us?"

Harry's face screwed into a quizzical look. "For what?"

"Remember our little get-togethers before a mission?"

"Great. Dare I ask who's bringing the food?"

"Ty and Bill drew the short straw for the food." Jackson winked at Harry. "Chief bought the beer…of course. Mikey chose the dessert, and since I'm a little tied up, I hope someone started the fire."

Mangus grinned. "I'm sure one of them did."

Harry held up his wedding ring. "JJ, you do remember I'm married now?"

Jackson paused for a few seconds. "Yeah, I vaguely remember you telling me that. Her name's Gabby, right?"

"Correct."

"Go grab your wife while I take a shower. I won't make a good impression on her covered in the blood and afterbirth from a mare."

"Roger." Harry gave him a thumbs up. He and Mangus headed to the house

Jackson pulled on Frank's sleeve. "Come on." They walked to the bunkhouse.

Jackson placed his foot on the bench of their wooden A-frame picnic table. He watched Chief throw logs into the glowing fire pit. "Thanks for starting the fire. Lady decided today's the day."

Chief turned after he covered the coals with a grate. "Colt or filly?"

"Colt."

"I'll have to go by later and check him out. Red like mom or brown like dad?"

"Red, with a blaze and socks on the two back feet."

Chief let out a boisterous laugh. "He'll be spoiled with you around."

"Funny. Be back in a few." Jackson walked into the bunkhouse. *Wait, those two don't know each other. Mikey told me he was the only one who spoke to Frank on the plane.* He stayed hidden in the corner of the doorway, watching Frank's reaction to Chief.

Frank cocked his head. "Socks?"

Chief pointed at his shoes. "The two back feet are white like a pair of socks. It's nice to see you again, Dr. Howard. Come to check on your wayward patient?"

"Yes, I did. Call me Frank. How're his nightmares?"

"Gone for the most part, along with the depression. Just an occasional bad dream. Since he talks about it right after they happen, including to his horse when no one else is around, they don't bother him anymore. The colonel is happy and loves it here, so he's doing great."

Frank scratched his chin. "I can see that. I almost didn't recognize him from the back since his upper body has bulked up so much. He still has skinny legs, but they have gotten larger. His waist looks like a man's, not an anorexic teenager."

Jackson shook his head. *Anorexic teenager? Really. I didn't look that bad.*

Chief stood taller at the compliment. "Yep, the colonel's worked hard to build up his legs since he lost so much muscle mass in his thighs. As for his waist until a few weeks ago, I could yank off his jeans with them buttoned. Now they fit perfectly. He uses the belt to hold his knife. Why don't we sit and talk until everyone gets here?"

Chief likes Frank. Jackson glanced at his watch. *Time for a Special Forces shower.*

Fifteen minutes later, Ty, Bill, and Mikey walked up with full paper sacks in their arms.

Mikey glanced at the open bunkhouse door. "Is the colonel okay?"

"He's taking a shower." Frank stood from the table. "One of the mares gave birth today. Jackson wound up on the icky side since he was in the stall with her. General Malone invited me here to check on Jackson. Harry's here too. He went to get his wife."

Jackson walked out of the bunkhouse with his hair still damp. "Hey, guys. Heard Frank tell you about Harry. They should be here soon. Who has grill duty? I did it last week."

"Me." Mikey's tone turned sheepish. "I'll try not to burn yours up like the last time."

"Yeah." Jackson scrunched his nose as he smacked his lips. "My burger looked like a charcoal briquette and was about as edible."

Frank pointed at the fire. "What're you guys having?"

Ty pulled everything out of the sacks on the table. "Steak and baked potatoes. Ribeyes for us. A sirloin for the colonel. The potatoes are cowboy style on the outside coals. I wish we'd known so we could've bought more food."

"Don't worry. I brought enough for the rest of us. My wife's joining us tonight," said Mangus' deep bass voice behind them. Everyone turned as Mangus set a large red ice chest next to the table.

Jackson pulled six collapsible blue canvas camp chairs out of the bunkhouse closet and set them around the fire.

Harry walked up, carrying four similar red chairs. Beside him, a dark-haired woman with a wrapped bundle in her arms.

Jackson stared as Sara set up a playpen on the grass, away from the fire. *What's that for?* He looked at the wrapped bundle. *Huh? Did Harry forget to tell me something?* He walked up to the woman standing next to Harry. "Hi, I'm Jackson."

The woman smiled. "I know who you are, JJ. Harry's told me all about you. I'm Gabby."

"It's nice to meet you." Jackson pointed at one of the chairs. "Please sit."

Gabby sat with bundle against her chest. "Thank you." She pulled the blanket back. A small brown-haired head appeared.

Harry flipped a St. John's medal on a silver chain around Jackson's neck. "Surprise. Meet Jackson Joseph Russell. Your godson."

Taken aback, Jackson felt a warmth spread through his body. He wiped a tear from his eyes. "The honor is mine. I hope to do as good a job as my godfather." *Harry got me good.*

"I know you will." Harry took the child from Gabby and faced Jackson. "Your turn."

Jackson held out his arms. "Thank you." He cradled the infant against his chest and walked around the fire, softly cooing to him.

"JJ, look this way. I want to try out my new Polaroid camera."

"Come on, Harry. Give me a few minutes."

"No. Smile." Harry put the camera to his eye.

"Whatever." Jackson tried for his cheesiest smile. Lips pulled back with his teeth showing and chin jutted out.

"You'll thank me when JJ's bigger." Harry pulled the photo from the camera and waved it back and forth.

Jackson handed little JJ to Gabby when he cried. "I think he's hungry?"

"Probably." Gabby unbuttoned her shirt, draped a large towel over her shoulder, and tucked her son underneath. Sucking noises came from under the towel.

Did she really do that? Jackson's jaw dropped. He couldn't take his eyes off Gabby.

Harry poked him in the shoulder. "You look like a tomato. It's called breastfeeding. The same as your little boy in the barn."

"Too much information." Jackson went into the bunkhouse to grab a cup of coffee. The guys deserved a chance to introduce themselves and meet the new addition to the family. As he set the coffee can on the countertop, the bunkhouse door opened. With each step behind him came the squeak of patent leather shoes. "Hey, Frank, I know it's you. Only a doctor would wear Corfams on a ranch. I hope you brought a pair of boots, or those shoes will need some serious cleaning before you wear them with your uniform."

Frank leaned against the cabinet. "Cute. I brought my combat boots, but these are broken in and comfortable. How are you doing?"

"Good. I haven't fully recovered. I'd put me at about eighty percent. I'll probably never get back to one-hundred and will deal with this for the rest of my life." Jackson tapped the side of this head. "I'll have my good days, and, unfortunately, a few bad ones when my demons pop up."

"I agree with your assessment. Where were you the last time I saw you?"

Jackson filled the empty pot with water. "That's easy, zero."

"I agree with that too. You're totally honest with me, and that's good. Did General Malone tell you I asked a psychiatrist friend about his treatment plan if you were in his care?"

"Yeah, he did." Jackson spooned four large scoops of fresh coffee into the basket. "The doctor was surprised I was doing it without drugs."

"Yes. What made the difference?"

"In my uneducated opinion, being out here with no constraints and the horse Uncle Manny gave me."

Frank's eyes widened. "The horse?"

After starting the brew cycle, Jackson turned to Frank. "Yeah, the horse. He gave me a reason to get out of bed in the mornings. I had to take care of Bandit. He's my responsibility. I fixated on him and beat the crap out of a heavy bag every morning. I could talk to Bandit when I couldn't talk to anyone else. I'm not sure I'd be here without him."

"It was that bad?" Frank cocked his head. "And the horse made that much of a difference?"

I can't tell anyone. Suicide crossed my mind that first week. One thing stopped me, Bandit. "Yes, it was that bad, and he made all the difference. Horses, like most animals, are nonjudgmental. Bandit knew I was in pain and stuck his head in my chest to comfort me."

"Wow. I can't believe an animal made such a difference. It's unique."

234

"Well, I can't speak for anyone else, but it worked for me."

Frank looked his friend up and down. "I can tell. Mangus said they can't keep you out of the refrigerator. He told me about your reaction during the Belmont. That's so out of character for you."

"True, but that was history." Jackson spread out his hands with a slight shrug. "I love horses, what else can I say, and, yes, I eat a lot now. That's why we bought a refrigerator for the bunkhouse and installed a cupboard. Sometimes we get hungry at night. No one cares if we go to the house for midnight snacks. We've startled Aunt Sara a few times in her bathrobe when she wasn't expecting us. We keep stuff here instead."

"Glad to hear it. Your huge appetite shows how far you've come in the last six months."

"Thanks. Where are you going to stay tonight? I'm sure Harry will hot bunk in the guesthouse with his wife. Do you want to sleep here or the main house?"

"My plan was to stick with you and Chief unless you don't want me to."

Jackson didn't stop to take a breath. The words poured out non-stop. "We'd love to have you stay with us. Do you want a tour of the ranch? If you do, I hope you can ride. I get up at 0500 to work out and take care of my horse. Breakfast is at 0800 hours. Be ready for a long day. I have a lot of ground to cover tomorrow."

Frank held both hands up, palms out. "Slow down, Mighty Mouth. I can hardly understand you. Yes, I can ride, and I'd love a tour. I'm in the army, so I get up early. Medically speaking, I want to see how well you move around during your workout. What about Harry?"

"Sorry. It's nice to have company for a change. Harry's never ridden a day in his life. He's a city boy. I'm not about to put him on a horse for the first time to have him fall off and need your services now that he has a family. I'll take him around in the truck after I finish my chores. In 'Nam, he told me that he always wanted a big covered porch. The main house has a nice one. He and Gabby can kick back and enjoy the ranch. Besides, Harry will be here all next week. We have plenty of time to talk. He may be on vacation, but I have to work." Jackson pointed at the door with his full coffee cup. "Let's go join the party."

Even before they walked through the open door, Jackson heard Chief regaling everyone with his version of *Born to be Wild.* Next, he belted out a new song, *Desperado,* making like he was riding a horse.

Frank stopped mid-step. "What's going on with Chief?"

"He says the song reminds him of me since my ranch duties include maintaining the fences and being AWOL makes I'm a desperado. When he heard the song on the radio last month, he pointed it out." Jackson chuckled at the irony. "He's right. The lyrics do sound like me."

"I agree with him."

"He's been practicing that song, using me as his audience and critic all month."

In full rapture, Chief had everyone's attention over the sounds of the crickets. At the end of the song, everyone stood and applauded.

Sara patted Chief on the shoulder. "You have a beautiful singing voice, honey. We need to get you on a stage somewhere and make a lot of money."

Chief kissed her cheek. "Thank you." He looked at Mikey. "See, someone thinks I sound like a real singer."

Mikey shook his head. "Guess I'm outvoted."

Jackson sat in an empty chair. He relaxed, feet out, ankles crossed, watching the clouds float overhead.

Frank pulled up a chair next to him, an open bottle in his hand. "No beer?"

"Nope. My stomach doesn't do alcohol very well now. Did Dr. Rose tell you what happened?"

Frank nodded. "About the bottle of Jack Daniels, yeah, he told me."

"There's another reason. My first day in 'Nam after being stateside for the Medal of Honor ceremony, General Thomas ordered me to report to the 6th Convalescent Center for a physical. Even though Dr. Green cleared me for full combat duty, he was on my butt about my weight. He gave me a stern warning that if I didn't follow his instructions to the letter, he would recommend forced retirement. I received written orders to report to Dr. Nicholson once a week for an evaluation of my progress." Jackson turned to look Frank in the eyes. "Bet you know how well I responded to an ultimatum."

"Yeah. Not well. What did you do?"

"I went to the local watering hole to blow off steam and got totally wasted. I started a drunken brawl with my West Point roommate." Jackson pointed at the large scar on his left forearm. "Chris threw a broken beer bottle. It cut the crap out of my arm. I don't even remember the trip to the hospital. When I woke up, Dr. Green said his staff sedated me after I tried to start another fight. The alcohol combined with the drugs gave me a huge hangover. It was too late to patch up our friendship. Chris left for his new duty assignment that morning. I don't drink because of what might happen if I drink too much."

Frank tapped his bottle on Jackson's chair. "You didn't have to tell me the story. You've come a long way to admit that to me."

"Yeah, I know. I thought I should explain."

"Are you ever going to patch things up with him?"

Jackson poked the fire with a sharp stick and followed the airborne sparks with his eyes. "If I ever get the chance, yes. I started the fight. But given my current situation, who knows when that might be."

On the other side of the fire, Mikey yelled. "Dinner's ready. Everyone grab your plates."

First in line, Mangus and Sara. Jackson stood behind them. As he stepped up to the fire, Mikey plopped the steak on his plate. Juices oozed from the meat as Jackson stabbed a baked potato in the coals with his fork. "Much better than last time, Mikey."

"Yes, sir." Mikey tapped the meat fork on the grate. "Kept a close eye on it tonight."

Jackson returned to his chair and balanced the plate in his lap.

Frank sat next to him. "That steak has to weigh two pounds. The baked potato's the size of a softball."

Jackson turned to Frank, knife in hand. "Please leave me alone for a few minutes so I can eat in peace. I'm starving. We can talk about this later."

The sun sank lower and lower until the blood-red dot snuck below the horizon. Mikey pulled out S'mores. The roaring wood fire was perfect for roasting marshmallows.

"Mmm." Jackson stuffed his face with chocolate, gooey white marshmallows, and graham crackers.

Sara poked Jackson in the shoulder. "You have chipmunk cheeks, honey." She brought up her camera. "Smile." *Click*, a flashbulb went off.

Aunt Sara and her camera. Jackson rolled his eyes. *I have chocolate on my teeth.* He licked the residue off his lips. *Hope she doesn't drag out my naked baby pictures. That would be embarrassing.* Harry handed him little JJ. He settled into the chair with his godson nestled protectively in his arms.

"Oh, that one's even better." Sara pointed her camera at them. "Hold him up so I can get your faces together." *Click*.

"Aunt Sara, you're blinding me!"

Little JJ became the focal point.

Bill tossed a paper ball in the fire. "Ty, remember when the colonel launched the food tray across his cell like a two-year-old?"

Ty tipped up his beer bottle. "Which time? There were so many. We had to wash potatoes out of his hair every week."

"Yeah. It was like scraping cement off his head. How about the day…"

Undeterred by the verbal assault, Jackson kept smiling. It didn't embarrass him anymore to hear about the events. Looking from the outside in, it was funny.

At 2145 hours, Harry stood in front of Jackson. "Sorry, buddy. We need to get little JJ into his crib."

"Okay. Easy. He's asleep. Don't wake him." Jackson gently placed his godson in Harry's waiting arms. He watched Harry and Gabby walk to the guesthouse. *It's nice to have such good friends.*

Sara and Mangus stood. She looped her arm around Mangus' extended elbow. "You kids enjoy yourselves. We're going to bed."

Jackson kissed Sara's cheek. "Have fun. I heard strange noises coming from the house last night."

"You're a brat." Sara pointed at Jackson. "I want grandchildren one of these days."

"Isn't that's what you were doing last night, Aunt Sara?"

"Hush, young man or you're grounded." Sara winked then walked with Mangus to the house.

Ty and Bill gathered the leftover food and beer.

"Where are you guys going?" Jackson looked at his watch. "It's only 2200 hours."

Bill fished his car keys out of his pocket. "To get the house presentable for Sunday dinner with our girlfriends."

"Bet it looks like a pigsty."

"Nag, nag, nag. You sound like an old woman. See you on Monday."

Bill jerked Ty's arm. Both men walked toward the driveway, each with a sack under their arm.

Mikey ran to catch up. "Can I catch a ride? The colonel has company."

Bill held out his hand. "Sure, for a price. You can help us clean up for an hour."

"I don't have a choice with no wheels." Mikey slapped Bill's palm. "Deal."

"What happened to loyalty, guys?" Jackson skipped a rock next to Ty's retreating feet.

Ty grinned over his shoulder. "Not when it comes to women, sir."

238

"Hmph!" Jackson placed his hands on the back of Frank and Chief's chairs and leaned between them. "Do you guys want to stay here or call it a night?"

"I'm going inside, boss." Chief rubbed his throat.

"Go gargle salt water to get your voice back unless you want Frank to help." Jackson grabbed the bucket next to the bunkhouse wall and dumped water on the fire to put it out.

Chief stacked the chairs against the wall. "No. I can take care of it. Don't need your doctor to help me."

Jackson grabbed his rifle from behind the bunkhouse door then spun Frank around by the shoulder. "You coming?"

"Checking on the foal?" Frank fell in step with him.

"Yep. I need to make sure he's okay for the night." Jackson whistled along the well-worn dirt path. A bounce to each step. He went inside the small barn and propped the rifle against the wall.

Lady's ears twitched with his footsteps. She nuzzled Jackson's chest as he petted her. In return, he fed her a handful of mints. Lady crunched then returned to her hay. Her foal squealed when she moved, milk dribbling from his mouth.

"Chief's right." Frank shook his finger at Jackson. "You're going to spoil that colt."

Jackson set his foot on the bottom rail of Lady's stall. "Got a question for you."

Frank copied his stance. "Sure."

"What have you heard, not what the army's telling the press?"

"They don't know where you went, and it has them stumped." Frank braced his elbows on the top rail. "The rumor circulating around CID is you're working as assassins for the highest bidder. They're trying to pin a few international murders on you, but the descriptions don't match."

Jackson stuck a piece of straw in his mouth. "We know that's not true. Anything else?"

"Yeah. An APB went out on Christmas Eve, requesting law enforcement agencies check medical facilities for a sick individual matching your description. When I pointed it out to my superiors, they told me to drop the issue if I knew what was good for me."

Lady's head jerked up when Jackson banged the rail with his toe. "Hammond calls me a liar when I couldn't hold my head up. The army announces I faked everything. They tell the police to look for a sick man.

It's hypocrisy. I would've died in that crappy cell. I have no way to prove it."

Frank leaned against the rail sideways. "Dr. Rose sent me your records and test results. He kept great notes and took pictures. If it ever comes to that, I can prove how close you came to dying."

"I've had this same discussion with Curtis. I'll tell you the same thing. If the army ever catches me, I won't go quietly. It took a lot of hard work to get this far in my recovery. I don't want to die, but I can't go through that pain again. I'll find a way out. You won't like the second option."

"No, I don't like it, but I do understand. I hope it never comes to that. If it does, I'll get you out. Even if I have to go all the way to the President."

"I thought you should know. I owe you that much."

Frank gripped Jackson's shoulder. "Thanks. It takes a lot to earn your trust."

Jackson pointed at the mare and foal. "Let's go. They're good for the night." He picked up his rifle, followed Frank outside then closed and locked the barn door.

As Jackson and Frank walked into the bunkhouse, Chief met them at the threshold. "Everything okay with the new momma?"

"Yeah, they're fine." Jackson leaned his rifle against the doorjamb then headed to the coffee pot.

Frank tossed his bag on the bunk across the aisle from Jackson's. "What's with the fan?"

"It gets stuffy in here at night." Chief plugged the cord into a socket. "The fan keep you cool and muffles the sounds of the animals. You'll love hearing the wolves howl in the early morning hours. It takes some getting used to. The colonel keeps his 30-30 next to the door in case one tries to climb in through the half-open windows."

"Thanks. Why'd they leave us alone earlier?"

Chief pulled off his shirt. Sweat gleamed on his chest. "They don't like the fire. The colonel's picked a few off prowling around the main living area. They steer clear of us. That's why the barn doors are locked at night. Don't be alarmed if he jumps up and grabs his rifle. Somethin' might be trying to get in."

Jackson set his coffee mug on the table next to his bunk. The birthday present from Uncle Manny. It was coffee-stained after months of use. He pulled off his boots and jeans then put on a faded pair of Army issue gray workout shorts from the surplus store in Billings.

Frank changed into the exact same shorts. His looked brand new.

Probably never wore them before today. Doctors don't have to do PT. Jackson leaned back into the pillows on his bunk and picked up a paperback book.

Frank sat on the next bunk. "What're you reading?"

Jackson eyed his friend over the novel. "*Smoky the Cowhorse*. Uncle Manny had it in the house. Never read it but saw the movie. They showed it at my firebase in '68. Everyone was rooting for the horse at the end. I guess it served a purpose by getting everyone's mind off the war."

"There was a movie? Was it any good?"

"The book's better than the movie, and the movie was good." Jackson took a sip of coffee.

Frank pointed at the mug. "Doesn't that keep you awake?"

"Nah, just used to it." Jackson grabbed a chocolate bar from his table, nibbling on it as he read his book. He saw Frank looking at the wall behind him. "Like the picture? That's my dad and me in Korea."

"Yeah, I can tell. He's the one wearing eagles. You're his younger mirror image with corporal stripes. Was that taken on a Marine base? The Marine Corps flag is behind you."

"Yep. I visited Dad on a one-day pass right before he died."

Frank picked up a framed photograph on Jackson's table. "Is this your family? Your mother was a beautiful woman."

"I was ten years old in that picture. It was taken after Dad received the Medal of Honor for his bravery at the battle of Okinawa." Jackson smiled at the good memory. Dad treated them to ice cream sundaes for acting like gentlemen for the photographer. "That's my older brother, Jim, next to me. I agree, Mom was beautiful."

"How did your mother die?"

"She was the head nurse of an Army MASH unit in Korea. Her jeep ran over a landmine after delivering supplies to an aid station. Killed her and the driver instantly. She died the same day as Dad." Jackson sniffed. He missed his family so much.

"Sorry to bring it up." Frank ran his hand along the glass. "You can see your love for each other in the photo."

Jackson took the picture and returned it to the table. "It's okay. I keep it next to my bed to remember the happy times."

"That tells me a lot."

Harry strolled into the building, a small green duffle bag slung over his shoulder.

Jackson eyeballed his friend. "Thought you were staying with your wife?"

"I haven't seen you in over nine months." Harry walked to Jackson's bunk with a cheeky grin. "You were so out of it the last time your sorry ass didn't even know I was in the room. You're my best friend. I'm worried about you. Gabby understands."

Jackson dog-eared a page corner, closed his book, and laid it on his table. "You're here for the same reason as Frank, to make sure everything's okay. Right?"

"Yeah." Harry rubbed his chin. "Pretty much."

"I'm fine, Harry."

"I can tell. You're back to your old self. I have to reassure myself for my peace of mind, okay. Wanna see my foot?"

"What foot, the left or the right one?" Jackson held up his finger. "Oh, you mean the plastic one."

"Funny." Harry tossed his bag on the bunk next to Jackson. He changed into a pair of red shorts and a white t-shirt, then removed his foot and waved it in the air.

Coffee poured out of Jackson's nose. "Your stump looks better than my back."

Harry grinned. "You're right. At least I can cover mine up, you goofball."

"I can too. With a shirt." Jackson flexed his right arm. "No bare-chested posing at the beach for me, showing off my beautiful muscles. You can hop around on one foot and drive the women wild with your fur-covered chest, Mr. Woolly Bear."

"Chicken legs!" Harry flapped his arms. "Bok, bok, bokok!"

"Aren't you the funny one tonight." Jackson shook his head. Harry got him good.

Harry pointed at Jackson's mug. "Got any more of that coffee?"

"Yeah, plenty. The cups are in the cabinet. Are you going to put that foot on or hop over there and back? The coffee won't stay in the cup. It'll spill all over my clean floor. I just mopped it."

"Brat." Harry strapped on his foot.

As Harry walked back, Jackson watched him carefully. *Not even a bobble. His leg looks like something from Popular Mechanics magazine.* "No limp?"

Harry set his coffee cup on his table. "Nope. Been working on that in rehab. Got it licked."

"Noticed. I wish I could've been there for you."

"I know. We could've helped each other."

"Yeah, things would've gone better if I had you to lean on for support." Jackson swung his legs off his bunk and stood.

Harry threw his arms around Jackson in a tight hug.

Jackson wrapped his arms around his best friend. He'd wanted to touch Harry in the visitation room to make sure he was real. He couldn't raise his arms with his handcuffs attached to the leather strap around his waist.

Time stood still until Harry backed away first.

Jackson fiddled with the St. John's medal around his neck. "I missed you so much."

"Same here. I was so worried. Dr. Howard called me after he talked to Dr. Rose. I wanted to see you. I couldn't take the chance with CID following us and tapping our phones."

"Figured they had you under surveillance." Jackson sat on his bunk. "Why'd they stop?"

Harry plopped down on his bunk. "Gabby asked the lawyer at the paper for help. He filed a cease and desist order in federal court since the army kept infringing on our fourth amendment rights. After the order went into effect, we received a written apology from the Secretary of the Army. Since I lost my foot, they didn't want the bad press. Good idea going through my doctor at the VA to keep me informed on your progress."

Jackson cocked his head in confusion. "Wasn't my idea."

Frank sat next to Harry. "It was mine. I figured you should know."

"Thanks so much for saving his life." Harry held out his hand.

Frank took it in a tight grip. He released Harry's hand and held up a silver chain. Dangling on the end, a St. Michael's medal. "What's this?"

"A token of my friendship. JJ gave us ones like it after the camp. Since you joined our little club, I had one engraved with your name."

Jackson smiled at his friend. "Nice touch. I agree with you."

"Thank you." Frank flipped the chain around his neck. "I just did my job. It still floors me that someone can break the unbreakable rules and override a doctor's recommendation, who, by regulation, can't be overridden. That's not supposed to happen."

Harry crossed his arms over his chest. "Well, it did. JJ almost died because of it."

"I'll keep harping on the subject with my superiors until I get an answer as to why." Frank tucked the medal under his t-shirt.

Jackson sighed at the rehash of the old argument. "Let's drop this conversation. There's nothing we can do about it anyway."

"True," Harry admitted.

"Do me a favor, Harry?"

"Anything? Name it." Harry flashed a grin as Jackson pulled electric hair clippers from the shelf above his bunk. "Do you want it the same as always?"

"Yep. Why change now? I've had the same haircut since I was nine years old."

"Just like your dad. Okay, one Marine regulation high and tight coming up." Harry plugged the clippers into the wall socket.

Jackson grabbed a folding chair and a towel from the hamper. *Why dirty a clean one?* He placed the chair in front of Harry and sat with the towel around his neck.

Harry gripped Jackson's shoulder. "You've gone gray."

Jackson vehemently shook his head. "No, I haven't. My hair's still blond."

"Yeah, grayish blond." Harry chuckled. "Too much stress from almost dying twice in a year."

"I'll agree with the dying part. Not the color of my hair."

"Okay, it's blond. Only in your mind," Harry muttered under his breath.

"I heard that," Jackson replied cheekily.

"Heard what? You're hallucinating. Maybe you're still having mental problems. I didn't hear anything." Harry turned on the clippers.

"Right. Only in my mind and your dreams, woolly bear."

Harry jerked up the clippers and burst out laughing.

"Why'd you stop?"

"Didn't want to cut a bald streak across your head."

"Oh…okay. Get control of yourself and finish." Jackson clapped his hands. "Chop, chop."

"Hush up, or I'll make you look funny." Harry hit the on/off switch several times.

Jackson stayed quiet as Harry buzzed the top of his head. He bit his tongue to keep from laughing as Harry ran the clippers over the sides. They tickled the skin above his ears.

"Done. Check it."

Jackson ran a hand across his head. The sides were nearly shaved with a quarter-inch of hair on top. "Perfect."

"Was there any doubt? Are you ready for bed, or do you wanna stay up for a while longer?"

Jackson pulled down the quilt on his bunk. "Consider lights out called. I have a lot of work to do tomorrow. You get to be a lazy ass."

"Funny." Harry's face lit up. "You're right. I get to watch you work."

Harry and Frank laughed as they lay down on their bunks.

"Shut off the coffee pot, JJ, since most of it's in your stomach." Harry pulled his blanket over his head.

"Whatever." Jackson flipped the switch on the Mr. Coffee then turned off the lights. He found his way in the dark by using the bunk footrests as a guide. As he climbed into his bunk, his big toe banged the metal leg. "Ouch!"

"Are you okay, Jackson?" Frank muttered.

"Yeah, go to sleep."

CHAPTER 20

July 1, 1973

At 0450 hours, Jackson stretched his lanky body and made his bed. He padded past his sleeping friends. The breeze from their fans made the hair on his bare legs stand up. *Wonder how long they watched me sleep.*

In the bathroom, Jackson put on his workout clothes, laced up his sneakers then tiptoed to his gym. He didn't want to wake his friends. They were adults. It wasn't his problem when they got up.

Jackson was twenty minutes into his run before Frank and Harry strolled into the room, rubbing the sleep from their eyes. They walked around the treadmill observing his technique.

"Your running style's a lot smoother since you've gained weight. In 'Nam, it was choppy and slow." Harry glanced at his watch. "How far and how fast?"

Jackson panted with each quick, long stride. "Six miles in thirty minutes."

"A five-minute mile. Excellent."

"Yeah, I thought so. Haven't done a five-minute mile since I was on the high school track team and training all the time."

Finished with his run, Jackson hopped off the treadmill, grabbed a towel, and dried the sweat from his face and head. He sat on the weight bench. Since Chief hadn't come in yet, he eyeballed his friends. "One of you wanna spot me?"

The first to move, Harry stood behind the bar. "What did you start with?"

"Just the empty bar." Jackson glanced at Frank, who kept scribbling in his black notebook. *Doctors.* He grabbed the bar, pushed it above his face, and brought it down to his chest.

"Take it easy. There's two hundred pounds on the bar. It weighs more than you do."

"Harry, can it! Your job is to keep me from dropping it on my neck. I don't think Frank wants to do an emergency tracheostomy with my knife and his pen." Jackson grunted through four sets of ten bench presses.

For the next part of his routine, Jackson removed fifty pounds from the bar. He pushed it over his head, and settled it across his shoulders.

Harry stood next to him. "Be careful, JJ."

"Harry, I'm trying to concentrate. Make sure I don't topple over. I've got this."

Jackson squatted four sets of ten with 150 pounds on the bar.

Frank's eyes widened. "That's impressive for someone who six months ago could barely walk and had skinny sticks for legs."

Jackson ignored Frank and did fifty arm curls.

Harry flexed his arm. "Look at his biceps. They look like bowling balls."

Finished with the weights, Jackson wrapped his hands and pulled on the boxing gloves. The eighty-pound heavy bag was an excellent way to remove stress. Circling the bag, he used lateral movement to set up his punches. He balanced on his toes, transferring weight from one foot to the other—using his legs to generate powerful punches at different ranges. Elbows in and hands up while moving. Ready to react as if facing an opponent.

Chief came in and grabbed a pair of focus mitts.

Jackson bobbed and weaved as he moved around Chief, who raised or lowered a pad for him to hit. Chief punched, making Jackson evade, pursue, and cut angles. Sharpening his boxing skills. Each four-minute round timed with the wall clock. Five in total with a minute rest in between.

He switched to the speed bag to improve his rhythm and his hand-eye coordination. The most painful part was last, three hundred crunches on the floor.

Chief handed Jackson a plastic cup.

Jackson grimaced at the pink liquid inside. "Strawberry's not any better than the chocolate." He gulped down the slimy, slightly berry-flavored concoction and headed into the main living quarters. "I need coffee to wash the aftertaste out of my mouth."

Frank and Harry stood in the doorway as Jackson poured the black liquid into his mug.

"You do that every morning?" Harry fiddled with the laces of a boxing glove. "You look more like a boxer than a cowboy."

Jackson pulled a set of clean clothes out of the community dresser. "Yep. Worked up to it the last few months."

"No wonder you look so good. I'm impressed." Harry looked at Frank, who nodded. "And the doc is too."

"Thanks. I'm headed to the shower unless someone wants to go first. My first stop is the foaling barn to check on Lady, then take care of Bandit if you want to come along."

"Not me. I'm hightailing it to the guesthouse before Gabby divorces me. I'll catch you at breakfast. You're right. You need a shower, my stinky friend."

"But it's a good, honest stink. Candy ass."

Harry's lip bulged out in a hurt look but he couldn't hold it. He threw the boxing glove at Jackson. It missed and skidded across the floor. Harry grabbed his bag and left the bunkhouse.

Frank pointed at the bathroom. "I'll only be a few minutes if you can wait?"

"Sure. Go ahead." Jackson held up his mug. "I'll drink coffee while you drain the hot water tank."

"Be out in a few." Frank grabbed his clothes from his messy bunk and disappeared into the bathroom.

"You looked great this morning, boss," Chief said. "Best I've seen you do. Your coordination has improved tenfold. The major's right, you look more like a boxer than a cowboy."

Jackson checked his watch. *I'll time, Frank.* "I'd rather be a cowboy, my friend. A lot less hitting involved. I have enough scars for one lifetime."

"Yeah. Don't get hurt again. You've had too many close calls."

"On that point, I agree with you."

Jackson looked at his watch when Frank exited the bathroom. *Fifteen minutes. Not bad. A little slow.* He showered, shaved and dressed in less than ten minutes. After dumping his dirty clothes in the hamper, he put on his cowboy hat, grabbed his rifle, and left the bunkhouse.

Frank ran to catch up. He eyed the 30-30 Jackson propped on his shoulder. "Why are you carrying the rifle?"

"The wolves are around at dawn. I bring it with me to the barn."

"The wolves are that bad?"

"Sometimes." Jackson chuckled at the irony. "Compliments of the US Government."

"Huh?"

"The Forest Service transplanted a bunch at Yellowstone a few years ago. Except, they don't stay in Yellowstone. They're more trouble than the mountain lions. They run in packs, find their own territory, and take down our livestock. It's a problem with no predators other than us with rifles to keep them thinned out. You heard them howling last night, right?"

Frank's head swiveled to look at him. "I thought you were asleep."

"I was. I woke up when I heard the noise. They were far away so I went back to sleep."

"How'd you get familiar so quickly with ranch life?"

Jackson pointed at the barn with his rifle muzzle. "Aunt Sara wanted to stop moving from base to base with their kids. Uncle Manny wanted a cattle ranch. A manager ran the place until he retired. Uncle Manny took his leaves while his kids were out of school. Dad and I trailered my horse from Pendleton here every summer until we retired him. Uncle Manny made sure I had a horse to ride after that. I spent many an hour in these pastures tending the cattle. This was my go-to place during breaks from West Point, and on leave until I married Carolyn. She liked JFK. He liked the Green Berets. She came looking for one and hooked me. It was only a few months before my first deployment to 'Nam. Bad choice, and an even worse mistake on my part. That's a whole other story for another time, and not one I want to talk about."

"That makes sense. Where'd you sleep?"

"The bunkhouse. It gave me more independence from Aunt Sara's prying eyes. She could always tell when Jim and I were up to something. It was more like camping out."

Frank's forehead furrowed. "Which bunk?"

"The same one I'm occupying now. The ones at the end give you more room and the wall space to hang things." Jackson rolled his eyes. "Bet you thought I wanted it for the corner to sit in."

"Yeah, I did. Mikey told me you were still pretty out of it when you guys arrived."

"I was, but I always sleep in that bunk."

Frank stopped Jackson with a hand on his arm. "Do they know?"

Jackson shook his head. "No, it's never come up." He started walking toward their destination on the well-worn path. "They probably wondered how I know the ranch so well."

"I don't know about them, but I did."

"Stop, Frank. There are fresh scratches on the door." Jackson brought the rifle to his shoulder with his finger on the trigger. He eased around the corner. Nothing but grass. "Good, they're gone." He unlocked the door and went inside. "You okay, girl?"

Lady shook her head over the stall door with a loud snort.

Frank cocked his head. "What's that mean?"

"She's hungry." Jackson stuck his palm filled with peppermints under her nose. Lady chewed the treats as he opened the turnout door at the back of the stall. She trotted into the pasture with her foal close on her heels.

Jackson pitched a load of dirty straw into the wheelbarrow then leaned on the pitchfork. "You can always help out."

Frank draped his upper body over the stall door. "That's okay. I'll watch you work. I have no idea what you're doing. I'd make a fool out of myself if I slipped in manure."

"Thanks a lot," Jackson huffed. "Mikey's more help than you." *Maybe he'll step in a soft, steamy pile and have to clean those shiny shoes. That'll be funny.*

With half of his chores completed, Jackson headed to the main barn. Even before they went inside, Bandit's forceful whinny echoed through the door. Jackson removed his hat and hung it on a nail near the tack room.

Bandit bobbed his head over the stall door and stomped his front feet.

"Guess you're hungry too, huh?" Jackson fed the horse a handful of peppermints.

Bandit jerked his head up and it landed on Jackson's. Slobber dripped on Jackson's head and ran down his neck.

Frank leaned against the wall and laughed.

Jackson wiped off the candy goo with a towel. "Glad you think this is funny."

Full of spunk, Bandit bucked, bit, kicked up his rear feet, nibbled on Jackson's hair and reared. To muck the stall without interruption, Jackson opened the turnout door. He flapped his arms to force his buddy into the pasture. Bringing him inside, much easier. Bandit walked up to his full feed bucket and shoved his hungry mouth in it. The distraction gave Jackson the time to groom him until his coat glistened bright red.

Jackson turned Bandit out into the pasture.

The hard-headed horse neighed and stomped his front feet like a five-year-old throwing a tantrum. He reared, bucked then trotted to the fence and whinnied.

"Didn't you just get enough of my attention?" Jackson fed him peppermints to quiet him down. The decision almost backfired when he glanced at his watch, 0755 hours. He grabbed Frank by the arm. "Let's go. Aunt Sara's as much a Marine as Uncle Manny. She doesn't understand the concept of late to any family function. Breakfast is a family function." He double-timed to the house with Frank at his side.

Frank looked back at the barn. "Why'd you put Bandit in the pasture instead of his stall?"

"Since this is your first time on a ranch, I'll give you a pointer. Horses crap a lot. I'm coming back after breakfast to saddle him. Why make more work for myself this afternoon?"

"Good point. Now I know how much work it is to take care of a horse. I can tell he made a difference in your recovery. You're right, he's more like a dog than a horse. He shoved his head into your chest first thing. When he plopped his head on yours, that was funny."

"He does things like that all the time. That damn horse would grab my hat if I didn't take it off. He tore up my first one pulling it from my head and shaking it like a toy."

Frank pointed at Jackson's shirt. "He slobbered all over you."

Jackson brushed at the hardened spots. "Yeah, Bandit does that when he shakes his head. It was on purpose if you didn't notice."

Harry and Gabby were at the table with their son drinking a bottle in his mother's arms.

Jackson kissed the baby's forehead. "I love you." He returned from the kitchen with a coffee cup and sat next to Harry.

Harry sniffed the air. "You smell better."

Oh, he had to start. My turn. Jackson elbowed his friend in the ribs. "Feels like jello."

Harry returned the favor. "Ouch!" He rubbed his elbow. "Is that a concrete wall under your shirt? Where's the doctor? I need a cast."

"There goes the unit drama queen." Jackson put two fingers behind Harry's head like rabbit ears.

Gabby rolled her eyes as she held her son. "Better you than me, Jackson. I'm ready for a break. My sides hurt constantly."

Chief eyes crinkled at the corners as he tried not to laugh.

Mangus shook his head.

Frank leaned back in his chair. "Leave me out of this."

Sara tittered like a schoolgirl in the doorway. "I'm glad Harry's back in your life. He makes you whole."

"Let me help you, Aunt Sara." Jackson stood, took the two serving platters from her and placed them on the table.

"Thank you. You're such a gentleman." Sara sat in her chair next to Mangus—the signal for the meal to begin.

Jackson sat in his chair then pulled four pancakes onto his plate and filled a bowl with eggs.

Frank picked up a mason jar. "What's with the honey? I've never seen anyone pour honey on pancakes before. Is that a ranch thing?"

Jackson paused with the bite halfway to his mouth. "Ever since the POW camp, store-bought syrup upsets my stomach. I use honey instead."

"Another one of your quirks. I'll add it to my notes."

"Whatever." Jackson pulled another stack of pancakes onto his plate.

Frank scratched his head. "How much are you going to eat?"

"Make up your mind. When I first met you, it was *you're too skinny*. Now, you're questioning my eating habits."

"No, I love it. I'll note that too."

Jackson rolled his eyes. "Doctors."

Time slowed as Frank ate. Each bite the size of a quarter. He chewed twenty times and swallowed.

City guys. Jackson carried his empty plate to the kitchen and grabbed the newspaper lying next to the stove. He read until Frank set his plate in the sink, folded the paper then picked up his rifle and hat next to the door.

Outside the house, Frank hit Jackson with a loaded look. "What is it with you two?"

"What do you mean...us two?"

"You and Harry. You keep ribbing the crap out of each other."

"Oh, that." Jackson nonchalantly flipped the rifle over his shoulder. "We've done that since Special Forces training. Harry pulled pranks in the barracks. I always joined him." *We carried Staff Sergeant West on his rack to the flagpole. He threw off his blanket completely naked. Everyone laughed. The hundreds of pushups and hours of front leaning rest were worth it. The guy had a big head.* "I joke around with the guys, and, yes, I did it in 'Nam. Never on duty. On duty, I was as serious as a heart attack. The men hated me because I didn't give them any slack. All bets were off when the day was over. It relieved the pressure for all of us. Especially me after the camp. I started a lot of it." He raised an eyebrow. "Is there a problem?"

"No. It's nice to see how close you are to your friends to say the things you do to make each other laugh. In the hospital, I only saw a man who felt betrayed by the army."

"True. It's nice to laugh again without remembering all the pain."

At the barn, Jackson saddled a black and white pinto named Duke and handed the reins to Frank. Bandit stood still as Jackson put on the bridle, cinched up the saddle, and placed his rifle in the scabbard. With his horse ready to go, Jackson strapped on his chaps, pulled on his riding gloves, and secured his hunting knife to his belt.

Frank patted his foot. "Where's your canteen? It's ninety degrees outside. Didn't you learn your lesson about dehydration?"

"Yeah. No more enemas." Jackson grabbed two round canteens from the tack room. He filled them in the sink, handed one to Frank, and hung the other one on his saddle horn.

"We can go now."

Jackson led Bandit to the road. He stood waiting for Frank to catch up. The second Duke's hooves touched the gravel, Jackson slipped his left foot in the stirrup and in one fluid motion mounted his horse.

Frank took a little longer. He hopped, jumped and stretched to climb onto Duke. As his right leg went over the saddle, a pained grimace crossed his face.

"Hurry up, slowpoke. We're burning daylight. I have a lot of ground to cover." Jackson sidestepped Bandit in a large circle around Duke, showing off.

"Oh, hush up. I'm a doctor, not a cowboy. I may be out of my element on the back of a horse. But I'm a tenacious bulldog, prideful and stubborn. I will follow you around all day. No way am I backing out of your tour." Frank spurred his horse forward. "Ouch! The saddle is rubbing my ass and balls. What have I gotten myself into?"

Jackson kicked open the latch on the north pasture gate from his horse and rode across the field.

Frank struggled to keep up. He bounced in the saddle like a ball.

An hour after they left the barn, Jackson opened the west pasture gate. He turned to Frank behind him. "I hope we don't find any newborn calves downed by the wolves. I found one yesterday. It was messy. Parts were scattered everywhere. They like babies because they're defenseless."

Frank cringed. "That's horrible."

Even though they didn't find any calves, a young steer wasn't so lucky.

Jackson pointed at the half-eaten carcass, covered in flies. "That's what the wolves do. It costs the ranch every time we lose a cow. They're averaging about forty dollars per every one hundred pounds this year. This guy was about nine hundred pounds. He would've pushed twelve hundred when he was ready for market. Do the math. That's four to five hundred dollars lost right here. Between the wolves and mountain lions, we lose about a dozen head a year. That's about a six-thousand-dollar loss on average."

"Now, I understand how the wolves are a problem."

To emphasize his point, Jackson patted his rifle scabbard. "If a pack can take down a nine-hundred-pound steer, think of what they can do if they catch you in the open without a gun. Bad news."

Frank pulled back on the reins when Duke stepped forward. "Whoa, boy. What are you going to do with the body?"

"When we head in, I'll send a ranch hand out here with the tractor. The only way to keep the flies and scavengers away from the house is to bury it in the pasture."

The shadows grew shorter as the sun climbed overhead while Jackson checked the horses in the south pasture. With them all accounted for, he checked the fence lines for breaks. All Frank did was sit on his horse and follow him around.

At each stop, Jackson pointed out various locations. The clearing where he saw his first bear. His secret fishing pond. The log fort he built with Jim. The creek where they found the arrowheads in his collection.

The most special place, at least for Jackson, a large oak tree in the south pasture. The burial site of his quarter horse, Taco. A wooden plaque nailed to the trunk inscribed with his name marked the grave for all to find.

Jackson patted the sign. "Hey, buddy. I'm here for my weekly visit."

Frank lifted himself in his stirrups. "How big is this ranch?"

"About ten thousand acres of rolling hills. I bet it feels huge on the back of a horse."

Frank rubbed between his legs.

Tonight will be interesting.

As the mid-day sun passed thirty-eight degrees toward the western horizon, around 1430 hours, Jackson and Frank approached the main house along the fence line. A passing truck backfired. A bay horse near the barn reared. The rider flipped backward out of the saddle as the horse bolted. His direction, straight for the open main gate and the highway.

Jackson spurred Bandit into a full gallop. He had to stop the animal from being a hood ornament on a passing semi. As they flew along the gravel road, he flipped the rope loop over his head in a circle several times. It left his hand and landed around the neck of the running horse. The noose tightened then the horse slowed. This allowed Bandit to catch up. They came to a stop together. Jackson turned Bandit with the panting horse walking behind them.

Frank sat still on Duke with his mouth wide open.

Jackson pulled back on the reins next to Frank. "Whoa, boy." Bandit stopped. Jackson handed the rope to Larry. "Like the show, Frank?"

"Sure did. You're a natural. If you hadn't gone into the army, you would've wound up a cowboy on this ranch working for your godfather."

"Maybe or after the Olympics, I would've joined FEI and made a name for myself on the professional jumping and dressage circuit. But we'll

254

never know." Jackson hung the coiled rope Larry gave him on his saddle horn. "I have to check the east pasture. You coming along, Frank?"

Frank slid off Duke and handed the reins to a waiting ranch hand, Clyde.

"Guess not." Jackson rode off.

Two hours later, Jackson returned to the bunkhouse and took a shower. The day wasn't over. Harry got his tour in the ranch truck on the perimeter road.

Harry stuck his nose to the passenger window. "What's with the guy on the yellow tractor?"

Jackson grinned. Time to get his revenge. "Uncle Manny loves luaus. I thought we'd cook a dead cow…kalua style."

"What do you mean, dead cow?" Harry paused for a few seconds. "This is a joke, right?"

"Yeah, you got me."

After dinner, they sat in the living room drinking coffee and discussing current events. Except for Frank—he soaked his medicated, saddle sore body in a warm bathtub.

"Something wrong, Frank?" Jackson faked a limp across the living room.

Frank glared at Jackson from the recliner with his feet up. "You think this is funny, don't you?"

"Yes, since you're the doctor, and I'm not the one doing the limping."

"Rub it in, funny guy."

"Sure. How about going back out with me tomorrow?" Jackson poked Frank in the shoulder. "You'll be so numb you won't feel a thing."

CHAPTER 21

December 1, 1973
Army/Navy Football Game

Mangus sat in front of the TV decked out in Navy blue and gold. Jackson wore a faded black and gold Army Black Knights sweatshirt with *MacKenzie* on the back.

Popcorn, beer cans, one coffee mug and plates filled with food dotted the end tables. Everyone else sat around the room. Each one wearing a shirt with the logo of their favorite school.

Mangus held out his hand. "Still want to go ahead with the bet?"

"Of course." Jackson slapped his hand into Mangus' open palm and tightened his grip. "Navy's going down again this year. Records mean nothing."

Two phrases rang out as the game started.

"Go Army, Beat Navy!" Jackson stood on the recliner, yelling and shaking a cowbell.

"Go Navy, Beat Army!" Mangus sat on the couch. His enthusiasm rang out in his voice, loud and proud.

Navy scored a touchdown on the first drive. Navy 7, Army 0.

Jackson glared at Mangus when his face erupted in a huge smile. "Lucky break. A game's four quarters."

By the second and third quarters, Jackson's upbeat mood went sour as the score turned lopsided. Navy scored touchdown after touchdown. Army kept fumbling the ball. At the end of the game, his shoulders slumped. He raised his hands in defeat. "My bad luck continues."

Mangus flashed a dazzling smile. "I win. Blowout 51-0 for Navy."

"Yeah, yeah." Jackson wadded up the paper in his hand and threw it across the room. "What do you want me to fix for dinner?"

"My favorite, liver and onions."

"Do I have to eat any?" Jackson screwed his face into a frown.

"You lost the bet, so, yes. Then you get to sing the Navy alma mater in front of everyone."

"Okay. Singing I can do. Don't get your knickers in a twist when I puke liver and onions all over the table. Next year, I'll have my revenge on the Naval Academy, and you fix me a steak dinner."

"Only if the Black Knights can do better than a perfect 0-10 record. They lost every game this season."

"Don't rub it in, Uncle Manny."

December 7, 1973

Exhausted after a long day of rounding up stray cattle, Jackson dragged his body out of the saddle at the barn and fed his horse. *Hope everyone forgot my thirty-ninth birthday.* As he brushed Bandit, his seventh birthday at Camp Pendleton entered his thoughts.

The clang of a phone broke the silence as Jackson sat at the table, fork and knife in hand. In front of his plate, Mom's pot roast, macaroni and cheese, corn-on-the-cob and rolls. Next to his hand, a vanilla milkshake. Behind him on the walnut china cabinet, a white birthday cake with seven candles and presents wrapped in blue paper.

His dad ran into the dining room in his khaki summer uniform, captain's bars on the collar, his garrison cap gripped in his hand. He kissed Jackson's forehead. "Sorry, squirt, I have to go."

"But, Dad, it's my birthday. You promised to take off today." Jackson whimpered, tears streaming down his cheeks.

"Something's come up." Dad rubbed Jackson's head. The front door slammed a minute later.

His mom, Kimberly, came into the dining room. She hugged Jackson as he cried in his chair. "It's okay, JJ."

His nine-year old brother, Jim, walked into the dining room. "Sorry, bubba." He squeezed Jackson's shoulder.

"Jim, sit down. We're going to eat JJ's birthday dinner. He'll open his presents when James comes back." Mom pulled out a chair next to Jackson. She placed the milkshake on his plate. "Drink this, honey. It'll help."

After dinner, Mom, Jim, and Jackson sat on the living room couch, listening to the radio. The attack on Pearl Harbor was the topic of conversation on every station.

Mom grabbed Jackson's and Jim's hands. In the hall, she went down on one knee in front of them. "Jim, go to bed. I'll be there in a few minutes to tuck you in."

"Take care of JJ first, Mom." Jim ruffled Jackson's hair then ran to his room.

She led Jackson to his room and tucked him into bed.

"Mom, are we going to war? Is Dad going to die?" Jackson wailed.

"I don't know, baby." She held Jackson as he cried himself to sleep in her arms.

Jackson awoke with a hand stroking his head the next morning. He looked into his father's eyes.

Dad smiled. "Hi, squirt. I'm sorry I broke my promise. I bought you something special. Wanna come look?"

"Sure, Dad." Jackson sat up, rubbing the sleep from his eyes. He climbed out of bed and followed his father.

At the threshold of the door, Dad stopped. Jackson walked up beside him. He placed an arm around his son's shoulder. "Hope you like him. I wanted to make it up to you for messing up your birthday."

Jackson peeked around the doorframe. In the yard stood a black and white Welsh pony, bridled and saddled. He threw his arms around his father's waist. "I love him, Dad. What's his name?"

"Scout."

A nibble on Jackson's head broke the memory. He pushed Bandit's wet nose away. "Quit that, you crazy horse." He dabbed peppermint slobber from his face with his sleeve then sniffed. *Boy, I stink. I smell like Harry's dirty, sweaty socks. Better take a shower before dinner.*

Still damp, Jackson pulled on his clothes then glanced at his watch. 1730 hours. *Crap.* He threw on his coat and ran through the snow to the house, crossing under a Happy Birthday banner at the threshold of the front door. *Oh well. They remembered.*

Jackson hung his coat on the rack. He shoved his hands into his pockets and walked into the dining room. On the loveseat Mangus and Sara sat holding hands. Next to the fireplace stood his friends with drinks in their hands, talking to Jason Nichols.

"Happy birthday," Jason said. "You look fantastic."

"Thank you." Jackson flexed both arms. The material around his biceps stretched to a breaking point.

"You've exceeded my expectations. The general has kept me informed. I'm glad I came."

Jackson waved his right arm back and forth. "Wanna arm wrestle?"

"After seeing your arms, no way." Jason patted his bicep. "You'd take me in a hot second."

Uncle Jason's proud of my hard work. Jackson flexed like a bodybuilder. He went into the kitchen, grabbed a cup of coffee and returned to the living room to take advantage of the moment. Jason's promised war story about serving in his father's company at Iwo Jima.

258

Sara interrupted Jason when she stood in the doorway at 1800 hours. "Dinner's ready."

Jackson beat everyone to the dining room and sat in his regular chair. On the table, roasted flank steak, baked potatoes, corn-on-the-cob, and rolls. He sniffed the air. "Mmmm. Smells good."

Mangus took his place at the head of the table. Sara beside him. Jason sat across from Jackson. Ty, Mikcy, Bill, and Chief grabbed their usual positions. The food disappeared quickly.

Sara picked up the empty roast platter. "This is a compliment. No leftovers."

Jackson stood from his chair. "Hand that to me. I'll take care of the dishes."

"Sit down, birthday boy." Mangus pushed Jackson down in the seat. "Not today."

Sara placed a Bundt cake on the table. "We wanted you to have a real birthday this year. I used pumpkin instead of oil to keep the cake moist. I made the glaze out of honey, milk, and powdered sugar."

"Thanks, Aunt Sara. It smells wonderful." Jackson blew out his forest fire of a cake. This time every candle went out with one breath of air. No one laughed at him huffing, puffing, and nearly spitting to make the flames go out.

Mangus stood with his arms out like a music director. "We won't sing unless you want us to."

"No way." Jackson slammed both hands over his ears. "My sensitive ears can't take the noise."

Jason waggled his finger at Jackson. "Hilarious, kid. Maybe we should sing just for that comment."

"Only if you want me to hide under the table, sir."

"Sir?"

Jackson grinned. "Okay, okay. Uncle Jason."

Sara cut a large chunk, added a scoop of ice cream on top, and set the plate in front of Jackson.

Since this was something new, Jackson ate a small taste. His stomach didn't revolt, so he devoured the rest in four large bites, along with the ice cream. He waited until everyone received a piece then helped himself to another slice with two more scoops of ice cream.

Sara's chest puffed out. "I guess it's good."

"Terrific," Jackson mumbled through the bite in his mouth.

"Want me to save you some? It's your birthday."

"Yeah, a couple of pieces. I'll have them as a midnight snack."

Mangus pushed back his chair. "Everybody report to the living room. That's an order."

Jackson hustled to the living room and grabbed his favorite chair. The overstuffed black leather one with the hassock next to the fireplace. He loved reading by the light of the fire. Jason sat in the recliner across from Jackson. Sara and Mangus took up residence on the loveseat against the wall separating the living room from the entry hall. Ty, Bill, Chief, and Mikey plopped down on the couch under the front window.

Jason handed Jackson a box covered in USMC wrapping paper. "Hope everything fits."

Like a ten-year-old expecting the toy of his dreams, Jackson ripped off the paper. "Thanks, Uncle Jason, I needed new workout clothes. My old ones have spent too many times going through the washing machine spin cycle. Are they all the same?"

"Yes. Five sets of standard red USMC running shorts with matching t-shirts. Check the shoes. Are they the right size? The general said yours are worn out from the hundreds of miles you've put on the treadmill."

Jackson pulled the black sneakers out of the box. "Yep, size twelve." He hugged Jason. "You know they'd drum me out of the army for wearing the Marine Corps colors."

"Thought they already did. The army didn't deserve you in its ranks. You would've made a much better Marine. Your dad would be proud of you for fighting your way through the pain."

"I know." His father's spirit lived in his heart. Jackson returned to his seat as his men produced presents wrapped in the Sunday comics. He opened the biggest box. "Just what I wanted, a case of coffee cans."

Mangus looked at Sara. "I think we should invest in coffee futures."

Jackson ripped the paper off the second box. He held up a pair of muck boots. "Thanks, guys. Now I won't get mine dirty in the mornings."

Chief whistled softly. "Check inside, boss."

"Sneaky." Jackson removed two pairs of tan riding gloves from the shank. He rubbed one pair between his fingertips. "Nice. They're made of soft goatskin."

"Keep digging. You ain't found everything yet."

"Okay." Jackson pulled out a brown stocking cap. "Great, now my ears won't get cold. Bandit chewed up my old one last week."

Mangus handed Jackson a brown cardboard box with a mailing label. "This one's from Harry."

"Yeah, he couldn't make it. His doc wanted to fit him for a new foot." Flipping the box on its end, Jackson slit the tape with his pocket knife. Inside was a new full-length, black terry-cloth robe. The MacKenzie Scottish crest embroidered on the front.

Chief gave Jackson a Buck folding Hunter's knife.

"I love it." Jackson snapped it open and ran his thumb down the blade. "And it's really sharp," he mumbled with his thumb in his mouth.

Ty, Chief, Bill, and Mikey crowded around him.

Jackson hugged his friends for their thoughtful gifts.

Sara handed Jackson three boxes wrapped in USMC paper.

Jackson examined the beautiful, straight creases. *Looks like she used a ruler.* He opened the first box. "Thanks. I needed a new pair of boots. My old ones are all scratched up from the brush. They look like crap."

Sara pinched her nose. "Smell like it too."

"Yes, ma'am." Jackson opened the second box. It held one of Sara's blue homemade quilts and two new pillows. "Thank you."

"You're welcome. Keep going."

Enclosed in the last box—a brown Carhartt jacket with matching lined pants. Jackson hugged his godparents. "You guys spent way too much on me."

Mangus held up a credit card. "No. We didn't spend enough. You're our godson. We love you. Besides, I don't want you freezing to death working for me."

Jackson rolled his eyes. *I'll never win that argument.* "Thanks, Uncle Manny. It's my best birthday in years."

"I'm glad. Wait until Christmas."

Caught off guard, Jackson turned defensive. "What! This was already too much, sir. Don't spend more money on me."

"Wrong." Mangus' brow furrowed like a wavy flag. "It's our money to spend. I want you to have an extra special Christmas this year. Last year you nearly died on that day."

"Don't remind me. I caused his collapse." Jason looked at the ground in a manner unlike a retired Marine Sgt. Major.

Jackson placed a hand on Jason's shoulder. "You didn't know. I stressed myself out. My mistake. It was too much for me too soon."

"And I should've believed you. You're James MacKenzie's son. You've always been honest about everything. I didn't believe the crap coming from the army anyway. I know you."

"Well, it's over now. I'm healthy and happy. Let's forget about it, okay."

Jason gripped Jackson's forearm. "I can live with that. I'm going home in the morning. I'll be back at Christmas with Rachel. She can't wait to see you."

Mangus poked the coals in the fireplace. "It'll be a big Christmas this year. Dr. Howard, Harry, and his family are coming. My kids are going to their in-laws. We trade off every year to make it fair. They'll be here after New Year's. That's when we'll do Christmas with their families. You'll get two Christmas dinners this year with a lot of football."

"Looking forward to it. I've spent so many Christmases living in the mud with dozens of stinky men. We decorated the fake tree in the barracks with ornaments made of soap and frag from mortar shells. Most of the time, the presents were whatever we could find lying around the base, wrapped in worn-out copies of Stars and Stripes." Jackson chuckled. "Aunt Sara's cooking will surpass the runny mashed potatoes and gray-colored turkey substitute in the chow hall by a mile."

"Oh yeah, expect Dr. Rose and Jerry this year. They want to check on you."

Jackson picked up the discarded wrapping paper. "They're coming too? Can't wait to see them."

Mangus grabbed the wadded up paper from Jackson. "I already told you about this. Sit down. Today, you don't clean up anything…Lieutenant Colonel MacKenzie."

Uncle Manny's pissed. Better follow orders. Jackson sat on the couch. "Yes, sir."

Mangus tossed the paper into the fireplace. They lit up into rings of glowing embers.

Jason walked up with two glasses of brown liquid and ice. He handed one to Mangus.

From the smell, Jackson knew it was Captain Morgan spiced rum, his godfather's favorite.

Mangus set the glass on the fireplace mantle. "I remember the day Jackson and Jim went fishing the south pasture pond. A bear…"

Jackson waved his hand. "Uncle Manny, hush. Please don't tell that story."

CHAPTER 22

December 23, 1973

Tired and ready to relax, Jackson headed to the bunkhouse. It had been a long day. The snow slowed him down. His shoulders ached from swinging a hatchet to break the inch-thick ice in the water troughs. He leaned his rifle next to the door. As he took off his coat, a hand fell on his shoulder from behind. He turned. "Hiya, Curtis. You guys came to me instead of the other way around."

Curtis crossed his arms. "Sure did. Stand there. Let me check you out." He walked around Jackson then pulled a stethoscope from his bag.

"Awww, come on."

"Don't use that tone with me. Take off your shirt."

Jackson unbuttoned his shirt and pulled his t-shirt over his head.

"Holy crap, Dad." Jerry's jaw dropped.

"Like what you see?" Jackson flexed his arms.

Curtis smiled. "Yes. Your body has filled out more than I expected. Stand still so I can listen to your heart."

Jackson flinched as Curtis placed the diaphragm on his chest. "Hey, it's cold."

"Shhh!" Curtis looped the tubing around his neck. "Sounds good. So do your lungs. You must work out and eat a lot to have that much muscle development in your chest and arms."

"I do. It's a far cry from one hard-boiled egg. I work out every morning. Don't be alarmed when I get up at 0500 hours." Jackson noticed them eyeballing his Winchester. "The wolves come out after dark. If I grab my rifle, they're close. If the buggers are far away, I don't bother. Since the windows are closed, the pack can't get in. They can still go after the stock. I don't want the rabid things around the houses or barns. If one comes close, it winds up with a 30-30 round between the eyes."

Curtis nodded. "Thanks for the warning. I watched the news this morning."

Jackson rubbed his chin. "And?"

"Nothing about you guys at all."

"Guess they moved on since we pulled out of 'Nam. The only thing I'm doing tomorrow besides taking care of my horse is feeding the cows. If you two want a tour, you can ride with me when I haul hay out to them and break the ice in the water troughs." *That hurts thinking about it.*

Jerry spoke up. "Yeah, we'd love a tour, right, Dad?"

"Of course. I want to keep an eye on you." Curtis pointed at Jackson's stomach.

"What is it with you doctors?" Jackson flipped a towel over his shoulder. "It won't be until after breakfast. Where's Frank?"

"At the house. He needed to check on a patient. You don't have a phone in here."

"Don't need one. I'm going to take a shower. Make yourselves at home. Dinner's at 1800 hours. We are never late. Aunt Sara doesn't do late for anything if you get my meaning."

Ten minutes later, Jackson emerged from the bathroom, clean and dressed with a damp towel around his neck. After depositing his dirty laundry in the hamper, he grabbed a cup of coffee and sat on his bunk.

Jerry made a drinking motion with his hand. "Some things don't change, Dad."

At 1730 hours, Jackson put on his coat and hat, grabbed his rifle and exited from the bunkhouse.

Chief, Curtis, and Jerry followed him.

The first one in the house, Jackson made a beeline for the dining room.

Harry handed off his child and the bottle.

Curtis and Jerry watched until Frank made the introductions. "This is Jackson's best friend, Major Harry Russell. The little boy is Jackson's godson, Jackson Joseph Russell."

"Nice looking boy, Major Russell." Curtis patted Harry's shoulder.

"Call me Harry."

Hungry little JJ sucked his bottle dry and pushed it away.

Harry draped a towel over Jackson's right shoulder. "Lay him against your chest. Rest his chin on your shoulder."

Jackson flipped the baby from the crook of his arm to his shoulder. "What now?"

"Gently pat or rub his back." Harry placed Jackson's left hand in the correct position.

Five pats later, little JJ didn't disappoint. A loud belch escaped his mouth with milk drool on the towel.

Harry squeezed Jackson's arm. "Make me a promise."

"Sure. What do you have in mind?"

"If anything ever happens to us, adopt my son."

Jackson teared up. "Bet on it. He'll never be alone. I know how that feels."

Sara broke her pattern. She placed the ham, mashed potatoes, buttered corn, green beans, salad, and rolls on the table five minutes early.

That's new. Jackson handed his godson to Gabby. He sat in his usual chair. After Sara took her seat next to Mangus, Jackson loaded his plate with everything. For dessert, two large slices of Sara's pumpkin cake with powdered sugar glaze.

As everyone pushed back their plates, Jackson grabbed an armload of dirty dishes and took them to the kitchen. Sara already had her hands in the soapy water. He dried and put everything away.

Curtis stopped Jackson as he left the kitchen. "You know something."

Jackson raised an eyebrow. "What?"

"I loved seeing how much you ate tonight. It is a far cry from one egg. You showed me your true character and gracious demeanor. Only a gentleman helps clean up after dinner. That only cemented your legend with me. Don't quit fighting. You'll win. Even with the United States Army's stacked deck against you."

"Thank you. That means a lot coming from you."

"What's going on for the evening?"

"Nothing. I'm headed to the bunkhouse. You can stay and talk to Uncle Manny or join me." Jackson grabbed his coat from the rack.

Curtis snagged Jerry by the shirtsleeve. "Let's go with Jackson. I'm tired."

"Great." Jackson propped the rifle on his shoulder. He flipped his hat on his head and opened the front door. A wolf howled as he led Frank, Chief, Curtis, and Jerry along the snow-covered path to the bunkhouse.

Jerry ran ahead and opened the door. "Colonel?"

"Don't worry." Jackson put the rifle stock against his shoulder as his friends walked into the bunkhouse. He followed them inside, closed the door, and leaned the rifle against the jamb. Time to get comfortable. He changed into shorts and a t-shirt.

Frank strolled up to Jackson's bunk. "Changing alliances?"

"Huh?" Jackson picked up *King of the Wind* by Marguerite Henry from his table. He had four chapters left and wanted to finish tonight.

"Marine Corps?" Frank pointed at the red shorts.

"Oh that. They were a gift from Jason for my birthday. The army threw me in the trash. If the Marines could get the charges dropped, I'd change service branches and start all over again."

"You're kidding, right?"

Jackson wrapped up in his bathrobe and kicked back on his bunk. A paperback book in one hand and a coffee cup in the other. "You figure it out. I'm not committing to anything."

December 24, 1973

Jackson ran the body brush across Bandit's flank. With each stroke, his coat glistened like a blood-red sun. *Jerry's wearing the Alabama crap again. Bandit will take care of it for me.* He stepped out and closed the stall door. "Have you ever been around horses before, Jerry?"

"No. First time." Jerry adjusted the crimson Alabama ball cap on his head.

"Want to feed him a treat?"

"Sure. What do I do?"

Jackson demonstrated with his hand out, palm up. "Hold your palm flat under his nose."

"Okay." Jerry copied the movement.

Don't curl your fingers or he'll nip you with his teeth." Jackson dropped a peppermint in Jerry's palm. "Give it a try."

Jerry stuck his hand under Bandit's nose. "Like this?"

"Yeah. Keep your hand still."

The horse snorted. Jerry jumped but kept his hand in place. Bandit grabbed the bill of Jerry's ball cap and shook it, flinging his head around as if laughing. Slobber flew all over Curtis and Jerry.

Curtis wiped the liquid from his face. "You got him good, Jackson."

"I've lost a couple of cowboy hats the same way, Jerry." Jackson bit down on his lip to keep from laughing.

Jerry's face was beet red in embarrassment. "Sure?"

Jackson retrieved the damp, but still intact hat from the horse's mouth. He handed it to his friend. "At least he didn't tear it up."

"Ewww." Jerry tucked the hat in his back pocket. "I'll wash it in the sink when we go back to the bunkhouse."

"It's horse slobber, not the plague. It gives your hat character and the worn-out look you kids love today."

"Whatever, Colonel."

"Do you want to play fetch with him?" Jackson pulled a softball out of his pocket.

"It's a horse, not a dog."

"Are you sure?" Jackson set the ball on the stall door.

Bandit picked it up in his mouth, bobbed his head a few times and released it in Jerry's direction.

Jerry ducked to the side as the ball rolled past. "Funny."

Curtis leaned against the wall, laughing. "You need to take the act on the road, Jackson."

"Yep. He's a smart horse." Jackson picked up the ball and stuck it in his coat pocket. "Let's head to the house. Breakfast is in ten minutes."

Jackson parked the flatbed truck next to the barn and walked into the bunkhouse. "Hope you liked the tour."

Curtis laid his magazine in his lap. "We did. Never seen cows up close before. It gives you a new perspective on much work it takes to buy steaks and hamburger at the store."

"Yeah." Jackson looked around the room. "Where's Jerry? Is he washing his hat?"

"No, he's in your workout room. My son has muscle envy."

Jackson pushed open the door and leaned against the jamb. He shook his head at the sight of Jerry lying on the weight bench, his arms shaking with the effort to push the bar above his chest. "With the way you're struggling and grunting, I think 275 pounds is too heavy for you."

Jerry dropped the bar on the holder. "Yeah, me too. I didn't want to take the time to change it. What do you need, sir?"

"Want to give me a hand? I need to grab the Christmas presents I hid in the workshop."

"Sure. Bandit's not around, is he?"

Jackson ran his hand through his hair. "No, he's in his stall. It's safe to wear your hat."

Light snow fell as they walked around the main barn to a wooden building with an overhead garage door.

Jackson pointed at a beat-up white Ford F-150 parked in front. "That's my work truck. Let's get the big stuff first." He pulled up the overhead door and pointed at an object wrapped in a tarp with a rope tied around it. "This one first."

"What is it?"

"A surprise." Jackson picked up one end while Jerry grabbed the other.

With the gift lying flat in the bed of the truck, they returned for the one with four legs and a top wrapped in plastic sheeting.

Jerry grasped two legs. "What's this? Looks like a weird table."

"Kinda." Jackson lifted his end.

They carried it to the truck then went back into the workshop.

Jackson pointed at the boxes spread across the workbench then picked up a roll of green wrapping paper. "I need to wrap everything else."

Jackson stepped back to admire his handiwork. "I think it looks great. What about you?"

"Not bad. Better than mine. My creases are crooked. Yours are straight. What were you doing with scissors?" Jerry pulled off a wad of tape stuck to his shirt.

"Feathering the ribbons. Saw Aunt Sara doing it yesterday. Let's take everything to the house." Jackson grabbed a fifty-five-gallon garbage bag from the shelf. "We'll use this to carry everything." He held it open. "Start stuffing."

"Okay." Jerry dropped boxes into the bag.

With two full bags, Jackson threw one over his shoulder and Jerry the other. Jackson shoved his bag into the middle of the bench seat then climbed behind the steering wheel.

Jerry placed his bag between his legs in the floorboard on the passenger side.

Jackson drove to the house at five miles an hour. No way would he take a chance on damaging the special gifts in the truck bed. They unloaded the two large items into the garage then carried the wrapped gifts into the house and placed them under the tree.

"You hungry, Jerry?" Jackson rubbed his rumbling stomach.

"Nah. Sara fixes a mean breakfast. I'm headed to the bunkhouse. It's siesta time. I'm on winter break from college."

"See you at dinner." Jackson grabbed a roast beef sandwich from a tray on the dining room table. He added raw vegetables to his plate and poured coffee into his favorite mug. Since the table was covered, he carried his snack to the living room.

"That's not a plate Jackson's carrying, it's a serving platter," Curtis said to Frank as Jackson sat in a recliner.

"Yeah, and he ate enough for a horse at breakfast. I think he installed a hollow leg to stuff all that food," Frank replied.

Jackson glanced at Curtis and Frank sitting on the couch. Still chewing, he set the sandwich on the plate in his lap and reached for his cup. "Something wrong, Frank? I can hear you. I'm like five feet away," he mumbled through the bite in his mouth.

"No. Just comparing notes. We remember when getting you to eat was like pulling wisdom teeth. Now you eat all the time, work out, and could even gain a few more pounds. Were your ears burning?"

"Nope. Not today." Jackson ate another bite of his sandwich. He heard his name again and again but ignored the doctors as he finished his snack.

Jackson saluted Curtis and Frank with his coffee cup. He went to the kitchen, washed his dirty dishes, and returned them to the cabinet.

Sara was peeling potatoes.

Rachel was sprinkling sugar on a fresh cherry pie.

"Need any help?" Jackson pointed at the food on the kitchen counter.

"No. We have this under control. Thanks for asking." Sara gently pushed her godson out of the kitchen. "Go relax until dinner."

Jackson grabbed a copy of *Leatherneck Magazine* from the bookshelf. The house was quiet. Too quiet. *Where are Uncle Manny, Jason, and Chief? Haven't seen them all afternoon.* He looked out the window. The Bronco wasn't in the driveway. *Wherever they are, they're together.* With nothing better to do, he sat in his favorite chair to read his magazine.

The loud rumble of a large engine rattled the living room windows.

Sounds like the Bronco. Jackson glanced at the clock. 1700 hours. When the front door opened, he checked the time. *Why did it take them fifteen minutes? The house is ten feet from the driveway.*

Mangus and Jason strolled into the house with Chief behind them shouldering a big red bag like Santa Claus.

Jackson wandered over as Chief placed presents under the tree. "Where've you guys been?"

"In town. Jason and I went with the General to pick up a few things. Mrs. Taylor wrapped everything. That's what took so long. It would've looked like crap if one of us tried. We wanted everything to look nice for Christmas."

Sara walked over and kissed Jackson's cheek. "Do you want to help me?"

Jackson snaked his arms around her back. "Yes, ma'am. What do you need?"

"Could you put the food away and set the table?"

"No problem."

Chief dusted off his hands. "Want some help, boss?"

"Sure. The more, the merrier. It'll go quicker." Jackson led the way into the dining room.

Chief gathered up the snack trays and carried them to the kitchen.

Jackson set the china plates in front of each chair. He placed the silverware on a folded linen napkin the way his mother taught him for special occasions.

Harry sat at the table and bounced his son on his lap.

Jackson picked up his godson. He walked around the house singing *Santa Claus is Coming to Town*. The little boy squealed in joy.

Sara and Rachel stepped out of the kitchen.

"Now it seems like Christmas," Sara said.

Jackson winked at them then sang *Jingle Bells*.

Ty, Mikey, and Bill came in and deposited their gifts in the pile under the tree.

"Where have you guys been? It's 1757 hours." Jackson gave them his wilting glare through squinted eyes.

It backfired. Instead of acknowledging his directive, Mikey, Ty, and Bill made funny faces at little JJ. In return, the baby grinned at them. All three men laughed.

Jackson walked to the dining room, shaking his head. *It's lecture time again.* He saw the grandfather clock. *Crap, it's 1803.* He carried his godson past Sara patting her foot in the doorway. "Sorry. Blame my men. They're late again."

Sara crossed her arms. "I noticed, but we know who kept them occupied, don't we Jackson."

"Yes, Aunt Sara." Jackson sat his namesake in his high chair as everyone entered the dining room.

Sara handed Mangus the carving knife. He expeditiously cut the turkey to get everything back on schedule. Once she sat down, hands shot out across table for the turkey and Sara's special mashed potatoes made with fresh sour cream.

Jackson grabbed his favorite. Sweet potato casserole with marshmallows and pecan streusel. He would load his plate with the rest—later.

270

"Where have you two been for the last hour?" Harry called from the couch.

Jackson threw a damp dishtowel at Harry. "Washing dishes. You decided to be a lazy ass, Major Russell."

With all the chairs and couches taken, Jackson and Jerry sat on the floor next to the fireplace.

Little Jackson played with his toys in his playpen next to the wall.

Sara turned on the radio. Christmas music filtered through the living room. "Since you have a baby, you're first, Harry."

Bill, Ty, Mikey, and Chief handed Harry boxes wrapped in the Sunday comics. Toy trucks, cars, a football, nerf ball, a G.I. Joe and one Evil Knievel stunt cycle wound up stacked next to Harry's chair.

Sara presented Gabby with a handmade blue checkerboard quilt. "Put this on his bed when you get home."

Mangus handed Harry a one-hundred-dollar bill. "Jumpstart his college fund with this."

Jason gave Harry a small box wrapped in USMC paper. "Hope you'll let him wear this."

Harry ripped off the paper. He held up baby-sized Marine Corps dress blue uniform with Sgt. Major stripes on the sleeves. "You bet he'll wear it. After what the army did to JJ, why would I give them my loyalty? My retirement checks say United States Government, not army."

Frank produced a four-foot teddy bear from behind the couch. "Couldn't find a big enough box."

"Wow." Harry placed it in the playpen next to his son.

Jackson handed Harry a box wrapped in green paper with a red bow. "This is from me."

Harry removed the paper, pulled off the top and tilted the box to show Gabby. "Honey, look."

Gabby held up a little Carhartt jacket, brown cowboy boots, jeans, a blue flannel shirt, and a tiny gray cowboy hat. "These are so cute. Thank you, JJ."

"You're welcome." Jackson bowed to his best friend. "Now your son can look like me."

"Keep holding them up, Gabby." The room lit up as Sara snapped a picture.

With Chief's appreciation of all things mechanical, Jackson pushed a large red OU toolbox across the living room floor.

Chief's eyes sparkled when he opened the lid. Inside—a brand new set of expensive tools. Then he opened the box next to it. "Thanks, boss." He flipped the OU sweatshirt and matching sweatpants over his shoulder and sang *Boomer Sooner*—loud and proud.

Gabby tore the green paper off her gift. She pulled a pink quilt-lined hooded coat out of the box then stood and kissed Jackson's forehead. "You're so sweet. I love it."

"That's my wife you're nearly open-mouthed kissing." Harry threw wadded up paper at Jackson.

Jackson dipped Gabby toward the ground like a dance partner.

"And you're both blushing. Time to let her go."

Jackson escorted Gabby back to her chair. "At your service, my lady."

Harry kissed Gabby's cheek. "Don't encourage him."

Gabby shrugged "Why not? He needs more happiness in his life and so do you, honey."

"Here, guys. No kissing allowed." Jackson handed Harry, Ty, Mikey, and Bill a green wrapped box. Paper piled on the floor around their feet as they opened their gifts.

Mikey put on his Carhartt jacket. "Thanks, Colonel. I needed a new coat."

"Same here. Beats my old army coat by a mile." Bill draped the jacket over the back of his chair.

Harry laid his jacket on top of his son's toys. "Now I look like you and my son."

"Yep." Jackson stuck his thumbs into his belt loops.

Ty flipped his Carhartt jacket over his shoulder. "I won't freeze in the office."

Undeterred by the betrayal, his loyalty to West Point remained strong. He gave Dr. Rose, Frank, and Jerry hooded sweatshirts silk-screened with the Black Knight logo.

Frank looked at the tag. "How did you get official sweatshirts from West Point delivered to Beaver Creek? Your name would throw up a red flag."

Jackson held up one finger. "Connections. Need to know…and you don't need to know."

"Yes, I do. What did this connection tell you?"

Leave it to Frank to put a damper on the festivities. He hadn't told anyone. Only his godfather knew since he was the tie to the Pentagon. Jackson glanced at Mangus then at Frank. "Well…scuttlebutt says there was a Russian spy in camp. He's the one who set up the mortar attack that killed Johnson."

"They think you're involved, right?"

"Not sure...maybe...I don't think so. We had a thief on base. Maybe it's the same person. We know how well intel guys figure stuff out."

"True. What about you?"

Jackson sighed. He didn't want to discuss this now. "That's a whole different ballgame."

Frank stomped his foot. "Then throw the first pitch. I won't let it go. They know Manny is involved. He requested to see you."

"The brass filed that under Marine Corps revenge because of Dad. Which surprises me. I would've thought they'd let him beat the shit out of me."

Mangus rubbed his hands together. "It's a good thing they didn't. I might've, as Jackson says, got stupid after seeing him in that cell. The army won't show up here. The Commandant told the Chief of Staff I wanted Jackson to die a slow death."

"Again, what about you?" Frank demanded.

"Our lives are considered...forfeit. We're traitors. Deadly force is authorized if we resist capture. It's that simple."

"Shit."

"Frank...don't worry about." *He doesn't need to know my demons still visit. My penance for not listening to my gut.* "If I have to live the rest of my life here, so be it. We're safe as long as we don't leave the area. The people around here respect Uncle Manny."

Frank flipped the sweatshirt over his shoulder. "If you're okay with it, I am."

"Good." The last two gifts, Jackson handed Jason and Rachel. He wanted to get the Christmas spirit back on track.

Jason removed the paper and pulled up the box flap. He held up the USMC flag for all to see. The red USMC sweatshirt he put on over his shirt and placed the brown felt cowboy hat on the end table. "Thanks, kid."

"You're welcome." Jackson two-stepped around the room. "Now you fit in on the ranch as a swinging Marine cowboy."

Jason stuck a toothpick between his teeth. He flipped the cowboy hat on his head with a flourish. "Nice dancin' there, Tex."

Torn wrapping paper drifted across the floor as Rachel exploded out of her chair. She grabbed Jackson in a hug. "How'd you know I wanted cast iron cookware?"

Jackson tapped his ear. "Overheard you talking to Aunt Sara yesterday. After my chores, I ran into town and bought a set."

"Thank you." Rachel kissed his cheek. "Stop blushing or I'll tell baby stories that'll really make you blush."

Jackson felt the heat rise his face in embarrassment. No way did he want that to happen. "Hey, Jerry, Chief, Mikey, can you give me a hand?"

Chief stood. "What do you need, boss?"

"Meet me in the garage, all three of you."

Mikey and Chief carried the new quilting frame into the house and set it in front of Sara.

Jerry and Jackson brought in a tarp-wrapped object and placed it in front of Mangus.

Sara sucked in a deep breath. "Jackson, honey. Thank you."

Mangus pulled off the cover. He stood open-mouthed in front of a large square wooden sign for the main entrance gate. In the middle—the logo of Double M ranch between two crossed sabers. Engraved in the lower-left corner—the USMC bulldog. On the right—the USMC Eagle, Globe, and Anchor. In each upper corner—an upside-down worn horseshoe off Bandit, for luck. "You made this?"

"Yes, sir. We'll hang it up for you tomorrow." Jackson squared his shoulders.

For several minutes, Mangus examined the exquisitely beautiful engraving and well-crafted ironwork. He ran a finger over each curve, and line then went down on one knee and brushed his palm over the smooth satin, dark brown finish. "It's beautiful. I love it. How long have you been working on this?"

"Every evening for the last two months in the workshop."

"How did you know Sara needed a new quilting frame? I priced one for her birthday. Those things cost five hundred dollars."

"Caught Chief repairing the legs. It's worth every penny to make Aunt Sara happy."

Mangus grabbed Jackson from one side. Sara joined him on the other. Together they smashed him in the middle. Jackson smiled from ear to ear. Their admiration of his gifts meant everything to him.

Jackson sat on the floor with his gifts. *Why do I get more than everyone else?* He chuckled after opening the first one. "Just what I wanted, more coffee cans."

"We want you stocked in Columbia's finest, sir." Mikey picked up Jackson's mug. "Your mood swings stay in check as long as you have one of these in your hand."

"True." Jackson pulled two pairs of long underwear out of the second box. "Are these to keep me from getting hypothermia?"

"Yep." Mikey fake shivered with his arms around his chest. "You almost wound up in the hospital last week when the truck broke down."

Chief handed Jackson a straight-bladed hunting knife. "Surprise, boss."

"Thanks. You can't have too many knives." Jackson slipped the leather sheath on his belt.

"You're welcome." Chief patted a matching knife hanging at his side.

Jackson opened Harry's gift. He held up a USMA Black Knight hooded sweatshirt, MacKenzie embroidered in gold on the right, even with the logo on the left. In the box, the matching sweatpants, ball cap, and a pair of black running shoes. "Thanks, Harry, Gabby. Thought I was the sneaky one."

"Great minds think alike." Harry flipped his friend a crisp salute.

Jackson carefully removed the USMC paper from Jason's gift to save as a memento. He smiled at the two pairs of Levis, two flannel shirts, two polo shirts, white t-shirts, socks, and underwear in the box. *Out of curiosity, he checked the tag on the jeans. One size bigger won't make a difference. They'll shrink up nicely in hot water.* "Thanks, Aunt Rachel, Uncle Jason."

Curtis handed Jackson a brown paper sack. "This is from Jerry and me. Sorry, we didn't wrap it."

"That's okay. I saw his wrapping prowess earlier." Jackson pulled out a set of blue and gold Fighting Irish sweats. "How'd you know I was a Notre Dame fan?"

"You're Catholic. Hard to find one who isn't."

Frank pulled a black sweatshirt from behind his back. "Sorry, I didn't wrap mine either."

Jackson held it up to look at the Marine Corps bulldog on the front. "Hmm. I wonder why you picked this."

Frank pointed at Mangus. "You know why. No way would I ever cross him."

"Me neither. I'm liable to wind up with a chunk missing from my ass."

"Jackson, come over here." Sara crooked her finger several times.

"Yes, Aunt Sara." Jackson jogged over to her. "What do you need?"

"This is for you." Sara handed him a box wrapped in green and white striped paper. Red ribbon crossed over each end. In the center, a red bow with feathered ends.

"It's almost too pretty to open." Jackson slit the tape so the paper came off in one piece. He thumbed through each item. A pair of pressed khaki pants, two pairs of Levis, and three short-sleeve, button-up shirts. "Nice."

"That's not everything." Sara opened the entry hall closet.

"Please, this is already too much."

"Be quiet." Sara handed him a garment bag.

Jackson pulled out a white dress shirt, a three-piece dark blue pinstriped suit, expensive black silk tie, and a pair of black dress shoes. "Thanks, Aunt Sara. Now I have classy clothes for special occasions instead of jeans and a denim shirt."

Sara pulled on Jackson's shirtsleeve. "I know. That's most of your current wardrobe. I want you to look nice instead of like a cowboy. You're way too handsome to stay alone forever. I want grandchildren."

Mangus handed Jackson a large, unwrapped box. Inside was a Model 39 Smith and Wesson 9mm pistol, two boxes of ammo, and a belt holster. He looked from the box to his godfather. "You already gave me a gun."

"It's for your protection." Mangus pointed at the Winchester leaning against the wall. "You're not always near the rifle when you're fixing a fence or something else. That way, you don't have to carry it everywhere you go." He pulled a KA-BAR in its USMC/Eagle, Globe, and Anchor embossed brown leather sheath from the rear waistband of his pants. "This is to replace the one you lost in Vietnam."

"Thanks, Uncle Manny."

Mangus squeezed Jackson's shoulder. "I'm the one who got the better end of the deal. I bought a gun and a knife. You designed and built me a beautiful sign. That makes it special."

"No. You're the special one for putting up with me. Thanks for screwing my head back on straight." *He made it happen by giving me Bandit.*

Once the used wrapping paper made its way into the fire, everyone sat around talking with various drinks in their hands, reminiscing about past holidays until well past midnight.

Sara grabbed Jackson's arm as he tried to sneak into the kitchen. "No one leaves until I take a picture next to the tree for my scrapbook. I want to remember this wonderful Christmas."

"Aww. Can't we skip it this year?" Jackson half-heartedly tried to pull away.

"No, go stand in front of that tree. You're as bad as my kids when it comes to taking pictures. No funny faces."

"Okay." Jackson stood in the back row next to Harry. He stuck two fingers up behind Harry's head as the timer clicked.

As everyone gathered up their things to leave, Jackson opened the front door and saw tracks in the snow across the sidewalk. "Crap. The wolves are prowling around tonight." He grabbed his rifle. "Harry, I'm walking with you, Gabby, and little JJ to the guesthouse."

"What's up?" Harry handed his son to Gabby.

Jackson flipped the Winchester on his shoulder. "Wolves. Don't want your family to be a quick meal."

Harry pointed at the door. "Escort away."

Thirty minutes later, Jackson pushed open the door to the bunkhouse. He held it open with his foot as he maneuvered his armload of presents through the opening. A Zenith color TV with rabbit ear antennas sat on the dresser. *That's why Uncle Manny took Chief into town.* Tired and emotionally drained, he changed into the USMA sweats, poured a cup of coffee, sat on his bunk, and loaded the pistol magazines.

Frank sat next to him. "A year ago, it would've been a mistake to give you that pistol."

After inserting the magazine, Jackson thumped the butt with his palm, chambered a round, and stuck the pistol in the holster. "Yes, but things have changed. I'll never get to that point again." He felt a demon tug on his thoughts. "At least, I hope I don't." He set the pistol on the shelf above his bunk.

"Me too." Frank returned to his bunk. He leaned against the headboard with a paperback book. *Smoky the Cowhorse.*

On the other side of the room, Chief, Curtis and Jerry sat in the folding chairs watching *Santa Claus is Coming to Town* on TV.

Jackson settled back against his pillows with his newest book, *Old Bones, The Wonder Horse* by Mildred Pace.

December 25, 1973

Jackson pulled out his chair for the traditional Christmas morning breakfast. The table was covered with platters of egg and cheese casserole, sausage, biscuits, gravy, fresh melon, and pancakes. Sara, ever the doting grandmother, gave a hand-decorated red Christmas sock to everyone at the table. Each one filled with fruit and candy.

Sara handed Jackson another sock after he washed the dishes.

"You already gave me one. Who's this for?" Jackson turned the sock around. "Bandit, since there's a little silver horse drawn on the side."

"Yes. The wonder horse deserved a bag of peppermints from me." Sara pointed at the front door. "Go get Bandit. Take him all brushed and saddled to the guesthouse."

"Yes, ma'am." Jackson ran to the barn. He made sure Bandit's coat had an extra shine and wiped down the saddle until it reflected his image. *Aunt Sara has something in mind.* As he rode up, Harry and Gabby were waiting outside with their son. Jackson looked at his clothes, Sara with her 35mm camera then his godson dressed in his matching mini outfit. *I know what Aunt Sara wants.* He dismounted and held onto Bandit's bridle.

Harry's face beamed as bright as the sun overhead when he placed his child on the horse's back. Bandit stood rock still while everyone crowded around him snapping pictures of the little boy on the big red horse.

Sara waved her camera. "Get on, Jackson. I want a few of you too."

Jackson mounted his horse. "Got something even better. Hand little JJ to me."

Harry placed his son in the saddle in front of his best friend. "Hold onto him."

"Of course." Jackson cradled his arm around the boy. Sitting on Bandit's back with little JJ was fine for pictures, but they needed to move. He urged Bandit forward. They moved in a slow circle around the group.

"Look this way, Jackson. You and little JJ are so cute together," Sara called out.

Jackson pulled back on the reins. Bandit stopped. Jackson clicked his tongue until Bandit looked at Gabby and Sara.

"Look, Bandit's smiling," Gabby exclaimed.

Camera shutter clicks went off for ten seconds.

Harry retrieved his son, leaving Jackson alone on his horse.

Bill, Ty, Chief, and Mikey crowded in front of him and turned to face the cameras.

Jackson took his rope off the saddle horn, flipped it over his head a few times and looped all of them. "You guys look like a herd of skinny cows."

Sara, Rachel, and Gabby snapped picture after picture.

Once he released his men and recoiled the rope, Jackson circled the group, sidestepping the horse. *Time for my fun.* "Showtime."

Bandit wheeled around in a circle then reared up on his hind legs. His front legs pawed the air. Jackson removed his hat and waved it over his head. "Yee-haw!"

The lawn looked like a paparazzi mob scene as Sara, Rachel, and Gabby jockeyed for position.

Jackson queued Bandit into a piaffe. Bandit trotted in place, moving neither forward nor backward. To show off, they did a half-pass across the lawn at a canter. Moving forward and sideways at the same time. Jackson threw in a flying leg change. With all four feet in the air, Bandit skipped, changing his right lead leg to his left. For the finale, they did a pirouette and a passage. Bandit's legs exploded from the ground as he moved across the ground at a highly elevated and extremely powerful trot.

Harry held his son on his shoulder. "Look at that. Your godfather trained Bandit as a dressage horse. And he's good at it, too. Looks like they're dancing."

Little JJ's single front tooth appeared as he squealed in high-pitched joy, clapping his little hands.

Jackson dismounted in front of Harry. "You betcha." He bowed with Bandit going down on one knee, his other leg out straight with his head dipped between them.

The applause ended. Jackson unsaddled Bandit and turned him out into the snow-covered pasture where they played their version of tag. Bandit nosed Jackson in the back as he ran, sending him face-first into the snow. He stood, brushed off his coat, picked up his hat, and shook his head to get the wet stuff out of his ears. When Bandit ran past, Jackson slapped the horse on the rear. They ended the game when Bandit trotted to the barn door and stomped his feet.

Jackson opened the door. "You're hungry. Me too." He couldn't resist hanging Bandit's sock on his stall door. After feeding him a few treats, Jackson returned to the house for the afternoon to enjoy the company of his close friends and family. *No one should be alone on Christmas Day, like so many of my past holidays.* Today was his best Christmas in years. Like the ending of *It's a Wonderful Life.* A day he didn't want to end.

Made in the USA
Middletown, DE
18 September 2020